FEELING VERY STRA

Feeling Very Strange

THE SLIPSTREAM ANTHOLOGY

James Patrick Kelly & John Kessel | *editors*

TACHYON PUBLICATIONS | SAN FRANCISCO

Feeling Very Strange: The Slipstream Anthology

Design & composition by John D. Berry
The text typeface is Aldus nova, with Whitney display type

Tachyon Publications
1459 18th Street #139
San Francisco, CA 94107
(415) 285-5615
www.tachyonpublications.com

Series Editor: Jacob Weisman

ISBN 10: 1-892391-35-X
ISBN 13: 978-1-892391-35-3

Printed in the United States of America
by Worzalla

9 8 7 6 5 4 3 2

Contents

Acknowledgments

WE'D LIKE TO THANK THE FOLLOWING PEOPLE for advice, suggestions, and recommendations: Wilton Barnhardt, Richard Butner, Matthew Cheney, Gregory Frost, Eileen Gunn, Rich Horton, Kelly Link, and David Moles.

Our thanks are also due to Jacob Weisman, Jill Roberts, and the other folks at Tachyon Publications who helped see this project through to completion.

None of these estimable people are responsible for errors of judgment or taste we committed in assembling this anthology.

Slipstream, the Genre That Isn't

James Patrick Kelly | John Kessel

Mist and Wishful Thinking

When we were first approached to edit this book, we had to ask ourselves a hard question. Did we actually believe that there was such a thing as slipstream? We knew that for many writers and critics we trusted, the answer was no. Those who would deny slipstream argue that a genre can't be defined by what it is not. Slipstream can't just be magic realism sliced away from its South American roots. Slipstream can't just be a kind of fantasy where nothing is explained, or science fiction where the science doesn't have to make sense. To assert that it inhabits the spaces between otherwise-accepted genres and realistic fiction is to say it is nowhere. And then there is the problem of including mainstream writers, like Michael Chabon, George Saunders, and Aimee Bender, in our understanding of slipstream. This is a term that arises from the genre of science fiction; while some mainstream writers may have heard of slipstream, it's clear that none of them set out to write it. In fact, it's probably safe to say that very few if any of the writers we include here – even those aware of the debate over slipstream – would acknowledge that they set out to write in this brave new genre. Several contributors to this book expressed surprise that we thought their work might be slipstream.

As if the problem of definition weren't daunting enough, we then had to pick stories and offer them up as examples of the genre that might not be. To form a canon out of mist and wishful thinking. In fact, picking the stories was the easiest part of our work on this book. Or perhaps it was the hardest, in that there were so many fine stories and talented writers we thought belonged here that we agonized over our selections. It is not as if there were only a handful of stories to choose from. Many writers who are primarily known for their work either in the mainstream or the various genres have dipped their toes into what we consider the slipstream. In fact, it was this depth and breadth of stories that encouraged us to make the attempt.

Call of the Ghetto

The term slipstream was coined by Bruce Sterling in a column he wrote for a fanzine called *SF Eye* in 1989. Sterling was attempting to understand a kind of fiction that he saw increasingly in science fiction publications and elsewhere. He quite rightly asserted that it was not true science fiction, and yet it bore some relation to science fiction. In a key passage of his essay, Sterling wrote,

> This genre is not category SF; it is not even "genre" SF. Instead, it is a contemporary kind of writing which has set its face against consensus reality. It is fantastic, surreal sometimes, speculative on occasion, but not rigorously so. It does not aim to provoke a "sense of wonder" or to systematically extrapolate in the manner of classic science fiction.
>
> Instead, this is a kind of writing which simply makes you feel very strange; the way that living in the late twentieth century makes you feel, if you are a person of a certain sensibility. We could call this kind of fiction Novels of a Postmodern Sensibility...for the sake of convenience and argument, we will call these books "slipstream."

Two points need to be made about Sterling's essay. First is that it includes a reading list of writers, of whom only a vanishingly small fraction were identified with a genre. From the outset, Sterling defined slipstream as largely a mutant form of the mainstream. The second point is that the essay was addressed to an audience of science fiction writers and readers. Nobody calls mainstream writers "mainstream" except for those of us in the ghetto of the fantastic. The very notion that slipstream writing needed to be placed in a genre of its own comes from measuring it against science fiction and fantasy. Building a wall to pen the mutant up is a very skiffy thing to do; the impulse is generated from an understanding of genre built up over fifty years of category publishing in the United States.

This is primarily a social distinction. Science fiction, since the birth of the genre magazines in the 1920s, has been seen as a category of pulp publishing more than as a literary form, and still carries this meaning (and associated stigma) despite fifty years of scholars and writers attempting to define it as a mode of writing rather than a mode of publishing. As such, SF was isolated from developments outside of pulp genres. Although the writers themselves may have been well read and educated in other forms of fiction, the genre for better or worse retained its separate identity.

So when the New Wave SF writers of the 1960s and 1970s adapted techniques and attitudes of literary modernism to SF materials (stream of consciousness, fragmented narrative, cinematic techniques, intense concentration of the sensibility of the protagonist, psychological "realism"), it was seen within the genre community as a revolution, even though these techniques had been commonplace in Dos Passos and Hemingway and Stein and Joyce since the 1920s.

Slipstream as a publishing category has meaning only to those coming from the genre side of the divide. Sterling, chief propagandist of the cyberpunk movement of the 1980s, was trying to come to grips with other forms of ambitious visionary fiction being written in the 1980s that could by no means be categorized as cyberpunk. In a way, his essay was an attempt to identify a form of fiction in opposition to cyberpunk so as to differentiate it. In the ensuing seventeen years, many writers in the genre who have been trying to establish an identity separate from category SF and fantasy, and in relation to literary fiction, have seized upon Sterling's formulation. They have taken it to places that Sterling did not intend, and created a subcategory of publications, editors, magazines, and critical opinion within the world of SF discourse and yet separate from it. But in all discussions of slipstream we have seen, at some point the relationship of slipstream to genre science fiction is entertained and defined.

So, for instance, the publication of Karen Joy Fowler's "What I Didn't See" by *SciFiction,* one of the major outlets for science fiction in the oughts, sparked a considerable debate among writers and fans of "slipstream" and those writers and readers of science fiction for whom Fowler's story had no legitimate place in the genre. The fact that "What I Didn't See" won the Nebula Award, one of science fiction's highest prizes, only adds to the irony.

Consider Jonathan Lethem's "Light and the Sufferer." Mysterious aliens are a staple of science fiction, their motives and actions the subject of much overheated speculation. They come in all flavors, from hostile to godlike to benevolent to inscrutable. Lethem's alien "Sufferers" are inscrutable, all right, but the story is not about them. Lethem ignores the commonplaces of the SF alien story; it's almost as if he cannot be bothered to take them seriously. On the other hand, Lethem uses his aliens to comment on a story of character, and somehow this story conveys more seriousness than the average alien story. Lethem obviously knows his aliens, and while that knowledge hovers in the background of the story, it never comes to the foreground. He also expects his readers to know of SF's idea of superior aliens, and to accept the conceit without flinching. In this sense a slipstream story quotes genre in pursuit of literary effect. A story like this would have had trouble being accepted in a science fiction magazine of forty years ago. SF traditionalists wring their hands when such stories appear in science fiction publications today.

The writers of slipstream who do not come from the genre side of the divide, however, never worry about its connection to science fiction, and do not talk about it unless prompted by questioners attempting to link their work to sf.

Dessert Topping or Floor Wax?

So what do we think slipstream is? How did we decide on the stories that follow?

The problem is that, in the years since Sterling coined it, the term has become smeared across several meanings. It is now a would-be literary form, a publishing category, and most recently a fluid but discrete group of writers who recognize in one another a common sensibility.

It is the literary form that most interests us. However, we see no profit in penning the mutant. Science fiction has not been well served by its seventy-year-long war of definition, and moreover, what right do we have to raise the walls of a new genre around writers who have no commitment to or even knowledge of what we think of as slipstream? For most of our contributors these stories are just stories. If they feel pressed to give them a label, they may use "metafiction" or "magic realism" or "fabulation" – or they may just tweak their noses at us. Definition does not matter to many of them, and that is a warning to us not to put too much faith in definitions. The concept of slipstream is a fuzzy set; it is easier to point to examples than to create "if-and-only-if" definitions. So take the following discussion as descriptive rather than definitive.

John Clute, in *The Encyclopedia of Science Fiction,* in an entry on "Slipstream SF" took the term literally, imagining slipstream to be mainstream writers following in the wake of SF, being drawn along by the force of its concepts. Clute preferred the term *fabulation,* popularized by Robert Scholes in the late 1970s to describe the work of Donald Barthelme, John Barth, Robert Coover, etc. Elsewhere in the encyclopedia, Clute writes intelligently about fabulation and identifies a thread within it that relates directly to slipstream as we see it: that such fiction abandons the assumption, common to both realism and science fiction, that the world can be "seen whole, and described accurately in words." Slipstream raises fundamental epistemological and ontological questions about reality that most other kinds of fiction are ill prepared to address.

We chose to call this book *Feeling Very Strange* for just this reason. While we will argue that slipstream has some identifiable attributes that might well be the beginnings of genre, it is primarily at this point in its evolution a psychological and literary effect that cuts across genre, in the same way that the effect of horror manifests in many different kinds of writing. Where horror is the literature of fear, slipstream is the literature of cognitive dissonance and of strangeness *triumphant.*

According to the theory of cognitive dissonance, we are often faced with competing and even contradictory cognitions, which can take the form of assumptions, emotions, values, and the like. This creates psychic dissonance, which we naturally seek to reduce. How long can you stand to both love and hate an abusive father? How can you rejoice in the success of a friend when it comes at your expense? If you believed destroying weapons of mass destruction justified the invasion of Iraq, how do you feel about the war now? If God created everything, then who created God? And don't even try to think about what happened before the Big Bang.

In a memorable fake commercial from the first season of *Saturday Night Live,* a husband and wife are arguing over a new product called Shimmer. He claims it's a dessert topping; she says it's a floor wax. Suddenly the announcer steps in and tells them that they're both right, demonstrates on the kitchen floor and a bowl of butterscotch pudding, and closes by saying, "Shimmer, for the greatest shine you ever tasted!" The skit works precisely because it tickles our cognitive dissonance. F. Scott Fitzgerald once wrote that "the true test of a first-rate mind is the ability to hold two contradictory ideas at the same time and still function." However, it is our fate to live in a time when it takes a first-rate mind just to get through the day. We have unprecedented access to information; cognitive dissonance is a banner headline in our morning paper and radiates silently from our computer screen. We contend that slipstream is an expression of the zeitgeist: it embraces cognitive dissonance rather than trying to reduce it. Again and again in the stories in this volume, writers present us with contradictions and then, deliberately and with great skill, elaborate on them without trying to resolve them. Is Shimmer a floor wax or a dessert topping? Is an electron a wave or a particle?

Slipstream tells us that the answer is yes.

How to Be Strange

So then, if slipstream is a literary effect rather than a fully developed genre, how is it accomplished?

1. Slipstream violates the tenets of realism.

2. Although slipstream stories pay homage to various popular genres and their conventions, they are not science fiction stories, traditional fantasies, dreams, historical fantasies, or alternate histories.

3. Slipstream is playfully postmodern. The stories often acknowledge their existence as fictions, and play against the

genres they evoke. They have a tendency to bend or break narrative rules.

The hardest thing to put a finger on is the strangeness that Sterling identifies as the essence of slipstream, but that all commentators have been at pains to define. It has been called a matter of making the familiar strange or the strange familiar. Carol Emshwiller, a writer we see as central to any understanding of slipstream, says, "estranging the everyday" is the motive for most of her fiction. But there is typically more to it than that.

In their commitment to cognitive dissonance, slipstream stories deploy many techniques to estrange us: they may use allegory ("The Little Magic Shop"), borrow forms from nonliterary sources ("Exhibit H: Torn Pages Discovered..."), literalize metaphor ("Lieserl"), inject genre elements into decidedly nongenre milieus ("Sea Oak"), play metafictional games ("The Rose in Twelve Petals"), invent faux-autobiography ("Bright Morning"), incorporate pastiche, parody, or collage ("The Lions Are Asleep This Night"), or externalize psychological and ontological distress ("You Have Never Been Here"). They play with older genre forms: "The God of Dark Laughter" reinvents Lovecraft, "The Specialist's Hat" the ghost story, and "Biographical Notes to 'A Discourse on the Nature of Causality, with Air-planes'" the 1930s pulp adventure. Frequently slipstream writers do two or three of these things in the same story, as Carol Emshwiller's "Al" mashes up James Hilton's *Lost Horizon* with an anthropologically informed sideways satire of the New York City art scene.

Not without risks. Benjamin Rosenbaum has praised slipstream for "playing with tropes such that the reader's awareness that you are playing, but playing seriously, is part of the story's joy.... [They explore] that interesting boundary between the distanced/ironic/cool/mocking and the emotionally engaged, and how a story that slips from one to the other can sometimes catch you unawares and move you more deeply than one that is frankly sentimental." But slipstream's cavalier attitude toward boundaries can lead to a lack of rigor. A failed slipstream story can seem like idle noodling, a grab bag of uncommitted allusions to genres without any investment in characters or the ideas behind them, or acknowledgment that genre tropes are anything more than pawns on a chess board.

You Have Never Been Here

In his essay "Kafka and His Precursors," Jorge Luis Borges said, "every writer creates his own precursors." New genres arise from existing genres. Mary Shelley, Jules Verne, and H.G. Wells were not "science fiction" writers when they wrote (are there three works more different than *Frankenstein, Twenty Thousand Leagues Under the Sea,* and *When the Sleeper Wakes*?), but in retrospect they can be identified as such once the genre has been "invented." Similarly, if we place Kafka's "In the Penal Colony," Borges' "The Library of Babel," John Collier's "Evening Primrose," Shirley Jackson's "One Ordinary Day, with Peanuts," Damon Knight's "The Handler," Robert Coover's "The Babysitter," Fritz Leiber's "The Man Who Made Friends with Electricity," Donald Barthelme's "Robert Kennedy – Saved from Drowning," Thomas Disch's "Descending," Italo Calvino's "The Argentine Ant," and Barry Malzberg's "The Man Who Loved the Midnight Lady" side by side, we can discern the shape of slipstream.

The ideal version of this anthology would include such precursors. Instead we have confined ourselves to writers active today, primarily in the period since Sterling's essay. We have included writers from both sides of the genre divide, and some who seem to traverse it without noticing. We have taken only stories published in the United States, though it would have been easy to extend the selection to Great Britain and Canada, and to work not originally published in English. We have tried to focus on writers who have spent much if not all of their careers writing slipstream. But still there are at least a dozen other writers who belong in the pages that follow, had we but enough space.

Where does slipstream go from here?

Within the last fifteen years, magazines and one-shots like *Crank, Lady Churchill's Rosebud Wristlet, Say..., McSweeney's, Polyphony, Zoetrope, Century, The Journal of Pulse-Pounding Narratives, Trampoline, The Third Alternative, All-Star Zeppelin Adventure Stories, The Infinite Matrix,* and *Strange Horizons* have provided a showcase for slipstream. This nascent publishing niche may or may not develop into a genre in the accepted sense of the word. However, it has already opened new territories to the fantastic.

Borges, as devoted to the word as any writer in the last century, did not make high-vs.-low genre distinctions. He drew on Poe and Wells and Chesterton – writers ignored or discounted by the modernist canon – without embarrassment, or even awareness that he ought to be embarrassed. Today, mainstream writers like George Saunders and Aimee Bender are more aware of genre conventions and icons, and less wary of them, than previous generations. From the other side of the genre divide, there are writers who appear regularly in the pages of *Asimov's Science Fiction Magazine* and *The Magazine of Fantasy & Science Fiction* who have more in common with Borges than with Isaac Asimov. They are committed to writing the kind of fiction we identify in this book.

We don't pretend to know where this will take us. Consider M. Rickert's "You Have Never Been Here," which has not been published before. We selected it, and placed it last in the anthology, because we think it an exemplar of what slipstream does best. It is at once hauntingly familiar and very, very strange. Who is the narrator? Who is he talking to? Who are you?

Slipstream can take you to a place where you have never been. An impossible place that cannot exist, and yet a place where you are expected. Your name is at the top of the list and your room is ready.

Have a nice stay.

FEELING VERY STRANGE

Al

Carol Emshwiller

SORT OF A PLANE CRASH in an uncharted region of the park.

We were flying fairly low over the mountains. We had come to the last ridge when there, before us, appeared this incredible valley....

Suddenly the plane sputtered. (We knew we were low on gas but we had thought to make it over the mountains.)

"I think I can bring her in." (John's last words.)

I was the only survivor.

A plane crash in a field of alfalfa, across the road from it the Annual Fall Festival of the Arts. An oasis on the edge of the parking area. One survivor. He alone, Al, who has spent considerable time in France, Algeria and Mexico, his paintings without social relevance (or so the critics say) and best in the darker colors, not a musician at all yet seems to be one of us. He, a stranger, wandering in a land he doesn't remember and not one penny of our kind of money, creeping from behind our poster, across from it the once-a-year art experience for music lovers. Knowing him as I do now, he must have been wary then; view from our poster, ENTRANCE sign, vast parking lot, our red and white tent, our EXIT on the far side, maybe the sound of a song – a frightening situation under the circumstance, all the others dead and Al having been unconscious for who knows how long? (the scar from that time is still on his cheek), stumbling across the road then and into our ticket booth.

"Hi."

I won't say he wasn't welcome. Even then we were wondering, were we facing stultification? Already some of our rules had become rituals. Were we, we wondered, doomed to a partial relevance in our efforts to make music meaningful in our time? And now Al, dropped to us from the skies (no taller than we are, no wider and not even quite so graceful). Later he was to say: "Maybe the artful gesture is lost forever."

We had a girl with us then as secretary, a long-haired changeling child, actually the daughter of a prince (there still are princes), left out in the picnic area of a western state forest to be found and brought up by an old couple in the upper middle class (she still hasn't found this out for sure, but has always suspected something of the sort), so when *I* asked Al to *my* (extra) bedroom it was too late. (By that time he had already pounded his head against the wall some so he seemed calm and happy and rather well adjusted to life in our valley.) The man from the *Daily* asked him how did he happen to become interested in art? He said he came from a land of cultural giants east of our outermost islands where the policemen were all poets. That's significant in two ways.

About the artful gesture being lost, so many lost arts and also soft, gray birds, etc., etc., etc. (The makers of toe shoes will have to go when the last toe dancer dies.)

However, right then, there was Al, mumbling to us in French, German and Spanish. We gave him two tickets to our early-evening concert even though he couldn't pay except in what looked like pesos. Second row, left side. (Right from the beginning there was something in him I couldn't resist.) We saw him craning his neck there, somehow already with our long-haired girl beside him. She's five hundred years old though she doesn't look a day over sixteen and plays the virginal like an angel. Did her undergraduate work at the University of Utah (around 1776, I would say). If she crossed the Alleghenies *now* she'd crumble into her real age and die, so later on I tried to get them to take a trip to the Ann Arbor Film Festival together, but naturally she had something else to do. Miss Haertzler.

As our plane came sputtering down I saw the tents below, a village of nomads, God knows how far from the nearest outpost of civilization. They had, no doubt, lived like this for thousands of years.

These thoughts went rapidly through my mind in the moments before we crashed and then I lost consciousness.

"COME, COME YE SONS OF ART." That's what our poster across the street says, quotes, that is. Really very nice in Day-Glo colors. "COME, COME AWAY..." etc., on to "TO CELEBRATE, TO CELEBRATE THIS TRIUMPHANT DAY," which meant to me, in some symbolic way even at that time, the day Al came out from behind it and stumbled across the road to our booth, as they say, "a leading force, from then on, among the new objectivists and continues to play a major role among them up to the present time" (which was a few years ago). Obtained his bachelor's degree in design at the University of Michigan with further study at the Atelier Chaumière in Paris. He always says, "Form speaks." I can say I knew him pretty well at that time. I know he welcomes criticism but not too early in the morning. Ralph had said (he was on the staff of the Annual Fall Festival), "Maybe artistic standards are no longer relevant." (We were wondering at the time how to get the immediacy of the war into our concerts more meaningfully than the "1812 Overture." Also something of the changing race relations.) Al answered, but just then a jet came by or some big oil truck and I missed the key word. That leaves me still not understanding what he meant. The next morning the same thing happened and it may have been more or less the answer to everything.

By then we had absorbed the major San Francisco influences. These have remained with us in some form or other up to the present time. Al changed the art exhibit we had in the vestibule to his kind of art as soon as Miss Haertzler went to bed with him. We had a complete new selection of paintings by Friday afternoon, all hung in time for the early performance (Ralph hung them) and by then, or at least by Saturday night, I knew I was, at last, really in love for the first time in my life.

When I came to, I found we had crashed in a cultivated field planted with some sort of weedlike bush entirely unfamiliar to me. I quickly ascertained that my three companions were beyond my help, then extricated myself from the wreckage and walked to the edge of the field. I found myself standing beneath a giant stele where strange symbols swirled in brilliant, jewellike colors. Weak and dazed though I was, I felt a surge of delight. Surely, I thought, the people who made this cannot be entirely uncivilized.

Miss Haertzler took her turn on stage like the rest of us. She was the sort who would have cut off her right breast the better to bow the violin, but, happily, she played the harpsichord. Perhaps Al wouldn't have minded, anyway. Strange man. From some entirely different land and I could never quite figure out where. Certainly he wouldn't have minded. She played only the very old and the very new, whereas *I* had suddenly discovered Beethoven (over again) and I talked about Romanticism during our staff meetings. Al said, "In some ways a return to Romanticism is like a return to the human figure." I believe he approved of the idea.

He spent the first night, Tuesday night, that was, the twenty-second, in our red and white tent under the bleachers at the back. A touch of hay fever woke him early.

By Wednesday Ralph and I had already spent two afternoons calculating our losses due to the rain, and I longed for a new experience of some sort that would lift me out of the endless problems of the Annual Fall Festival of the Arts. I returned dutifully, however, to the area early the next day to continue my calculations in the quiet of the morning and found him there.

"Me, Al. You?" Pointing finger.

"Ha, ha." (I *must* get rid of my nervous laugh!)

I wanted to redefine my purposes not only for his sake, but for my own.

I wanted to find out just what role the audience should play.

I wanted to figure out, as I mentioned before, how we could best incorporate aspects of the war and the changing race relations into our concerts.

I wondered how to present musical experiences in order to enrich the lives of others in a meaningful way, how to engage, in other words, their total beings. I wanted to expand their musical horizons.

"I've thought about these things all year," I said, "ever since I knew I would be a director of the Annual Fall Festival. I also want to mention the fact," I said, "that there's a group from the college who would like to disrupt the unity of our performances (having other aims and interests) but," I told him, "the audience has risen to the occasion, at least by last night, when we had not only good weather, but money and an enthusiastic reception."

"I have recognized," he replied, "here in this valley, a fully realized civilization with a past history, a rich present, and a future all its own, and I have understood, even in my short time here, the vast immigration to urban areas that must have taken place and that must be continuing into the present time."

How could I help but fall in love with him? He may have spent the second night in Miss Haertzler's bed (if my conjectures are correct) but, I must say, it was with me he had all his discussions.

I awoke the next morning extremely hungry, with a bad headache and with sniffles and no handkerchief, yet somehow, in spite of this, in fairly good spirits though I did long for a good hot cup of almost anything. Little did I realize then, or I might not have felt so energetic, the hardships I was to encounter here in this strange, elusive, never-never land. Even just getting something to eat was to prove difficult.

Somewhat later that day I asked him out to lunch and I wish I could describe his expression eating his first grilled cheese and bacon, sipping his first clam chowder....

Ralph, I tell you, this really happened and just as if we haven't *all* crash-landed here in some sort of (figurative) unknown alfalfa field. As if we weren't *all* penniless or about to be, waiting for you to ask us out to lunch. Three of our friends are dead and already there are several misunderstandings. You may even be in love with me for all I know, though that may have been before I had gotten to be your boss in the Annual Fall Festival.

That afternoon I gave Al a job, Ralph, cleaning up candy wrappers and crumpled programs with a nail on a stick, and I invited him to our after-performance party for the audience. Paid him five dollars in advance. That's how much in love I was, so there's no sense in you coming over anymore. Besides, I'm tired of people who play instruments by blowing.

I found the natives to be a grave race, sometimes inattentive, but friendly and smiling, even though more or less continuously concerned about the war. The younger ones frequently live communally with a charming innocence, by threes or fours or even up to sixes or eights in quite comfortable apartments, sometimes forming their own family groups from a few chosen friends, and, in their art, having a strange return to the very old or the primitive along with their logical and very right interest in the new, though some liked Beethoven.

We had invited the audience to our party after the performance. The audience was surprised and pleased. It felt privileged. It watched us now with an entirely different point of view and it wondered at its own transformation while I wondered why I hadn't thought of doing this before and said so to Al as the audience gasped, grinned, clapped, fidgeted and tried to see into the wings.

We had, during that same performance, asked the audience to come forward, even to dance if it was so inclined. We had discussed this thoroughly beforehand in our staff meetings. It wasn't as though it was not a completely planned thing, and we had thought some Vivaldi would be a good way to start them off. Al had said, "Certainly something new must happen every day." Afterward I said to the audience, "Let me introduce Al, who has just arrived by an unfortunate plane crash from a far-off land, a leading force among the new objectivists, but penniless at the moment, sleeping out under our bleachers.... However, that very night I heard that Miss Haertzler and Al either went for a walk after our party up to the gazebo on the hill or they went rowing on the lake, and I heard someone say, though not necessarily referring to them, "Those are two thin young people in the woods and they're quite conscious that they don't have clothes on and that they're very free spirits." And someone said, "She has a rather interesting brassiere," though that was at a different time, and also, "I wonder if he's a faggot because of the two fingers coming down so elegantly."

I found it hard to adjust to some of the customs of this hardy and lively people. This beautiful, slim young girl invited me to her guest room on my second night there and then entered as I lay in bed, dropping her simple, brightly colored shift at her feet. Underneath she wore only the tiniest bit of pink lace, and while I was wondering, was she, perhaps, the king's daughter or the chief's mistress? what dangers would I be opening myself up to? and thinking besides that this was my first night in a really comfortable bed after a very enervating two days, also my first night with a full stomach and would I be able to? she moved, not toward me, but to the harpsichord....

I had much to learn.

Mornings, sometimes as early as nine-thirty, Al could be found painting in purples, browns, grays and blacks in the vestibule area at the front of our tent. The afternoons many of us, Al included, frequently spent lounging on the grass outside the tent (on those days when it didn't rain), candidly confessing the ages of and the natures of our very first sexual experiences and discussing other indiscretions, with the sounds of the various rehearsals as our background music. (Miss Haertzler's first sexual experience, from what I've been told, may have actually taken place fairly recently and in our own little red ticket booth.) Thinking back to those evening concerts I can still see Al, as though it were yesterday, in his little corner backstage scribbling on his manifesto of the new art:

"Why should painting remain shackled by outmoded laws? Let us proclaim, here and at once, a new world for art where each work is judged by its own internal structures, by the manifestations of its own being, by its self-established decrees, by its self-generated commands.

"Let us proclaim the universal properties of the thing itself without the intermediary of fashion.

"Let us proclaim the fragment, the syllable, the single note (or sound) as the supreme elements out of which everything else flows...."

And so forth.

(Let us also proclaim what a friend [Tom Disch] has said: "I don't understand people who have a feeling of comfortableness about art. There's a kind of art that they feel comfortable seeing and will go and see that kind of thing again and again. I get very bored with known sensations....")

But, even as Al worked, seemingly so contented, and even as he welcomed color TV, the discovery of DNA and the synthesizing of an enzyme, he had his doubts and fears just like anyone else.

Those mountains that caught the rays of the setting sun and burned so red in the evenings! That breathtaking view! How many hours did I spend gazing at them when I should have been writing on my manifesto, aching with their beauty and yet wondering whether I would ever succeed in crossing them? How many times did my conversation at that time contain hidden references to bearers and guides? Once I learned of a trail that I might follow by myself if I could get someone to furnish me with a map. It was said to be negotiable only through the summer to the middle of October and to be too steep for mule or motorcycle. Later on I became acquainted with a middle-aged homosexual flute player named Ralph, who was willing to answer all my questions quite candidly. We became good friends and, as I got to know him better, I was astounded at the sophistication of his views on the nature of the universe. He was a gentle, harmless person, tall and tanned from a sun lamp. Perhaps I should mention that he never made any sexual advances to me, that I was aware of at any rate.

"After the meeting between Ralph A. and Al W.," the critics write, "Ralph A.'s work underwent an astonishing change. Obviously he was impressed by the similarities between art and music and he attempted to interpret in musical terms those portions of Al W.'s manifesto that would lend themselves to this transposition. His 'Three Short Pieces for Flute, Oboe and Prepared Piano' is, perhaps, the finest example of his work of this period."

By then Al had lent his name to our town's most prestigious art gallery. We had quoted him often in our programs. I had discussed with him the use of public or private funds for art. I had also discussed, needless to say, the problem of legalized abortion and whether the state should give aid to parochial schools. Also the new high-yield rice. I mentioned our peace groups including our Women's March for Peace. I also tried to tell him Miss Haertzler's real age and I said that, in spite of her looks, it would be very unlikely that she could ever have any children, whereas I, though not particularly young anymore, could at least do that, I'm (fairly) sure.

And then, all too soon, came the day of the dismantling of the Annual Fall Festival tent and the painting over of our billboard, which Al did (in grays, browns, purples and blacks), making it into an ad for the most prestigious art gallery, and I, I was no longer a director of anything at all. The audience, which had grown fat and satiated on our sounds, now walked in town as separate entities...factions...fragments...will-o'-the-wisp...meaningless individuals with their separate reactions. Al walked with them, wearing his same old oddly cut clothes as unself-consciously as ever, and, as ever, with them but not of them. He had worked for us until the very last moment, but now I had no more jobs to give. He couldn't find any other work and, while the critics and many others, too, liked his paintings, no one wanted to buy them. They were fairly expensive and the colors were too somber. I helped him look into getting a grant, but in the end it went to a younger man (which I should have anticipated). I gave him, at about that time, all my cans of corned beef hash even though I knew he still spent some time in Miss Haertzler's guest room, though, by then, a commune (consisting of six young people of both sexes in a three-room apartment) had accepted him as one of them. (I wonder sometimes that he never asked Miss Haertzler to marry him, but he may have been unfamiliar with marriage as we know it. We never discussed it that I remember and not too many people in his circle of friends were actually married to each other.)

Ralph had established himself as the local college musical figure, musician in residence really, and began to walk with a stoop and a slight limp and to have a funny way of clearing his throat every third or fourth word. I asked him to look into a similar job for Al, but they already had an artist in residence, a man in his sixties said to have a fairly original eye and to be profoundly concerned with the disaffection of the young, so they couldn't do a thing for Al for at least a year, they said, aside from having him give a lecture or two, but even that wouldn't be possible until the second semester.

Those days I frequently saw Al riding around on a borrowed motor scooter (sometimes not even waving), Miss Haertzler on the back with her skirts pulled up. He still painted. The critics have referred to this time in his life as one of hardship and self-denial while trying to get established.

Meanwhile it grew colder.

Miss Haertzler bought him a shearling lamb jacket. Also one for herself. I should have suspected something then, but I knew it was the wrong time of year for a climb. There was already a little bit of snow on the top of the highest of our mountains and the weatherman had forecast a storm front on the way that was to be there by that night or the next afternoon. We all thought it was too early for a blizzard.

> *I was to find Miss (Vivienne) Haertzler an excellent traveling companion. Actually a better climber than I was myself in many ways and yet, for all that vigor, preserving an essential femininity. Like many others of her race, she had small hands and feet and a fair-skinned look of transparency, and yet an endurance that matched my own. But I did notice about her that day an extraordinary anxiety that wasn't in keeping with her nature at all (nor of the natives in general). I didn't give a second thought, however, to any of the unlikely rumors I had heard, but I assumed it was due to the impending storm that we hoped would hide all traces of our ascent.*

A half day later a good-sized group of our more creative people were going after one of the most exciting minds in the arts with bloodhounds. A good thing for Miss Haertzler, too, since the two of them never even got halfway. I saw them back in town a few days afterward, still looking frostbitten, and it wasn't long after that that I had a very pleasant discussion with Al. I had asked him out to our town's finest continental restaurant. We talked, among other things, about alienation in our society, population control, impending world famine and other things of international concern including the anxiety prevalent among our people of impending atomic doom. In passing I mentioned a psychologist I had once gone to for certain anxieties of my own of a more private nature. Soon after that I heard that Al was in therapy himself and had learned to accept his perennial urge to cross the mountains and, as the psychologist put it, "leave our happy valley in his efforts to escape from something in himself." It would be a significant moment in both modern painting and modern music (and perhaps in literature, too) when Al would finally be content to remain in his new-found artistic milieu. I can't help but feel that the real beginning of Al's participation (sponsored) within our culture as a whole was right here on my couch in front of the fireplace with a cup of hot coffee and a promise of financial assistance from two of our better-known art patrons. It was right here that he began living out some sort of universal human drama of life and death in keeping with his special talents.

The Little Magic Shop

Bruce Sterling

THE EARLY LIFE of James Abernathy was rife with ominous portent.

His father, a New England customs inspector, had artistic ambitions; he filled his sketchbooks with mossy old Puritan tombstones and spanking new Nantucket whaling ships. By day, he graded bales of imported tea and calico; during evenings he took James to meetings of his intellectual friends, who would drink port, curse their wives and editors, and give James treacle candy.

James's father vanished while on a sketching expedition to the Great Stone Face of Vermont; nothing was ever found of him but his shoes.

James's mother, widowed with her young son, eventually married a large and hairy man who lived in a crumbling mansion in upstate New York.

At night the family often socialized in the nearby town of Albany. There, James's stepfather would talk politics with his friends in the National Anti-Masonic Party; upstairs, his mother and the other women chatted with prominent dead personalities through spiritualist table rapping.

Eventually, James's stepfather grew more and more anxious over the plotting of the Masons. The family ceased to circulate in society. The curtains were drawn and the family ordered to maintain a close watch for strangers dressed in black. James's mother grew thin and pale, and often wore nothing but her houserobe for days on end.

One day, James's stepfather read them newspaper accounts of the angel Moroni, who had revealed locally buried tablets of gold that detailed the Biblical history of the Mound Builder Indians. By the time he reached the end of the article, the stepfather's voice shook and his eyes had grown quite wild. That night, muffled shrieks and frenzied hammerings were heard.

In the morning, young James found his stepfather downstairs by the hearth, still in his dressing gown, sipping teacup after teacup full of brandy and absently bending and straightening the fireside poker.

James offered morning greetings with his usual cordiality. The stepfather's eyes darted frantically under matted brows. James was informed that his mother was on a mission of mercy to a distant family stricken by scarlet fever. The conversation soon passed to a certain upstairs storeroom whose door was now nailed shut. James's stepfather strictly commanded him to avoid this forbidden portal.

Days passed. His mother's absence stretched to weeks. Despite repeated and increasingly strident warnings from his stepfather, James showed no interest whatsoever in the upstairs room. Eventually, deep within the older man's brain, a ticking artery burst from sheer frustration.

During his stepfather's funeral, the family home was struck by ball lightning and burned to the ground. The insurance money, and James's fate, passed into the hands of a distant relative, a muttering, trembling man who campaigned against liquor and drank several bottles of Dr. Rifkin's Laudanum Elixir each week.

James was sent to a boarding school run by a fanatical Calvinist deacon. James prospered there, thanks to close study of the scriptures and his equable, reasonable temperament. He grew to adulthood, becoming a tall, studious young man with a calm disposition and a solemn face utterly unmarked by doom.

Two days after his graduation, the deacon and his wife were both found hacked to bits, their half-naked bodies crammed into their one-horse shay. James stayed long enough to console the couple's spinster daughter, who sat dry-eyed in her rocking chair, methodically ripping a handkerchief to shreds.

James then took himself to New York City for higher education.

It was there that James Abernathy found the little shop that sold magic.

James stepped into this unmarked shop on impulse, driven inside by muffled screams of agony from the dentist's across the street.

The shop's dim interior smelled of burning whale-oil and hot lantern-brass. Deep wooden shelves, shrouded in cobwebs, lined the walls. Here and there, yellowing political broadsides requested military help for the rebel Texans. James set his divinity texts on an apothecary cabinet, where a band of stuffed, lacquered frogs brandished tiny trumpets and guitars. The proprietor appeared from behind a red curtain. "May I help the young master?" he said, rubbing his hands. He was a small, spry Irishman. His ears rose to points lightly shrouded in hair; he wore bifocal spectacles and brass-buckled shoes.

"I rather fancy that fantod under the bell jar," said James, pointing.

"I'll wager we can do much better for a young man like yourself," said the proprietor with a leer. "So fresh, so full of life."

James puffed the thick dust of long neglect from the fantod jar. "Is business all it might be, these days?"

"We have a rather specialized clientele," said the other, and he introduced himself. His name was Mr. O'Beronne, and he had recently fled his country's devastating potato famine. James shook Mr. O'Beronne's small papery hand.

"You'll be wanting a love-potion," said Mr. O'Beronne with a shrewd look. "Fellows of your age generally do."

James shrugged. "Not really, no."

"Is it budget troubles, then? I might interest you in an ever-filled purse." The old man skipped from behind the counter and hefted a large bearskin cape.

"Money?" said James with only distant interest.

"Fame then. We have magic brushes – or if you prefer newfangled scientific arts, we have a camera that once belonged to Montavarde himself."

"No, no," said James, looking restless. "Can you quote me a price on this fantod?" He studied the fantod critically. It was not in very good condition.

"We can restore youth," said Mr. O'Beronne in sudden desperation.

"Do tell," said James, straightening.

"We have a shipment of Dr. Heidegger's Patent Youthing Waters," said Mr. O'Beronne. He tugged a quagga hide from a nearby brass-bound chest and dug out a square glass bottle. He uncorked it. The waters fizzed lightly, and the smell of May filled the room. "One bottle imbibed," said Mr. O'Beronne, "restores a condition of blushing youth to man or beast."

"Is that a fact," said James, his brows knitting in thought. "How many teaspoons per bottle?"

"I've no idea," Mr. O'Beronne admitted. "Never measured it by the spoon. Mind you, this is an old folks' item. Fellows of your age usually go for the love-potions."

"How much for a bottle?" said James.

"It is a bit steep," said Mr. O'Beronne grudgingly. "The price is everything you possess."

"Seems reasonable," said James. "How much for two bottles?"

Mr. O'Beronne stared. "Don't get ahead of yourself, young man." He recorked the bottle carefully. "You've yet to give me all you possess, mind."

"How do I know you'll still have the waters, when I need more?" James said.

Mr. O'Beronne's eyes shifted uneasily behind his bifocals. "You let me worry about that." He leered, but without the same conviction he had shown earlier. "I won't be shutting up this shop – not when there are people of your sort about."

"Fair enough," said James, and they shook hands on the bargain. James returned two days later, having sold everything he owned. He handed over a small bag of gold specie and a bank draft conveying the slender remaining funds of his patrimony. He departed with the clothes on his back and the bottle.

Twenty years passed.

The United States suffered civil war. Hundreds of thousands of men were shot, blown up with mines or artillery, or perished miserably in septic army camps. In the streets of New York, hundreds of antidraft rioters were mown down with grapeshot, and the cobbled street before the little magic shop was strewn with reeking dead. At last, after stubborn resistance and untold agonies, the Confederacy was defeated. The war became history.

James Abernathy returned.

"I've been in California," he announced to the astonished Mr. O'Beronne. James was healthily tanned and wore a velvet cloak, spurred boots, and a silver sombrero. He sported a large gold turnip-watch, and his fingers gleamed with gems.

"You struck it rich in the goldfields," Mr. O'Beronne surmised.

"Actually, no," said James. "I've been in the grocery business. In Sacramento. One can sell a dozen eggs there for almost their weight in gold dust, you know." He smiled and gestured at his elaborate clothes. "I did pretty well, but I don't usually dress this extravagantly. You see, I'm wearing my entire worldly wealth. I thought it would make our transaction simpler." He produced the empty bottle.

"That's very farsighted of you," said Mr. O'Beronne. He examined James critically, as if looking for hairline psychic cracks or signs of moral corruption. "You don't seem to have aged a day."

"Oh, that's not quite so," said James. "I was twenty when I first came here; now I easily look twenty-one, even twenty-two." He put the bottle on the counter. "You'll be interested to know there were twenty teaspoons exactly."

"You didn't spill any?"

"Oh, no," said James, smiling at the thought. "I've only opened it once a year."

"It didn't occur to you to take two teaspoons, say? Or empty the bottle at a draught?"

"Now what would be the use of that?" said James. He began stripping off his rings and dropping them on the counter with light tinkling sounds. "You did keep the Youthing Waters in stock, I presume."

"A bargain's a bargain," said Mr. O'Beronne grudgingly. He produced another bottle. James left barefoot, wearing only shirt and pants, but carrying his bottle.

The 1870s passed and the nation celebrated its centennial. Railroads stitched the continent. Gaslights were installed in the streets of New York. Buildings taller than any ever seen began to soar, though the magic shop's neighborhood remained obscure.

James Abernathy returned. He now looked at least twenty-four. He passed over the title deeds to several properties in Chicago and departed with another bottle.

Shortly after the turn of the century, James returned again, driving a steam automobile, whistling the theme of the St. Louis Exhibition and stroking his waxed mustache. He signed over the deed to the car, which was a fine one, but Mr. O'Beronne showed little enthusiasm. The old Irishman had shrunken with the years, and his tiny hands trembled as he conveyed his goods.

Within the following period, a great war of global empires took place, but America was mostly spared the devastation. The 1920s arrived, and James came laden with a valise crammed with rapidly appreciating stocks and bonds. "You always seem to do rather well for yourself," Mr. O'Beronne observed in a quavering voice.

"Moderation's the key," said James. "That, and a sunny disposition." He looked about the shop with a critical eye. The quality of the junk had declined. Old engine parts lay in reeking grease next to heaps of moldering popular magazines and spools of blackened telephone wire. The exotic hides, packets of spice and amber, ivory tusks hand-carved by cannibals, and so forth, had now entirely disappeared. "I hope you don't mind these new bottles," croaked Mr. O'Beronne, handing him one. The bottle had curved sides and a machine-fitted cap of cork and tin.

"Any trouble with supply?" said James delicately.

"You let me worry about that!" said Mr. O'Beronne, lifting his lip with a faint snarl of defiance.

James's next visit came after yet another war, this one of untold and almost unimaginable savagery. Mr. O'Beronne's shop was now crammed with military surplus goods. Bare electric bulbs hung over a realm of rotting khaki and rubber.

James now looked almost thirty. He was a little short by modern American standards, but this was scarcely noticeable. He wore high-waisted pants and a white linen suit with jutting shoulders.

"I don't suppose," muttered Mr. O'Beronne through his false teeth, "that it ever occurs to you to share this? What about wives, sweethearts, children?"

James shrugged. "What about them?"

"You're content to see them grow old and die?"

"I never see them grow all *that* old," James observed. "After all, every twenty years I have to return here and lose everything I own. It's simpler just to begin all over again."

"No human feelings," Mr. O'Beronne muttered bitterly.

"Oh, come now," said James. "After all, I don't see *you* distributing elixir to all and sundry, either."

"But I'm in the magic shop *business*," said Mr. O'Beronne, weakly. "There are certain unwritten rules."

"Oh?" said James, leaning on the counter with the easy patience of a youthful centenarian. "You never mentioned this before. Supernatural law – it must be an interesting field of study."

"Never you mind that," Mr. O'Beronne snapped. "You're a *customer*, and a human being. You mind your business and I'll mind mine."

"No need to be so touchy," James said. He hesitated. "You know, I have some hot leads in the new plastics industry. I imagine I could make a great deal more money than usual. That is, if you're interested in selling this place." He smiled. "They say an Irishman never forgets the Old Country. You could go back into your old line – pot o' gold, bowl of milk on the doorstep...."

"Take your bottle and go," O'Beronne shouted, thrusting it into his hands.

Another two decades passed. James drove up in a Mustang convertible and entered the shop. The place reeked of patchouli incense, and Day-Glo posters covered the walls. Racks of demented comic books loomed beside tables littered with hookahs and handmade clay pipes.

Mr. O'Beronne dragged himself from behind a hanging beaded curtain. "You again," he croaked.

"Right on," said James, looking around. "I like the way you've kept the place up to date, man. Groovy."

O'Beronne gave him a poisonous glare. "You're a hundred and forty years old. Hasn't the burden of unnatural life become insupportable?"

James looked at him, puzzled. "Are you kidding?"

"Haven't you learned a lesson about the blessings of mortality? About how it's better not to outlive your own predestined time?"

"Huh?" James said. He shrugged. "I did learn something about material possessions, though.... Material things only tie a cat down. You can't have the car this time, it's rented." He dug a hand-stitched leather wallet from his bell-bottom jeans. "I have some fake ID and credit cards." He shook them out over the counter.

Mr. O'Beronne stared unbelieving at the meager loot. "Is this your idea of a joke?"

"Hey, it's all I possess," James said mildly. "I could have bought Xerox at fifteen, back in the '50s. But last time I talked to you, you didn't seem interested. I figured it was like, you know, not the bread that counts, but the spirit of the thing."

Mr. O'Beronne clutched his heart with a liver-spotted hand. "Is this never going to end? Why did I ever leave Europe? They know how to respect a tradition there...." He paused, gathering bile. "Look at this place! It's an insult! Call this a magic shop?" He snatched up a fat mushroom-shaped candle and flung it to the floor.

"You're overwrought," James said. "Look, you're the one who said a bargain's a bargain. There's no need for us to go on with this any longer. I can see your heart's not in it. Why not put me in touch with your wholesaler?"

"Never!" O'Beronne swore. "I won't be beaten by some cold-blooded... bookkeeper."

"I never thought of this as a contest," James said with dignity. "Sorry to see you take it that way, man." He picked up his bottle and left.

The allotted time elapsed, and James repeated his pilgrimage to the magic shop. The neighborhood had declined. Women in spandex and net hose lurked on the pavement, watched from the corner by men in broad-brimmed hats and slick polished shoes. James carefully locked the doors of his BMW.

The magic shop's once-curtained windows had been painted over in black. A neon sign above the door read ADULT PEEP 25¢.

Inside, the shop's cluttered floor space had been cleared. Shrink-wrapped magazines lined the walls, their fleshy covers glaring under the bluish corpse-light of overhead fluorescents. The old counter had been replaced by a long glass-fronted cabinet displaying knotted whips and flavored lubricants. The bare floor clung stickily to the soles of James's Gucci shoes.

A young man emerged from behind a curtain. He was tall and bony, with a small, neatly trimmed mustache. His smooth skin had a waxy subterranean look. He gestured fluidly. "Peeps in the back," he said in a high voice, not meeting James's eyes. "You gotta buy tokens. Three bucks."

"I beg your pardon?" James said.

"Three bucks, man!"

"Oh." James produced the money. The man handed over a dozen plastic tokens and vanished at once behind the curtains.

"Excuse me?" James said. No answer. "Hello?"

The peep machines waited in the back of the store, in a series of curtained booths. The vinyl cushions inside smelled of sweat and butyl nitrate. James inserted a token and watched.

He then moved to the other machines and examined them as well. He returned to the front of the shop. The shopkeeper sat on a stool, ripping the covers from unsold magazines and watching a small television under the counter.

"Those films," James said. "That was Charlie Chaplin. And Douglas Fairbanks. And Gloria Swanson..."

The man looked up, smoothing his hair. "Yeah, so? You don't like silent films?"

James paused. "I can't believe Charlie Chaplin did porn."

"I hate to spoil a magic trick," the shopkeeper said, yawning. "But they're genuine peeps, pal. You ever hear of Hearst Mansion? San Simeon? Old Hearst, he liked filming his Hollywood guests on the sly. All the bedrooms had spy holes."

"Oh," James said. "I see. Ah, is Mr. O'Beronne in?"

The man showed interest for the first time. "You know the old guy? I don't get many nowadays who knew the old guy. His clientele had pretty special tastes, I hear."

James nodded. "He should be holding a bottle for me."

"Well, I'll check in the back. Maybe he's awake." The shopkeeper vanished again. He reappeared minutes later with a brownish vial. "Got some love-potion here."

James shook his head. "Sorry, that's not it."

"It's the real stuff, man! Works like you wouldn't believe!" The shopkeeper was puzzled. "You young guys are usually into love-potions. Well, I guess I'll have to rouse the old guy for you. Though I kind of hate to disturb him."

Long minutes passed, with distant rustling and squeaking. Finally the shopkeeper backed through the curtains, tugging a wheelchair. Mr. O'Beronne sat within it, wrapped in bandages, his wrinkled head shrouded in a dirty nightcap. "Oh," he said at last. "So it's you again."

"Yes, I've returned for my – "

"I know, I know." Mr. O'Beronne stirred fitfully on his cushions. "I see you've met my...associate. Mr. Ferry."

"I kind of manage the place, these days," said Mr. Ferry. He winked at James, behind Mr. O'Beronne's back.

"I'm James Abernathy," James said. He offered his hand.

Ferry folded his arms warily. "Sorry, I never do that."

O'Beronne cackled feebly and broke into a fit of coughing. "Well, my boy," he said finally, "I was hoping I'd last long enough to see you one more time... Mr. Ferry! There's a crate, in the back, under those filthy movie posters of yours...."

"Sure, sure," Ferry said indulgently. He left.

"Let me look at you," said O'Beronne. His eyes, in their dry, leaden sockets, had grown quite lizardlike. "Well, what do you think of the place? Be frank."

"It's looked better," James said. "So have you."

"But so has the world, eh?" O'Beronne said. "He does bang-up business, young Ferry. You should see him manage the books...."

He waved one hand, its tiny knuckles warped with arthritis. "It's such a blessing, not to have to care anymore."

Ferry reappeared, lugging a wooden crate, crammed with dusty six-packs of pop-top aluminum cans. He set it gently on the counter.

Every can held Youthing Water. "Thanks," James said, his eyes widening. He lifted one pack reverently, and tugged at a can.

"Don't," O'Beronne said. "This is for you, all of it. Enjoy it, son. I hope you're satisfied."

James lowered the cans, slowly. "What about our arrangement?"

O'Beronne's eyes fell, in an ecstasy of humiliation. "I humbly apologize. But I simply can't keep up our bargain any longer. I don't have the strength, you see. So this is yours now. It's all I could find."

"Yeah, this must be pretty much the last of it," nodded Ferry, inspecting his nails. "It hasn't moved well for some time – I figure the bottling plant shut up shop."

"So many cans, though..." James said thoughtfully. He produced his wallet. "I brought a nice car for you, outside...."

"None of that matters now," said Mr. O'Beronne. "Keep all of it, just consider it my forfeit." His voice fell. "I never thought it would come to this, but you've beaten me, I admit it. I'm done in." His head sagged limply.

Mr. Ferry took the wheelchair's handles. "He's tired now," he said soothingly. "I'll just wheel him back out of our way, here...." He held the curtains back and shoved the chair through with his foot. He turned to James. "You can take that case and let yourself out. Nice doing business – goodbye." He nodded briskly.

"Goodbye, sir!" James called. No answer.

James hauled the case outside to his car, and set it in the backseat. Then he sat in front for a while, drumming his fingers on the steering wheel.

Finally he went back in.

Mr. Ferry had pulled a telephone from beneath his cash register. When he saw James he slammed the headset down. "Forget something, pal?"

"I'm troubled," James said. "I keep wondering...what about those unwritten rules?"

The shopkeeper looked at him, surprised. "Aw, the old guy always talked like that. Rules, standards, quality." Mr. Ferry gazed meditatively over his stock, then looked James in the eye. "What *rules*, man?"

There was a moment of silence.

"I was never quite sure," James said. "But I'd like to ask Mr. O'Beronne."

"You've badgered him enough," the shopkeeper said. "Can't you see he's a dying man? You got what you wanted, so scram, hit the road." He folded his arms. James refused to move.

The shopkeeper sighed. "Look, I'm not in this for my health. You want to hang around here, you gotta buy some more tokens."

"I've seen those already," James said. "What else do you sell?"

"Oh, machines not good enough for you, eh?" Mr. Ferry stroked his chin. "Well, it's not strictly in my line, but I might sneak you a gram or two of Señor Buendia's Colombian Real Magic Powder. First taste is free. No? You're a hard man to please, bub."

Ferry sat down, looking bored. "I don't see why I should change my stock, just because you're so picky. A smart operator like you, you ought to have bigger fish to fry than a little magic shop. Maybe you just don't belong here, pal."

"No, I always liked this place," James said. "I used to, anyway. I even wanted to own it myself."

Ferry tittered. "You? Gimme a break." His face hardened. "If you don't like the way I run things, take a hike."

"No, no, I'm sure I can find something here," James said quickly. He pointed at random to a thick hardbound book, at the bottom of a stack, below the counter. "Let me try that."

Mr. Ferry shrugged with bad grace and fetched it out. "You'll like this," he said unconvincingly. "Marilyn Monroe and Jack Kennedy at a private beach house."

James leafed through the glossy pages. "How much?"

"You want it?" said the shopkeeper. He examined the binding and set it back down. "Okay, fifty bucks."

"Just cash?" James said, surprised. "Nothing magical?"

"Cash *is* magical, pal." The shopkeeper shrugged. "Okay, forty bucks and you have to kiss a dog on the lips."

"I'll pay the fifty," James said. He pulled out his wallet. "Whoops!" He fumbled, and it dropped over the far side of the counter.

Mr. Ferry lunged for it. As he rose again, James slammed the heavy book into his head. The shopkeeper fell with a groan.

James vaulted over the counter and shoved the curtains aside. He grabbed the wheelchair and hauled it out. The wheels thumped twice over Ferry's outstretched legs. Jostled, O'Beronne woke with a screech.

James pulled him toward the blacked-out windows. "Old man," he panted. "How long has it been since you had some fresh air?" He kicked open the door.

"No!" O'Beronne yelped. He shielded his eyes with both hands. "I have to stay inside here! That's the rules!" James wheeled him out onto the pavement. As sunlight hit him, O'Beronne howled in fear and squirmed wildly. Gouts of dust puffed from his cushions, and his bandages flapped. James yanked open the car door, lifted O'Beronne bodily, and dropped him into the passenger seat. "You can't do this!" O'Beronne screamed, his nightcap flying off. "I belong behind walls, I can't go into the world...."

James slammed the door. He ran around and slid behind the wheel. "It's dangerous out here," O'Beronne whimpered as the engine roared into life. "I was safe in there...."

James stamped the accelerator. The car laid rubber. He glanced behind him in the rearview mirror and saw an audience of laughing, whooping hookers. "Where are we going?" O'Beronne said meekly.

James floored it through a yellow light. He reached into the backseat one-handed and yanked a can from its six-pack. "Where was this bottling plant?"

O'Beronne blinked doubtfully. "It's been so long...Florida, I think."

"Florida sounds good. Sunlight, fresh air..." James weaved deftly through traffic, cracking the pop-top with his thumb. He knocked back a hefty swig, then gave O'Beronne the can. "Here, old man. Finish it off."

O'Beronne stared at it, licking dry lips. "But I can't. I'm an owner, not a customer. I'm simply not allowed to do this sort of thing. I own that magic shop, I tell you."

James shook his head and laughed.

O'Beronne trembled. He raised the can in both gnarled hands and began chugging thirstily. He paused once to belch, and kept drinking.

The smell of May filled the car.

O'Beronne wiped his mouth and crushed the empty can in his fist. He tossed it over his shoulder.

"There's room back there for those bandages, too," James told him. "Let's hit the highway."

The Healer

Aimee Bender

THERE WERE TWO MUTANT GIRLS in the town: one had a hand made of fire and the other had a hand made of ice. Everyone else's hands were normal. The girls first met in elementary school and were friends for about three weeks. Their parents were delighted; the mothers in particular spent hours on the phone describing over and over the shock of delivery day.

I remember one afternoon, on the playground, the fire girl grabbed hold of the ice girl's hand and – Poof – just like that, each equalized the other. Their hands dissolved into regular flesh – exit mutant, enter normal. The fire girl panicked and let go, finding that her fire reblazed right away, while the ice spun back fast around the other girl's fingers like a cold glass turban. They grasped hands again; again, it worked. Delighted by the neat new trick, I think they even charged money to perform it for a while and made a pretty penny.

Audiences loved to watch the two little girls dabbling in the elements with their tiny powerful fists.

After a while, the ice girl said she was tired of the trick and gave it up and they stopped being friends. I'd never seen them together since but now they were both sixteen and in the same science class. I was there too; I was a senior then.

The fire girl sat in the back row. Sparks dripped from her fingertips like sweat and fizzed on the linoleum. She looked both friendly and lonely. After school, she was most popular with the cigarette kids who found her to be the coolest of lighters.

The ice girl sat in the front row and wore a ponytail. She kept her ice hand in her pocket but you knew it was there because it leaked. I remember when the two met, at the start of the school year, face-to-face for the first time in years, the fire girl held out her fire hand, I guess to try the trick again, but the ice girl shook her head. I'm not a shaker, she said. Those were her exact words. I could tell the fire girl felt bad. I gave her a sympathetic look but she missed it. After school let out, she passed along the brick wall, lighting cigarette after cigarette, tiny red circles in a line. She didn't keep the smokers company; just did her duty and then walked home, alone.

Our town was ringed by a circle of hills and because of this no one really came in and no one ever left. Only one boy made it out. He'd been very gifted at public speech and one afternoon he climbed over Old Midge, the shortest of the ring, and vanished forever. After six months or so he mailed his mother a postcard with a fish on it that said: In the Big City. Giving Speeches All Over. Love, J. She Xeroxed the postcard and gave every citizen a copy. I stuck it on the wall by my bed. I made up his speeches, regularly, on my way to school; they always involved me. Today we focus on Lisa, J.'s voice would sail out, Lisa with the two flesh hands. This is generally where I'd stop – I wasn't sure what to add.

During science class that fall, the fire girl burnt things with her fingers. She entered the room with a pile of dry leaves in her book bag and by the time the bell rang, there was ash all over her desk. She seemed to need to do this. It prevented some potential friendships, however, because most people were too scared to approach her. I tried but I never knew what to say. For Christmas that year I bought her a log. Here, I said, I got this for you to burn up. She started to cry. I said: Do you hate it? but she said No. She said it was a wonderful gift and from then on she remembered my name.

I didn't buy anything for the ice girl. What do you get an ice girl anyway? She spent most of her non-school time at the hospital, helping sick people. She was a great soother, they said. Her water had healing powers.

What happened was the fire girl met Roy. And that's when everything changed.

I found them first, and it was accidental, and I told no one, so it wasn't my fault. Roy was a boy who had no parents and lived alone.

He was very rarely at school and he was a cutter. He cut things into his skin with a razor blade. I saw once; some Saturday when everyone was at a picnic and I was bored, I wandered into the boys' bathroom and he was in there and he showed me how he carved letters into his skin. He'd spelled out OUCH on his leg. Raised and white. I put out a hand and touched it and then I walked directly home. It was hard to feel those letters. They still felt like skin.

I don't know exactly how the fire girl met Roy but they spent their afternoons by the base of the mountains and she would burn him. A fresh swatch of skin every day. I was on a long walk near Old Midge after school, wondering if I'd ever actually cross it, when I passed the two of them for the first time. I almost waved and called out Hi but then I saw what was going on. Her back was to me, but still I could see that she was leaning forward with one fire finger pressed against his inner elbow and his eyes were shut and he was moaning. The flames hissed and crisped on contact. She sucked in her breath, sss, and then she pulled her hand away and they both crumpled back, breathing hard. Roy had a new mark on his arm. This one did not form a letter. It swirled into itself, black and detailed, a tiny whirlpool of lines.

I turned and walked away. My own hands were shaking. I had to force myself to leave instead of going back and watching more. I kept walking until I looped the entire town.

All during the next month, both Roy and the fire girl looked really happy. She stopped bringing leaves into science class and started participating and Roy smiled at me in the street which had never happened before. I continued my mountain walks after school, and usually I'd see them pressed into the shade, but I never again allowed myself to stop and watch. I didn't want to invade their privacy but it was more than that; something about watching them reminded me of quicksand, slide and pull in, as fast as that. I just took in what I could as I passed by. It always smelled a bit like barbecue, where they were. This made me hungry, which made me uncomfortable.

It was some family, off to the base of Old Midge to go camping, that saw and told everyone.

The fire girl is hurting people! they announced, and Roy tried to explain but his arms and thighs were pocked with fingerprint scars and it said OUCH in writing on his thigh and no one believed him, they believed the written word instead, and placed him in a foster home. I heard he started chewing glass.

They put the fire girl in jail. She's a danger, everyone said, she burns things, she burns people. She likes it. This was true: at the jail she grabbed the forearm of the guard with her fire fist and left a smoking tarantula handprint; he had to go to the hospital and be soothed by the ice girl.

The whole town buzzed about the fire girl all week. They said: She's crazy! Or: She's primitive! I lay in my bed at night, and thought of her concentrating and leaning in to Roy. I thought of her shuddering out to the trees like a drum.

I went to the burn ward and found the ice girl. If anyone, I thought, she might have some answers.

She was holding her hand above a sick man in a bed with red sores all over his body, and her ice was dripping into his mouth and he looked thrilled.

I want you to come to the jail, I said, and give her a little relief.

The ice girl looked over at me. Who are you? she asked.

I was annoyed. I'm in your science class, I said, Lisa.

She gave a nod. Oh right, she said. You sit in the middle.

I looked at the man in the hospital bed, the bliss on his face, the gloom on hers.

This can't be too fun for you, I said.

She didn't answer. Come to the jail, I said, please, she's so unhappy, maybe you can help.

The ice girl checked the watch on her flesh hand. The man beneath her made something close to a purring sound. If you come back in an hour, she said at last, I'll go for a little bit.

Thank you, I said, this is another good deed.

She raised her slim eyebrows. I have enough good deeds, she said. It's just that I've never seen the jail.

I returned in exactly an hour, and we went over together.

The guard at the jail beamed at the ice girl. My wife had cancer, he said, and you fixed her up just fine. The ice girl smiled. Her smile was small. I asked where the fire girl was and the guard pointed. Careful, he said, she's nutso. He coughed and crossed his legs. We turned to his point, and I led the way down.

The fire girl was at the back of her cell, burning up the fluffy inside of the mattress. She recognized me right away.

Hi, Lisa, she said, how's it going?

Fine, I said. We're on frogs now in science.

She nodded. The ice girl stood back, looking around at the thick stone walls and the low ceiling. The room was dank and smelled moldy.

Look who I brought, I said. Maybe she can help you.

The fire girl looked up. Hey, she said. They exchanged a nod. It was all so formal. I was annoyed. It seems to me that in a jail, you don't need to be that formal, you can let some things loose.

So, wanting to be useful, I went right over to the ice girl and pulled her hand out of her pocket, against her half-protests. I held it forward, and stuck it through the bars of the cell. It was surprisingly heavy which filled me with new sympathy. It felt like a big cold rock.

Here, I said, shaking it a little, go to it.

The fire girl grasped the ice girl's hand. I think we weren't sure it would work, if the magic had worn off in junior high, but it hadn't; as soon as they touched, the ice melted away and the fire burned out and they were just two girls holding hands through the bars of a jail. I had a hard time recognizing them this way. I looked at their faces and they looked different. It was like seeing a movie star nude, no makeup, eyes small and blinking.

The fire girl started to shiver and she closed her eyes. She held on hard.

It's so much quieter like this, she murmured.

The other girl winced. Not for me, she said. Her face was beginning to flush a little.

The fire girl opened her eyes. No, she said, nodding, of course. It would be different for you.

I clasped my own hands together. I felt tepid. I felt out of my league.

I don't suppose I can hold your hand all day, the fire girl said in a low voice.

The ice girl shook her head. I have to be at the hospital, she said, I need my hand. She seemed uncomfortable. Her face was getting redder. She held on a second longer. I need my hand, she said. She let go.

The fire girl hung her head. Her hand blazed up in a second, twirling into turrets. I pictured her at the mountains again – that ribbon of pleasure, tasting Roy with her fingertips.

Ice whirled back around the other girl's hand. She stepped back, and the color emptied out of her face.

It's awful, the fire girl said, shaking her wrist, sending sparks flying, starting to pace her cell. I want to burn everything. I want to burn *everything*. She gripped the iron frame of the cot until it glowed red under her palm. Do you understand? she said, it's all I think about.

We could cut it off, said the ice girl then.

We both stared at her.

Are you kidding? I said, you can't cut off the *fire* hand, it's a beautiful thing, it's a wonderful thing –

But the fire girl had released the bed and was up against the bars. Do you think it would work? she said. Do you think that would do something?

The ice girl shrugged. I don't know, she said, but it might be worth a try.

I wanted to give a protest here but I was no speechwriter; the speechwriter had left town forever and taken all the good speeches with him. I kept beginning sentences and dropping them off. Finally, they sent me out to find a knife. I don't know what they talked about while I was gone. I wasn't sure where to go so I just ran home, grabbed a huge sharp knife from the kitchen, and ran back. In ten minutes I was in the cell again, out of breath, the wooden knife handle tucked into my belt like a sword.

The fire girl was amazed. You're fast, she said. I felt flattered. I thought maybe I could be the fast girl. I was busy for a second renaming myself Atalanta when I looked over and saw how nervous and scared she was.

Don't do this, I said, you'll miss it.

But she'd already reached over and grabbed the knife and was pacing her cell again, flicking sparks onto the wall. She spoke mainly to herself. It would all be so much easier, she said.

The ice girl had no expression. I'll stay, she said, tightening her ponytail, in case you need healing. I wanted to kick her. There was a horrible ache growing in my stomach.

The fire girl took a deep breath. Then, kneeling down, she laid her hand, leaping with flames, on the stone jail floor and slammed the knife down right where the flesh of her wrist began. After sawing for a minute, she let out a shout and the hand separated and she ran over to the ice girl who put her healing bulb directly on the wound.

Tears streaked down the fire girl's face and she shifted her weight from foot to foot. The cut-off hand was hidden in a cloud of smoke on the floor. The ice girl leaned in, her soother face intent, but something strange was happening. The ice bulb wasn't working. There was no ice at all. The ice girl found herself with just a regular flesh hand, clasping the sawed-off tuber of a wrist. Equalized and normal. The fire girl looked down in horror.

Oh, pleaded the fire girl, never let go, *please*, don't, *please*, but it was too late. Her wrist had already been released to the air.

The fire girl's arm blazed up to the elbow. It was a bigger blaze now, a looser one, a less dexterous flame with no fingers to guide it. Oh no, she cried, trying to shake it off, oh *no*. The ice girl was silent, holding her hand as it reiced in her flesh palm, turning it slowly, numbing up. I was twisting in the corner, the ache in my stomach fading, trying to think of the right thing to say. But her body was now twice as burning and twice as loud and twice as powerful and twice everything. I still thought it was beautiful, but I was just an observer. The ice girl slipped silently down the hallway and I only stayed for a few more minutes. It was too hard to see. The fire girl started slamming her arm against the brick wall. When I left, she was sitting down with her chopped-off hand, burning it to pieces, one finger at a time.

They let her out a week later, but they made her strap her arm to a metal bucket of ice. The ice girl even dripped a few drops into it, to make it especially potent. The bucket would heat up on occasion but her arm apparently quieted. I didn't go to see her on the day she got out; I stayed at home. I felt responsible and ashamed: it was me who'd brought the ice girl to the jail, I'd fetched the knife, and worst, I was still so relieved it hadn't worked. Instead, I sat in my room at home that day and thought about J. in the Big City. He didn't give speeches about me anymore. Now we stood together in the middle of a busy street, dodging whizzing cars, and I'd pull him tight to me and begin to learn his skin.

All sorts of stories passed through the town about the fire girl on her day of release: She was covered in ash! She was all fire with one flesh hand! My personal favorite was that even her teeth were little flaming squares. The truth was, she found a shack in the back of town by the mountains, a shack made of metal, and she set up a home there.

The funny thing is what happened to the ice girl after all of it. She quit her job at the hospital, and she split. I thought I'd leave, I thought the fire girl would leave, but it was the ice girl who left. I passed her on the street the day before.

How are you doing, I said, how is the hospital?

She turned away from me, still couldn't look me in the eye. Everyone is sick in the hospital, she said. She stood there and I waited for her to continue. Do you realize, she said, that if I cut off my arm, my entire body might freeze?

Wow, I said. Think of all the people you could cure. I couldn't help it. I was still mad at her for suggesting the knife at all.

Yeah, she said, eyes flicking over to me for a second, think of that.

I watched her. I was remembering her face in the jail, waiting to see what would happen when the fire hand was removed. Hoping, I suppose, for a different outcome. I put my hands in my pockets. I guess I never told you, she said, but I feel nothing. I just feel ice.

I nodded. I wasn't surprised.

She turned a bit. I'm off now, she said, bye.

When the town discovered she had disappeared, there was a big uproar, and everybody blamed the fire girl. They thought she'd burned her up or something. The fire girl who never left her metal shack, sitting in her living room, her arm in that bucket. The whole town blamed her until a hungry nurse opened the hospital freezer and found one thousand Dixie cups filled with magic ice. They knew it was *her* ice because as soon as they brought a cup to a stroke patient, he improved and went home in two days. No one could figure it out, why the ice girl had left, but they stopped blaming the fire girl. Instead, they had an auction for the ice cups. People mortgaged their houses for one little cup; just in case, even if everyone was healthy; just in case. This was a good thing to hoard in your freezer.

The ones who didn't get a cup went to the fire girl. When they were troubled, or lonely, or in pain, they went to see her. If they were lucky, she'd remove her blazing arm from the ice bucket and gently touch their faces with the point of her wrist. The burns healed slowly, leaving marks on their cheeks. There was a whole group of scar people who walked around town now. I asked them: Does it hurt? And the scar people nodded, yes. But it felt somehow wonderful, they said. For one long second, it felt like the world was holding them close.

I Want My 20th-Century Schizoid Art, I

[*On May 3, 2005, new writer David Moles posted a question on his blog, Chrononautic Log (www.chrononaut.org/log/). We found the ensuing discussion to be fascinating, in part because it attracted so many young writers we consider to be among the best of their generation. We are excerpting it in four sections throughout* Feeling Very Strange. – JAMES PATRICK KELLY AND JOHN KESSEL]

When, exactly, did *slipstream* stop meaning "a kind of writing which simply makes you feel very strange; the way that living in the late twentieth century makes you feel, if you are a person of a certain sensibility," which is what Bruce Sterling wrote in his *Catscan 5* essay from *SF Eye,* and start meaning stories that "feel a bit like magical realism...[that] make the familiar strange – by taking a familiar context and disturbing it with SFnal/fantastical intrusions," as Rich Horton said, quoted in Jim Kelly's column in *Asimov's*? Because that seems to be what it means now. And it's not cutting it for me.

DAVID MOLES, 3:00PM, MAY 3, 2005

Good one, Dave. I was talking to somebody about this yesterday afternoon and we agreed that "rigorous" doesn't necessarily only mean what some folks think it means, either. I'd say more, but you've said it so well, above.

CHRISTOPHER ROWE, 5:04 PM, TUESDAY, MAY 3, 2005

I don't know, man. Telling me that a piece should make you "feel strange, like living the late twentieth century," doesn't do a lot for me, mainly because the 20th century didn't make me feel strange. Heck, neither does the 21st. It's like saying "feel strange, like breathing oxygen." Clearly I don't have the certain sensibility Sterling's referring to. And if slipstream has shifted to Horton's definition, then that suggests a whole bunch of other writers felt the same way. Of course, when dealing with vague categories, I can also understand why something prescriptive would be more popular than descriptive. Easier to get a handle on.

Having said that, if you're truly unhappy, then you should start calling Horton's classification "New Slipstream" and make a case for an immediate return to "Classic Slipstream."

JON HANSEN, 6:19 PM, TUESDAY, MAY 3, 2005

What's not good about the shift is that it took a very broad category and narrowed it down to perhaps one kind of story that fit that category and left out of the definition any of the other sorts. It's an attempt, I think, to control and define something that was hard to get a grip on. I can remember a lot of debates about this about seven or eight years ago now. People really didn't know what slipstream meant. They still don't. But what most people have decided is that it means magical realism. And the sad thing is, they think it means a very banal sort of magical realism.

CHRIS BARZAK, 8:28 PM, TUESDAY, MAY 3, 2005

I'm not entirely certain that I see a clear difference between the two pull quotes. At least, they read to me a bit like a Venn diagram. This may be because I'm with Jon in that living in the late 20th century doesn't in of itself feel strange.

My guess would be that people felt they needed a word for that vaguely-magical-realism-written-by-non-South-American writers, and there was this one for kinda sorta the same thing?

HANNAH BOWEN, 9:01 PM, TUESDAY, MAY 3, 2005

I think it gets to what Barzak's saying, that Anglo magical realism was only one small part of what Sterling was trying to define when he coined the word *slipstream*. And that what most SFnal folks seem to mean when they use it, is, in fact, not just magical realism but a very banal sort of magical realism.

And it's okay if living in the 20th century didn't make you feel strange; there's nothing wrong with not being a person of a certain sensibility. But there should still be fiction that makes you feel strange.

DAVID MOLES, 9:45 AM, WEDNESDAY, MAY 4, 2005

The difference is that the second definition defines it in relation to – or opposition to – traditional SF or fantasy. It causes problems because it doesn't take the work for what it is, but instead wants to say, "This could be SF if the science was better" or "This could be fantasy, except it's not clear whether there's really magic happening or not." It has trouble getting past those considerations and taking the work on its own merits.

I have to confess to a certain amount of bewilderment over the need for definitions and labels. From a marketing/publishing standpoint it has validity, but should we as writers be worrying about what to call our writing?

DAVE SCHWARTZ, 9:52 AM, WEDNESDAY, MAY 4, 2005

Dave, I think you're pretty much right about what's wrong with the definition of *slipstream*. It's a little like old-school literary folks talking about SF: "Well, but 'The Specialist's Hat' and 'One Ordinary Day, With Peanuts' can't be slipstream – *they're* good!"

But I think you're wrong about the usefulness of having a critical vocabulary of distinctions, as long as categorizing isn't the end of the discussion, as in "What pigeonhole can I put this in?" but the beginning, as in "What can I read that will take me closer to the heart of what this is trying to do?"

BENJAMIN ROSENBAUM, 10:47 AM, WEDNESDAY, MAY 4, 2005

The Specialist's Hat

Kelly Link

"WHEN YOU'RE DEAD," Samantha says, "you don't have to brush your teeth..."

"When you're Dead," Claire says, "you live in a box, and it's always dark, but you're not ever afraid."

Claire and Samantha are identical twins. Their combined age is twenty years, four months, and six days. Claire is better at being Dead than Samantha.

The babysitter yawns, covering up her mouth with a long white hand. "I said to brush your teeth and that it's time for bed," she says. She sits crosslegged on the flowered bedspread between them. She has been teaching them a card game called Pounce, which involves three decks of cards, one for each of them. Samantha's deck is missing the Jack of Spades and the Two of Hearts, and Claire keeps on cheating. The babysitter wins anyway. There are still flecks of dried shaving cream and toilet paper on her arms. It is hard to tell how old she is – at first they thought she must be a grownup, but now she hardly looks older than them. Samantha has forgotten the babysitter's name.

Claire's face is stubborn. "When you're Dead," she says, "you stay up all night long."

"When you're dead," the babysitter snaps, "it's always very cold and damp, and you have to be very, very quiet or else the Specialist will get you."

"This house is haunted," Claire says.

"I know it is," the babysitter says. "I used to live here."

Something is creeping up the stairs,
Something is standing outside the door,
Something is sobbing, sobbing in the dark;
Something is sighing across the floor.

Claire and Samantha are spending the summer with their father, in the house called Eight Chimneys. Their mother is dead. She has been dead for exactly 282 days.

Their father is writing a history of Eight Chimneys and of the poet Charles Cheatham Rash, who lived here at the turn of the century, and who ran away to sea when he was thirteen, and returned when he was thirty-eight. He married, fathered a child, wrote three volumes of bad, obscure poetry, and an even worse and more obscure novel, *The One Who Is Watching Me Through the Window*, before disappearing again in 1907, this time for good. Samantha and Claire's father says that some of the poetry is actually quite readable and at least the novel isn't very long.

When Samantha asked him why he was writing about Rash, he replied that no one else had, and why didn't she and Samantha go play outside. When she pointed out that she was Samantha, he just scowled and said how could he be expected to tell them apart when they both wore blue jeans and flannel shirts, and why couldn't one of them dress all in green and the other in pink?

Claire and Samantha prefer to play inside. Eight Chimneys is as big as a castle, but dustier and darker than Samantha imagines a castle would be. There are more sofas, more china shepherdesses with chipped fingers, fewer suits of armor. No moat.

The house is open to the public, and, during the day, people – families – driving along the Blue Ridge Parkway will stop to tour the grounds and the first story; the third story belongs to Claire and Samantha. Sometimes they play explorers, and sometimes they follow the caretaker as he gives tours to visitors. After a few weeks, they have memorized his lecture, and they mouth it along with him. They help him sell postcards and copies of Rash's poetry to the tourist families who come into the little gift shop.

When the mothers smile at them and say how sweet they are, they stare back and don't say anything at all. The dim light in the house makes the mothers look pale and flickery and tired. They leave Eight Chimneys, mothers and families, looking not quite as real as they did before they paid their admissions, and of course Claire and Samantha will never see them again, so maybe they aren't real. Better to stay inside the house, they want to tell the families, and if you must leave, then go straight to your cars.

The caretaker says the woods aren't safe.

Their father stays in the library on the second story all morning, typing, and in the afternoon he takes long walks. He takes his pocket recorder along with him and a hip flask of Gentleman Jack, but not Samantha and Claire.

The caretaker of Eight Chimneys is Mr. Coeslak. His left leg is noticeably shorter than his right. He wears one stacked heel. Short black hairs grow out of his ears and his nostrils and there is no hair at all on top of his head, but he's given Samantha and Claire permission to explore the whole of the house. It was Mr. Coeslak who told them that there are copperheads in the woods, and that the house is haunted. He says they are all, ghosts and snakes, a pretty badtempered lot, and Samantha and Claire should stick to the marked trails, and stay out of the attic.

Mr. Coeslak can tell the twins apart, even if their father can't; Claire's eyes are grey, like a cat's fur, he says, but Samantha's are *gray*, like the ocean when it has been raining.

Samantha and Claire went walking in the woods on the second day that they were at Eight Chimneys. They saw something. Samantha thought it was a woman, but Claire said it was a snake. The staircase that goes up to the attic has been locked. They peeked through the keyhole, but it was too dark to see anything.

And so he had a wife, and they say she was real pretty. There was another man who wanted to go with her, and first she wouldn't, because she was afraid of her husband, and then she did. Her husband found out, and they say he killed a snake and got some of this snake's blood and put it in some whiskey and gave it to her. He had learned this from an island man who had been on a ship with him. And in about six months snakes created in her and they got between her meat and the skin. And they say you could just see them running up and down her legs. They say she was just hollow to the top of her body, and it kept on like that till she died. Now my daddy said he saw it.

—AN ORAL HISTORY OF EIGHT CHIMNEYS

Eight Chimneys is over two hundred years old. It is named for the eight chimneys that are each big enough that Samantha and Claire can both fit in one fireplace. The chimneys are red brick, and on each floor there are eight fireplaces, making a total of twenty-four. Samantha imagines the chimney stacks stretching like stout red tree trunks, all the way up through the slate roof of the house. Beside each fireplace is a heavy black firedog, and a set of wrought iron pokers shaped like snakes. Claire and Samantha pretend to duel with the snake-pokers before the fireplace in their bedroom on the third floor. Wind rises up the back of the chimney. When they stick their faces in, they can feel the air rushing damply upwards, like a river. The flue smells old and sooty and wet, like stones from a river.

Their bedroom was once the nursery. They sleep together in a poster bed which resembles a ship with four masts. It smells of mothballs, and Claire kicks in her sleep. Charles Cheatham Rash slept here when he was a little boy, and also his daughter. She disappeared when her father did. It might have been gambling debts. They may have moved to New Orleans. She was fourteen years old, Mr. Coeslak said. What was her name, Claire asked. What happened to her mother, Samantha wanted to know. Mr. Coeslak closed his eyes in an almost wink. Mrs. Rash had died the year before her husband and daughter disappeared, he said, of a mysterious wasting disease. He can't remember the name of the poor little girl, he said.

Eight Chimneys has exactly one hundred windows, all still with the original wavery panes of handblown glass. With so many windows, Samantha thinks, Eight Chimneys should always be full of light, but instead the trees press close against the house, so that the rooms on the first and second story – even the third-story rooms – are green and dim, as if Samantha and Claire are living deep under the sea. This is the light that makes the tourists into ghosts. In the morning, and again towards evening, a fog settles in around the house. Sometimes it is grey like Claire's eyes, and sometimes it is gray, like Samantha's eyes.

I met a woman in the wood,
Her lips were two red snakes.
She smiled at me, her eyes were lewd
And burning like a fire.

A few nights ago, the wind was sighing in the nursery chimney. Their father had already tucked them in and turned off the light. Claire dared Samantha to stick her head into the fireplace, in the dark, and so she did. The cold wet air licked at her face and it almost sounded like voices talking low, muttering. She couldn't quite make out what they were saying.

Their father has mostly ignored Claire and Samantha since they arrived at Eight Chimneys. He never mentions their mother. One evening they heard him shouting in the library, and when they came downstairs, there was a large sticky stain on the desk, where a glass of whiskey had been knocked over. It was looking at me, he said, through the window. It had orange eyes.

Samantha and Claire refrained from pointing out that the library is on the second story.

At night, their father's breath has been sweet from drinking, and he is spending more and more time in the woods, and less in the library. At dinner, usually hot dogs and baked beans from a can, which they eat off of paper plates in the first floor dining room, beneath the Austrian chandelier (which has exactly 632 leaded crystals shaped like teardrops), their father recites the poetry of Charles Cheatham Rash, which neither Samantha nor Claire cares for.

He has been reading the ship diaries that Rash kept, and he says that he has discovered proof in them that Rash's most famous poem, "The Specialist's Hat," is not a poem at all, and in any case, Rash didn't write it. It is something that one of the men on the whaler used to say, to conjure up a whale. Rash simply copied it down and stuck an end on it and said it was his.

The man was from Mulatuppu, which is a place neither Samantha nor Claire has ever heard of. Their father says that the man was supposed to be some sort of magician, but he drowned shortly before Rash came back to Eight Chimneys. Their father says that the other sailors wanted to throw the magician's chest overboard, but Rash persuaded them to let him keep it until he could be put ashore, with the chest, off the coast of North Carolina.

The specialist's hat makes a noise like an agouti;
The specialist's hat makes a noise like a collared peccary;
The specialist's hat makes a noise like a white-lipped peccary;
The specialist's hat makes a noise like a tapir;
The specialist's hat makes a noise like a rabbit;
The specialist's hat makes a noise like a squirrel;
The specialist's hat makes a noise like a curassow;
The specialist's hat moans like a whale in the water;
The specialist's hat moans like the wind in my wife's hair;
The specialist's hat makes a noise like a snake;
I have hung the hat of the specialist upon my wall.

The reason that Claire and Samantha have a babysitter is that their father met a woman in the woods. He is going to see her tonight, and they are going to have a picnic supper and look at the stars. This is the time of year when the Perseids can be seen, falling across the sky on clear nights. Their father said that he has been walking with the woman every afternoon. She is a distant relation of Rash and besides, he said, he needs a night off and some grownup conversation.

Mr. Coeslak won't stay in the house after dark, but he agreed to find someone to look after Samantha and Claire. Then their father couldn't find Mr. Coeslak, but the babysitter showed up precisely at seven o'clock. The babysitter, whose name neither twin quite caught, wears a blue cotton dress with short floaty sleeves. Both Samantha and Claire think she is pretty in an old-fashioned sort of way.

They were in the library with their father, looking up Mulatuppu in the red leather atlas, when she arrived. She didn't knock on the front door, she simply walked in and then up the stairs, as if she knew where to find them.

Their father kissed them goodbye, a hasty smack, told them to be good and he would take them into town on the weekend to see the Disney film. They went to the window to watch as he walked into the woods. Already it was getting dark and there were fireflies, tiny yellow-hot sparks in the air. When their father had entirely disappeared into the trees, they turned around and stared at the babysitter instead. She raised one eyebrow. "Well," she said. "What sort of games do you like to play?"

Widdershins around the chimneys,
Once, twice, again.
The spokes click like a clock on the bicycle;
They tick down the days of the life of a man.

First they played Go Fish, and then they played Crazy Eights, and then they made the babysitter into a mummy by putting shaving cream from their father's bathroom on her arms and legs, and wrapping her in toilet paper. She is the best babysitter they have ever had.

At nine-thirty, she tried to put them to bed. Neither Claire nor Samantha wanted to go to bed, so they began to play the Dead game. The Dead game is a let's pretend that they have been playing every day for 274 days now, but never in front of their father or any other adult. When they are Dead, they are allowed to do anything they want to. They can even fly by jumping off the nursery bed, and just waving their arms. Someday this will work, if they practice hard enough.

The Dead game has three rules.

One. Numbers are significant. The twins keep a list of important numbers in a green address book that belonged to their mother. Mr. Coeslak's tour has been a good source of significant amounts and tallies: they are writing a tragical history of numbers.

Two. The twins don't play the Dead game in front of grownups. They have been summing up the babysitter, and have decided that she doesn't count. They tell her the rules.

Three is the best and most important rule. When you are Dead, you don't have to be afraid of anything. Samantha and Claire aren't sure who the Specialist is, but they aren't afraid of him.

To become Dead, they hold their breath while counting to thirty-five, which is as high as their mother got, not counting a few days.

"You never lived here," Claire says. "Mr. Coeslak lives here."

"Not at night," says the babysitter. "This was my bedroom when I was little."

"Really?" Samantha says. Claire says, "Prove it."

The babysitter gives Samantha and Claire a look, as if she is measuring them: how old, how smart, how brave, how tall. Then she nods. The wind is in the flue, and in the dim nursery light they can see the milky strands of fog seeping out of the fireplace. "Go stand in the chimney," she instructs them. "Stick your hand as far up as you can, and there is a little hole on the left side, with a key in it."

Samantha looks at Claire, who says, "Go ahead." Claire is fifteen minutes and some few uncounted seconds older than Samantha, and therefore gets to tell Samantha what to do. Samantha remembers the muttering voices and then reminds herself that she is Dead. She goes over to the fireplace and ducks inside.

When Samantha stands up in the chimney, she can only see the very edge of the room. She can see the fringe of the mothy blue rug, and one bed leg, and beside it, Claire's foot, swinging back and forth like a metronome. Claire's shoelace has come undone and there is a Band-Aid on her ankle. It all looks very pleasant and peaceful from inside the chimney, like a dream, and for a moment she almost wishes she didn't have to be Dead. But it's safer, really.

She sticks her left hand up as far as she can reach, trailing it along the crumbly wall, until she feels an indentation. She thinks about spiders and severed fingers, and rusty razorblades, and then she reaches inside. She keeps her eyes lowered, focused on the corner of the room and Claire's twitchy foot.

Inside the hole, there is a tiny cold key, its teeth facing outward. She pulls it out, and ducks back into the room. "She wasn't lying," she tells Claire.

"Of course I wasn't lying," the babysitter says. "When you're Dead, you're not allowed to tell lies."

"Unless you want to," Claire says.

Dreary and dreadful beats the sea at the shore.
Ghastly and dripping is the mist at the door.
The clock in the hall is chiming one, two, three, four.
The morning comes not, no, never, no more.

Samantha and Claire have gone to camp for three weeks every summer since they were seven. This year their father didn't ask them if they wanted to go back and, after discussing it, they decided that it was just as well. They didn't want to have to explain to all their friends how they were half-orphans now. They are used to being envied, because they are identical twins. They don't want to be pitiful.

It has not even been a year, but Samantha realizes that she is forgetting what her mother looked like. Not her mother's face so much as the way she smelled, which was something like dry hay, and something like Chanel No. 5, and like something else too. She can't remember whether her mother had gray eyes, like her, or grey eyes, like Claire. She doesn't dream about her mother anymore, but she does dream about Prince Charming, a bay whom she once rode in the horse show at her camp. In the dream, Prince Charming did not smell like a horse at all. He smelled like Chanel No. 5. When she is Dead, she can have all the horses she wants, and they all smell like Chanel No. 5.

"Where does the key go to?" Samantha says.

The babysitter holds out her hand. "To the attic. You don't really need it, but taking the stairs is easier than the chimney. At least the first time."

"Aren't you going to make us go to bed?" Claire says.

The babysitter ignores Claire. "My father used to lock me in the attic when I was little, but I didn't mind. There was a bicycle up there and I used to ride it around and around the chimneys until my mother let me out again. Do you know how to ride a bicycle?"

"Of course," Claire says.

"If you ride fast enough, the Specialist can't catch you."

"What's the Specialist?" Samantha says. Bicycles are okay, but horses can go faster.

"The Specialist wears a hat," says the babysitter. "The hat makes noises."

She doesn't say anything else.

> *When you're dead, the grass is greener*
> *Over your grave. The wind is keener.*
> *Your eyes sink in, your flesh decays. You*
> *Grow accustomed to slowness; expect delays.*

The attic is somehow bigger and lonelier than Samantha and Claire thought it would be. The babysitter's key opens the locked door at the end of the hallway, revealing a narrow set of stairs. She waves them ahead and upwards.

It isn't as dark in the attic as they had imagined. The oaks that block the light and make the first three stories so dim and green and mysterious during the day, don't reach all the way up. Extravagant moonlight, dusty and pale, streams in the angled dormer windows. It lights the length of the attic, which is wide enough to hold a softball game in, and lined with trunks where Samantha imagines people could sit, could be hiding and watching. The ceiling slopes down, impaled upon the eight thickwaisted chimney stacks. The chimneys seem too alive, somehow, to be contained in this empty, neglected place; they thrust almost angrily through the roof and attic floor. In the moonlight they look like they are breathing. "They're so beautiful," she says.

"Which chimney is the nursery chimney?" Claire says.

The babysitter points to the nearest righthand stack. "That one," she says. "It runs up through the ballroom on the first floor, the library, the nursery."

Hanging from a nail on the nursery chimney is a long black object. It looks lumpy and heavy, as if it were full of things. The babysitter takes it down, twirls it on her finger. There are holes in the black thing and it whistles mournfully as she spins it. "The Specialist's hat," she says.

"That doesn't look like a hat," says Claire. "It doesn't look like anything at all." She goes to look through the boxes and trunks that are stacked against the far wall.

"It's a special hat," the babysitter says. "It's not supposed to look like anything. But it can sound like anything you can imagine. My father made it."

"Our father writes books," Samantha says.

"My father did too." The babysitter hangs the hat back on the nail. It curls blackly against the chimney. Samantha stares at it. It nickers at her. "He was a bad poet, but he was worse at magic."

Last summer, Samantha wished more than anything that she could have a horse. She thought she would have given up anything for one – even being a twin was not as good as having a horse. She still doesn't have a horse, but she doesn't have a mother either, and she can't help wondering if it's her fault. The hat nickers again, or maybe it is the wind in the chimney.

"What happened to him?" Claire asks.

"After he made the hat, the Specialist came and took him away. I hid in the nursery chimney while it was looking for him, and it didn't find me."

"Weren't you scared?"

There is a clattering, shivering, clicking noise. Claire has found the babysitter's bike and is dragging it towards them by the handlebars. The babysitter shrugs. "Rule number three," she says.

Claire snatches the hat off the nail. "I'm the Specialist!" she says, putting the hat on her head. It falls over her eyes, the floppy shapeless brim sewn with little asymmetrical buttons that flash and catch at the moonlight like teeth. Samantha looks again and sees that they are teeth. Without counting, she suddenly knows that there are exactly fifty-two teeth on the hat, and that they are the teeth of agoutis, of curassows, of white-lipped peccaries, and of the wife of Charles Cheatham Rash. The chimneys are moaning, and Claire's voice booms hollowly beneath the hat. "Run away, or I'll catch you and eat you!"

Samantha and the babysitter run away, laughing as Claire mounts the rusty, noisy bicycle and pedals madly after them. She rings the bicycle bell as she rides, and the Specialist's hat bobs up and down on her head. It spits like a cat. The bell is shrill and thin, and the bike wails and shrieks. It leans first towards the right and then to the left. Claire's knobby knees stick out on either side like makeshift counterweights.

Claire weaves in and out between the chimneys, chasing Samantha and the babysitter. Samantha is slow, turning to look behind. As Claire approaches, she keeps one hand on the handlebars and stretches the other hand out towards Samantha. Just as she is about to grab Samantha, the babysitter turns back and plucks the hat off Claire's head.

"Shit!" the babysitter says, and drops it. There is a drop of blood forming on the fleshy part of the babysitter's hand, black in the moonlight, where the Specialist's hat has bitten her.

Claire dismounts, giggling. Samantha watches as the Specialist's hat rolls away. It picks up speed, veering across the attic floor, and disappears, thumping down the stairs. "Go get it," Claire says. "You can be the Specialist this time."

"No," the babysitter says, sucking at her palm. "It's time for bed."

When they go down the stairs, there is no sign of the Specialist's hat. They brush their teeth, climb into the ship-bed, and pull the covers up to their necks. The babysitter sits between their feet. "When you're Dead," Samantha says, "do you still get tired and have to go to sleep? Do you have dreams?"

"When you're Dead," the babysitter says, "everything's a lot easier. You don't have to do anything that you don't want to. You don't have to have a name, you don't have to remember. You don't even have to breathe."

She shows them exactly what she means.

When she has time to think about it (and now she has all the time in the world to think), Samantha realizes with a small pang that she is now stuck indefinitely between ten and eleven years old, stuck with Claire and the babysitter. She considers this. The number 10 is pleasing and round, like a beach ball, but all in all, it hasn't been an easy year. She wonders what 11 would have been like. Sharper, like needles maybe. She has chosen to be Dead, instead. She hopes that she's made the right decision. She wonders if her mother would have decided to be Dead, instead of dead, if she could have.

Last year they were learning fractions in school, when her mother died. Fractions remind Samantha of herds of wild horses, piebalds and pintos and palominos. There are so many of them, and they are, well, fractious and unruly. Just when you think you have one under control, it throws up its head and tosses you off. Claire's favorite number is 4, which she says is a tall, skinny boy. Samantha doesn't care for boys that much. She likes numbers. Take the number 8 for instance, which can be more than one thing at once. Looked at one way, 8 looks like a bent woman with curvy hair. But if you lay it down on its side, it looks like a snake curled with its tail in its mouth. This is sort of like the difference between being Dead and being dead. Maybe when Samantha is tired of one, she will try the other.

On the lawn, under the oak trees, she hears someone calling her name. Samantha climbs out of bed and goes to the nursery window. She looks out through the wavy glass. It's Mr. Coeslak. "Samantha, Claire!" he calls up to her. "Are you all right? Is your father there?" Samantha can almost see the moonlight shining through him. "They're always locking me in the tool room. Goddamn spooky things," he says. "Are you there, Samantha? Claire? Girls?"

The babysitter comes and stands beside Samantha. The babysitter puts her finger to her lip. Claire's eyes glitter at them from the dark bed. Samantha doesn't say anything, but she waves at Mr. Coeslak. The babysitter waves too. Maybe he can see them waving, because after a little while he stops shouting and goes away. "Be careful," the babysitter says. "*He'll* be coming soon. It will be coming soon."

She takes Samantha's hand, and leads her back to the bed, where Claire is waiting. They sit and wait. Time passes, but they don't get tired, they don't get any older.

Who's there?
Just air.

The front door opens on the first floor, and Samantha, Claire, and the babysitter can hear someone creeping, creeping up the stairs. "Be quiet," the babysitter says. "It's the Specialist."

Samantha and Claire are quiet. The nursery is dark and the wind crackles like a fire in the fireplace.

"Claire, Samantha, Samantha, Claire?" The Specialist's voice is blurry and wet. It sounds like their father's voice, but that's because the hat can imitate any noise, any voice. "Are you still awake?"

"Quick," the babysitter says. "It's time to go up to the attic and hide."

Claire and Samantha slip out from under the covers and dress quickly and silently. They follow her. Without speech, without breathing, she pulls them into the safety of the chimney. It is too dark to see, but they understand the babysitter perfectly when she mouths the word, *Up*. She goes first, so they can see where the finger-holds are, the bricks that jut out for their feet. Then Claire. Samantha watches her sister's foot ascend like smoke, the shoelace still untied.

"Claire? Samantha? Goddammit, you're scaring me. Where are you?" The Specialist is standing just outside the half-open door. "Samantha? I think I've been bitten by something. I think I've been bitten by a goddamn snake." Samantha hesitates for only a second. Then she is climbing up, up, up the nursery chimney.

Light and the Sufferer

Jonathan Lethem

MY BROTHER showed me the gun. I'd never seen one up close before. He kept it in a knapsack under his bed at the Y. He held it out and I looked at the black metal.

"You want me to hold it?" I said.

"What, at the place?"

"No, I mean now. I mean, do you want me to touch it or something. Now. I mean like, get comfortable with it."

He stared.

"Don't look at me like I'm crazy. What do you want me to do with the gun?"

"Nothing. I'm just showing it to you, like 'Look, I got it.' Like, 'Here's the gun.'"

My brother was two years younger than me. I was just back from dropping out of my junior year of college, at Santa Cruz, and was living, quite unhappily, at my parents' tiny new house in Plainview, Long Island.

Our parents, Jimmy and Marilla, had kicked Don out for the final time while I was away at school. They hadn't heard from him for almost a year. I went and hung out at Washington Square and found him within a few hours.

"Okay," I said. "Right. Nice gun."

"Don't get freaked."

"I'm not freaked, Don." I paused.

"Then let's go, right?"

"Let's go, Don," I said, and I swear I almost added: *This is good, we're brothers, we still do things together.* I almost said: *See, Don.*

Our parents named my brother Donovan because all their friends had already named their kids Dylan, I guess. It wasn't important to Don. His only chance of ever hearing Donovan was if MC Death sampled "Season of the Witch" or "Hurdy Gurdy Man" in a rap.

Myself being a bit older, I knew those songs in their original versions, not from the radio, of course, but from the days when our parents still played their records.

I followed my brother downstairs. It was night. We walked the short distance to Washington Square Park but stopped half a block away. I stopped.

"What?" said Don.

"Nothing. Should we call the airport? Find out – "

"Like you said, there's always gonna be a plane, Paul."

We went into the park, through the evening throngs, the chessplayers and skatebladers, and I stood on the pathway waiting, shrugging off offers of nickel bags, while Don found his two friends, the ones who were supposed to kill him for stealing drugs.

" – gotta *talk* to you."

"Randall sick of yo shit, Light."

"Can we go up to your apartment, Kaz? Please?"

Don walked them towards me. A fat black man with a gigantic knitted hat: Kaz. Another black man, smaller in every way, with a little beard, and wearing a weirdly glossy, puffed-out gold coat: Drey.

Nobody my brother knew had a regular name. And they all called him "Light," for his being white, I suppose.

"The fuck is this?" said Drey, looking at me.

"Paul," Don mumbled.

"Looks like yo fuckin' brother, man."

"All us white dudes look like brothers to you, nigger."

Drey grinned, then tightened his mouth, as though remembering that he was supposed to be angry at Don.

We walked out of the park, east on Third Street. All the way Kaz mumbled at Don: "Can't believe you, man; you fuckin' come around here; you took Randall; can't believe you, man; fuck you think you doin'; look at you stupid face; you think you talk you way out of this; I should be doin' you; fuckin' crackhead; can't believe you man." Et cetera.

And Don just kept saying, every thirty seconds or so: "Shut up, Kaz, man." Or: "Gimme a minute, man."

We went into a door beside a storefront on First Avenue, and up a flight of stairs. Don and I ahead of Kaz and Drey, through the dark.

Kaz stepped around and let us in, and I looked down and saw Don take the gun out of his coat. Don wanted to pull it coming in; he'd said he knew that Kaz kept guns in the house. But not on his person. That was crucial.

We all got inside and Kaz closed the door, and Don turned around. "You're dead," said the fat black man the minute he saw the gun.

The place was just about empty: crumbling walls, a bed. And a cheap safe, nailed instead of bolted to the floor, price tag still showing. A safe house, literally. Crash and stash, as Don would say.

Don waved the gun between Kaz and Drey. "You're dead," said Kaz again. Drey said: "Shit."

"Shut up. Paul, take their shit. Clean Drey up, then Kaz. Find the keys on Kaz."

I stepped up to play my part. Keys on Kaz. I put my hand on Drey, who hissed: "Motherfucker." It turned out the weird shiny gold coat was on inside out; the gold was the *lining* of a rabbit-fur fake leopard. Strange. I ran my hands through the fur, searching out Drey's pockets.

I found a wad, singles on the outside, which I pocketed. Then an Exacto knife, which I tossed on the floor behind me, at Don's feet. He kicked it to the wall.

When I turned to Kaz he slapped my hands away, a strangely girlish move.

"You a chump, Light," he said, ignoring me. "Randall shoulda killed your ass already. He gonna now."

"We're all Randall's chumps, Kaz, man. Now I'm taking and you can tell Randall what you want."

"I ain't no chump, man, Light. You the chump. Randall tried to treat you right. You fuckin' smokehead. You could be playing with the cash like me, like Randall says. 'Staid you *usin'*." He hurled the word like it was the only real insult he knew.

It was true. Don had used the drugs he was supposed to deal for Randall.

"Playing with the cash now, Kaz."

I reached for Kaz's pockets again, and again he slapped me away. "You dead, brother."

Don stepped up and clapped Kaz's temple with the side of the gun.

"Ain't no cash, Light, man," Kaz whimpered. He looked down. "Ain't sold it yet, you stupid fuck."

"Open the safe."

"What did you mean 'You dead, *brother*,'?" I asked. "Don told you I'm not his brother. Or are you just using that as an expression?"

Kaz just shook his head and got out the key to the safe. Drey said: "Fuckin' idiot."

Inside the safe was all bottles. Crack. Nothing else. Two big plastic bags full of ten- and five-dollar bottles. I'd never seen that much in one place. Don had, of course; specifically, when Kaz and Randall brought him up here to entrust him with a load of bottles to sell.

That time there had also been a large supply of cash, which was what we were here supposedly to steal.

"Fuck you expected?" said Drey.

"You dead," said Kaz.

Don didn't hesitate. He took the two bags of bottles and quickly felt behind them, but there was nothing else in the safe. He slammed the door shut and pushed the gun up at Kaz's face again. "Your roll, Kaz."

"You a fuckin' chump." Kaz got out his money, another fat wad with ones on the outside. Don took it and stuffed it in his pocket. Then he shook the two bags of bottles into the two big side pockets of his parka, tossing the plastic bags aside when they were empty.

"Fuck you gonna do?" said Drey. "Sell the shit? Randall gun you down."

"Gimme the keys," said Don to Kaz. "Sit down. Both of you."

"Shit."

Don waved the gun some more, and Kaz and Drey sat down on the floor. Don pushed me back out into the hallway ahead of him, then shut the door and locked it from the outside with Kaz's key.

That was when we saw the Sufferer. It was sitting on the landing of the stairway above us, looking down. On its haunches in the dark it looked just like a giant panther, eyes shining.

I assumed it was waiting for someone else. I'd only seen the aliens twice before, each time trailing after somebody in trouble. That was what they liked to do.

Don didn't even glance at it. I guess leading his lifestyle, he passed them pretty often. He put the gun in his belt and ran downstairs, and I followed him. The Sufferer padded down after us.

Don hailed a cab on First Avenue. "La Guardia," he said, leaning in the window.

"Manhattan only," said the cabbie. Don pulled out Kaz's money and began peeling off ones. I looked behind us, thinking of Kaz and Drey and the unlocated guns in the apartment. Had Don really locked them in? Even if he had, they could shoot us from the front windows, or off the fire escape, while we haggled with the cabbie.

I saw the Sufferer push out of the door and settle on the sidewalk to watch us.

"Fifteen dollars before the fare," said Don. "C'mon."

The driver popped the locks, and Don and I scooted into the back, Don's coat-load of bottles clinking against the door.

"La Guardia," said Don again.

"Take the Manhattan Bridge," I said. "Canal Street."

"He knows where the Manhattan Bridge is, Paul."

"He said Manhattan only."

"You picking somebody up?" said the driver.

"Domestic departures," I said.

"What airline?"

"Uh, Pan Am."

"There is no more Pan Am," said the driver.

"Wow. Okay, uh, Delta?"

"Does it matter?" said Don.

"He has to take us *somewhere,*" I explained patiently. Sometimes it seemed like Don and I grew up in separate universes. "The airport is big. Delta should have a lot of flights to California. We can start there, anyway."

The cab went down first to Canal and entered the funnel of traffic leading onto the bridge. I always mention the Manhattan Bridge because a lot of people just reflexively take the Brooklyn, though it isn't really faster or more convenient. People prefer the Brooklyn Bridge, I guess because it's prettier, but I like the way you can be driving alongside a *subway train* on the Manhattan Bridge.

So I looked out the window, and what I saw was the Sufferer, running alongside the cab, keeping time even when the traffic smoothed out and we accelerated across the empty middle of the bridge. It loped along right beside us, almost under my window. Our cabbie was going faster than the other cars, and when we passed one the Sufferer would drop back, trailing us, until the space beside my door was clear again.

Don was in his own world, leafing through the roll he'd stolen and counting the bottles in his pockets by feel. I didn't draw his attention to the Sufferer. The cabbie hadn't noticed either.

"You can't take the gun on the plane," I said to Don, quietly.

"Big news," said Don sarcastically.

"It's okay," I said, responding to his annoyance as some kind of plea for reassurance, as I always had. "We won't need it in Cali."

"Yeah," he said dreamily.

"We're really going," I said. "Things'll be different there." I felt it slipping away, the hold my proposal had had on him an hour ago.

"What," he snorted. "Nobody has guns in California?"

"You're going to live different, there." I looked up to see if the cabbie was listening. "So why don't you leave the gun here in the cab, okay, Don? Just push it under the seat. Because it's crazy going into the airport with it. Crazy enough just carrying all the drugs."

"I'll put it in a locker. Just in case."

"What? In case of what?"

We pulled off onto the BQE and headed for the airport. I checked the window. There was the Sufferer, rushing along with us, leaping potholes.

"What?" said Don, noticing.

"One of those aliens."

"The one from Kaz's?"

I shrugged – a lie, since I knew. "How much money did you get from Kaz?" I said, trying to change the subject.

"Four hundred. Chump change from a chump. Fuck is it doing out there?" He leaned over me to look out the window.

"Hey," said the cabbie. "You got a Sufferer."

"Just drive," said Don.

"I don't want trouble. Why's it following you?"

"It's not following anyone," I said. "Anyway, they don't cause trouble. They *prevent* it. They keep people out of trouble."

"Right. So if they follow you, you must be trouble."

Don took the gun out of his belt, but kept it below the level of the Plexiglas barrier above the seat. I tried to scowl at him, but he ignored me.

"You don't like it, why don't you try to kill it with the car?" he said to the driver in a low, insinuating voice.

"You're crazy."

"Right. So just take us to the airport and shut up." He looked at me. "How much you get?"

"Two hundred and fifty dollars. Sidekick change from a sidekick." The joke was out before I thought to wonder: but who's the sidekick *here*? It was possibly a very important question.

Don snorted. "Barely afford the tickets." He put the gun back into his belt.

The Sufferer accompanied us through the maze of exits and into the roundabout of the airport. We pulled up in front of Delta. Don paid the cabfare and rolled off twenty extra, then paused, and rolled off another twenty. "Pull up there and wait ten minutes," he said.

"Don, we're getting on a plane. Besides, even if we weren't, it isn't hard to catch a cab at the *airport*."

"Just in case. Me and this dude got an understanding. Right, man?" He cocked his head at the driver.

The cabbie shrugged, then smiled. "Sure. I'll wait."

I sighed. Don was always turning passersby into accomplices. Even when it didn't mean anything. It was a kind of compulsive seduction, like *Women Who Love Too Much*.

"You're getting me worried, Don. We're flying out of here, right?"

"Relax. We're at the airport, right? Just wait a minute." He put his mouth at the driver's little money window. "Pull up over there, man.

We'll walk back, we don't have bags or anything. Just get out of the light, okay?"

We pulled past the terminal entrance, into a dead zone of baggage carts. The Sufferer trotted alongside, on the pedestrian ramp, weaving around the businessmen and tourists leaking out of the terminal.

Don rolled his window down a couple of inches, then got out a glass pipe and shook out the contents of a five-dollar vial into the bowl.

"Donnie."

"Hey, not in the cab!"

"Minute, man." He flicked his lighter and the little rocks flared blue and pink and disappeared. So practiced, so fast.

The Sufferer leaned close in to my window and watched. When Don noticed he said: "Open your door and whack that fuckin' thing in the face."

"Don't smoke that crap in my cab," said the driver.

"Okay, okay," said Don, palming the pipe away. He pointed a finger at the cabbie. "You'll wait, right?"

"I'll wait, but don't do that in my cab."

"Let's go, Don."

"Okay."

I opened my door and the Sufferer stepped aside to let us pass. We got out onto the walkway. Don stopped and shook his head, straightened his parka, which was burdened with the loaded pockets, and pushed the gun out of sight under his sweatshirt. We walked up to the entrance. The doors were operated by electric eye, and they slid open for us, then stayed open as the Sufferer followed.

Don and I both instinctively hurried into a mass of people, but no crowd could have been big enough to keep it from being obvious who the alien was with. A baggage guy stood and watched, his eyes going from the Sufferer to us and back again. He could as easily have been airport security – maybe he was.

"We've got a problem here, Don," I said.

"Yeah." He made a mugging face, but didn't meet my eye.

"Let's – here, you've gotta find a place for the gun, anyway." I steered him out of the flow near the ticket agents, to a relatively empty stretch of terminal: newspaper vending machines, hotel phones, and a shoeshine booth. I didn't see any lockers, though.

The Sufferer sat and cocked its head at us, waiting.

"What do your friends do when this happens?"

"What?" said Don sarcastically. "You mean when some big black animal from space follows them to the airport after an armed robbery?"

"When these things – when one of these things shows up, Don. I mean, it must happen to people you know."

"One dude, Rolando. Thing started trailing him. Rolando fell in love, like him and the thing fucking eloped. Last I saw Rolando. Just that one dude, though."

As people passed us they'd stare first at the Sufferer, then follow its gaze to us.

"Ironic," I said. "It wants to help you, right? At least, I assume so. But it doesn't know that you're planning to go to California to dry out. It probably doesn't even understand how airports work, how it's fucking this up for you. How important it is for you to leave the city."

I was babbling. I couldn't help myself. I wanted to hear him say *Yes, I mean to get on a plane and change my life in California, Paul. You had a good idea.* Instead of his grunting, distracted assent. It didn't help that his big last farewell heist had netted pockets full of crack instead of cash.

And I didn't for the life of me know what to do with the Sufferer.

"It doesn't want to help me," Don said.

"Yeah, well, in this case, anyway, it isn't. We're already gonna fit a bad profile, buying tickets at the last minute with cash. If there's a Sufferer trailing around they'll search us for sure."

"They let it on the plane?"

"I don't think so. I mean, how could they? So all we have to do is dump the drugs *and* the gun, then they can search us all they want, doesn't matter, we're gone."

"Uh-uh."

"What?"

"I'm on parole, Paul. Breaking parole to go. I can't get checked out."

"What? You never told me you were in prison!"

"Shut up, Paul. *Sentenced* to parole, one year. Nothing, man."

"For what?"

"*Nothing,* man. Now shut up. What, you think I wasn't breaking the *law*?"

"Okay, okay, but listen, we just have to get on a plane. We have to try. So stash the stuff – "

"Nah. This is no good. I got an idea." He headed back to the terminal exits.

"Don!"

The Sufferer and I followed him out. He jogged back to the cab, hands protectively over the flaps of his coat pockets. We got back in and Don said: "Get us out of here."

"Back."

"Yeah, that direction. But get off the fuckin' freeway."

"Have to be on the freeway – "

"Yeah, yeah, I mean as soon as you can."

I actually thought we'd lost the Sufferer when we exited into a blasted neighborhood of boarded-up and gutted storefronts, but by the time we'd driven, at Don's request, back under the freeway and into a dark, empty cobblestone lot, the alien came loping up behind us.

The freeway roared above us, but the nearby streets were vacant. The people in the cars might as well have been in flying saucers, whistling past stragglers in the desert.

Don gave the cabbie another ten and said: "Get lost for fifteen minutes. Leave us here and circle around, find yourself a cup of coffee or something." The cabbie and I exchanged a look that said *Coffee? Here?* but Don was already out of the cab.

I got out and the cab rumbled away over the cobblestones and around a corner. The Sufferer didn't glance at it, just sat like an obedient dog and watched us.

Don ignored it, or pretended to, and walked over and took a seat on the fender of a wrecked truck. It was getting cold. I thought, stupidly, about the meal we would have been eating, about the movie we would have been watching, on the plane.

Don took out the pipe again and loaded it with a rock of crack. The wind bent the blue column of flame from his lighter one way, then Don sucked it the other, into the pipe. The Sufferer hurried up like a hunting cat to where Don sat. I stepped back.

Don curled his shoulder protectively around the pipe and glared back at the alien. "Fuck *you* want?"

The Sufferer nudged at his elbow with its hand-like paw.

"Leave me the fuck alone."

"Don, what are you doing? It can't help it. What are you trying to do, bait it?"

Don ignored me. He flicked his lighter again, tried to get a hit. The Sufferer jogged his elbow. Don kicked at it. The alien danced back easily out of the way, like a boxer, then stepped back in, trying to square its face with Don's, trying to look him in the eye.

Don kicked out again, brushing the Sufferer back, then pocketed the pipe and drew out his gun.

The alien cocked his head.

"Hey, Don – "

Don fired the gun straight into the Sufferer's chest, and the alien jumped back and fell onto the cobblestones, then got back on its feet and walked in a little circle, shaking its head, blinking its eyes.

Don said: "Ow, fuck, I think I sprained my arm."

"How? What happened?"

"The gun, man. It bucked back on me. Shit."

"You can't kill it, Don. Everybody knows that. The shots'll just bring the police."

Don looked at me. His expression was dazed and cynical at the same time. "I just wanted to give it a piece of my fuckin' mind, okay, Paul?"

"Okay, Don. Now what about going back to the airport?"

"Nah. We gotta lose this thing."

The Sufferer circled back around to where Don sat still holding the gun, kneading his injured forearm with his free hand. The alien sat up like a perky cat and tapped at Don's jacket pocket, rattling the load of bottles.

"I guess it just wants to see you get clean, Don. If you get rid of the bottles it'll leave us alone and we can fly to California."

"You believe that shit, Paul? Where'd you read that, *Newsweek*?"

"What?"

"That this thing is like some kind of vice cop? That it wants me to kick?"

"Isn't that the idea?" The stuff I'd read about them wasn't clear on much except that they followed users around, actually.

"Yeah? Watch this." Don clicked the safety on the gun and handed it to me, then got out his pipe and loaded it. He braised the rock with flame from the lighter, but this time when he got it glowing he turned it around and offered it to the Sufferer. The alien grasped the pipe in its dexterous paw and stuck the end in its mouth and toked.

"I think I read about that," I said, lying. "It's like an empathy thing. They want to earn your trust."

Don just smirked at me, then snatched his pipe away from the Sufferer, who didn't protest.

"I'm cold," I said. "You think that cab is coming back?"

"Fuck yes," said Don. "You kidding? We're a fucking gold mine." He shook out another rock.

The Sufferer and I both watched. Suddenly I wanted some. I'd done a lot of uncooked coke with some of my Upper West Side friends the last year of high school, but I'd only smoked rock twice before, with Don each time.

"Give me a hit, Don," I said.

He loaded the pipe and handed it and the lighter to me, ungrudgingly.

I drew in a hit, and felt the crazy rush of the crack hit me. Like snorting a line of coke while plummeting over the summit of a roller coaster.

The Sufferer opened its weird, toothless black mouth and leaned towards me, obviously wanting another hit.

"Maybe the idea is to help run through your stash," I said. "Help use up your stuff, keep you from O.D.ing. Because their bodies can take it, like the bullets. Doesn't hurt them."

"Maybe they're just fucking crackheads, Paul."

The cab's reappearance startled me, the sound of its approach masked by the rush of cars overhead. And of course, I was thinking of cops.

Don took his gun back, jammed it in his waistband, and we got into the back. Don held the door open for the Sufferer. "Might as well get it off the freeway," he said. "Gonna be with us next place we go either way." The Sufferer didn't hesitate to clamber in over our feet and settle down on the floor of the back, pretty much filling the space.

"Okay, but we need a plan, Donnie." I heard myself beginning to whine.

"Where to?" said the cabbie.

"Back to Manhattan," said Don. "East, uh, 83rd and, uh, Park." He turned to me. "Chick I know."

"You can't go back to the city."

"Manhattan is a big place, Paul. Far as Randall and Kaz is concerned, 83rd Street might as well be California."

"Don't talk to me about California. Like you know something about California."

"Paul, man, I didn't say shit about California. I'm just saying we can hide out uptown, figure some shit out, okay? Take care of the Crackhead from Space here, right?"

"Uptown. New York is a world to you, you don't know anything but uptown or downtown or Brooklyn. California's a whole other place, Donnie, you can't imagine. It'll be *different*. The things you're dealing with here, they don't have to be – you don't have to have these *issues*, Donnie. Randall, uptown, whatever."

"Okay, Paul. But I just wanna take care of two things, okay, and then we'll go, let's just get rid of the Creature and just move this stuff to some people I know, okay? Get cash for this product, then we'll go."

The Sufferer shifted, stepping on my foot, and looked up at us.

"Okay." I was defeated, by the two of them. It was like they were in collusion now. "Just don't talk about California like it's *Mars*, for God's sake. We're going there, you'll see how it is, and then you can tell me what you think. It'll blow your mind, Donnie, to see how different it can be."

"Yeah," he said, far away.

We were silent into Manhattan. At 83rd Street and Park Avenue Don paid the cab fare, and we got out. The three of us. The street was full of cars, mainly cabs, actually – nobody up here owned a car – but the sidewalk was dead, except for doormen. In a way Don was right about New York. This was another place. The thought of him selling crack on Park Avenue gave me a quick laugh.

Don led us into a brightly lit foyer. "Annette Sweeney," he told the doorman.

The doorman eyed the Sufferer. "Is she expecting visitors?"

"Tell her it's Light."

We went up to the ninth floor and found Annette Sweeney's door. Annette Sweeney lived well – I knew that before we even got inside.

She opened the door before we could knock. "You can't just always come up here, Light."

"Annette, chill out. I got some stuff for you. If it's not a good time – "

Annette baited easily. Don's hook gave me an idea what they had in common. "No, Light, I'm just saying why don't you call? Why don't you *ever* call me? What do you have?"

"Just some stuff." He stepped in. "This my brother."

"Hi." She was staring at the Sufferer. "Light, look."

"I know. Forget it."

I stepped in, and so did the Sufferer. Like it owned the place.

"What do you mean? When did this happen?"

"Shut up, forget it. It's a temporary thing."

"What did you do?"

Don went past her, left the rest of us in the doorway, and flopped on her couch. The apartment was big and spare, the architectural detail as lush as the outside of the building, the furniture modern, all aluminum and glass.

"I haven't seen you for weeks, Annette. What did I do? I did a lot of shit, you want to know it all? I come here and you ask me questions?"

Annette fazed easily. She tilted her head so that her hair fell, then brushed it away and pursed her lips and said: "*Sorry*, Light." I saw a rich girl who thought that when she hung out with my brother she was slumming. And I saw my brother twisting her incredible need around his fingers, and hated them both for a second.

Then she turned to me and smiled weakly and said: "Hi. I'm

Annette...I didn't know Light had a brother," and I felt immediately guilty for judging. It didn't hurt that she was beautiful, really striking, with black hair and big black eyes.

I took her hand. The Sufferer pushed past us, brushing my hip, and leapt onto the couch beside Don. "Yeah, well, he does," I said. "I'm Paul."

"It's funny, 'cause my brother is staying with me right now. That's why I was so weird about Light just dropping by."

"You got a brother?" said Don, distractedly. He'd pulled all the little bottles out of his pockets and piled them on her rug. The Sufferer just sat upright on the couch and watched him.

"Yeah. He's out right now, but he might come back."

"That's cool," said Don. "We'll party."

"Um, Douglas might not really wanna...*Jesus,* Light."

"What?"

"Well, just – your new friend. And all that stuff."

"I guess the two kind of go together," I said.

"Very funny," said Don. "He's harmless, he's our – what, *mascot.* Like Tony the Tiger. Smoke rock – it's grrrreat!"

"Doesn't it freak you out?"

"Nah." Don chucked the Sufferer on the chin. "You can't believe all that shit you hear. It just wants to hang. That's all they want. Came from space to party with me. You should of seen it following the cab, though – it was like a video game."

Annette shook her head, grinning.

"Hey, Paul, come here for a minute," said Don, jumping up, nodding his head at the door to the bedroom.

"What?"

"Nothing. Lemme talk to you for a minute though."

We left Annette and the drugs and the Sufferer in the living room, and sat on the edge of the bed. "Don't talk about this California thing," Don said in a low voice. "Don't let Annette hear about us leaving because she'll fucking flip out if she hears I'm going away and I don't need that, okay?"

"Okay," I said, then: "Don?"

"What?"

"Maybe we should call Jimmy and Marilla. Let them know you're okay."

"They kicked me out. They don't care."

"Just because they couldn't let you live there anymore doesn't mean they don't worry about you. Just to let them know you're still *alive* – "

"Okay, but later, okay?" He had a distracted expression, one I was beginning to recognize: *I want a hit.*

"Okay."

Don tapped me on the back and we went back out. The Sufferer had the pipe, but Annette looked like she'd had possession of it recently enough. The room was filled with that sour ozone smell.

She didn't ask what we'd been talking about in private. Didn't even seem to wonder. In general, her self-esteem around my brother seemed kind of low.

"Here," said Don, plucking the pipe away from the alien. I knelt down on the carpet with them and accepted the offer. Between Don and Annette and the Sufferer it was seriously questionable whether any of the drugs would get sold – which was fine with me. Whether or not using up Don's supply was part of the alien's strategy – assuming the alien had a strategy – didn't matter. It could be my strategy.

Annette got up and found her cigarettes and brought one back lit, adding to the haze. Then she brushed her hair back and, seemingly emboldened by the cocaine and nicotine, began talking. "Really, though, Light, you should look out, with this thing hanging around you. I heard about how there are people who'll beat you up just because you've got one of these things following you around. It's a reactionary thing, like AIDS-bashing, you know, blaming the victim. Also won't the police, like, search you or something, hassle you, if they see it?"

"The police know me. They already hassle me. I don't mean shit to the police. Tony the Tiger doesn't change that."

"It's just weird, Light."

"Of course it's weird," said Don. "That's why we love it, right, Paul? It's from another dimension, it's fucking weird, it's science fiction." The Sufferer cocked its head at Don as if it was considering his words. Don raised his fists like a boxer. The Sufferer opened its mouth at him, a black O, and its ears, or what I was mistaking for its ears, wrinkled forward. Now that I could see it up close, it really didn't look so much like a cat. The face was really more human, like the sphinx with a toothless octopus mouth.

Don waved his hands in its face and said: "Dee-nee dee-nee, dee-nee dee-nee" – Twilight Zone Theme.

"Well, when's it going to leave you alone?" She took another rock of crack and stuffed it into the end of an unlit cigarette.

"I'm gonna lose it," he said.

"That's supposed to be pretty hard, Light. I mean, it's like an *obsession* for them."

"Would you stop quoting the, whatever, the Geraldo Rivera version, or wherever you got that crap? I said I'm gonna lose it. You can help. We can trap it in your bedroom and I'll cut out."

"I think it can hear you, Don," I said.

"That's so fucking stupid, man. It's from another planet."

Of course we all turned to look at it now. It stared back and then pawed at the pile of bottles on the carpet.

"Hey, cut it out," said Don. He reached out to push it away, then winced. "Fuck."

"What?"

"You think you could rub my arm? I sprained it or something." He reached under his sweatshirt and freed himself of the gun, dropping it with a clatter on a little table beside the couch.

"Uh, sure, Light," Annette said absently, goggling at the gun. She put her cigarette in her mouth and scooted up beside Don and took his arm in her lap. The Sufferer went on rattling the bottles.

"What about at the airport?" Don said. "You didn't think it could understand us then."

"I'm wrong, it was just a feeling."

"Why'd you have to say that? You creeped me the fuck out."

"Airport?" said Annette.

"Uh, that's where we had to go to get the stuff," I said, gesturing at the rug, taking up the burden of covering Don's slip out of guilt, out of habit.

"You scored at the *airport*?"

Don shrugged at her, and said: "Sure."

Annette lit the loaded cigarette. The rock hissed as it hit the flame. "What are you doing with all this?"

"Well, I really gotta sell some," said Don. "I was wondering if you wanted to call some of your friends. I don't wanna go downtown now."

"I don't know, Light." She looked at the Sufferer, who was still rattling at the vials. "Won't it narc on us?"

"Don't be stupid."

"Even if it doesn't, that's what everybody'll think if they see it here."

"Just set it up, okay? We can arrange something so they don't have to meet Tony the Tiger." He lit a rock and toked.

"Well, anyway, my brother is coming back tonight so I don't think you can deal out of my house, Light."

"What does that have to do with it? It's *your* house, right?"

"Well, I don't know. He's my *older* brother."

"Paul is my older fucking brother," Don said. "So what?"

Maybe Annette's older brother knows how to take care of his sibling, I thought. Like I obviously don't.

There was a sound of a key fumbling in a lock. "Speak of the devil," said Annette.

Douglas turned out to be quite a bit older than Annette, or at least the way he dressed and held himself made it seem that way. He came up to where we all were sprawled on the couch and the carpet and said, to me: "Are you Light?"

"No," said Don, "that's me."

Douglas's eyes played over the scene: the gun, the vials, the alien sitting like a giant snake-skinned cougar on the carpet.

He reached down and picked up the gun.

"Ann, why don't you go lock yourself in the bedroom," he said.

"*Doug*-las," she whined.

"Do it."

"Don't be a chump," said Don. "This is her place."

"Shut up. I know all about you. We're going to have a little talk. *Go*, Ann."

"I told you," Annette said to Don as she got up from the couch. "Uh, nice to meet you, Paul. Sorry."

As she slouched her way to the bedroom, the Sufferer jumped up and followed her. Douglas took a step back, startled. I watched the gun. Douglas handled it badly, but I was pretty sure the safety was still in place.

The Sufferer was suddenly, inexplicably agitated. It ran ahead of her into the bedroom, looked out the far window at the lights of the building across 83rd Street, and back at us.

"What's it doing?" said Doug angrily.

Don shrugged. Annette stood waiting at the doorway.

"Get it out of there," said Doug, gesturing with the gun.

"Hey, that's not my responsibility," said Don. "You're the dude who's taking charge."

The Sufferer wrinkled its ears forward and stared glumly at Don. Don glowered at Douglas.

"Here," I said. I went in and pushed at the Sufferer. Its flesh was like a dense black pudding, and it felt like it weighed about a thousand pounds. I tried to prod it towards the door, but it wouldn't budge. Annette came into the bedroom and tried to help me push, to no avail.

Don, his movements exaggerated and slow, put a rock of coke into the glass pipe and flicked his lighter enticingly. The Sufferer trotted forward, like it had read the script, and Annette and I almost fell on our faces.

Douglas didn't find it funny. "Get back out here," he said to me, and when I obliged he reached over and slammed the door shut with Annette inside. "Sit down," he told me, and I did it.

The Sufferer, of course, paid him no mind. It went past us all, into the kitchen.

"What's on your mind?" said Don drawlingly, lighting the pipe.

"I want you and your monster out of Annette's life, *Light*," said Douglas. "She's told me plenty about you."

"Why not? I'm her boyfriend."

"You're not her boyfriend," snarled Douglas. "You're her dealer. Only you're not even around enough to do a good job of that." From the kitchen came a crash of breaking glass. Douglas looked in, then turned back to Don. "You get Annette hooked and then she's gotta go out and find her own because you smoked up your whole shipment.

You pathetic piece of human garbage."

"Fuck told you that shit?"

"What, is it a shock to find out that you're known, you sleazeball?"

Another crash from the kitchen, and then a sound like chimes: the Sufferer wading through the glass or ceramic it had broken.

"What's your – monster-thing doing?" said Douglas. I got the feeling that his castigating Don was the fulfillment of a long-standing fantasy, only the Sufferer wasn't part of the scenario.

"I told you, it's not my thing, I don't tell it what to do, man."

"Is that why you're trying to unload all this stuff on my sister – the monster won't let you use it anymore?"

Don just smirked. "The monster's 'using it' with me. I don't tell it what to do and it don't tell me what to do."

"It's following you because you're dead, you loser. You're smoking your life away – it's like your death angel."

"That's not right," I said. "It's nothing like that. It's an empathy thing, it's responding to the *life* in Don – "

"Yeah, right. The life. You people are walking corpses. And I'll finish you off myself if you don't leave my sister alone."

"You wanna kill me, huh?" said Don.

"I will if I have to. Before you destroy my sister's life like you destroyed your own. Before one of those death creatures comes prowling around for her."

"You don't know what you're talking about," I said. "You never met a Sufferer before, you have no idea how they operate."

"You never met me before, either," said Don.

"I heard all I need to know from your sleazebag pusher friends," said Douglas.

"What?" said Don, suddenly attentive.

"When you disappeared, Annette started buying from this black dude who called around for you. Real pimpy type of guy. I had to call the cops on him. I *should* call the cops on you."

"Who – Annette!" Don jumped up.

"Randall," said Douglas. "Randall whose shipment you singlehandedly smoked up. I'm surprised you're not dead by now."

Annette looked out of the bedroom. "You gave him my number,

Light, remember? He called here looking for you about, I don't know, four or five days ago – "

"Let's get the fuck out of here," said Don. "Give me my gun." He knelt down and began scooping the vials back into his parka.

"Take your crap with you," said Douglas. "Go get nice and high on it. But I think I'd better keep the gun."

"*Fuck* you, man – "

"No, fuck *you*." Douglas clicked the safety off. I was surprised he knew how. Then he put his foot on Don's shoulder and shoved him back on his ass on the carpet. "No more bullshit, Light. You leave Annette alone, no calls, no late-night visits, got it? And I'm keeping the gun. You're lucky I don't call the cops."

"Call the cops, see if I give a damn, man. You don't have a fucking clue." Don stood up. He came up to Douglas's shoulder, but he was crowding the gun, and Douglas took a step back. I thought about trying to step in and realized my whole body was trembling.

The Sufferer came out of the kitchen, pumping forward on its massive black legs, and rushed up to where Douglas stood. It opened its strange black mouth and emitted a sound, something between a howl and a moan. Actually, it sounded like a man bellowing as he fell down a bottomless well, complete with echoes and Doppler effects.

At the same time chunks of broken glass fell out of its mouth at Douglas's feet, and on his shoes.

Douglas pointed the gun and fired, at almost the exact same spot on the alien's big bulldog chest. The noise, in the quiet apartment, was deafening. Douglas dropped the weapon and grabbed his hand, wincing.

Don immediately picked it up.

"Go," he said to me, and nodded at the door. Then he bent back down to collect the last of his vials, sweeping up the empties along with them.

Douglas stood holding his hand, watching the Sufferer. The creature had rolled back on its haunches at the impact of the gunshot, and now it was shaking its head vigorously, and spitting out more shards of glass.

Don pushed the gun back into his belt and hustled me towards the door, and then turned and slapped Douglas ever so lightly on the cheek. Like he wanted to wake him up, not hurt him. "You mess up your hand?" he said.

Douglas didn't say anything.

"Maybe your sister can rub it for you. See ya."

We ran to the elevator, the Sufferer leaping after us.

Out on the street Don said: "Hell was it doing?"

"It got you your gun back," I said.

"Yeah, but what was it doing, eating the dishes?" He knelt down and looked in the Sufferer's mouth. "Jesus." He reached in and pulled out a chunk of glass that was lodged there. The Sufferer snorted and shook its head.

"It's like the one soft spot, the whatchacallit, Achilles tendon," Don said. "I wonder if I could kill it by shooting it in the mouth?"

"*Donnie!* That's not cool. It saved you up there. Besides, you can't kill them, I read it – "

"Okay, shut up." He tossed the glass out into the street, under a parked car.

"Now what?" I said, and then quickly made my nomination: "The airport? Or Port Authority, catch a Greyhound upstate?"

Don didn't say anything.

"Upstate, New York State, isn't breaking parole, right? You can do anything you want, doesn't matter if the Sufferer's following you. I bet they've never seen one of these guys up there, huh?"

"I gotta sell the shit," said Don. "The triangle on 72nd and Broadway. I can move it there. C'mon, we can walk across." He started towards Central Park.

We ran after him, me and the Sufferer. "Don, wait. Why can't we just go? What are you stalling for?"

"Damn, Paul, you can't just show up with this idea and *rush* me out of town. Maybe I don't *want* to go to California. Maybe at least you ought to let me clear up my damn business before we go, okay?"

"What? *What?*" As if the robbery hadn't happened, or as if it weren't connected to the plan, a plan he'd already agreed to.

"Relax, okay. Damn. We'll go. Just let me unload the stuff, okay?"

We walked to the edge of the park on the empty streets, the three of us. In silence, until Don said, without turning: "It's been a while since we were in touch."

"What? Yeah, I guess. What do you mean?"

"That's all, just it's been a while. We didn't, like, keep up on each other's lives or anything."

"Yeah," I said, chilled.

Central Park at night made me think of high school, of smoking pot with my Upper West Side friends. White people's drugs, drugs for the kids who stay in school, go to college. While back in Brooklyn, Don was finding the other kind, the drugs for the black kids, the ones who wouldn't go to college even if they bluffed it through high school.

Now my West Side friends were all off at college, in various parts of the country, and I was back in town to sell drugs at 72nd and Broadway, under their parents' windows.

The Sufferer seemed to like the park. Several times it roamed wide of us, disappearing briefly in the trees. When we crossed Central Park West, though, it was back close at our heels.

We set up at the benches on the triangle, along with some sleeping winos. There was a black kid, too, who kept crossing the street to the subway and ducking inside, then crossing back to the triangle. He and the Sufferer exchanged a long look, then the kid went back to his pacing routine, and the Sufferer jumped over the bench, into the little plot of land the pavement and benches encircled. I hoped it would stay there, more or less out of sight from the street.

"This is dead, Don."

"Relax. It's where you come, up here. It's the only place to score."

"It's Tuesday night."

"Junkies don't know weekends, man."

"We're gonna get arrested. This is just like a target, like sitting in the middle of a target."

"Shut up. You're being a chump. Forget the cops."

A chump. The unkindest cut. I shut up. Don got out his pipe and smoked away another rock of the product. I had a hit too. The Sufferer didn't seem as interested.

And we waited.

The traffic on Broadway was all cabs, and – surprise! – two of them pulled over and transacted business with Don. One was slumming West Side yuppies on their way to a club, men overdressed, women waiting in the back of the cab, relieved laughter when the males returned safely. The other was two blacks in the front seat, the cabbie and a pal, with the cab still available. I ached to push Don in the back and take off, but I stayed shut up.

Another customer walked up, from the park side. He caught up with the kid, who shook his head, nodded at us, and made his jog across the street to the subway station again while the street was clear. Don made the sale and the guy headed back the way he'd come.

I was just noticing that this time the kid hadn't come back to the triangle when the truck pulled up. A van, really, like a UPS delivery truck but covered with layers of graffiti and minor dents, and missing doors on both sides. It pulled around the triangle the wrong way, bringing down a plague of honking from cabs.

Don said: "Oh shit."

"What?"

"That's Randall's truck." But he didn't move, or reach for the gun.

The driver kicked the emergency brake down and turned to us holding a toy-like machine gun. I figured it wasn't a toy. "Is that Randall?" I said.

"Nah. Shut up now."

The man in the passenger seat came around the front. Well dressed, unarmed. "Light," he said.

"Yo, Randall."

"Get in the back. This your man?" He raised his chin at me. His voice had a slight Caribbean lilt.

Don shrugged.

"You took my safe house tonight, my man?" Randall asked me. He was clean and pretty, like some young, unbeaten boxer. But he had a boiled-looking finger-thick scar running all along the right underside of his jaw, and where it would have crossed his ear the lobe was missing.

"That's me," I said, dorkily.

"Come along." He made it sound jolly. He opened the back. Inside were Kaz and Drey, sitting on tires, looking miserable.

I tried to catch Don's eye, but he just trudged forward and stepped up into the back. I went after him.

I glanced over my shoulder, but didn't spot the Sufferer. Randall climbed in behind us, slammed the two doors shut, and went up to the front. There wasn't any divider, just a big open metal box with two bucket seats in front of the window, and a steering wheel on a post to the floor. The driver handed Randall the little machine gun and took off across Broadway, down 72nd Street.

Don and I leaned against the back. I looked out the back window and just caught sight of the pay phone on the far side of the subway entrance.

We rattled to the end of 72nd, under the West Side Highway and parked out on the stretch of nothing before the water. It's always amazing to get to the edge of Manhattan and see how much stuff there is between the city – you know, the city that you think of, the city people use – and the real edge of the island. You think of it as being like a raft of skyscrapers, buildings to the edge, and instead there's the edge of the island. Boathouses, concrete and weeds, places that nobody cares about.

Unfortunately, at the moment.

The driver serving as gunman again, Randall opened the back and steered us out into a dark, empty garage, a sort of cinderblock shell full of rusted iron drums and piles of rotting linoleum tile. The floor was littered with glass and twisted, rusty cable. A seagull squawked out of our path, flapping but not taking off, then refolded its wings and wobbled outside once we were safely past. Kaz and Drey both looked back dubiously, acting more like fellow captives than Randall's henchmen, but Randall kept nodding us forward, until the moonlight from the garage entrance petered out and we all stood in darkness.

"You messin' up, Light," said Randall.

"Here's your stuff," said Don, scooping in his parka pockets. He sounded afraid. I wondered where the Sufferer was.

"That's good. Give it to Drey. You make a little green out there?"

"Yeah."

"You smoke up a little, there, too?"

Before Don could squeak "Yeah" again Randall stepped forward and smacked him, viciously hard, across the mouth. Don's foot slipped and skidded through the broken glass, but he kept from falling.

"Relax, relax," said Randall suddenly, as though some protest had been raised. "We ain't killing you tonight, Light. But we gotta talk about this funny stuff, you chumps playing with my money. You think you takin' Kaz but it's all my money, right?"

"Yeah."

"It's like it's all a game, like *Monopoly* money, you and Kaz can just fuckin' *play* with it."

"Kaz didn't do anything wrong," said Don.

"Kaz a sucker get taken by a chump like you." He raised his hand and Kaz flinched. Leaving his hand in the air, he turned to me. "Who's your man here?"

"Paul."

"He your brother?"

"Nah."

Randall looked at Kaz and Drey. "This the dude?"

Kaz nodded.

Randall stared at me, but he was still talking to Don. "You tell him Randall got some easy money, some play money, just laying around? You tell him I'm a fuckin' chump?"

"Randall, we didn't even take your money. Just some dope, man. We only took money off Kaz and Drey."

"My dope *is* money, stupid. My dope is *product*. Not for you to fuckin' smoke. Why you so stupid, crackhead?"

At that moment a shadow slipped in through the moonlit garage entrance, then almost disappeared into the darkness. The Sufferer. I felt relieved, like it was the cavalry. But when it came into the circle it stepped up beside Randall, and then I saw that it wasn't the same.

It was bigger than ours, its eyes were longer, slits instead of ovals, and the strangely human nose was pushed to one side. A scarred Sufferer, for Randall.

"Here's my thing," said Randall. "I heard you got a thing, yourself. You been seen around *town* together."

"Uh, yeah. So what?"

"So what? That the only reason I came up here to talk to you myself, you think I bother with a fuckin' chump like you? Only reason my man didn't do you in a drive-by on Broadway."

"What, you like them? You can have mine."

"Naw, why you have to get fresh, Light?" He leaned over and slapped Don again, but lightly. It was the same slap Don had used on Douglas, exactly the same. Don was a reflexive mimic. "You disappoint me."

Don didn't speak.

"What does it want?" said Randall.

"I don't know."

Randall made a face. "I can't get rid of the sucker. It wants me to stop – stop livin' the life?"

"I said I don't know."

"Because I'm not a *user*, Light, I'm not like you. What's it trying to say to me?" Randall lurched forward and Don flinched. Intimidation, I sensed, was a way of life for Randall. It even leaked into interactions where he wanted to propagate trust. He couldn't help it.

"Nothing," said Don.

Randall turned and paced in a tight, impatient circle. "I wanna know, Light. Why this thing in my life, what the *meaning* is. Tell me."

It occurred to me that Randall thought Don knew because he was *white*.

"Nothing."

"Must want something, everybody wants something, Light. It stop you from using?"

"It doesn't give a shit, Randall. It smokes rock. It's a party animal, man."

"Gonna turn me in? Working for the Narcotics?"

"Sure, I don't know. This is fuckin' stupid, Randall."

Randall wheeled. "What you sayin'? It's gathering *evidence*, man? Tell me what you know!"

Kaz and Drey shifted nervously. The gun man cleared his throat.

"Nothing, Randall, man. It can't fuckin' talk, it's from another *planet*, man. Can't turn you in. Relax. It's really got you rattled, man."

"So tell me what it wants."

"Nothing. It's just...trying to, you know, get along." Don sighed. "Really, Randall. Everybody wants it to be *about* something, or up *to* something, but it's just, like...*attracted*. All the explanations are bullshit."

"That's not right," I blurted. "It's like a guardian angel. It's drawn to you because it senses something – "

I hesitated, and saw that I had everyone's undivided attention.

" – because it feels this sense that you're, uh, *important*, your life is important, and so it's drawn to you." I was going in circles. "It's not *judging* you, it's not moralistic. That's why it doesn't try to stop you, try to change your behavior, why it'll even share the pipe. Drugs aren't the point, it's not some simplistic thing like they make it out to be, it's more subtle than that. It wants to be around you and protect you because – your life is important. And it's afraid that you don't – care enough. So it's trying to do that, to *care* – "

I wanted to convince them, somehow, because I wanted to convince myself.

While I was talking, Don's Sufferer had crept in, like some kind of affirmation of my words. It padded past Don and Randall, stopping a foot or so away from Randall's Sufferer. I stopped talking. The two aliens stared at each other, and the distance between them suddenly seemed very small.

I thought of the aliens' incredible strength. I wished Don's was bigger than Randall's, instead of the reverse.

"Guardian angel," mused Randall. "That your guardian angel, Light?" The sneer in his voice made me sorry I'd spoken at all.

"Yeah," said Don. "It'll always be with you now, Randall. Gonna live your life with you, see everything you do."

"Fuck you trying to say?"

"Nothing. Just that you gotta live right, now, Randall. You're being watched." Don wasn't saying it because it meant anything to him. He was just yanking Randall's chain.

"Huh." Randall thought this over. "Light, you don't know shit about shit. You don't know what I do, how I live."

"Maybe not, Randall."

"I gotta get my money back, Light. Drey, take the money off Light."

Don handed it over, preemptively. I thought of the gun.

"I gotta put a hurt on you, Light, like you put on me. How'm I gonna do that?"

"I dunno."

"What you got that I can take? You ain't got nothing."

The Sufferers suddenly both stood, and I braced for some kind of violence between them. Instead they turned and walked out of the garage together, into the frame of moonlight, and then disappeared around the corner, heading towards the water. To settle their differences?

With them gone I felt naked, doomed.

"Kaz," said Randall, "you gotta do my hurtin' for me, my man. For what Light did to you."

"Naw, Randall," whined Kaz. "Naw, man."

"Hit him."

"Naw. He still got a gun, Randall, anyway. You didn't take it off him."

"So take it off him." Randall pointed at me. "You go, chump. You got lucky. Don't fuck with me no more. Don't go around with this dude Light, he's bad news. Go."

"What?" I said.

"Get lost. I ain't gonna fuck with you. You didn't know what you was doing."

"We'll go together," I said. "He's, uh, my brother."

"Go." Randall pointed, and the driver raised the gun at me.

"Go ahead, Paul," said Don.

"No, I'm his *brother*," I said, getting hysterical. "No."

Randall shoved me towards the door, and the driver followed. I took a few steps.

"Take him, Kaz," commanded Randall, done with me. "Take his gun."

"Naw, don't make me, Randall."

"Do it!"

"I'm his *brother* – "

The driver kicked me, and aimed the gun at my stomach. Inside, Kaz was advancing sheepishly on Don.

I ran, into the glare of moonlight.

Where was the Sufferer? I ran towards the water. Behind me, the clatter of voices: Don, Randall, Kaz. I ran, gasping.

When I found the Sufferers I thought they were killing each other. They were half hidden behind a pile of shredded, stinking tires, in a puddle of stagnant water streaked with oil rainbows. They lay entwined, limbs twisted together, both moaning like echoing wells, their bodies twitching, paws treading air, ears wrinkled back.

Fucking. Making love – the moment it hit me was the moment I heard the shot.

I turned in time to see the four shadows sprinting for the truck. Kaz's voice: "You made me, you made me, you shouldn't of fuckin' made me – "

They'd driven off before I got back to Don.

He was lying on the floor scrabbling in the glass with a hand already sticky with blood. In the dark the blood looked black, and watching it seep out of his stomach was like watching his white sweatshirt disappear into the gloom. It was happening fast.

"Fuck, Paul," he said, when he saw me.

"I'm going to get help," I said.

"Wait, don't leave me – "

"I'll be back – "

I ran out, back under the freeway, and found a woman walking her dog in the park. "For God's sake, my brother got shot, down in the old garage down there, please can you call an ambulance, please – " I fumbled it out between gasps, repeated everything, pointing, and when she agreed I turned and ran back, clutching a knot in my side; a cramp from running, but it felt like a sympathetic wound.

Moving too fast, I slid in his blood, and my knees buckled at seeing how little of the white of the sweatshirt was left. I sat down, in blood and glass, and held his hand.

His gun lay to one side, and I felt suddenly sure that he'd been shot with his own gun, Kaz trying to take it from him. The gun we could have left behind so many times in so many different places.

"I can't see you, man," said Don.

"Your eyes?" My voice was trembling, on the verge of sobs.

"No, stupid, I mean move around here, don't sit behind me."

I shifted. "An ambulance is coming, okay, Donnie? So just hang on. Guess you'll have to talk to the police or something, huh?"

An hour ago I was still picturing Don in California. Now the dream of seeing him in a hospital bed seemed maybe too much to dare hope for.

"You're so stupid about the cops, Paul." His voice was husky, and as he went on, it got rougher and softer. "I don't care about the cops. When they arrested me before I told the guy 'Thank you, you saved me.' 'Cause I was a skeleton, I weighed about ninety pounds, and I knew I would dry out, get healthy in jail. That's all jail is, man, guys gettin' fed, getting healthy again, doing pushups, so they can go out and do it again. Shit, if they'd given me time instead of parole I might be off rock now."

I started weeping.

"C'mon, Paul, relax."

"We could be on a plane right now," I said. "We were right there, we were at the airport. The Sufferer, the Sufferer ruined everything."

"Nah, man, I didn't want to go. Tony the Tiger didn't blow it."

"Why? Why couldn't we just go?"

"I was all freaked out. I mean, it sounds great, right? Start over, cut out, leave all the shit behind. But I wasn't ready. I was just going along, I didn't want to disappoint you."

"What do you mean?"

"If California is my big second chance, Paul, I don't wanna go fuck it up with my pockets full of rock. I wanted it to be like you said, but I wasn't ready, I was afraid. If I went and I was still all fucked up there – I didn't want to disappoint you, Paul. At least if we didn't go I hadn't fucked up *California*. It was still there, like this beautiful picture you were painting, you know – "

His voice was trailing off, and I could barely hear him for my own sobbing.

"It was sort of hard for me to think about California or whatever, anything else, with all that rock in my coat, Paul. When we took Kaz for rock instead of cash...I had to get rid of it, and if I had to get rid of it, why not get high, you know? You don't know... you don't know how much I...like to get *high*, Paul. You haven't been around me that much.

We haven't been in touch. I'm not just, like, the little kid you knew. I been...*doing* stuff – "

"My fault, the whole thing about robbing Kaz. You did that because of my stupid idea, to get cash for the tickets."

"Yeah, yeah, let's blame it all on you and the monster. Whatever. But the California thing...wasn't stupid. It was a good idea, so relax now, okay?"

"Okay."

"Shut up now and stop making me talk so much, right?"

"Okay."

"We'll go...we'll still go to California."

I didn't say anything, and Don closed his eyes, and we were quiet. The pace of blood leaking through his shirt slowed down. Time seemed to slow with it.

"I'm gonna pass out now," he said.

"Okay," I managed.

"I'm just...passing out, right, I'm not *dying*."

He couldn't see his sweatshirt. "Right," I said.

He was dead for almost five minutes before I finally heard sirens, and they weren't even close yet.

I made a quick calculation about talking to a long series of people about what happened, starting with the ambulance people and the police and ending with our parents, versus getting the hell out of there. It wasn't a hard call.

I took Don's pipe and lighter and put them in my pocket and ran, south under the highway, and circled around a couple of blocks back to Broadway.

I hopped the turnstile and took the IRT downtown, to the Village, then walked across West 3rd Street to Washington Square Park, where life went on as usual, all night every night, every night for the last thirty years, probably. I sat on the same bench I'd been on at noon, waiting for Don to turn up, finding him after so long. Now I had to share it with a guy who was sleeping, but his smell and my stare kept anyone else away.

I wondered if I was waiting for Kaz. I couldn't think of what I would do or say if he showed, so I guessed I wasn't.

I started feeling sleepy about the same time the sky began to lighten up. The deadest hour in the park, when the night is officially over. A few businessmen walked across, and joggers. It was their park now, for a few short hours.

I got off my bench and managed to find someone dealing. There's always someone dealing. If I'd said to him: "You seen Kaz?" or "You seen Light?" he probably would have said: "Naw, man. But he be around later. What you want him for?"

Instead I just scored a five-dollar vial and went back to my bench.

I put it into Don's pipe and flickered the lighter over it and drew a hit, and at that moment the Sufferer walked up. It sat down in front of me and cocked its head.

I tried to ignore it, which worked for about five seconds. Then, riding the rush from the crack, I jumped on it and started beating its face with my fists. "You didn't do anything!" I screamed. The Sufferer just twisted slowly away from my blows, squinting its big eyes, shifting its feet to accommodate my assault. "You didn't help him at all! You didn't change anything!"

A crowd began to gather around us. "You were fucking, you were fucking when they killed him!" My voice cracked with rage, and I tasted my snot and tears as they ran down my face. I beat at it, my fists aching, then tried to reach for its mouth, its "Achilles tendon," but it just butted me away with its cheek. "You didn't help him at all!"

A couple of Rastafarians came forward out of the crowd and plucked me away. "Easy there, little man, come on. It didn't hurt you now, you just hurting youself. Easy up."

I squirmed out of their grasp and fell to the pavement in front of the Sufferer. The alien opened its mouth and moaned silently at me, then took a step away from me. The crowd ducked quickly out of its way, though it hadn't made a sudden or violent movement yet.

Sickened, trembling, I crawled off the pavement, into the grassy section behind the benches.

Soon enough the little knot of attention that had gathered around us was dissolved back into the park. The Sufferer wandered away too.

When the trembling passed I got up and staggered out of the park, half blind with hunger and exhaustion. The Village swirled around me, oblivious. I thought about Don weighing ninety pounds, reaching the end of his run, thanking the cops for taking him off the street, for noticing him at all.

I don't know how long I walked before I passed out on the bench on Sixth Avenue, in front of the basketball courts, but when I woke again, the sun was low. People were going home from work. I was freezing. The Sufferer was staring at me, its face inches from mine.

I reached out, weak, wanting to hit it or twist its ears and to take its warmth at the same time.

It pulled away, and turned and trotted down Sixth. "You fucker," I said. "It would have been better if you'd never come at all."

I could have been talking to myself. Maybe I was.

I watched the Sufferer turn the corner, and I never saw it again after that.

The Brooklyn Bridge has a walkway. The Manhattan used to, but doesn't anymore. I crossed the bridge under an orange sky. I walked through downtown Brooklyn to Flatbush Avenue, and took the Long Island Railroad to Plainview, to tell Jimmy and Marilla that I knew what had happened to Don, to Donovan, to Light.

Sea Oak

George Saunders

AT SIX Mr. Frendt comes on the P.A. and shouts, "Welcome to Joysticks!" Then he announces Shirts Off. We take off our flight jackets and fold them up. We take off our shirts and fold them up. Our scarves we leave on. Thomas Kirster's our beautiful boy. He's got long muscles and bright-blue eyes. The minute his shirt comes off two fat ladies hustle up the aisle and stick some money in his pants and ask will he be their Pilot. He says sure. He brings their salads. He brings their soups. My phone rings and the caller tells me to come see her in the Spitfire mock-up. Does she want me to be her Pilot? I'm hoping. Inside the Spitfire is Margie, who says she's been diagnosed with Chronic Shyness Syndrome, then hands me an Instamatic and offers me ten bucks for a close-up of Thomas's tush.

Do I do it? Yes I do.

It could be worse. It is worse for Lloyd Betts. Lately he's put on weight and his hair's gone thin. He doesn't get a call all shift and waits zero tables and winds up sitting on the P-51 wing, playing solitaire in a hunched-over position that gives him big gut rolls.

I Pilot six tables and make forty dollars in tips plus five an hour in salary.

After closing we sit on the floor for Debriefing. "There are times," Mr. Frendt says, "when one must move gracefully to the next station in life, like for example certain women in Africa or Brazil, I forget which, who either color their faces or don some kind of distinctive headdress upon achieving menopause. Are you with me? One of our ranks must now leave us. No one is an island in terms of being thought cute forever, and so today we must say good-bye to our friend Lloyd. Lloyd, stand up so we can say good-bye to you. I'm sorry. We are all so very sorry."

"Oh God," says Lloyd. "Let this not be true."

But it's true. Lloyd's finished. We give him a round of applause, and Frendt gives him a Farewell Pen and the contents of his locker in a trash bag and out he goes. Poor Lloyd. He's got a wife and two kids and a sad little duplex on Self-Storage Parkway.

"It's been a pleasure!" he shouts desperately from the doorway, trying not to burn any bridges.

What a stressful workplace. The minute your Cute Rating drops you're a goner. Guests rank us as Knockout, Honeypie, Adequate, or Stinker. Not that I'm complaining. At least I'm working. At least I'm not a Stinker like Lloyd.

I'm a solid Honeypie/Adequate, heading home with forty bucks cash.

At Sea Oak there's no sea and no oak, just a hundred subsidized apartments and a rear view of FedEx. Min and Jade are feeding their babies while watching *How My Child Died Violently*. Min's my sister. Jade's our cousin. *How My Child Died Violently* is hosted by Matt Merton, a six-foot-five blond who's always giving the parents shoulder rubs and telling them they've been sainted by pain. Today's show features a ten-year-old who killed a five-year-old for refusing to join his gang. The ten-year-old strangled the five-year-old with a jump rope, filled his mouth with baseball cards, then locked himself in the bathroom and wouldn't come out until his parents agreed to take him to FunTimeZone, where he confessed, then dove screaming into a mesh cage full of plastic balls. The audience is shrieking threats at the parents of the killer while the parents of the victim urge restraint and forgiveness to such an extent that finally the audience starts shrieking threats at them too. Then it's a commercial. Min and Jade put down the babies and light cigarettes and pace the room while studying aloud for their GEDs. It doesn't look good. Jade says "regicide" is a virus. Min locates Biafra one planet from Saturn. I offer to help and they start yelling at me for condescending.

"You're lucky, man!" my sister says. "You did high school. You got your frigging diploma. We don't. That's why we have to do this GED shit. If we had our diplomas we could just watch TV and not be all distracted."

"Really," says Jade. "Now shut it, chick! We got to study. Show's almost on."

They debate how many sides a triangle has. They agree that Churchill was in opera. Matt Merton comes back and explains that last week's show on suicide, in which the parents watched a reenactment of their son's suicide, was a healing process for the parents, then shows a video of the parents admitting it was a healing process.

My sister's baby is Troy. Jade's baby is Mac. They crawl off into the kitchen and Troy gets his finger caught in the heat vent. Min rushes over and starts pulling.

"Jesus freaking Christ!" screams Jade. "Watch it! Stop yanking on him and get the freaking Vaseline. You're going to give him a really long arm, man!"

Troy starts crying. Mac starts crying. I go over and free Troy no problem. Meanwhile Jade and Min get in a slap fight and nearly knock over the TV.

"Yo, chick!" Min shouts at the top of her lungs. "I'm sure you're slapping me? And then you knock over the freaking TV? Don't you care?"

"I care!" Jade shouts back. "You're the slut who nearly pulled off her own kid's finger for no freaking reason, man!"

Just then Aunt Bernie comes in from DrugTown in her DrugTown cap and hobbles over and picks up Troy and everything calms way down.

"No need to fuss, little man," she says. "Everything's fine. Everything's just hunky-dory."

"Hunky-dory," says Min, and gives Jade one last pinch.

Aunt Bernie's a peacemaker. She doesn't like trouble. Once this guy backed over her foot at FoodKing and she walked home with ten broken bones. She never got married, because Grandpa needed her to keep house after Grandma died. Then he died and left all his money to a woman none of us had ever heard of, and Aunt Bernie started in at DrugTown. But she's not bitter. Sometimes she's so nonbitter it gets on my nerves. When I say Sea Oak's a pit she says she's just glad to have a roof over her head. When I say I'm tired of being broke she says

Grandpa once gave her pencils for Christmas and she was so thrilled she sat around sketching horses all day on the backs of used envelopes. Once I asked was she sorry she never had kids and she said no, not at all, and besides, weren't we her kids?

And I said yes we were.

But of course we're not.

For dinner it's beanie-wienies. For dessert it's ice cream with freezer burn.

"What a nice day we've had," Aunt Bernie says once we've got the babies in bed.

"Man, what an optometrist," says Jade.

Next day is Thursday, which means a visit from Ed Anders from the Board of Health. He's in charge of ensuring that our penises never show. Also that we don't kiss anyone. None of us ever kisses anyone or shows his penis except Sonny Vance, who does both, because he's saving up to buy a FaxIt franchise. As for our Penile Simulators, yes, we can show them, we can let them stick out the top of our pants, we can even periodically dampen our tight pants with spray bottles so our Simulators really contour, but our real penises, no, those have to stay inside our hot uncomfortable oversized Simulators.

"Sorry fellas, hi fellas," Anders says as he comes wearily in. "Please know I don't like this any better than you do. I went to school to learn how to inspect meat, but this certainly wasn't what I had in mind. Ha ha!"

He orders a Lindbergh Enchilada and eats it cautiously, as if it's alive and he's afraid of waking it. Sonny Vance is serving soup to a table of hairstylists on a bender and for a twenty shoots them a quick look at his unit.

Just then Anders glances up from his Lindbergh.

"Oh for crying out loud," he says, and writes up a Shutdown and we all get sent home early. Which is bad. Every dollar counts. Lately I've been sneaking toilet paper home in my briefcase. I can fit three rolls in. By the time I get home they're usually flat and don't work so great on the roller but still it saves a few bucks.

I clock out and cut through the strip of forest behind FedEx. Very pretty. A raccoon scurries over a fallen oak and starts nibbling at a rusty bike. As I come out of the woods I hear a shot. At least I think it's a shot. It could be a backfire. But no, it's a shot, because then there's another one, and some kids sprint across the courtyard yelling that Big Scary Dawgz rule.

I run home. Min and Jade and Aunt Bernie and the babies are huddled behind the couch. Apparently they had the babies outside when the shooting started. Troy's walker got hit. Luckily he wasn't in it. It's supposed to look like a duck but now the beak's missing.

"Man, fuck this shit!" Min shouts.

"Freak this crap you mean," says Jade. "You want them growing up with shit-mouths like us? Crap-mouths I mean?"

"I just want them growing up, period," says Min.

"Boo-hoo, Miss Dramatic," says Jade.

"Fuck off, Miss Ho," shouts Min.

"I mean it, jagoff, I'm not kidding," shouts Jade, and punches Min in the arm.

"Girls, for crying out loud!" says Aunt Bernie. "We should be thankful. At least we got a home. And at least none of them bullets actually hit nobody."

"No offense, Bernie?" says Min. "But you call this a freaking home?"

Sea Oak's not safe. There's an ad hoc crackhouse in the laundry room and last week Min found some brass knuckles in the kiddie pool. If I had my way I'd move everybody up to Canada. It's nice there. Very polite. We went for a weekend last fall and got a flat tire and these two farmers with bright-red faces insisted on fixing it, then springing for dinner, then starting a college fund for the babies. They sent us the stock certificates a week later, along with a photo of all of us eating cobbler at a diner. But moving to Canada takes bucks. Dad's dead and left us nada and Ma now lives with Freddie, who doesn't like us, plus he's not exactly rich himself. He does phone polls. This month he's asking divorced women how often they backslide and sleep with their exes. He gets ten bucks for every completed poll.

So not lucrative, and Canada's a moot point.

I go out and find the beak of Troy's duck and fix it with Elmer's.

"Actually you know what?" says Aunt Bernie. "I think that looks even more like a real duck now. Because sometimes their beaks are cracked? I seen one like that downtown."

"Oh my God," says Min. "The kid's duck gets shot in the face and she says we're lucky."

"Well, we are lucky," says Bernie.

"Somebody's beak is cracked," says Jade.

"You know what I do if something bad happens?" Bernie says. "I don't think about it. Don't take it so serious. It ain't the end of the world. That's what I do. That's what I always done. That's how I got where I am."

My feeling is, Bernie, I love you, but where are you? You work at DrugTown for minimum. You're sixty and own nothing. You were basically a slave to your father and never had a date in your life.

"I mean, complain if you want," she says. "But I think we're doing pretty darn good for ourselves."

"Oh, we're doing great," says Min, and pulls Troy out from behind the couch and brushes some duck shards off his sleeper.

Joysticks reopens on Friday. It's a madhouse. They've got the fog on. A bridge club offers me fifteen bucks to oil-wrestle Mel Turner. So I oil-wrestle Mel Turner. They offer me twenty bucks to feed them chicken wings from my hand. So I feed them chicken wings from my hand. The afternoon flies by. Then the evening. At nine the bridge club leaves and I get a sorority. They sing intelligent nasty songs and grope my Simulator and say they'll never be able to look their boyfriends' meager genitalia in the eye again. Then Mr. Frendt comes over and says phone. It's Min. She sounds crazy. Four times in a row she shrieks get home. When I tell her calm down, she hangs up. I call back and no one answers. No biggie. Min's prone to panic. Probably one of the babies is puky. Luckily I'm on FlexTime.

"I'll be back," I say to Mr. Frendt.

"I look forward to it," he says.

I jog across the marsh and through FedEx. Up on the hill there's a light from the last remaining farm. Sometimes we take the boys to the adjacent car wash to look at the cow. Tonight however the cow is elsewhere.

At home Min and Jade are hopping up and down in front of Aunt Bernie, who's sitting very very still at one end of the couch.

"Keep the babies out!" shrieks Min. "I don't want them seeing something dead!"

"Shut up, man!" shrieks Jade. "Don't call her something dead!"

She squats down and pinches Aunt Bernie's cheek.

"Aunt Bernie?" she shrieks. "Fuck!"

"We already tried that like twice, chick!" shrieks Min. "Why are you doing that shit again? Touch her neck and see if you can feel that beating thing!"

"Shit shit shit!" shrieks Jade.

I call 911 and the paramedics come out and work hard for twenty minutes, then give up and say they're sorry and it looks like she's been dead most of the afternoon. The apartment's a mess. Her money drawer's empty and her family photos are in the bathtub.

"Not a mark on her," says a cop.

"I suspect she died of fright," says another. "Fright of the intruder?"

"My guess is yes," says a paramedic.

"Oh God," says Jade. "God, God, God."

I sit down beside Bernie. I think: I am so sorry. I'm sorry I wasn't here when it happened and sorry you never had any fun in your life and sorry I wasn't rich enough to move you somewhere safe. I remember when she was young and wore pink stretch pants and made us paper chains out of DrugTown receipts while singing "Froggie Went A-Courting." All her life she worked hard. She never hurt anybody. And now this.

Scared to death in a crappy apartment.

Min puts the babies in the kitchen but they keep crawling out. Aunt Bernie's in a shroud on this sort of dolly and on the couch are a bunch of forms to sign.

We call Ma and Freddie. We get their machine.

"Ma, pick up!" says Min. "Something bad happened! Ma, please freaking pick up!"

But nobody picks up.

So we leave a message.

Lobton's Funeral Parlor is just a regular house on a regular street. Inside there's a rack of brochures with titles like "Why Does My Loved One Appear Somewhat Larger?" Lobton looks healthy. Maybe too healthy. He's wearing a yellow golf shirt and his biceps keep involuntarily flexing. Every now and then he touches his delts as if to confirm they're still big as softballs.

"Such a sad thing," he says.

"How much?" asks Jade. "I mean, like for basic. Not superfancy."

"But not crappy either," says Min. "Our aunt was the best."

"What price range were you considering?" says Lobton, cracking his knuckles. We tell him and his eyebrows go up and he leads us to something that looks like a moving box.

"Prior to usage we'll moisture-proof this with a spray lacquer," he says. "Makes it look quite woodlike."

"That's all we can get?" says Jade. "Cardboard?"

"I'm actually offering you a slight break already," he says, and does a kind of push-up against the wall. "On account of the tragic circumstances. This is Sierra Sunset. Not exactly cardboard. More of a fiberboard."

"I don't know," says Min. "Seems pretty gyppy."

"Can we think about it?" says Ma.

"Absolutely," says Lobton. "Last time I checked this was still America."

I step over and take a closer look. There are staples where Aunt Bernie's spine would be. Down at the foot there's some writing about Folding Tab A into Slot B.

"No freaking way," says Jade. "Work your whole life and end up in a Mayflower box? I doubt it."

We've got zip in savings. We sit at a desk and Lobton does what he calls a Credit Calc. If we pay it out monthly for seven years we can afford the Amber Mist, which includes a double-thick balsa box and two coats of lacquer and a one-hour wake.

"But seven years, jeez," says Ma.

"We got to get her the good one," says Min. "She never had anything nice in her life."

So Amber Mist it is.

We bury her at St. Leo's, on the hill up near BastCo. Her part of the graveyard's pretty plain. No angels, no little rock houses, no flowers, just a bunch of flat stones like parking bumpers and here and there a Styrofoam cup. Father Brian says a prayer and then one of us is supposed to talk. But what's there to say? She never had a life. Never married, no kids, work work work. Did she ever go on a cruise? All her life it was buses. Buses buses buses. Once she went with Ma on a bus to Quigley, Kansas, to gamble and shop at an outlet mall. Someone broke into her room and stole her clothes and took a dump in her suitcase while they were at the Roy Clark show. That was it. That was the extent of her tourism. After that it was DrugTown, night and day. After fifteen years as Cashier she got demoted to Greeter. People would ask where the cold remedies were and she'd point to some big letters on the wall that said Cold Remedies.

Freddie, Ma's boyfriend, steps up and says he didn't know her very long but she was an awful nice lady and left behind a lot of love, etc. etc. blah blah blah. While it's true she didn't do much in her life, still she was very dear to those of us who knew her and never made a stink about anything but was always content with whatever happened to her, etc. etc. blah blah blah.

Then it's over and we're supposed to go away.

"We gotta come out here like every week," says Jade.

"I know I will," says Min.

"What, like I won't?" says Jade. "She was so freaking nice."

"I'm sure you swear at a grave," says Min.

"Since when is freak a swear, chick?" says Jade.

"Girls," says Ma.

"I hope I did okay in what I said about her," says Freddie in his full-of-crap way, smelling bad of English Navy. "Actually I sort of surprised myself."

"Bye-bye, Aunt Bernie," says Min.

"Bye-bye, Bern," says Jade.

"Oh my dear sister," says Ma.

I scrunch my eyes tight and try to picture her happy, laughing, poking me in the ribs. But all I can see is her terrified on the couch. It's awful. Out there, somewhere, is whoever did it. Someone came in our house, scared her to death, watched her die, went through our stuff, stole her money. Someone who's still living, someone who right now might be having a piece of pie or running an errand or scratching his ass, someone who, if he wanted to, could drive west for three days or whatever and sit in the sun by the ocean.

We stand a few minutes with heads down and hands folded.

Afterward Freddie takes us to Trabanti's for lunch. Last year Trabanti died and three Vietnamese families went in together and bought the place, and it still serves pasta and pizza and the big oil of Trabanti is still on the wall but now from the kitchen comes this very pretty Vietnamese music and the food is somehow better.

Freddie proposes a toast. Min says remember how Bernie always called lunch dinner and dinner supper? Jade says remember how when her jaw clicked she'd say she needed oil?

"She was a excellent lady," says Freddie.

"I already miss her so bad," says Ma.

"I'd like to kill that fuck that killed her," says Min.

"How about let's don't say fuck at lunch," says Ma.

"It's just a word, Ma, right?" says Min. "Like pluck is just a word? You don't mind if I say pluck? Pluck pluck pluck?"

"Well, shit's just a word too," says Freddie. "But we don't say it at lunch."

"Same with puke," says Ma.

"Shit puke, shit puke," says Min.

The waiter clears his throat. Ma glares at Min.

"I love you girls' manners," Ma says.

"Especially at a funeral," says Freddie.

"This ain't a funeral," says Min.

"The question in my mind is what you kids are gonna do now," says Freddie. "Because I consider this whole thing a wake-up call, meaning it's time for you to pull yourselfs up by the bootstraps like I done and get out of that dangerous craphole you're living at."

"Mr. Phone Poll speaks," says Min.

"Anyways it ain't that dangerous," says Jade.

"A woman gets killed and it ain't that dangerous?" says Freddie.

"All's we need is a dead bolt and a eyehole," says Min.

"What's a bootstrap," says Jade.

"It's like a strap on a boot, you doof," says Min.

"Plus where we gonna go?" says Jade. "Can we move in with you guys?"

"I personally would love that and you know that," says Freddie. "But who would not love that is our landlord."

"I think what Freddie's saying is it's time for you girls to get jobs," says Ma.

"Yeah right, Ma," says Min. "After what happened last time?"

When I first moved in, Jade and Min were working the info booth at HardwareNiche. Then one day we picked the babies up at day care and found Troy sitting naked on top of the washer and Mac in the yard being nipped by a Pekingese and the day-care lady sloshed and playing KillerBirds on Nintendo.

So that was that. No more HardwareNiche.

"Maybe one could work, one could baby-sit?" says Ma.

"I don't see why I should have to work so she can stay home with her baby," says Min.

"And I don't see why I should have to work so she can stay home with her baby," says Jade.

"It's like a freaking veece versa," says Min.

"Let me tell you something," says Freddie. "Something about this country. Anybody can do anything. But first they gotta try. And you guys ain't. Two don't work and one strips naked? I don't consider that trying. You kids make squat. And therefore you live in a dangerous craphole. And what happens in a dangerous craphole? Bad tragic shit. It's the freaking American way – you start out in a dangerous craphole and work hard so you can someday move up to a somewhat less dangerous craphole. And finally maybe you get a mansion. But at this rate you ain't even gonna make it to the somewhat less dangerous craphole."

"Like you live in a mansion," says Jade.

"I do not claim to live in no mansion," says Freddie. "But then again I do not live in no slum. The other thing I also do not do is strip naked."

"Thank God for small favors," says Min.

"Anyways he's never actually naked," says Jade.

Which is true. I always have on at least a T-back.

"No wonder we never take these kids out to a nice lunch," says Freddie.

"I do not even consider this a nice lunch," says Min.

For dinner Jade microwaves some Stars-n-Flags. They're addictive. They put sugar in the sauce and sugar in the meat nuggets. I think also caffeine. Someone told me the brown streaks in the Flags are caffeine. We have like five bowls each.

After dinner the babies get fussy and Min puts a mush of ice cream and Hershey's syrup in their bottles and we watch *The Worst That Could Happen,* a half-hour of computer simulations of tragedies that have never actually occurred but theoretically could. A kid gets hit by a train and flies into a zoo, where he's eaten by wolves. A man cuts his hand off chopping wood and while wandering around screaming for help is picked up by a tornado and dropped on a preschool during recess and lands on a pregnant teacher.

"I miss Bernie so bad," says Min.

"Me too," Jade says sadly.

The babies start howling for more ice cream.

"That is so cute," says Jade. "They're like, *Give it the fuck up!*"

"We'll give it the fuck up, sweeties, don't worry," says Min. "We didn't forget about you."

Then the phone rings. It's Father Brian. He sounds weird. He says he's sorry to bother us so late. But something strange has happened. Something bad. Something sort of, you know, unspeakable. Am I sitting? I'm not but I say I am.

Apparently someone has defaced Bernie's grave.

My first thought is there's no stone. It's just grass. How do you deface grass? What did they do, pee on the grass on the grave? But Father's nearly in tears.

So I call Ma and Freddie and tell them to meet us, and we get the babies up and load them into the K-car.

"Deface," says Jade on the way over. "What does that mean, deface?"

"It means like fucked it up," says Min.

"But how?" says Jade. "I mean, like what did they do?"

"We don't know, dumbass," says Min. "That's why we're going there."

"And why?" says Jade. "Why would someone do that?"

"Check out Miss Shreelock Holmes," says Min. "Someone done that because someone is a asshole."

"Someone is a big-time asshole," says Jade.

Father Brian meets us at the gate with a flashlight and a golf cart.

"When I saw this," he says. "I literally sat down in astonishment. Nothing like this has ever happened here. I am so sorry. You seem like nice people."

We're too heavy and the wheels spin as we climb the hill, so I get out and jog alongside.

"Okay, folks, brace yourselves," Father says, and shuts off the engine.

Where the grave used to be is just a hole. Inside the hole is the Amber Mist, with the top missing. Inside the Amber Mist is nothing. No Aunt Bernie.

"What the hell," says Jade. "Where's Bernie?"

"Somebody stole Bernie?" says Min.

"At least you folks have retained your feet," says Father Brian. "I'm telling you I literally sat right down. I sat right down on that pile of dirt. I dropped as if shot. See that mark? That's where I sat."

On the pile of grave dirt is a butt-shaped mark.

The cops show up and one climbs down in the hole with a tape measure and a camera. After three or four flashes he climbs out and hands Ma a pair of blue pumps.

"Her little shoes." says Ma. "Oh my God."

"Are those them?" says Jade.

"Those are them," says Min.

"I am freaking out," says Jade.

"I am totally freaking out," says Min.

"I'm gonna sit," says Ma, and drops into the golf cart.

"What I don't get is who'd want her?" says Min.

"She was just this lady," says Jade.

"Typically it's teens?" one cop says. "Typically we find the loved one nearby? Once we found the loved one nearby with, you know, a cigarette between its lips, wearing a sombrero? These kids today got a lot more nerve than we ever did. I never would've dreamed of digging up a dead corpse when I was a teen. You might tip over a stone, sure, you might spray-paint something on a crypt, you might, you know, give a wino a hotfoot."

"But this, jeez," says Freddie. "This is a entirely different ballgame."

"Boy howdy," says the cop, and we all look down at the shoes in Ma's hands.

Next day I go back to work. I don't feel like it but we need the money. The grass is wet and it's hard getting across the ravine in my dress shoes. The soles are slick. Plus they're too tight. Several times I fall forward on my briefcase. Inside the briefcase are my T-backs and a thing of mousse.

Right off the bat I get a tableful of MediBen women seated under a banner saying BEST OF LUCK, BEATRICE, NO HARD FEELINGS. I take off my shirt and serve their salads. I take off my flight pants and serve their soups. One drops a dollar on the floor and tells me feel free to pick it up.

I pick it up.

"Not like that, not like that," she says. "Face the other way, so when you bend we can see your crack."

I've done this about a million times, but somehow I can't do it now.

I look at her. She looks at me.

"What?" she says. "I'm not allowed to say that? I thought that was the whole point."

"That is the whole point, Phyllis," says another lady. "You stand your ground."

"Look," Phyllis says. "Either bend how I say or give back the dollar. I think that's fair."

"You go, girl," says her friend.

I give back the dollar. I return to the Locker Area and sit awhile. For the first time ever, I'm voted Stinker. There are thirteen women at the MediBen table and they all vote me Stinker. Do the MediBen women know my situation? Would they vote me Stinker if they did? But what am I supposed to do, go out and say, Please ladies, my aunt just died, plus her body's missing?

Mr. Frendt pulls me aside.

"Perhaps you need to go home," he says. "I'm sorry for your loss. But I'd like to encourage you not to behave like one of those Comanche ladies who bite off their index fingers when a loved one dies. Grief is good, grief is fine, but too much grief, as we all know, is excessive. If your aunt's death has filled your mouth with too many bitten-off fingers, for crying out loud, take a week off, only don't take it out on our Guests, they didn't kill your dang aunt."

But I can't afford to take a week off. I can't even afford to take a few days off.

"We really need the money," I say.

"Is that my problem?" he says. "Am I supposed to let you dance without vigor just because you need the money? Why don't I put an ad in the paper for all sad people who need money? All the town's sad could come here and strip. Good-bye. Come back when you feel halfway normal."

From the pay phone I call home to see if they need anything from the FoodSoQuik.

"Just come home," Min says stiffly. "Just come straight home."

"What is it?" I say.

"Come home," she says.

Maybe someone's found the body. I imagine Bernie naked, Bernie chopped in two, Bernie posed on a bus bench. I hope and pray that something only mildly bad's been done to her, something we can live with.

At home the door's wide open. Min and Jade are sitting very still on the couch, babies in their laps, staring at the rocking chair, and in the rocking chair is Bernie. Bernie's body.

Same perm, same glasses, same blue dress we buried her in.

What's it doing here? Who could be so cruel? And what are we supposed to do with it?

Then she turns her head and looks at me.

"Sit the fuck down," she says.

In life she never swore.

I sit. Min squeezes and releases my hand, squeezes and releases, squeezes and releases.

"You, mister," Bernie says to me, "are going to start showing your cock. You'll show it and show it. You go up to a lady, if she wants to see it, if she'll pay to see it, I'll make a thumbprint on the forehead. You see the thumbprint, you ask. I'll try to get you five a day, at twenty bucks a pop. So a hundred bucks a day. Seven hundred a week. And that's cash, so no taxes. No withholding. See? That's the beauty of it."

She's got dirt in her hair and dirt in her teeth and her hair is a mess and her tongue when it darts out to lick her lips is black.

"You, Jade," she says. "Tomorrow you start work. Andersen Labels, Fifth and Rivera. Dress up when you go. Wear something nice. Show a little leg. And don't chomp your gum. Ask for Len. At the end of the month, we take the money you made and the cock money and get a new place. Somewhere safe. That's part one of Phase One. You, Min. You baby-sit. Plus you quit smoking. Plus you learn how to cook. No more food out of cans. We gotta eat right to look our best. Because I am getting me so many lovers. Maybe you kids don't know this but I died a freaking virgin. No babies, no lovers. Nothing went in, nothing came out. Ha ha! Dry as a bone, completely wasted, this pretty little thing God gave me between my legs. Well I am going to have lovers now, you fucks! Like in the movies, big shoulders and all, and a summer house, and nice trips, and in the morning in my room a big vase of flowers, and I'm going to get my nipples hard standing in the breeze from the ocean, eating shrimp from a cup, you sons of bitches, while my lover watches me from the veranda, his big shoulders shining, all hard for me, that's one damn thing I will guarantee you kids! Ha ha! You think I'm joking? I ain't freaking joking. I never got nothing! My life was shit! I was never even up in a freaking plane. But that was that life and this is this life. My new life. Cover me up now! With a blanket. I need my beauty rest. Tell anyone I'm here, you all die. Plus they die. Whoever you tell, they die. I kill them with my mind. I can do that. I am very freaking strong now. I got powers! So no visitors. I don't exactly look my best. You got it? You all got it?"

We nod. I go for a blanket. Her hands and feet are shaking and she's grinding her teeth and one falls out.

"Put it over me, you fuck, all the way over!" she screams, and I put it over her.

We sneak off with the babies and whisper in the kitchen.

"It looks like her," says Min.

"It is her," I say.

"It is and it ain't," says Jade.

"We better do what she says," Min says.

"No shit," Jade says.

All night she sits in the rocker under the blanket, shaking and swearing.

All night we sit in Min's bed, fully dressed, holding hands.

"See how strong I am!" she shouts around midnight, and there's a cracking sound, and when I go out the door's been torn off the microwave but she's still sitting in the chair.

In the morning she's still there, shaking and swearing.

"Take the blanket off!" she screams. "It's time to get this show on the road."

I take the blanket off. The smell is not good. One ear is now in her lap. She keeps absentmindedly sticking it back on her head.

"You, Jade!" she shouts. "Get dressed. Go get that job. When you meet Len, bend forward a little. Let him see down your top. Give him some hope. He's a sicko, but we need him. You, Min! Make breakfast. Something homemade. Like biscuits."

"Why don't you make it with your powers?" says Min.

"Don't be a smartass!" screams Bernie. "You see what I did to that microwave?"

"I don't know how to make freaking biscuits," Min wails.

"You know how to read, right?" Bernie shouts. "You ever heard of a recipe? You ever been in the grave? It sucks so bad! You regret all the things you never did. You little bitches are gonna have a very bad time in the grave unless you get on the stick, believe me! Turn down the thermostat! Make it cold. I like cold. Something's off with my body. I don't feel right."

I turn down the thermostat. She looks at me.

"Go show your cock!" she shouts. "That is the first part of Phase One.

After we get the new place, that's the end of the first part of Phase Two. You'll still show your cock, but only three days a week. Because you'll start community college. Pre-law. Pre-law is best. You'll be a whiz. You ain't dumb. And Jade'll work weekends to make up for the decrease in cock money. See? See how that works? Now get out of here. What are you gonna do?"

"Show my cock?" I say.

"Show your cock, that's right," she says, and brushes back her hair with her hand, and a huge wad comes out, leaving her almost bald on one side.

"Oh God," says Min. "You know what? No way me and the babies are staying here alone."

"You ain't alone," says Bernie. "I'm here."

"Please don't go," Min says to me.

"Oh, stop it," Bernie says, and the door flies open and I feel a sort of invisible fist punching me in the back.

Outside it's sunny. A regular day. A guy's changing his oil. The clouds are regular clouds and the sun's the regular sun and the only nonregular thing is that my clothes smell like Bernie, a combo of wet cellar and rotten bacon.

Work goes well. I manage to keep smiling and hide my shaking hands, and my midshift rating is Honeypie. After lunch this older woman comes up and says I look so much like a real Pilot she can hardly stand it.

On her head is a thumbprint. Like Ash Wednesday, only sort of glowing.

I don't know what to do. Do I just come out and ask if she wants to see my cock? What if she says no? What if I get caught? What if I show her and she doesn't think it's worth twenty bucks?

Then she asks if I'll surprise her best friend with a birthday table dance. She points out her friend. A pretty girl, no thumbprint. Looks somehow familiar.

We start over and at about twenty feet I realize it's Angela.

Angela Silveri.

We dated senior year. Then Dad died and Ma had to take a job at Patty-Melt Depot. From all the grease Ma got a bad rash and could barely wear a blouse. Plus Min was running wild. So Angela would come over and there'd be Min getting high under a tarp on the carport and Ma sitting in her bra on a kitchen stool with a fan pointed at her gut. Angela had dreams. She had plans. In her notebook she pasted a picture of an office from the J.C. Penney catalogue and under it wrote, *My (someday?) office.* Once we saw this black Porsche and she said very nice but make hers red. The last straw was Ed Edwards, a big drunk, one of Dad's cousins. Things got so bad Ma rented him the utility room. One night Angela and I were making out on the couch late when Ed came in soused and started peeing in the dishwasher.

What could I say? He's only barely related to me? He hardly ever does that?

Angela's eyes were like these little pies.

I walked her home, got no kiss, came back, cleaned up the dishwasher as best I could. A few days later I got my class ring in the mail and a copy of *The Prophet.*

> *You will always be my first love,* she'd written inside. *But now my path converges to a higher ground. Be well always. Walk in joy. Please don't think me cruel, it's just that I want so much in terms of accomplishment, plus I couldn't believe that guy peed right on your dishes.*

No way am I table dancing for Angela Silveri. No way am I asking Angela Silveri's friend if she wants to see my cock. No way am I hanging around here so Angela can see me in my flight jacket and T-backs and wonder to herself how I went so wrong etc. etc.

I hide in the kitchen until my shift is done, then walk home very, very slowly because I'm afraid of what Bernie's going to do to me when I get there.

Min meets me at the door. She's got flour all over her blouse and it looks like she's been crying.

"I can't take any more of this," she says. "She's like falling apart. I mean shit's falling off her. Plus she made me bake a freaking pie."

On the table is a very lumpy pie. One of Bernie's arms is now disconnected and lying across her lap.

"What are you thinking of!" she shouts. "You didn't show your cock even once? You think it's easy making those thumbprints? You try it, smartass! Do you or do you not know the plan? You gotta get us out of here! And to get us out, you gotta use what you got. And you ain't got much. A nice face. And a decent unit. Not huge, but shaped nice."

"Bernie, God," says Min.

"What, Miss Priss?" shouts Bernie, and slams the severed arm down hard on her lap, and her other ear falls off.

"I'm sorry, but this is too fucking sickening," says Min. "I'm going out."

"What's sickening?" says Bernie. "Are you saying I'm sickening? Well, I think you're sickening. So many wonderful things in life and where's your mind? You think with your lazy ass. Whatever life hands you, you take. You're not going anywhere. You're staying home and studying."

"I'm what?" says Min. "Studying what? I ain't studying. Chick comes into my house and starts ordering me to study? I freaking doubt it."

"You don't know nothing!" Bernie says. "What fun is life when you don't know nothing? You can't find your own town on the map. You can't name a single president. When we go to Rome you won't know nothing about the history. You're going to study the World Book. Do we still have those World Books?"

"Yeah right," says Min. "We're going to Rome."

"We'll go to Rome when he's a lawyer," says Bernie.

"Dream on, chick," says Min. "And we'll go to Mars when I'm a stock-breaker."

"Don't you dare make fun of me!" Bernie shouts, and our only vase goes flying across the room and nearly nails Min in the head.

"She's been like this all day," says Min.

"Like what?" shouts Bernie. "We had a perfectly nice day."

"She made me help her try on my bras," says Min.

"I never had a nice sexy bra," says Bernie.

"And now mine are all ruined," says Min. "They got this sort of goo on them."

"You ungrateful shit!" shouts Bernie. "Do you know what I'm doing for you? I'm saving your boy. And you got the nerve to say I made goo on your bras! Troy's gonna get caught in a crossfire in the courtyard. In September. September eighteenth. He's gonna get thrown off his little trike. With one leg twisted under him and blood pouring out of his ear. It's a freaking prophecy. You know that word? It means prediction. You know that word? You think I'm bullshitting? Well I ain't bullshitting. I got the power. Watch this: All day Jade sat licking labels at a desk by a window. Her boss bought everybody subs for lunch. She's bringing some home in a green bag."

"That ain't true about Troy, is it?" says Min. "Is it? I don't believe it."

"Turn on the TV!" Bernie shouts. "Give me the changer."

I turn on the TV. I give her the changer. She puts on *Nathan's Body Shop*. Nathan says washboard abs drive the women wild. Then there's a close-up of his washboard abs.

"Oh yes," says Bernie. "Them are for me. I'd like to give those a lick. A lick and a pinch. I'd like to sort of straddle those things."

Just then Jade comes through the door with a big green bag.

"Oh God," says Min.

"Told you so!" says Bernie, and pokes Min in the ribs. "Ha ha! I really got the power!"

"I don't get it," Min says, all desperate. "What happens? Please. What happens to him? You better freaking tell me."

"I already told you," Bernie says. "He'll fly about fifteen feet and live about three minutes."

"Bernie, God," Min says, and starts to cry. "You used to be so nice."

"I'm still so nice," says Bernie, and bites into a sub and takes off the tip of her finger and starts chewing it up.

Just after dawn she shouts out my name.

"Take the blanket off," she says. "I ain't feeling so good."

I take the blanket off. She's basically just this pile of parts: both arms in her lap, head on the arms, heel of one foot touching the heel of the other, all of it sort of wrapped up in her dress.

"Get me a washcloth," she says. "Do I got a fever? I feel like I got a fever. Oh, I knew it was too good to be true. But okay. New plan. New plan. I'm changing the first part of Phase One. If you see two thumbprints, that means the lady'll screw you for cash. We're in a fix here. We gotta speed this up. There ain't gonna be nothing left of me. Who's gonna be my lover now?"

The doorbell rings.

"Son of a bitch," Bernie snarls.

It's Father Brian with a box of doughnuts. I step out quick and close the door behind me. He says he's just checking in. Perhaps we'd like to talk? Perhaps we're feeling some residual anger about Bernie's situation? Which would of course be completely understandable. Once when he was a young priest someone broke in and drew a mustache on the Virgin Mary with a permanent marker, and for weeks he was tortured by visions of bending back the finger of the vandal until he or she burst into tears of apology.

"I knew that wasn't appropriate," he says. "I knew that by indulging in that fantasy I was honoring violence. And yet it gave me pleasure. I also thought of catching them in the act and boinking them in the head with a rock. I also thought of jumping up and down on their backs until something in their spinal column cracked. Actually I had about a million ideas. But you know what I did instead? I scrubbed and scrubbed our Holy Mother, and soon she was as good as new. Her statue, I mean. She herself of course is always good as new."

From inside comes the sound of breaking glass. Breaking glass and then something heavy falling, and Jade yelling and Min yelling and the babies crying.

"Oops, I guess?" he says. "I've come at a bad time? Look, all I'm trying to do is urge you, if at all possible, to forgive the perpetrators, as I forgave the perpetrator that drew on my Virgin Mary. The thing lost, after all, is only your aunt's body, and what is essential, I assure you, is elsewhere, being well taken care of."

I nod. I smile. I say thanks for stopping by. I take the doughnuts and go back inside.

The TV's broke and the refrigerator's tipped over and Bernie's parts are strewn across the living room like she's been shot out of a cannon.

"She tried to get up," says Jade.

"I don't know where the hell she thought she was going," says Min.

"Come here," the head says to me, and I squat down. "That's it for me. I'm fucked. As per usual. Always the bridesmaid, never the bride. Although come to think of it I was never even the freaking bridesmaid. Look, show your cock. It's the shortest line between two points. The world ain't giving away nice lives. You got a trust fund? You a genius? Show your cock. It's what you got. And remember: Troy in September. On his trike. One leg twisted. Don't forget. And also. Don't remember me like this. Remember me like how I was that night we all went to Red Lobster and I had that new perm. Ah Christ. At least buy me a stone."

I rub her shoulder, which is next to her foot.

"We loved you," I say.

"Why do some people get everything and I got nothing?" she says. "Why? Why was that?"

"I don't know," I say.

"Show your cock," she says, and dies again.

We stand there looking down at the pile of parts. Mac crawls toward it and Min moves him back with her foot.

"This is too freaking much," says Jade, and starts crying.

"What do we do now?" says Min.

"Call the cops," Jade says.

"And say what?" says Min.

We think about this awhile.

I get a Hefty bag. I get my winter gloves.

"I ain't watching," says Jade.

"I ain't watching either," says Min, and they take the babies into the bedroom.

I close my eyes and wrap Bernie up in the Hefty bag and twistie-tie the bag shut and lug it out to the trunk of the K-car. I throw in a shovel. I drive up to St. Leo's. I lower the bag into the hole using a bungee cord, then fill the hole back in.

Down in the city are the nice houses and the so-so houses and the lovers making out in dark yards and the babies crying for their moms, and I wonder if, other than Jesus, this has ever happened before. Maybe it happens all the time. Maybe there's angry dead all over, hiding in rooms, covered with blankets, bossing around their scared, embarrassed relatives. Because how would we know?

I for sure don't plan on broadcasting this.

I smooth over the dirt and say a quick prayer: If it was wrong for her to come back, forgive her, she never got beans in this life, plus she was trying to help us.

At the car I think of an additional prayer: But please don't let her come back again.

When I get home the babies are asleep and Jade and Min are watching a phone-sex infomercial, three girls in leather jumpsuits eating bananas in slo-mo while across the screen runs a constant disclaimer: "Not Necessarily the Girls Who Man the Phones! Not Necessarily the Girls Who Man the Phones!"

"Them chicks seem to really be enjoying those bananas," says Min in a thin little voice.

"I like them jumpsuits though," says Jade.

"Yeah them jumpsuits look decent," says Min.

Then they look up at me. I've never seen them so sad and beat and sick.

"It's done," I say.

Then we hug and cry and promise never to forget Bernie the way she really was, and I use some Resolve on the rug and they go do some reading in their World Books.

Next day I go in early. I don't see a single thumbprint. But it doesn't matter. I get with Sonny Vance and he tells me how to do it. First you ask the woman would she like a private tour. Then you show her the fake P-40, the Gallery of Historical Aces, the shower stall where we get oiled up, etc. etc. and then in the hall near the rest room you ask if there's anything else she'd like to see. It's sleazy. It's gross. But when I do it I think of September. September and Troy in the crossfire, his little leg bent under him etc. etc.

Most say no but quite a few say yes.

I've got a place picked out at a complex called Swan's Glen. They've never had a shooting or a knifing and the public school is great and every Saturday they have a nature walk for kids behind the clubhouse.

For every hundred bucks I make, I set aside five for Bernie's stone.

What do you write on something like that? LIFE PASSED HER BY?

DIED DISAPPOINTED? CAME BACK TO LIFE BUT FELL APART? All true, but too sad, and no way I'm writing any of those.

BERNIE KOWALSKI, it's going to say: BELOVED AUNT.

Sometimes she comes to me in dreams. She never looks good. Sometimes she's wearing a dirty smock. Once she had on handcuffs. Once she was naked and dirty and this mean cat was clawing its way up her front. But every time it's the same thing.

"Some people get everything and I got nothing," she says. "Why? Why did that happen?"

Every time I say I don't know.

And I don't.

I Want My 20th-Century Schizoid Art, II

BEN, I'LL GRANT THAT there is a use for critical language, certainly. I was speaking from my knee-jerk writer's perspective. I doubt if any of us start writing by deciding on the genre first, but perhaps I'm wrong. I rarely worry about such things until I'm deciding where to submit something.

But on the critical side, I question whether slipstream, under either definition, is a useful term. I just boned up on the original Sterling essay, and while he makes some interesting points – including questioning the adequacy of the term itself – the shorthand for what he's saying is essentially what Horton is saying above. Despite its attractiveness, it's a vague and unsatisfying expression of a genre. Try telling someone that you write fiction that makes people feel strange, and when they ask for clarification, see if you can do so without referencing the genres in some way. The layperson's definitions of fantasy and SF are reductive and incomplete, but they do have something at the heart of them; fantasy is about the impossible, while SF is about possibilities. Maybe the layperson's definitions shouldn't matter, but they do, because once a term takes on a meaning for someone, it's pretty tough to get them to accept a redefinition. And definitions will always get reduced, because that's how the human mind works.

I guess what I'm trying to say is that the problem with Sterling's essay, and the term *slipstream*, is that it doesn't reduce well. Horton's distillation of *slipstream* is reductive and incomplete, but in some ways it gets at the heart of Sterling's essay, which is something like, "There is some interesting writing going on that doesn't fit easily into either the literary or SF/fantasy genres, and here are some examples." That's not much to go on, because it mostly consists of defining that writing by what it isn't. If there's really a need to distinguish what many of us do at least part of the time from what the rest of the field does most of the time, we need better terminology for it.

DAVE SCHWARTZ, 12:50 PM, WEDNESDAY, MAY 4, 2005

I don't think the definitions are really commensurable. Rich Horton's defining it in terms of content – which is how the SF world tends to draw the SF/non-SF boundary – whereas Sterling's defining it in terms of effect, or even process.

DAVID MOLES, 12:58 PM, WEDNESDAY, MAY 4, 2005

I think that's what Dave means. Back in the Golden Age, the writers talked a lot about science fiction as something that "inspires a sense of wonder." Don't hear that any more, or at least I don't. It became reduced to its content.

JON HANSEN, 1:06 PM, WEDNESDAY, MAY 4, 2005

I certainly don't start with picking a genre or subgenre. But a critical understanding of genres and their history is a tool in the toolbox. It's useful to be able to say, "Now should I do the Philip K. Dick thing here, or the William Gibson thing, or the Italo Calvino thing, or the Dickens thing?" And to know what kind of constraints, reader expectations, costs, and advantages go with it. Like learning chess openings and end-games. Thinking too hard about it can also get in the way; that's a risk that comes with the territory.

SFnal/fantastical intrusions into mundane contexts do not necessarily make me feel strange at all. Did the movie *Ghost* make you feel strange in an eerie, postmodernist way? Did it challenge your ideas about who you are, make you feel like the edges of your reality might unravel at any moment? How about *Independence Day* with Will Smith? *Love at First Bite*? Feeling any eerie postmodernist unease yet?

If you want to see the difference between "literature that makes you feel very strange" (postmodernist, irrealist literature) and "SFnal/fantastical intrusions into familiar contexts" (contemporary fantasy), try these, from Sterling's list:

BANKS, IAIN – *The Wasp Factory*
FRISCH, MAX – *Homo Faber*
PYNCHON, THOMAS – *The Crying of Lot 49*

Genre intrusions? Not a one. But after reading *The Crying of Lot 49*, I spent a haunted train ride staring out a dark window into the night, wondering if I was real....

BENJAMIN ROSENBAUM, 2:01 PM, WEDNESDAY, MAY 4, 2005

I'm familiar with those works and to me they just underline the original point that Sterling was making, that mainstream fiction had co-opted the tropes of genre in order to create some really challenging fiction. I happen to agree; I find that feeling of strangeness much more often in mainstream or translated works than in genre fiction, at least at the novel-length.

I understand the distinction Ben and David are trying to make. But the more closely I look at the definitions, the less pronounced the distinction appears. Granted that Horton is talking about trappings to some extent, and Sterling is not. But consider this, from the Sterling: "It is a contemporary kind of writing which has set its face against consensus reality. It is fantastic, surreal sometimes, speculative on occasion, but not rigorously so." And Horton again: "Slipstream tries to make the familiar strange – by taking a familiar context and disturbing it with SFnal/fantastical intrusions." The difference there is pretty subtle; I wonder if that's what Hannah meant when she said she wasn't sure she saw the difference.

DAVE SCHWARTZ, 2:39 PM, WEDNESDAY, MAY 4, 2005

Where, in any of those examples I gave, do you see any co-opting of genre tropes?

I'm perfectly willing to admit that some works are both – that genre tropes are perfectly at home in postmodernist/irreal fiction. But they aren't necessary. And most genre fiction is not disruptive of consensus reality at all – quite the contrary, by playing its "What if" game it solidifies consensus reality. It says "We all know there are no ghosts; now here's a ghost story." Most genre fiction is deeply epistemologically conservative. *Especially* most urban fantasy of the "Here's a NYC love story – with a mermaid!" school, which, if you read the Horton quote, sounds like it could be *exactly* what he's talking about – and which seems to be the *opposite* of what Sterling is talking about.

But perhaps that isn't what Horton means by "making the familiar strange." In that case, perhaps he's talking about a subset of irrealist/strange fiction that happens to use genre tropes. But even then, it seems ass-backwards to me to say that that makes this postmodern-alienation fiction a kind of SF. By that logic, *Even Cowgirls Get the Blues* proves that absurdism is a subset of the Western.

Does anyone know the publication date of Sterling's *Catscan 5* essay?

BENJAMIN ROSENBAUM, 3:01 PM, WEDNESDAY, MAY 4, 2005

It appeared in *SF Eye* sometime in 1989. So, about seventeen years ago.

JON HANSEN, 3:21 PM, WEDNESDAY, MAY 4, 2005

Exhibit H: Torn Pages Discovered in the Vest Pocket of an Unidentified Tourist

(Note the blood-red discoloration in the lower left corner.)

An Excerpt from Hoegbotton's
COMPREHENSIVE TRAVEL GUIDE TO THE SOUTHERN CITY OF AMBERGRIS
Chapter 77: An In-depth Explanation For the City's Apparent Lack of Sanitation Workers
(And Why Tourists Should Not Be Afraid)

Jeff VanderMeer

UPON THE TRAVELER'S first visit to the legendary city of Ambergris, he will soon espy crimson, rectangular flags, no bigger than a scrap of silk cloth, attached to the tops of pencil-thin stakes hammered into dirt or between pavement cracks. Such a traveler, as he peruses the Religious Quarter, the various merchant districts, or even the rundown Industrial District, may also notice the complete absence of rotten food, human excrement, paper refuse, flotsam, jetsam, and the like on the streets – as well as the almost "spit-cleaned" quality of the gutters, the embankments, the front steps of public buildings – and no doubt with a measure of puzzlement, for this sparkling condition contrasts sharply with the disheveled state of Belezar, Stockton, Tratnor, and the other picturesque southern cities that straddle the silt-mad River Moth.

Such a naïve traveler (unless having had the good sense to buy this particular guidebook, available in Ambergris itself only at The Borges Bookstore [see Ch. 8, "Cultural Attractions"]) may not at first, or even on second or third glance, discern the connection between the flags, as uniform and well-positioned as surveyors' marks, and the preternaturally clean quality of the city's convoluted alleyways. The unobservant or naïve traveler, therefore, may never come to understand the city itself, for these flags mark out the territory, and are the only daylight sign, of those unique inhabitants of Ambergris known in the vernacular as "mushroom dwellers."[1]

Travelers should expect a certain tight-lipped anxiety from the locals upon any query as to (1) the red flags, often as clotted and numerous as common weeds, (2) the preternaturally clean nature of the city, or, especially, (3) "mushroom dwellers." The curious outsider should not be particularly surprised or alarmed at the stone-faced non-response, or even hostile extremity of response, engendered by such questions. (See Ch. 6, "Survival," for a list of mannerisms, sayings, and articulations that will charm or mollify angry locals.) A corollary to these questions, "When is the Festival of the Freshwater Squid?" should also be avoided if possible. (See Ch. 5, "The Festival of the Freshwater Squid: Precautions, Preferred Weapons, Hoegbotton Safe Houses.")

However, given a choice between satisfying rampant curiosity on these matters through consultation with the locals or through interrogation of the mushroom dwellers themselves, it would be advisable for even the adventurous traveler to seek out the nearest local. The mushroom dwellers generally remain mute on any subject related to their close-knit clan, nor are they likely to help the disoriented or lost traveler find his way to a safer part of the city.[2] Nor are they likely to converse with the casual passerby on *any* topic, especially as their only documented language consists of equal parts clicks, grunts, and moist slapping sounds that have thus far frustrated even the most prominent linguists.

Nor should it be expected that the average visitor will actually ever set eyes upon a mushroom dweller. These shy citizens[3] of Ambergris

---

1 Please see "Exploration of a Theme," the rather inaccurate if pleasant rendering by the famous collage artist of the last century, Michael Shores. Shores has included in his montage an even earlier and more whimsical drawing of the "monkfish" by the celebrated draftsman Nablodsky. "Exploration" is currently on display at the Voss Bender Memorial Art Museum.

2 For a list of inexpensive Hoegbotton Safe Houses, please refer to Appendix A.

3 Sometimes referred to as "mushies" by the locals when drunk, but never when sober;

sleep from dawn until dusk, and although the red flags often do indicate the close proximity of mushroom dwellers, they are likely to be resting below ground. Such flags – always found in clumps, except when a single flag marks the doorstep to a house or building[4] – may simply indicate an opening to the network of old sewage conduits and catacombs that have existed since the First Construction Empire presided over by Trillian the Great Banker. (See Ch. 3, "Rulers, Tyrants, and Minor Merchant Barons.")

It has been put forth by the noted naturalist and social scientist Loqueem Bender – cousin to the great opera composer Voss Bender (see Ch. 2, "Native Celebrities") – from the bloodstained notes discovered near the sewer duct where he was last seen (see Ch. 15, "Unsolved Mysteries of the City") that the mushroom dwellers have excellent night vision, but that as a consequence of their generations-old sleeping patterns, their eyes can no longer bear any but the weakest sunlight. If true, this intolerance would certainly explain the wide-brimmed floppy gray felt hats they wear during the day (and which, in combination with their short statures, diurnal habits, and long necks, have no doubt given them their eccentric reputation).[5] Bender's notes include fascinating physical details about the "mushroom dwellers," whom he once, during the early days of his research, described as "merry little pranksters": "I find they are remarkably strong, this strength at least partially due to a low center of gravity combined with thick, flat feet, extremely well-developed, almost rootlike leg muscles, and very large yet supple hands." Although it is not advisable to attack a mushroom dweller, or even to defend oneself from an attack (L. Bender, in his later notes, recommends standing quite still if charged by a mushroom dweller), it should be noted that their long, strangely delicate necks will break eas-

---

indeed, if the mischievous traveler wishes to provoke a full-scale riot, he simply need shout into a crowded tavern or church, "You're all a load of stupid 'mushies'!"

4 Do Not Enter any such marked house or building. Often, these dwellings will, on closer inspection, prove to contain relatives mourning a late relative still encased in a living-room casket. The mushroom dwellers seem particularly sensitive to the presence of death.

5 Incidentally, L. Bender posthumously received the Manque Kashmir Award of Achievement from the Morrow Institute of Social Research for "his close friendship with and in-depth studies of the mushroom dwellers." The book of his notes published by the Institute is on sale at the aforementioned Borges Bookstore.

ily if the traveler can get past the clinging, flailing hands thrown up in defense (and which, coincidentally, may be groping for the traveler's own neck).

It was L. Bender who first conducted credible scientific studies[6] of the mushroom dwellers' two main preoccupations: mushroom harvesting and the daily cleansing of Ambergris. L. Bender discovered that the ritual cleaning of the city's streets provided them rich leavings with which to propagate their midnight crop of fungus. "Although the mushrooms are grown underground for the most part, and may reach heights of four feet, weights of 60 pounds," L. Bender wrote, "on occasion a trail of mushrooms – like a vein of rich gold or silver – will burst out from the netherworld to riot in a spray of mauve, azure, yellow ochre, violet, and dead man's gray upon the walls of a merchant's pavilion or across the ceiling of a mortician's practice."

L. Bender's studies further proved that the mushroom dwellers' nightly mastery of city refuse was due not to incredible efficiency so much as to a large population – they simply exist in greater numbers than previously thought by so-called "experts," much as a single cockroach seen implies the existence of a dozen cockroaches unseen. Second, by studying the few civil records still in existence, as well as the 30-year writings of the obsessed statistician Marmey Gort,[7] L.

---

6 Previously, there had only been such romantic renderings as a slight description in Voss Bender's famous opera *The Refraction of Light in a Prison* sung by the distraught, suicidal Frange when he looks out of his window to exclaim:

What mystery fringed by dusky dawn
has given the soul of misery form?
Has the face of love come stumbling
crippled and confused to mewl 'neath
a sneering moon? No, 'tis only the elders
of the city eager to cleanse, and pray.

More descriptive is this melodramatic passage from Dradin Kashmir's semi-autobiographical short novel *Dradin, In Love*: "Positioned as he was at the mouth of the alley, Dradin felt as though he were spying on a secret, forbidden world. Did [the mushroom dwellers] dream of giant mushrooms, gray caps agleam with the dark light of a midnight sun? Did they dream of a world lit only by the phosphorescent splendor of their charges?"

7 Gort kept minutely detailed records of city denizens' sanitary habits, including their storage of refuse. A typical entry reads: "X – outhouse use increase: av. 7x/day (5 min. av. ea.); note: garbage output up 3x for week: connex?"

Bender discovered that over hundreds of years Ambergris' citizens had altered their patterns of consumption and refuse disposal to accommodate easy pickup by the mushroom dwellers.

The locals' treatment of the mushroom dwellers varies drastically between valley residents and city residents (see Ch, 9, "Cultural Differences Between Valley and City, and How to Exploit These Differences to Get Better Bargains"), no doubt because the city folk have spun a complex series of legends around the mushroom dwellers, while the valley folk, who rarely see them, know them only from the watered-down versions of such stories.[8]

These legends run the gamut from the inspired to the inane, although the traveler will, as mentioned previously, find it hard going to pry even a word or two from the lips of locals. Some folk believe the mushroom dwellers whisper and plot among themselves in a secret language so old that no one else, even in the far, far Occident, can speak it. Others weave tales of an origin in the subterranean caves and tunnels beneath Ambergris, inferring that they are not of human stock. Still others claim they are escaped convicts who gathered in the darkness many years ago and now shun the light from guilt over their forebears' crimes. The sailors on the docks have their own stories of mushroom dwellers as defilers of priests and murderers of young women to provide nutrients for their crop of fungus. The poor and under-educated spread rumors that the mushroom dwellers have supernatural powers – that newts, golliwogs, slugs, and salamanders follow in their path while above bats, nighthawks, and whippoorwills shadow them. And, even among the literati, especially among the Shortpin Group led by the noted author Sirin, irresponsible gossip has revived the old chestnut that the mushroom dwellers can "control our minds simply by spreading certain mushroom spores throughout the city's public places, where they may be inhaled all unknowing by the general populace, this inhalation soon followed by an unnatural fascination with fungus, and, of course, an unwavering devotion to the mushroom dwellers."[9]

---

8 As recently as three years ago, a mushroom dweller that wandered into the valley, presumably by mistake, was lynched by an angry mob of tradesmen. (Coincidentally, short travelers, defined as "under four feet six inches tall," are advised not to visit the valley without several sets of corroborating identification.)

9 L. Bender seems to have disproved this once and for all in his final set of notes, when

However, the most ridiculous version of their origin postulates that they once belonged to a guild of janitors, ordained by the Priests of the Seven-Edged Star when that order ruled the city so many centuries ago (see Ch. 21, "Conflicting Religions") and that, during the lawless Days of the Burning Sun, they became feral, seeking haven underground as a desperate remedy for unemployment and the persecution meted out to public workers as a form of protest against the government. (See Ch. 1, "A History of the City.") While this theory provides an explanation for the mushroom dwellers' need to "cleanse" the city of refuse, it ignores the blatantly spiritual nature of their many rituals.

In any event, anecdotal evidence from rare eyewitnesses (including two of the compilers of this book) suggests that the city folk secretly worship the mushroom dwellers,[10] setting out plates of eggs and moist bread or mugs of milksop for them at night, while some young girls and boys, strangely unafraid, have been known to feed them by hand as they would pigeons or squirrels. For the traveler interested in a more scholarly pursuit of the mushroom dweller myth, the L. Bender Memorial Museum, until recently kept up by his wife, Galendrace Bender,[11] provides a good starting and ending point. The museum contains the actual bloodstained notes discovered near L. Bender's last known location. It also displays items L. Bender stole from an underground mushroom dweller religious site, including such enigmatic objects as an ancient umbrella, a duck embryo preserved in ether, a

---

he writes, "Not only did I allow them to sprinkle my entire naked body with the spores, but I readily breathed them in. At no point did I lose control of my mind. At no point did I fall asleep, or come under the spell of a hypnotic trance." Thus, the spores appear to be a friendly form of ritual welcome.

10 Two editors, it should be noted, preferred the phrase "secretly fear," followed by "setting out placatory plates."

11 Sadly, Ms. Bender, a noted specialist on fungus reproduction, did not long survive her husband's death. She disappeared one month before this revised guide went to press, leaving behind a letter in which she indicated she had decided to live in the catacombs among the mushroom dwellers. A postscript to the letter which read in part, "I believe the mushroom dwellers are doomed angles [angels?] who have lost their wings, their position, and even any knowledge of their glorious past, and now consigned to a lugubrious state of semi-awareness," does not say much for her current mental state and it is only to be hoped that she will indeed someday emerge from the catacombs. [Ms. Bender was a frequent contributor to the Ambergris travel guide – she contributed greatly to this very article – and her expertise will be sorely missed. – Eds.]

mop even more ancient than the umbrella, and the steering wheel to a now-extinct motored vehicle.

As with most attractions in Ambergris, however, the careful traveler should not visit the museum after dark. To reiterate the safety precautions set out in Ch. 13, the wise tourist should avoid the following areas after nightfall: the Religious Quarter, the Industrial District, the Majori Merchant District, the Hoegbotton Merchant District (save for the Hoegbotton Safe Houses, half-price during the monsoon season), the docks, and the old bureaucratic center. Mushroom dwellers are notoriously near-sighted despite their fabled night vision, and have been known to mistake even the best-dressed gentleman as an exotic form of refuse, fit to be processed and dragged underground.

If confronted by mushroom dwellers (they often travel in groups of fifty or more), safe places (in addition to the Hoegbotton Safe Houses) include: (1) the top floors of tall buildings, especially buildings that do not possess dumbwaiters or air ducts; (2) the topmost branches of tall trees; mushroom dwellers are mediocre climbers at best and will, at dawn, forget their prey and return below ground, allowing the traveler ample opportunity to escape any light-sensitive sentry they might leave behind; (3) the center of large groups of fellow tourists (groups of locals may be inclined to give up the unsuspecting traveler).

The traveler planning a vacation to Ambergris this year should not be unduly alarmed by the information set out above. In fact, there have been far fewer tourist fatalities this year than in the previous three years combined, no doubt due in part to the extensive citywide bloodletting that occurred at last year's Festival of the Freshwater Squid (see Ch. 5). For this reason, it is the opinion of the editors of this guide[12] that even travelers who too closely investigate the apparent absence of sanitation workers in Ambergris will enjoy a pleasant stay.

---

12 Six in agreement, two in abstention.

Hell Is the Absence of God

Ted Chiang

THIS IS THE STORY of a man named Neil Fisk, and how he came to love God. The pivotal event in Neil's life was an occurrence both terrible and ordinary: the death of his wife Sarah. Neil was consumed with grief after she died, a grief that was excruciating not only because of its intrinsic magnitude, but because it also renewed and emphasized the previous pains of his life. Her death forced him to reexamine his relationship with God, and in doing so he began a journey that would change him forever.

Neil was born with a congenital abnormality that caused his left thigh to be externally rotated and several inches shorter than his right; the medical term for it was proximal femoral focus deficiency. Most people he met assumed God was responsible for this, but Neil's mother hadn't witnessed any visitations while carrying him; his condition was the result of improper limb development during the sixth week of gestation, nothing more. In fact, as far as Neil's mother was concerned, blame rested with his absent father, whose income might have made corrective surgery a possibility, although she never expressed this sentiment aloud.

As a child Neil had occasionally wondered if he was being punished by God, but most of the time he blamed his classmates in school for his unhappiness. Their nonchalant cruelty, their instinctive ability to locate the weaknesses in a victim's emotional armor, the way their own friendships were reinforced by their sadism: he recognized these as examples of human behavior, not divine. And although his classmates often used God's name in their taunts, Neil knew better than to blame Him for their actions.

But while Neil avoided the pitfall of blaming God, he never made the jump to loving Him; nothing in his upbringing or his personality led him to pray to God for strength or for relief. The assorted trials he faced growing up were accidental or human in origin, and he relied on strictly human resources to counter them. He became an adult who – like so many others – viewed God's actions in the abstract until they impinged upon his own life. Angelic visitations were events that befell other people, reaching him only via reports on the nightly news. His own life was entirely mundane; he worked as a superintendent for an upscale apartment building, collecting rent and performing repairs, and as far as he was concerned, circumstances were fully capable of unfolding, happily or not, without intervention from above.

This remained his experience until the death of his wife.

It was an unexceptional visitation, smaller in magnitude than most but no different in kind, bringing blessings to some and disaster to others. In this instance the angel was Nathanael, making an appearance in a downtown shopping district. Four miracle cures were effected: the elimination of carcinomas in two individuals, the regeneration of the spinal cord in a paraplegic, and the restoration of sight to a recently blinded person. There were also two miracles that were not cures: a delivery van, whose driver had fainted at the sight of the angel, was halted before it could overrun a busy sidewalk; another man was caught in a shaft of Heaven's light when the angel departed, erasing his eyes but ensuring his devotion.

Neil's wife Sarah Fisk had been one of the eight casualties. She was hit by flying glass when the angel's billowing curtain of flame shattered the storefront window of the café in which she was eating. She bled to death within minutes, and the other customers in the café – none of whom suffered even superficial injuries – could do nothing but listen to her cries of pain and fear, and eventually witness her soul's ascension toward Heaven.

Nathanael hadn't delivered any specific message; the angel's parting words, which had boomed out across the entire visitation site, were the typical *Behold the power of the Lord*. Of the eight casualties that day, three souls were accepted into Heaven and five were not, a closer ratio than the average for deaths by all causes. Sixty-two people received medical treatment for injuries ranging from slight concussions to ruptured eardrums to burns requiring skin grafts. Total property damage was estimated at $8.1 million, all of it excluded by private insurance companies due to the cause. Scores of people became devout worshipers in the wake of the visitation, either out of gratitude or terror.

Alas, Neil Fisk was not one of them.

After a visitation, it's common for all the witnesses to meet as a group and discuss how their common experience has affected their lives. The witnesses of Nathanael's latest visitation arranged such group meetings, and family members of those who had died were welcome, so Neil began attending. The meetings were held once a month in a basement room of a large church downtown; there were metal folding chairs arranged in rows, and in the back of the room was a table holding coffee and doughnuts. Everyone wore adhesive name tags made out in felt-tip pen.

While waiting for the meetings to start, people would stand around, drinking coffee, talking casually. Most people Neil spoke to assumed his leg was a result of the visitation, and he had to explain that he wasn't a witness, but rather the husband of one of the casualties. This didn't bother him particularly; he was used to explaining about his leg. What did bother him was the tone of the meetings themselves, when participants spoke about their reaction to the visitation: most of them talked about their newfound devotion to God, and they tried to persuade the bereaved that they should feel the same.

Neil's reaction to such attempts at persuasion depended on who was making it. When it was an ordinary witness, he found it merely irritating. When someone who'd received a miracle cure told him to love God, he had to restrain an impulse to strangle the person. But what he found most disquieting of all was hearing the same suggestion from a man named Tony Crane; Tony's wife had died in the visitation too, and he now projected an air of groveling with his every movement. In hushed, tearful tones he explained how he had accepted his role as one of God's subjects, and he advised Neil to do likewise.

Neil didn't stop attending the meetings – he felt that he somehow owed it to Sarah to stick with them – but he found another group to go to as well, one more compatible with his own feelings: a support group devoted to those who'd lost a loved one during a visitation, and were angry at God because of it. They met every other week in a room at the local community center, and talked about the grief and rage that boiled inside of them.

All the attendees were generally sympathetic to one another, despite differences in their various attitudes toward God. Of those who'd been devout before their loss, some struggled with the task of remaining so, while others gave up their devotion without a second glance. Of those who'd never been devout, some felt their position had been validated, while others were faced with the near impossible task of becoming devout now. Neil found himself, to his consternation, in this last category.

Like every other nondevout person, Neil had never expended much energy on where his soul would end up; he'd always assumed his destination was Hell, and he accepted that. That was the way of things, and Hell, after all, was not physically worse than the mortal plane.

It meant permanent exile from God, no more and no less; the truth of this was plain for anyone to see on those occasions when Hell manifested itself. These happened on a regular basis; the ground seemed to become transparent, and you could see Hell as if you were looking through a hole in the floor. The lost souls looked no different than the living, their eternal bodies resembling mortal ones. You couldn't communicate with them – their exile from God meant that they couldn't apprehend the mortal plane where His actions were still felt – but as long as the manifestation lasted you could hear them talk, laugh, or cry, just as they had when they were alive.

People varied widely in their reactions to these manifestations. Most devout people were galvanized, not by the sight of anything frightening, but at being reminded that eternity outside paradise was a possibility. Neil, by contrast, was one of those who were unmoved; as far as he could tell, the lost souls as a group were no unhappier than he was, their existence no worse than his in the mortal plane, and in some ways better: his eternal body would be unhampered by congenital abnormalities.

Of course, everyone knew that Heaven was incomparably superior, but to Neil it had always seemed too remote to consider, like wealth or fame or glamour. For people like him, Hell was where you went when you died, and he saw no point in restructuring his life in hopes of avoiding that. And since God hadn't previously played a role in Neil's life, he wasn't afraid of being exiled from God. The prospect of living without interference, living in a world where windfalls and misfortunes were never by design, held no terror for him.

Now that Sarah was in Heaven, his situation had changed. Neil wanted more than anything to be reunited with her, and the only way to get to Heaven was to love God with all his heart.

This is Neil's story, but telling it properly requires telling the stories of two other individuals whose paths became entwined with his. The first of these is Janice Reilly.

What people assumed about Neil had in fact happened to Janice. When Janice's mother was eight months pregnant with her, she lost control of the car she was driving and collided with a telephone pole during a sudden hailstorm, fists of ice dropping out of a clear blue sky and littering the road like a spill of giant ball bearings. She was sitting in her car, shaken but unhurt, when she saw a knot of silver flames – later identified as the angel Bardiel – float across the sky. The sight petrified her, but not so much that she didn't notice the peculiar settling sensation in her womb. A subsequent ultrasound revealed that the unborn Janice Reilly no longer had legs; flipperlike feet grew directly from her hip sockets.

Janice's life might have gone the way of Neil's, if not for what happened two days after the ultrasound. Janice's parents were sitting at their kitchen table, crying and asking what they had done to deserve this, when they received a vision: the saved souls of four deceased relatives appeared before them, suffusing the kitchen with a golden glow. The saved never spoke, but their beatific smiles induced a feeling of serenity in whoever saw them. From that moment on, the Reillys were certain that their daughter's condition was not a punishment.

As a result, Janice grew up thinking of her legless condition as a gift; her parents explained that God had given her a special assignment because He considered her equal to the task, and she vowed that she would not let Him down. Without pride or defiance, she saw it as her responsibility to show others that her condition did not indicate weakness, but rather strength.

As a child, she was fully accepted by her schoolmates; when you're as pretty, confident, and charismatic as she was, children don't even notice that you're in a wheelchair. It was when she was a teenager that she realized that the able-bodied people in her school were not the ones who most needed convincing. It was more important for her to set an example for other handicapped individuals, whether they had been touched by God or not, no matter where they lived. Janice began speaking before audiences, telling those with disabilities that they had the strength God required of them.

Over time she developed a reputation, and a following. She made a living writing and speaking, and established a nonprofit organization dedicated to promoting her message. People sent her letters thanking her for changing their lives, and receiving those gave her a sense of fulfillment of a sort that Neil had never experienced.

This was Janice's life up until she herself witnessed a visitation by the angel Rashiel. She was letting herself into her house when the tremors began; at first she thought they were of natural origin, although she didn't live in a geologically active area, and waited in the doorway for them to subside. Several seconds later she caught a glimpse of silver in the sky and realized it was an angel, just before she lost consciousness.

Janice awoke to the biggest surprise of her life: the sight of her two new legs, long, muscular, and fully functional.

She was startled the first time she stood up: she was taller than she expected. Balancing at such a height without the use of her arms was unnerving, and simultaneously feeling the texture of the ground through the soles of her feet made it positively bizarre. Rescue workers, finding her wandering down the street dazedly, thought she was in shock until she – marveling at her ability to face them at eye level – explained to them what had happened.

When statistics were gathered for the visitation, the restoration of Janice's legs was recorded as a blessing, and she was humbly grateful for her good fortune. It was at the first of the support group meetings that a feeling of guilt began to creep in. There Janice met two individuals with cancer who'd witnessed Rashiel's visitation, thought their cure was at hand, and been bitterly disappointed when they realized they'd been passed over. Janice found herself wondering, why had she received a blessing when they had not?

Janice's family and friends considered the restoration of her legs a reward for excelling at the task God had set for her, but for Janice, this interpretation raised another question. Did He intend for her to stop? Surely not; evangelism provided the central direction of her life, and there was no limit to the number of people who needed to hear her message. Her continuing to preach was the best action she could take, both for herself and for others.

Her reservations grew during her first speaking engagement after the visitation, before an audience of people recently paralyzed and now wheelchair-bound. Janice delivered her usual words of inspiration, assuring them that they had the strength needed for the challenges ahead; it was during the Q&A that she was asked if the restoration of her legs meant she had passed her test. Janice didn't know what to say; she could hardly promise them that one day their marks would be erased. In fact, she realized, any implication that she'd been rewarded could be interpreted as criticism of others who remained afflicted, and she didn't want that. All she could tell them was that she didn't know why she'd been cured, but it was obvious they found that an unsatisfying answer.

Janice returned home disquieted. She still believed in her message, but as far as her audiences were concerned, she'd lost her greatest source of credibility. How could she inspire others who were touched by God to see their condition as a badge of strength, when she no longer shared their condition?

She considered whether this might be a challenge, a test of her ability to spread His word. Clearly God had made her task more difficult than it was before; perhaps the restoration of her legs was an obstacle for her to overcome, just as their earlier removal had been.

This interpretation failed her at her next scheduled engagement. The audience was a group of witnesses to a visitation by Nathanael; she was often invited to speak to such groups in the hopes that those who suffered might draw encouragement from her. Rather than side-step the issue, she began with an account of the visitation she herself had recently experienced. She explained that while it might appear she was a beneficiary, she was in fact facing her own challenge: like them, she was being forced to draw on resources previously untapped.

She realized, too late, that she had said the wrong thing. A man in the audience with a misshapen leg stood up and challenged her: was she seriously suggesting that the restoration of her legs was comparable to the loss of his wife? Could she really be equating her trials with his own?

Janice immediately assured him that she wasn't, and that she couldn't imagine the pain he was experiencing. But, she said, it wasn't God's intention that everyone be subjected to the same kind of trial, but only that each person face his or her own trial, whatever it might be. The difficulty of any trial was subjective, and there was no way to compare two individuals' experiences. And just as those whose suffering seemed greater than his should have compassion for him, so should he have compassion for those whose suffering seemed less.

The man was having none of it. She had received what anyone else would have considered a fantastic blessing, and she was complaining about it. He stormed out of the meeting while Janice was still trying to explain.

That man, of course, was Neil Fisk. Neil had had Janice Reilly's name mentioned to him for much of his life, most often by people who were convinced his misshapen leg was a sign from God. These people cited her as an example he should follow, telling him that her attitude was the proper response to a physical handicap. Neil couldn't deny that her leglessness was a far worse condition than his distorted femur. Unfortunately, he found her attitude so foreign that, even in the best of times, he'd never been able to learn anything from her. Now, in the depths of his grief and mystified as to why she had received a gift she didn't need, Neil found her words offensive.

In the days that followed, Janice found herself more and more plagued by doubts, unable to decide what the restoration of her legs meant. Was she being ungrateful for a gift she'd received? Was it both a blessing and a test? Perhaps it was a punishment, an indication that she had not performed her duty well enough. There were many possibilities, and she didn't know which one to believe.

There is one other person who played an important role in Neil's story, even though he and Neil did not meet until Neil's journey was nearly over. That person's name is Ethan Mead.

Ethan had been raised in a family that was devout, but not profoundly so. His parents credited God with their above-average health and their comfortable economic status, although they hadn't witnessed any visitations or received any visions; they simply trusted that God was, directly or indirectly, responsible for their good fortune. Their devotion had never been put to any serious test, and might not have withstood one; their love for God was based in their satisfaction with the status quo.

Ethan was not like his parents, though. Ever since childhood he'd felt certain that God had a special role for him to play, and he waited for a sign telling him what that role was. He'd have liked to have become a preacher, but felt he hadn't any compelling testimony to offer; his vague feelings of expectation weren't enough. He longed for an encounter with the divine to provide him with direction.

He could have gone to one of the holy sites, those places where – for reasons unknown – angelic visitations occurred on a regular basis, but he felt that such an action would be presumptuous of him. The holy sites were usually the last resort of the desperate, those people seeking either a miracle cure to repair their bodies or a glimpse of Heaven's light to repair their souls, and Ethan was not desperate. He decided that he'd been set along his own course, and in time the reason for it would become clear. While waiting for that day, he lived his life as best he could: he worked as a librarian, married a woman named Claire, raised two children. All the while, he remained watchful for signs of a greater destiny.

Ethan was certain his time had come when he became witness to a visitation by Rashiel, the same visitation that – miles away – restored Janice Reilly's legs. Ethan was by himself when it happened; he was walking toward his car in the center of a parking lot, when the ground began to shudder. Instinctively he knew it was a visitation, and he assumed a kneeling position, feeling no fear, only exhilaration and awe at the prospect of learning his calling.

The ground became still after a minute, and Ethan looked around, but didn't otherwise move. Only after waiting for several more minutes did he rise to his feet. There was a large crack in the asphalt, beginning directly in front of him and following a meandering path down the street. The crack seemed to be pointing him in a specific direction, so he ran alongside it for several blocks until he encountered other survivors, a man and a woman climbing out of a modest fissure that had opened up directly beneath them. He waited with the two of them until rescuers arrived and brought them to a shelter.

Ethan attended the support group meetings that followed and met the other witnesses to Rashiel's visitation. Over the course of a few meetings, he became aware of certain patterns among the witnesses. Of course there were those who'd been injured and those who'd received miracle cures. But there were also those whose lives were changed in other ways: the man and woman he'd first met fell in love and were soon engaged; a woman who'd been pinned beneath a collapsed wall was inspired to become an EMT after being rescued. One business owner formed an alliance that averted her impending bankruptcy, while another whose business was destroyed saw it as a message that he change his ways. It seemed that everyone except Ethan had found a way to understand what had happened to them.

He hadn't been cursed or blessed in any obvious way, and he didn't know what message he was intended to receive. His wife Claire suggested that he consider the visitation a reminder that he appreciate what he had, but Ethan found that unsatisfying, reasoning that *every* visitation – no matter where it occurred – served that function, and the fact that he'd witnessed a visitation firsthand had to have greater significance. His mind was preyed upon by the idea that he'd missed an opportunity, that there was a fellow witness whom he was intended to meet but hadn't. This visitation had to be the sign he'd been waiting for; he couldn't just disregard it. But that didn't tell him what he was supposed to do.

Ethan eventually resorted to the process of elimination: he got hold of a list of all the witnesses, and crossed off those who had a clear interpretation of their experience, reasoning that one of those remaining must be the person whose fate was somehow intertwined with his. Among those who were confused or uncertain about the visitation's meaning would be the one he was intended to meet.

When he had finished crossing names off his list, there was only one left: JANICE REILLY.

In public Neil was able to mask his grief as adults are expected to, but in the privacy of his apartment, the floodgates of emotion burst open. The awareness of Sarah's absence would overwhelm him, and then he'd collapse on the floor and weep. He'd curl up into a ball, his body racked by hiccuping sobs, tears and mucus streaming down his face, the anguish coming in ever-increasing waves until it was more than he could bear, more intense than he'd have believed possible. Minutes or hours later it would leave, and he would fall asleep, exhausted. And the next morning he would wake up and face the prospect of another day without Sarah.

An elderly woman in Neil's apartment building tried to comfort him by telling him that the pain would lessen in time, and while he would never forget his wife, he would at least be able to move on. Then he would meet someone else one day and find happiness with her, and he would learn to love God and thus ascend to Heaven when his time came.

This woman's intentions were good, but Neil was in no position to find any comfort in her words. Sarah's absence felt like an open wound, and the prospect that someday he would no longer feel pain at her loss seemed not just remote, but a physical impossibility. If suicide would have ended his pain, he'd have done it without hesitation, but that would only ensure that his separation from Sarah was permanent.

The topic of suicide regularly came up at the support group meetings, and inevitably led to someone mentioning Robin Pearson, a woman who used to come to the meetings several months before Neil began attending. Robin's husband had been afflicted with stomach cancer during a visitation by the angel Makatiel. She stayed in his hospital room for days at a stretch, only for him to die unexpectedly when she was home doing laundry. A nurse who'd been present told Robin that his soul had ascended, and so Robin had begun attending the support group meetings.

Many months later, Robin came to the meeting shaking with rage. There'd been a manifestation of Hell near her house, and she'd seen her husband among the lost souls. She'd confronted the nurse, who admitted to lying in the hopes that Robin would learn to love God, so that at least she would be saved even if her husband hadn't been. Robin wasn't at the next meeting, and at the meeting after that the group learned she had committed suicide to rejoin her husband.

None of them knew the status of Robin's and her husband's relationship in the afterlife, but successes were known to happen; some couples had indeed been happily reunited through suicide. The support group had attendees whose spouses had descended to Hell, and they talked about being torn between wanting to remain alive and wanting to rejoin their spouses. Neil wasn't in their situation, but his first response when listening to them had been envy: if Sarah had gone to Hell, suicide would be the solution to all his problems.

This led to a shameful self-knowledge for Neil. He realized that if he had to choose between going to Hell while Sarah went to Heaven, or having both of them go to Hell together, he would choose the latter: he would rather she be exiled from God than separated from him. He knew it was selfish, but he couldn't change how he felt: he believed Sarah could be happy in either place, but he could only be happy with her.

Neil's previous experiences with women had never been good. All too often he'd begin flirting with a woman while sitting at a bar, only to have her remember an appointment elsewhere the moment he stood up and his shortened leg came into view. Once, a woman he'd been dating for several weeks broke off their relationship, explaining that while she herself didn't consider his leg a defect, whenever they were seen in public together other people assumed there must be something wrong with her for being with him, and surely he could understand how unfair that was to her?

Sarah had been the first woman Neil met whose demeanor hadn't changed one bit, whose expression hadn't flickered toward pity or horror or even surprise when she first saw his leg. For that reason alone it was predictable that Neil would become infatuated with her; by the time he saw all the sides of her personality, he'd completely fallen in love with her. And because his best qualities came out when he was with her, she fell in love with him too.

Neil had been surprised when Sarah told him she was devout. There weren't many signs of her devotion – she didn't go to church, sharing Neil's dislike for the attitudes of most people who attended – but in her own, quiet way she was grateful to God for her life. She never tried to convert Neil, saying that devotion would come from within or not at all. They rarely had any cause to mention God, and most of the time it would've been easy for Neil to imagine that Sarah's views on God matched his own.

This is not to say that Sarah's devotion had no effect on Neil. On the contrary, Sarah was far and away the best argument for loving God that he had ever encountered. If love of God had contributed to making her the person she was, then perhaps it did make sense. During the years that the two of them were married, his outlook on life improved, and it probably would have reached the point where he was thankful to God, if he and Sarah had grown old together.

Sarah's death removed that particular possibility, but it needn't have closed the door on Neil's loving God. Neil could have taken it as a reminder that no one can count on having decades left. He could have been moved by the realization that, had he died with her, his soul would've been lost and the two of them separated for eternity. He could have seen Sarah's death as a wake-up call, telling him to love God while he still had the chance.

Instead Neil became actively resentful of God. Sarah had been the greatest blessing of his life, and God had taken her away. Now he was expected to love Him for it? For Neil, it was like having a kidnapper demand love as ransom for his wife's return. Obedience he might have managed, but sincere, heartfelt love? That was a ransom he couldn't pay.

This paradox confronted several people in the support group. One of the attendees, a man named Phil Soames, correctly pointed out that thinking of it as a condition to be met would guarantee failure. You couldn't love God as a means to an end, you had to love Him for Himself. If your ultimate goal in loving God was a reunion with your spouse, you weren't demonstrating true devotion at all.

A woman in the support group named Valerie Tommasino said they shouldn't even try. She'd been reading a book published by the humanist movement; its members considered it wrong to love a God who inflicted such pain, and advocated that people act according to their own moral sense instead of being guided by the carrot and the stick. These were people who, when they died, descended to Hell in proud defiance of God.

Neil himself had read a pamphlet of the humanist movement; what he most remembered was that it had quoted the fallen angels. Visitations of fallen angels were infrequent, and caused neither good fortune nor bad; they weren't acting under God's direction, but just passing through the mortal plane as they went about their unimaginable business. On the occasions they appeared, people would ask them questions: Did they know God's intentions? Why had they rebelled? The fallen angels' reply was always the same: *Decide for yourselves. That is what we did. We advise you to do the same.*

Those in the humanist movement had decided, and if it weren't for Sarah, Neil would've made the identical choice. But he wanted her back, and the only way was to find a reason to love God.

Looking for any footing on which to build their devotion, some attendees of the support group took comfort in the fact that their loved ones hadn't suffered when God took them, but instead died instantly. Neil didn't even have that; Sarah had received horrific lacerations when the glass hit her. Of course, it could have been worse. One couple's teenage son had been trapped in a fire ignited by an angel's visitation, and received full-thickness burns over eighty percent of his body before rescue workers could free him; his eventual death was a mercy. Sarah had been fortunate by comparison, but not enough to make Neil love God.

Neil could think of only one thing that would make him give thanks to God, and that was if He allowed Sarah to appear before him. It would give him immeasurable comfort just to see her smile again; he'd never been visited by a saved soul before, and a vision now would have meant more to him than at any other point in his life.

But visions don't appear just because a person needs one, and none ever came to Neil. He had to find his own way toward God.

The next time he attended the support group meeting for witnesses of Nathanael's visitation, Neil sought out Benny Vasquez, the man whose eyes had been erased by Heaven's light. Benny didn't always attend because he was now being invited to speak at other meetings; few visitations resulted in an eyeless person, since Heaven's light entered the mortal plane only in the brief moments that an angel emerged from or reentered Heaven, so the eyeless were minor celebrities, and in demand as speakers to church groups.

Benny was now as sightless as any burrowing worm: not only were his eyes and sockets missing, his skull lacked even the space for such features, the cheekbones now abutting the forehead. The light that had brought his soul as close to perfection as was possible in the mortal plane had also deformed his body; it was commonly held that this illustrated the superfluity of physical bodies in Heaven. With the limited expressive capacity his face retained, Benny always wore a blissful, rapturous smile.

Neil hoped Benny could say something to help him love God. Benny described Heaven's light as infinitely beautiful, a sight of such compelling majesty that it vanquished all doubts. It constituted incontrovertible proof that God should be loved, an explanation that made it as obvious as 1+1=2. Unfortunately, while Benny could offer many analogies for the effect of Heaven's light, he couldn't duplicate that effect with his own words. Those who were already devout found Benny's descriptions thrilling, but to Neil, they seemed frustratingly vague. So he looked elsewhere for counsel.

Accept the mystery, said the minister of the local church. If you can love God even though your questions go unanswered, you'll be the better for it.

Admit that you need Him, said the popular book of spiritual advice he bought. When you realize that self-sufficiency is an illusion, you'll be ready.

Submit yourself completely and utterly, said the preacher on the television. Receiving torment is how you prove your love. Acceptance may not bring you relief in this life, but resistance will only worsen your punishment.

All of these strategies have proven successful for different individuals; any one of them, once internalized, can bring a person to devotion. But these are not always easy to adopt, and Neil was one who found them impossible.

Neil finally tried talking to Sarah's parents, which was an indication of how desperate he was: his relationship with them had always been tense. While they loved Sarah, they often chided her for not being demonstrative enough in her devotion, and they'd been shocked when she married a man who wasn't devout at all. For her part, Sarah had always considered her parents too judgmental, and their disapproval of Neil only reinforced her opinion. But now Neil felt he had something in common with them – after all, they were all mourning Sarah's loss – and so he visited them in their suburban colonial, hoping they could help him in his grief.

How wrong he was. Instead of sympathy, what Neil got from Sarah's parents was blame for her death. They'd come to this conclusion in the weeks after Sarah's funeral; they reasoned that she'd been taken to send him a message, and that they were forced to endure her loss solely because he hadn't been devout. They were now convinced that, his previous explanations notwithstanding, Neil's deformed leg was in fact God's doing, and if only he'd been properly chastened by it, Sarah might still be alive.

Their reaction shouldn't have come as a surprise: throughout Neil's life, people had attributed moral significance to his leg even though God wasn't responsible for it. Now that he'd suffered a misfortune for which God was unambiguously responsible, it was inevitable that someone would assume he deserved it. It was purely by chance that Neil heard this sentiment when he was at his most vulnerable, and it could have the greatest impact on him.

Neil didn't think his in-laws were right, but he began to wonder if he might not be better off if he did. Perhaps, he thought, it'd be better to live in a story where the righteous were rewarded and the sinners were punished, even if the criteria for righteousness and sinfulness eluded him, than to live in a reality where there was no justice at all. It would mean casting himself in the role of sinner, so it was hardly a comforting lie, but it offered one reward that his own ethics couldn't: believing it would reunite him with Sarah.

Sometimes even bad advice can point a man in the right direction. It was in this manner that his in-laws' accusations ultimately pushed Neil closer to God.

More than once when she was evangelizing, Janice had been asked if she ever wished she had legs, and she had always answered – honestly – no, she didn't. She was content as she was. Sometimes her questioner would point out that she couldn't miss what she'd never known, and she might feel differently if she'd been born with legs and lost them later on. Janice never denied that. But she could truthfully say that she felt no sense of being incomplete, no envy for people with legs; being legless was part of her identity. She'd never bothered with prosthetics, and had a surgical procedure been available to provide her with legs, she'd have turned it down. She had never considered the possibility that God might restore her legs.

One of the unexpected side effects of having legs was the increased attention she received from men. In the past she'd mostly attracted men with amputee fetishes or sainthood complexes; now all sorts of men seemed drawn to her. So when she first noticed Ethan Mead's interest in her, she thought it was romantic in nature; this possibility was particularly distressing since he was obviously married.

Ethan had begun talking to Janice at the support group meetings, and then began attending her public speaking engagements. It was when he suggested they have lunch together that Janice asked him about his intentions, and he explained his theory. He didn't know *how* his fate was intertwined with hers; he knew only that it was. She was skeptical, but she didn't reject his theory outright. Ethan admitted that he didn't have answers for her own questions, but he was eager to do anything he could to help her find them. Janice cautiously agreed to help him in his search for meaning, and Ethan promised that he wouldn't be a burden. They met on a regular basis and talked about the significance of visitations.

Meanwhile Ethan's wife Claire grew worried. Ethan assured her that he had no romantic feelings toward Janice, but that didn't alleviate her concerns. She knew that extreme circumstances could create a bond between individuals, and she feared that Ethan's relationship with Janice – romantic or not – would threaten their marriage.

Ethan suggested to Janice that he, as a librarian, could help her do some research. Neither of them had ever heard of a previous instance where God had left His mark on a person in one visitation and removed it in another. Ethan looked for previous examples in hopes that they might shed some light on Janice's situation. There were a few instances of individuals receiving multiple miracle cures over their lifetimes, but their illnesses or disabilities had always been of natural origin, not given to them in a visitation. There was one anecdotal report of a man being struck blind for his sins, changing his ways, and later having his sight restored, but it was classified as an urban legend.

Even if that account had a basis in truth, it didn't provide a useful precedent for Janice's situation: her legs had been removed before her birth, and so couldn't have been a punishment for anything she'd done. Was it possible that Janice's condition had been a punishment for something her mother or father had done? Could her restoration mean they had finally earned her cure? She couldn't believe that.

If her deceased relatives were to appear in a vision, Janice would've been reassured about the restoration of her legs. The fact that they didn't made her suspect something was amiss, but she didn't believe that it was a punishment. Perhaps it had been a mistake, and she'd received a miracle meant for someone else; perhaps it was a test, to see how she would respond to being given too much. In either case, there seemed only one course of action: she would, with utmost gratitude and humility, offer to return her gift. To do so, she would go on a pilgrimage.

Pilgrims traveled great distances to visit the holy sites and wait for a visitation, hoping for a miracle cure. Whereas in most of the world one could wait an entire lifetime and never experience a visitation, at a holy site one might only wait months, sometimes weeks. Pilgrims knew that the odds of being cured were still poor; of those who stayed long enough to witness a visitation, the majority did not receive a cure. But they were often happy just to have seen an angel, and they returned home better able to face what awaited them, whether it be imminent death or life with a crippling disability. And of course, just living through a visitation made many people appreciate their situations; invariably, a small number of pilgrims were killed during each visitation.

Janice was willing to accept the outcome whatever it was. If God saw fit to take her, she was ready. If God removed her legs again, she would resume the work she'd always done. If God let her legs remain, she hoped she would receive the epiphany she needed to speak with conviction about her gift.

She hoped, however, that her miracle would be taken back and given to someone who truly needed it. She didn't suggest to anyone that they accompany her in hopes of receiving the miracle she was returning, feeling that that would've been presumptuous, but she privately considered her pilgrimage a request on behalf of those who were in need.

Her friends and family were confused at Janice's decision, seeing it as questioning God. As word spread, she received many letters from followers, variously expressing dismay, bafflement, and admiration for her willingness to make such a sacrifice.

As for Ethan, he was completely supportive of Janice's decision, and excited for himself. He now understood the significance of Rashiel's visitation for him: it indicated that the time had come for him to act. His wife Claire strenuously opposed his leaving, pointing out that he had no idea how long he might be away, and that she and their children needed him too. It grieved him to go without her support, but he had no choice. Ethan would go on a pilgrimage, and at the next visitation, he would learn what God intended for him.

Neil's visit to Sarah's parents caused him to give further thought to his conversation with Benny Vasquez. While he hadn't gotten a lot out of Benny's words, he'd been impressed by the absoluteness of Benny's devotion. No matter what misfortune befell him in the future, Benny's love of God would never waver, and he would ascend to Heaven when he died. That fact offered Neil a very slim opportunity, one that had seemed so unattractive he hadn't considered it before; but now, as he was growing more desperate, it was beginning to look expedient.

Every holy site had its pilgrims who, rather than looking for a miracle cure, deliberately sought out Heaven's light. Those who saw it were always accepted into Heaven when they died, no matter how selfish their motives had been; there were some who wished to have their ambivalence removed so they could be reunited with their loved ones, and others who'd always lived a sinful life and wanted to escape the consequences.

In the past there'd been some doubt as to whether Heaven's light could indeed overcome *all* the spiritual obstacles to becoming saved. The debate ended after the case of Barry Larsen, a serial rapist and murderer who, while disposing of the body of his latest victim, witnessed an angel's visitation and saw Heaven's light. At Larsen's execution, his soul was seen ascending to Heaven, much to the outrage of his victims' families. Priests tried to console them, assuring them – on the basis of no evidence whatsoever – that Heaven's light must have subjected Larsen to many lifetimes' worth of penance in a moment, but their words provided little comfort.

For Neil this offered a loophole, an answer to Phil Soames's objection; it was the one way that he could love Sarah more than he loved God, and still be reunited with her. It was how he could be selfish and still get into Heaven. Others had done it; perhaps he could too. It might not be just, but at least it was predictable.

At an instinctual level, Neil was averse to the idea: it sounded like undergoing brainwashing as a cure for depression. He couldn't help but think that it would change his personality so drastically that he'd cease to be himself. Then he remembered that everyone in Heaven had undergone a similar transformation; the saved were just like the eyeless except that they no longer had bodies. This gave Neil a clearer image of what he was working toward: no matter whether he became devout by seeing Heaven's light or by a lifetime of effort, any ultimate reunion with Sarah couldn't re-create what they'd shared in the mortal plane. In Heaven, they would both be different, and their love for each other would be mixed with the love that all the saved felt for everything.

This realization didn't diminish Neil's longing for a reunion with Sarah. In fact it sharpened his desire, because it meant that the reward would be the same no matter what means he used to achieve it; the shortcut led to precisely the same destination as the conventional path.

On the other hand, seeking Heaven's light was far more difficult than an ordinary pilgrimage, and far more dangerous. Heaven's light leaked through only when an angel entered or left the mortal plane, and since there was no way to predict where an angel would first appear, light-seekers had to converge on the angel after its arrival and follow it until its departure. To maximize their chances of being in the narrow shaft of Heaven's light, they followed the angel as closely as possible during its visitation; depending on the angel involved, this might mean staying alongside the funnel of a tornado, the wavefront of a flash flood, or the expanding tip of a chasm as it split apart the landscape. Far more light-seekers died in the attempt than succeeded.

Statistics about the souls of failed light-seekers were difficult to compile, since there were few witnesses to such expeditions, but the numbers so far were not encouraging. In sharp contrast to ordinary pilgrims who died without receiving their sought-after cure, of which roughly half were admitted into Heaven, every single failed light-seeker had descended to Hell. Perhaps only people who were already lost ever considered seeking Heaven's light, or perhaps death in such circumstances was considered suicide. In any case, it was clear to Neil that he needed to be ready to accept the consequences of embarking on such an attempt.

The entire idea had an all-or-nothing quality to it that Neil found both frightening and attractive. He found the prospect of going on with his life, trying to love God, increasingly maddening. He might try for decades and not succeed. He might not even have that long; as he'd been reminded so often lately, visitations served as a warning to prepare one's soul, because death might come at any time. He could die tomorrow, and there was no chance of his becoming devout in the near future by conventional means.

It's perhaps ironic that, given his history of not following Janice Reilly's example, Neil took notice when she reversed her position. He was eating breakfast when he happened to see an item in the newspaper about her plans for a pilgrimage, and his immediate reaction was anger: how many blessings would it take to satisfy that woman? After considering it more, he decided that if she, having received a blessing, deemed it appropriate to seek God's assistance in coming to terms with it, then there was no reason he, having received such terrible misfortune, shouldn't do the same. And that was enough to tip him over the edge.

Holy sites were invariably in inhospitable places: one was an atoll in the middle of the ocean, while another was in the mountains at an elevation of twenty thousand feet. The one that Neil traveled to was in a desert, an expanse of cracked mud reaching miles in every direction; it was desolate, but it was relatively accessible and thus popular among pilgrims. The appearance of the holy site was an object lesson in what happened when the celestial and terrestrial realms touched: the landscape was variously scarred by lava flows, gaping fissures, and impact craters. Vegetation was scarce and ephemeral, restricted to growing in the interval after soil was deposited by floodwaters or whirlwinds and before it was scoured away again.

Pilgrims took up residence all over the site, forming temporary villages with their tents and camper vans; they all made guesses as to what location would maximize their chances of seeing the angel while minimizing the risk of injury or death. Some protection was offered by curved banks of sandbags, left over from years past and rebuilt as needed. A site-specific paramedic and fire department ensured that paths were kept clear so rescue vehicles could go where they were needed. Pilgrims either brought their own food and water or purchased them from vendors charging exorbitant prices; everyone paid a fee to cover the cost of waste removal.

Light-seekers always had off-road vehicles to better cross rough terrain when it came time to follow the angel. Those who could afford it drove alone; those who couldn't formed groups of two or three or four. Neil didn't want to be a passenger reliant on another person, nor did he want the responsibility of driving anyone else. This might be his final act on earth, and he felt he should do it alone. The cost of Sarah's funeral had depleted their savings, so Neil sold all his possessions in order to purchase a suitable vehicle: a pickup truck equipped with aggressively knurled tires and heavy-duty shock absorbers.

As soon as he arrived, Neil started doing what all the other light-seekers did: crisscrossing the site in his vehicle, trying to familiarize himself with its topography. It was on one of his drives around the site's perimeter that he met Ethan; Ethan flagged him down after his own car had stalled on his return from the nearest grocery store, eighty miles away. Neil helped him get his car started again, and then, at Ethan's insistence, followed him back to his campsite for dinner. Janice wasn't there when they arrived, having gone to visit some pilgrims several tents over; Neil listened politely while Ethan – heating prepackaged meals over a bottle of propane – began describing the events that had brought him to the holy site.

When Ethan mentioned Janice Reilly's name, Neil couldn't mask his surprise. He had no desire to speak with her again, and immediately excused himself to leave. He was explaining to a puzzled Ethan that he'd forgotten a previous engagement when Janice arrived.

She was startled to see Neil there, but asked him to stay. Ethan explained why he'd invited Neil to dinner, and Janice told him where she and Neil had met. Then she asked Neil what had brought him to the holy site. When he told them he was a light-seeker, Ethan and Janice immediately tried to persuade him to reconsider his plans. He might be committing suicide, said Ethan, and there were always better alternatives than suicide. Seeing Heaven's light was not the answer, said Janice; that wasn't what God wanted. Neil stiffly thanked them for their concern, and left.

During the weeks of waiting, Neil spent every day driving around the site; maps were available, and were updated after each visitation, but they were no substitute for driving the terrain yourself. On occasion he would see a light-seeker who was obviously experienced in off-road driving, and ask him – the vast majority of the light-seekers were men – for tips on negotiating a specific type of terrain. Some had been at the site for several visitations, having neither succeeded nor failed at their previous attempts. They were glad to share tips on how best to pursue an angel, but never offered any personal information about themselves. Neil found the tone of their conversation peculiar, simultaneously hopeful and hopeless, and wondered if he sounded the same.

Ethan and Janice passed the time by getting to know some of the other pilgrims. Their reactions to Janice's situation were mixed: some thought her ungrateful, while others thought her generous. Most found Ethan's story interesting, since he was one of the very few pilgrims seeking something other than a miracle cure. For the most part, there was a feeling of camaraderie that sustained them during the long wait.

Neil was driving around in his truck when dark clouds began coalescing in the southeast, and the word came over the CB radio that a visitation had begun. He stopped the vehicle to insert earplugs into his ears and don his helmet; by the time he was finished, flashes of lightning were visible, and a light-seeker near the angel reported that it was Barakiel, and it appeared to be moving due north. Neil turned his truck east in anticipation and began driving at full speed.

There was no rain or wind, only dark clouds from which lightning emerged. Over the radio other light-seekers relayed estimates of the angel's direction and speed, and Neil headed northeast to get in front of it. At first he could gauge his distance from the storm by counting how long it took for the thunder to arrive, but soon the lightning bolts were striking so frequently that he couldn't match up the sounds with the individual strikes.

He saw the vehicles of two other light-seekers converging. They began driving in parallel, heading north, over a heavily cratered section of ground, bouncing over small ones and swerving to avoid the larger ones. Bolts of lightning were striking the ground everywhere, but they appeared to be radiating from a point south of Neil's position; the angel was directly behind him, and closing.

Even through his earplugs, the roar was deafening. Neil could feel his hair rising from his skin as the electric charge built up around him. He kept glancing in his rearview mirror, trying to ascertain where the angel was while wondering how close he ought to get.

His vision grew so crowded with afterimages that it became difficult to distinguish actual bolts of lightning among them. Squinting at the dazzle in his mirror, he realized he was looking at a continuous bolt of lightning, undulating but uninterrupted. He tilted the driver's-side mirror upward to get a better look, and saw the source of the lightning bolt, a seething, writhing mass of flames, silver against the dusky clouds: the angel Barakiel.

It was then, while Neil was transfixed and paralyzed by what he saw, that his pickup truck crested a sharp outcropping of rock and became airborne. The truck smashed into a boulder, the entire force of the impact concentrated on the vehicle's left front end, crumpling it like foil. The intrusion into the driver's compartment fractured both of Neil's legs and nicked his left femoral artery. Neil began, slowly but surely, bleeding to death.

He didn't try to move; he wasn't in physical pain at the moment, but he somehow knew that the slightest movement would be excruciating. It was obvious that he was pinned in the truck, and there was no way he could pursue Barakiel even if he weren't. Helplessly, he watched the lightning storm move further and further away.

As he watched it, Neil began crying. He was filled with a mixture of regret and self-contempt, cursing himself for ever thinking that such a scheme could succeed. He would have begged for the opportunity to do it over again, promised to spend the rest of his days learning to love God, if only he could live, but he knew that no bargaining was possible and he had only himself to blame. He apologized to Sarah for losing his chance at being reunited with her, for throwing his life away on a gamble instead of playing it safe. He prayed that she understood that he'd been motivated by his love for her, and that she would forgive him.

Through his tears he saw a woman running toward him, and recognized her as Janice Reilly. He realized his truck had crashed no more than a hundred yards from her and Ethan's campsite. There was nothing she could do, though; he could feel the blood draining out of him, and knew that he wouldn't live long enough for a rescue vehicle to arrive. He thought Janice was calling to him, but his ears were ringing too badly for him to hear anything. He could see Ethan Mead behind her, also starting to run toward him.

Then there was a flash of light and Janice was knocked off her feet as if she'd been struck by a sledgehammer. At first he thought she'd been hit by lightning, but then he realized that the lightning had already ceased. It was when she stood up again that he saw her face, steam rising from newly featureless skin, and he realized that Janice had been struck by Heaven's light.

Neil looked up, but all he saw were clouds; the shaft of light was gone. It seemed as if God were taunting him, not only by showing him the prize he'd lost his life trying to acquire while still holding it out of reach, but also by giving it to someone who didn't need it or even want it. God had already wasted a miracle on Janice, and now He was doing it again.

It was at that moment that another beam of Heaven's light penetrated the cloud cover and struck Neil, trapped in his vehicle.

Like a thousand hypodermic needles the light punctured his flesh and scraped across his bones. The light unmade his eyes, turning him into not a formerly sighted being, but a being never intended to possess vision. And in doing so the light revealed to Neil all the reasons he should love God.

He loved Him with an utterness beyond what humans can experience for one another. To say it was unconditional was inadequate, because even the word "unconditional" required the concept of a condition and such an idea was no longer comprehensible to him: every phenomenon in the universe was nothing less than an explicit reason to love Him. No circumstance could be an obstacle or even an irrelevancy, but only another reason to be grateful, a further inducement to love. Neil thought of the grief that had driven him to suicidal recklessness, and the pain and terror that Sarah had experienced before she died, and still he loved God, not in spite of their suffering, but because of it.

He renounced all his previous anger and ambivalence and desire for answers. He was grateful for all the pain he'd endured, contrite for not previously recognizing it as the gift it was, euphoric that he was now being granted this insight into his true purpose. He understood how life was an undeserved bounty, how even the most virtuous were not worthy of the glories of the mortal plane.

For him the mystery was solved, because he understood that everything in life is love, even pain, especially pain.

So minutes later, when Neil finally bled to death, he was truly worthy of salvation.

And God sent him to Hell anyway.

Ethan saw all of this. He saw Neil and Janice remade by Heaven's light, and he saw the pious love on their eyeless faces. He saw the skies become clear and the sunlight return. He was holding Neil's hand, waiting for the paramedics, when Neil died, and he saw Neil's soul leave his body and rise toward Heaven, only to descend into Hell.

Janice didn't see it, for by then her eyes were already gone. Ethan was the sole witness, and he realized that this was God's purpose for him: to follow Janice Reilly to this point and to see what she could not.

When statistics were compiled for Barakiel's visitation, it turned out that there had been a total of ten casualties, six among light-seekers and four among ordinary pilgrims. Nine pilgrims received miracle cures; the only individuals to see Heaven's light were Janice and Neil. There were no statistics regarding how many pilgrims had felt their lives changed by the visitation, but Ethan counted himself among them.

Upon returning home, Janice resumed her evangelism, but the topic of her speeches has changed. She no longer speaks about how the physically handicapped have the resources to overcome their limitations; instead she, like the other eyeless, speaks about the unbearable beauty of God's creation. Many who used to draw inspiration from her are disappointed, feeling they've lost a spiritual leader. When Janice had spoken of the strength she had as an afflicted person, her message was rare, but now that she's eyeless, her message is commonplace. She doesn't worry about the reduction in her audience, though, because she has complete conviction in what she evangelizes.

Ethan quit his job and became a preacher so that he too could speak about his experiences. His wife Claire couldn't accept his new mission and ultimately left him, taking their children with her, but Ethan was willing to continue alone. He's developed a substantial following by telling people what happened to Neil Fisk. He tells people that they can no more expect justice in the afterlife than in the mortal plane, but he doesn't do this to dissuade them from worshiping God; on the contrary, he encourages them to do so. What he insists on is that they not love God under a misapprehension, that if they wish to love God, they be prepared to do so no matter what His intentions. God is not just, God is not kind, God is not merciful, and understanding that is essential to true devotion.

As for Neil, although he is unaware of any of Ethan's sermons, he would understand their message perfectly. His lost soul is the embodiment of Ethan's teachings.

For most of its inhabitants, Hell is not that different from Earth; its principal punishment is the regret of not having loved God enough when alive, and for many that's easily endured. For Neil, however, Hell bears no resemblance whatsoever to the mortal plane. His eternal body has well-formed legs, but he's scarcely aware of them; his eyes have been restored, but he can't bear to open them. Just as seeing Heaven's light gave him an awareness of God's presence in all things in the mortal plane, so it has made him aware of God's absence in all things in Hell. Everything Neil sees, hears, or touches causes him distress, and unlike in the mortal plane this pain is not a form of God's love, but a consequence of His absence. Neil is experiencing more anguish than was possible when he was alive, but his only response is to love God.

Neil still loves Sarah, and misses her as much as he ever did, and the knowledge that he came so close to rejoining her only makes it worse. He knows his being sent to Hell was not a result of anything he did; he knows there was no reason for it, no higher purpose being served. None of this diminishes his love for God. If there were a possibility that he could be admitted to Heaven and his suffering would end, he would not hope for it; such desires no longer occur to him.

Neil even knows that by being beyond God's awareness, he is not loved by God in return. This doesn't affect his feelings either, because unconditional love asks nothing, not even that it be returned.

And though it's been many years that he has been in Hell, beyond the awareness of God, he loves Him still. That is the nature of true devotion.

Lieserl

Karen Joy Fowler

EINSTEIN RECEIVED the first letter in the afternoon post. It had traveled in bags and boxes all the way from Hungary, sailing finally through the brass slit in Einstein's door. *Dear Albert,* it said. *Little Lieserl is here. Mileva says to tell you that your new daughter has tiny fingers and a head as bald as an egg. Mileva says to say that she loves you and will write you herself when she feels better.* The signature was Mileva's father's. The letter was sent at the end of January, but arrived at the beginning of February, so even if everything in it was true when written, it was entirely possible that none of it was true now. Einstein read the letter several times. He was frightened. Why could Mileva not write him herself? The birth must have been a very difficult one. Was the baby really as bald as all that? He wished for a picture. What kind of little eyes did she have? Did she look like Mileva? Mileva had an aura of thick, dark hair. Einstein was living in Bern, Switzerland, and Mileva had returned to her parents' home in Titel, Hungary, for the birth. Mileva was hurt because Einstein sent her to Hungary alone, although she had not said so. The year was 1902. Einstein was twenty-two years old. None of this is as simple as it sounds, but one must start somewhere even though such placement inevitably entails the telling of a lie.

Outside Einstein's window, large star-shaped flakes of snow swirled silently in the air like the pretend snow in a glass globe. The sky darkened into evening as Einstein sat on his bed with his papers. The globe had been shaken and Einstein was the still ceramic figure at its swirling heart, the painted Father Christmas. Lieserl. How I love her already, Einstein thought, dangerously. Before I even know her, how I love her.

The second letter arrived the next morning. *Liebes Schatzerl,* Mileva wrote. *Your daughter is so beautiful. But the world does not suit her at all. With such fury she cries! Papa is coming soon, I tell her. Papa will change everything for you, everything you don't like, the whole world if this is what you want. Papa loves Lieserl. I am very tired still. You must hurry to us. Lieserl's hair has come in dark and I think she is getting a tooth.* Einstein stared at the letter.

A friend of Einstein's will tell Einstein one day that he, himself, would never have the courage to marry a woman who was not absolutely sound. He will say this soon after meeting Mileva. Mileva walked with a limp, although it is unlikely that a limp is all this friend meant. Einstein will respond that Mileva had a lovely voice.

Einstein had not married Mileva yet when he received this letter, although he wanted to very badly. She was his *Lieber Dockerl,* his little doll. He had not found a way to support her. He had just run an advertisement offering his services as a tutor. He wrote Mileva back. *Now you can make observations,* he said. *I would like once to produce a Lieserl myself, it must be so interesting. She certainly can cry already, but to laugh she'll learn later. Therein lies a profound truth.* On the bottom of the letter he sketched his tiny room in Bern. It resembled the drawings he would do later to accompany his gedanken, or thought experiments, how he would visualize physics in various situations. In this sketch, he labeled the features of his room with letters. Big B for the bed. Little b for a picture. He was trying to figure a way to fit Mileva and Lieserl into his room. He was inviting Mileva to help.

In June he will get a job with the Swiss Civil Service. A year after Lieserl's birth, the following January, he will marry Mileva. Years later when friends ask him why he married her, his answer will vary. Duty, he will say sometimes. Sometimes he will say that he has never been able to remember why.

A third letter arrived the next day. *Mein liebes bose Schatzerl!* it said. *Lieserl misses her Papa. She is so clever, Albert. You will never believe it. Today she pulled a book from the shelf. She opened it, sucking hard on her fingers. Can Lieserl read? I asked her, joking. But she pointed to the letter*

E, making such a sweet, sticky fingerprint beside it on the page. E, she said. You will be so proud of her. Already she runs and laughs. I had not realized how quickly they grow up. When are you coming to us? Mileva.

His room was too small. The dust collected over his books and danced in the light with Brownian-like movements. Einstein went out for a walk. The sun shone, both from above him and also as reflected off the new snowbanks in blinding white sheets. Icicles shrank visibly at the roots until they cracked, falling from the eaves like knives into the soft snow beneath them. Mileva is a book, like you, his mother had told him. What you need is a housekeeper. What you need is a wife.

Einstein met Mileva in Zurich at the Swiss Federal Polytechnical School. Entrance to the school required the passage of a stiff examination. Einstein himself failed the General Knowledge section on his first try. She will ruin your life, Einstein's mother said. No decent family will have her. Don't sleep with her. If she gets a child, you'll be in a pretty mess.

It is not clear what Einstein's mother's objection to Mileva was. She was unhappy that Mileva had scholastic ambitions and then more unhappy when Mileva failed her final examinations twice and could not get her diploma.

Five days passed before Einstein heard from Mileva again. *Mein Liebster. If she has not climbed onto the kitchen table, then she is sliding down the banisters, Mileva complained. I must watch her every minute. I have tried to take her picture for you as you asked, but she will never hold still long enough. Until you come to her, you must be content with my descriptions. Her hair is dark and thick and curly. She has the eyes of a doe. Already she has outgrown all the clothes I had for her and is in proper dresses with aprons. Papa, papa, papa, she says. It is her favorite word. Yes, I tell her. Papa is coming. I teach her to throw kisses. I teach her to clap her hands. Papa is coming, she says, kissing and clapping. Papa loves his Lieserl.*

Einstein loved his Lieserl, whom he had not met. He loved Mileva. He loved science. He loved music. He solved scientific puzzles while playing the violin. He thought of Lieserl while solving scientific puzzles. Love is faith. Science is faith. Einstein could see that his faith was being tested.

Science feels like art, Einstein will say later, but it is not. Art involves inspiration and experience, but experience is a hindrance to the scientist. He has only a few years in which to invent, with his innocence, a whole new world that he must live in for the rest of his life. Einstein would not always be such a young man. Einstein did not have all the time in the world.

Einstein waited for the next letter in the tiny cell of his room. The letters were making him unhappy. He did not want to receive another so he would not leave, even for an instant, and risk delaying it. He had not responded to Mileva's last letters. He did not know how. He made himself a cup of tea and stirred it, noticing that the tea leaves gathered in the center of the cup bottom, but not about the circumference. He reached for a fresh piece of paper and filled it with drawings of rivers, not the rivers of a landscape but the narrow, twisting rivers of a map.

The letter came only a few hours later in the afternoon post, sliding like a tongue through the slit in the door. Einstein caught it as it fell. *Was treibst Du, Schatzerl?* it began. *Your little Lieserl has been asked to a party and looks like a princess tonight. Her dress is long and white like a bride's. I have made her hair curl by wrapping it over my fingers. She wears a violet sash and violet ribbons. She is dancing with my father in the hallway, her feet on my father's feet, her head only slightly higher than his waist. They are waltzing. All the boys will want to dance with you, my father said to her, but she frowned. I am not interested in boys, she answered. Nowhere is there a boy I could love like I love my papa.*

In 1899 Einstein began writing to Mileva about the electrodynamics of moving bodies, which became the title of his 1905 paper on relativity. In 1902 Einstein loved Mileva, but in 1916 in a letter to his friend Besso, Einstein will write that he would have become mentally and physically exhausted if he had not been able to keep his wife at a distance, out of sight and out of hearing. You cannot know, he will tell his friends, the tricks a woman such as my wife will play.

Mileva, trained as a physicist herself, though without a diploma, will complain that she has never understood the special theory of relativity. She will blame Einstein who, she will say, has never taken the time to explain it properly to her.

Einstein wrote a question along the twisting line of one river. Where are you? He chose another river for a second question. How are you moving? He extended the end of the second river around many curves until it finally merged with the first.

Liebes Schatzerl! the next letter said. It came four posts later. *She is a lovely young lady. If you could only see her, your breath would catch in your throat. Hair like silk. Eyes like stars. She sends her love. Tell my darling Papa, she says, that I will always be his little Lieserl, always running out into the snowy garden, caped in red, to draw angels. Suddenly I am frightened for her, Albert. She is as fragile as a snowflake. Have I kept her too sheltered? What does she know of men? If only you had been here to advise me.* Even after its long journey, the letter smelled of roses.

Two friends came for dinner that night to Einstein's little apartment. One was a philosophy student named Solovine. One was a mathematician named Habicht. The three together called themselves the Olympia Academy, making fun of the serious bent of their minds.

Einstein made a simple dinner of fried fish and bought wine. They sat about the table, drinking and picking the last pieces of fish out with their fingers until nothing remained on their plates but the spines with the smaller bones attached like the naked branches of winter trees. The friends argued loudly about music. Solovine's favorite composer was Beethoven, whose music, Einstein suddenly began to shout, was emotionally overcharged, especially in c minor. Einstein's favorite composer was Mozart. Beethoven created his beautiful music, but Mozart discovered it, Einstein said. Beethoven wrote the music of the human heart, but Mozart transcribed the music of God. There is a perfection in the humanless world which will draw Einstein all his life. It is an irony that his greatest achievement will be to add the relativity of men to the objective Newtonian science of angels.

He did not tell his friends about his daughter. The wind outside was a choir without a voice. All his life, Einstein will say later, all his life he tried to free himself from the chains of the *merely personal*. Einstein rarely spoke of his personal life. Such absolute silence suggests that he escaped from it easily or, alternatively, that its hold was so powerful he was afraid to ever say it aloud. One or both or neither of these things must be true.

Let us talk about the merely personal. The information received through the five senses is appallingly approximate. Take sight, the sense on which humans depend most. Man sees only a few of all the colors in the world. It is as if a curtain has been drawn over a large window, but not drawn so that it fully meets in the middle. The small gap at the center represents the visual abilities of man.

A cat hears sounds that men must only imagine. It has an upper range of 100,000 cycles per second as opposed to the 35,000 to 45,000 a dog can hear or the 20,000 which marks the upper range for men. A cat can distinguish between two sounds made only eighteen inches apart when the cat, itself, is at a distance of sixty feet.

Some insects can identify members of their own species by smell at distances nearing a mile.

A blindfolded man holding his nose cannot distinguish the taste of an apple from an onion.

Of course man fumbles about the world, perceiving nothing, understanding nothing. In a whole universe, man has been shut into one small room. Of course, Einstein could not begin to know what was happening to his daughter or to Mileva, deprived even of these blundering senses. The postman was careless with Mileva's next letter. He failed to push it properly through the door slit so that it fell back into the snow, where it lay all night and was ice the next morning. Einstein picked the envelope up on his front step. It was so cold it burnt his fingers. He breathed on it until he could open it.

Another quiet evening with your Lieserl. We read until late and then sat together, talking. She asked me many questions tonight about you, hoping, I think, to hear something, anything, I had not yet told her. But she settled, sweetly, for the old stories all over again. She got out the little drawing you sent just after her birth; have I told you how she treasures it? When she was a child she used to point to it. Papa sits here, she would say, pointing. Papa sleeps here. I wished that I could gather her into my lap again. It would have been so silly, Albert. You must picture her with her legs longer than mine and new gray in the black of her hair. Was I silly to want it, Schatzerl? Shouldn't someone have warned me that I wouldn't be able to hold her forever?

Einstein set the letter back down into the snow. He had not yet found it. He had never had such a beautiful daughter. Perhaps he had not even met Mileva yet, Mileva whom he still loved, but who was not sound and who liked to play tricks.

Perhaps, he thought, he will find the letter in the spring when the snow melts. If the ink has not run, if he can still read it, then he will decide what to do. Then he will have to decide. It began to snow again. Einstein went back into his room for his umbrella. The snow covered the letter. He could not even see the letter under the snow when he stepped over it on his way to the bakery. He did not want to go home where no letter was hidden by the door. He was twenty-two years old and he stood outside the bakery, eating his bread, reading a book in the tiny world he had made under his umbrella in the snow.

Several years later, after Einstein has married Mileva and neither ever mentions Lieserl, after they have had two sons, a colleague will describe a visit to Einstein's apartment. The door will be open so that the newly washed floor can dry. Mileva will be hanging dripping laundry in the hall. Einstein will rock a baby's bassinet with one hand and hold a book open with the other. The stove will smoke. How does he bear it? the colleague will ask in a letter which still survives, a letter anyone can read. That genius. How can he bear it?

The answer is that he could not. He will try for many years and then Einstein will leave Mileva and his sons, sending back to them the money he wins along with the Nobel Prize.

When the afternoon post came, the postman had found the letter again and included it with the new mail. So there were two letters, only one had been already opened.

Einstein put the new letter aside. He put it under his papers. He hid it in his bookcase. He retrieved it and opened it clumsily because his hands were shaking. He had known this letter was coming, known it perhaps with Lieserl's first tooth, certainly with her first dance. It was exactly what he had expected, worse than he could have imagined. *She is as bald as ice and as mad as a goddess, my Albert,* Mileva wrote. *But she is still my Lieber Dockerl, my little doll. She clings to me, crying if I must leave her for a minute. Mama, Mama! Such madness in her eyes and her mouth. She is toothless and soils herself. She is my baby. And yours, Schatzerl. Nowhere is there a boy I could love like my Papa, she says, lisping again just the way she did when she was little. She has left a message for you. It is a message from the dead. You will get what you really want, Papa, she said. I have gone to get it for you. Remember that it comes from me. She was weeping and biting her hands until they bled. Her eyes were white with madness. She said something else. The brighter the light, the more shadows, my Papa, she said. My darling Papa. My poor Papa. You will see.*

The room was too small. Einstein went outside where his breath rose in a cloud from his mouth, tangible, as if he were breathing on glass. He imagined writing on the surface of a mirror, drawing one of his gedanken with his finger into his own breath. He imagined a valentine. *Lieserl,* he wrote across it. He loved Lieserl. He cut the word in half, down the *s*, with the stroke of his nail. The two halves of the heart opened and closed, beating against each other, faster and faster, like wings, until they split apart and vanished from his mind.

Bright Morning

Jeffrey Ford

IF THERE IS one thing that distinguishes my books from others it is the fact that in the review blurbs that fill the back cover and the page that precedes the title page inside, the name of "Kafka" appears no less than eight times. Kafka, Kafkaesque, Kafka-like, in the tradition of Kafka. Certainly more Kafka than one man deserves – a veritable embarrassment of Kafka riches. My novels are fantasy/adventure stories with a modicum of metaphysical whim-wham that some find to be insightful and others have termed "overcooked navel gazing." Granted, there are no elves or dragons or knights or wizards in these books, but they are still fantasies, none the less. I mean, if you have a flying head, a town with a panopticon that floats in the clouds, a monster that sucks the essence out of hapless victims through their ears, what the hell else can you call it? At first glance, it would seem that any writer would be proud to have their work compared to that of one of the twentieth century's greatest writers, but upon closer inspection it becomes evident that in today's publishing world, when a novel does not fit a prescribed format, it immediately becomes labeled as Kafkaesque. The hope is, of course, that this will be interpreted as meaning exotic, when, in fact, it translates to the book-buying public as obscure. Kafka has become a place, a condition, a boundary to which it is perceived only the pretentious are drawn and only total lunatics will cross.

As my neighbor, a retired New York City transit cop, told me while holding up one of my novels and pointing to the cover, "Ya know, this Kafka shit isn't doing you any favors. All I know is he wrote a book about a guy who turned into a bug. What the fuck?"

"He's a great writer," I said in defense of my blurbs.

"Tom Clancy's a great writer, Kafka's a putz."

What could I say? We had another beer and talked about the snow.

Don't get me wrong, I like what I've read of Kafka's work. The fact that Gregor Samsa wakes from a night of troubling dreams to find that he has been transformed into a giant cockroach is, to my mind, certain proof of existential genius firing with all six pistons. Likewise, a guy whose profession is sitting in a cage and starving himself while crowds throng around and stare, is classic everyman discourse. But my characters run a lot. There's not a lot of running in Kafka. His writing is unfettered by parenthetical phrases, introductory clauses, and adjectival exuberance. My sentences sometimes have the quality of Arabic penmanship, looping and knotting, like some kind of Sufi script meant to describe one of the names given to God in order to avoid using his real name. In my plots, I'm usually milking some nostalgic sentiment resulting from unrequited love or working toward a punch line of revelation like an old Borscht Belt comic with a warmed-over variation of the one about the traveling salesman, whereas Kafka seems like he's trying to curtly elicit that ambiguous perplexity that makes every man an island, every woman an isthmus, every child a continental divide.

My friend, Quigley, once described the book *The Autobiography of a Yogi* as "a miracle a page," and that's the kind of effect I'm striving for, building up marvels until it just becomes a big, hallucinogenic shitstorm of wonder. Admittedly, sometimes the forecast runs into a low-pressure system and all I get is a brown drizzle; such are the vicissitudes of the fiction writer. On the other hand, Kafka typically employed only one really weird element in each story (a giant mole, a machine that inscribes a person's crime upon their back) that he treats as if it were as mundane as putting your shoes on. Then he inspects it six ways to Sunday, turning the microscope on it, playing out the string, until it eventually curls up into a question mark at the end. There are exceptions, "A Country Doctor," for instance, that swing from start to finish. I don't claim to be anywhere near as accomplished a writer as Kafka. If I was on a stage with Senator Lloyd Benson and he said to me, "I knew Kafka, and you, sir, are no Franz Kafka," I'd be the first to agree with him. I'd shake his damn hand.

I often wondered what Kafka would make of it, his name bandied about, a secret metaphor for *fringe* and *destination remainder bin*. For a while it really concerned me, and I would have dreams where I'd wake in the middle of the night to find Kafka standing at the foot of my bed, looking particularly grim, half in, half out of the shaft of light coming in from the hallway. He'd appear dressed in a funeral suit with a thin tie. His hair would be slicked back and his narrow head would taper inevitably to the sharp point of his chin. Ninety pounds soaking wet, but there would be this kind of almost visible tension surrounding him.

"Hey, Franz," I'd say, and get out of bed to shake his hand, "I swear it wasn't my idea."

Then he'd get a look on his face like he was trying to pass the Great Wall of China and haul off and kick me right in the nuts. From his stories, you might get the idea that he was some quiet little dormouse, a weary, put upon pencil pusher in an insurance office, but, I'm telling you, in those nightmares of mine, he really ripped it up.

Do you think Kafka would be the type of restless spirit to reach out from beyond the pale? On the one hand, he was so unassuming that he asked Max Brod to burn all of his remaining manuscripts when he died, while on the other hand, he wrote an awful lot about judgment. He might not have as much to do with my writing as some people say, but me and Franz, we go way back, and I'm here to warn you: the less you have to do with him the better. His pen still works.

It was 1972 and I was a junior at West Islip High School on Long Island. I was a quiet kid and didn't have a lot of friends. I liked to smoke pot and I liked to read, so sometimes I'd combine those two pleasures. I'd blow a joint in the woods behind the public library and then go inside and sit and read or just wander through the stacks, looking through different books. In those days, I was a big science fiction fan, and I remember reading *Martians, Go Home, Adam Link, Space Paw, Time Out of Joint*, etc. In our library, the science fiction books had a rocket ship on the plastic cover down at the bottom of the spine. There were three shelves of these books and I read just about all of them.

One afternoon at the library, I ran into Bettleman, a guy in my class. Bettleman was dwarfish short with a dismorphic body – long chimp arms, a sort of hunchback, and a pouch of loose skin under his chin. He was also a certified math genius and had the glasses to prove it – big mothers with lenses thick as ice cubes. I came around a corner of the stacks and there he was: long, beautiful woman fingers paging through a book he held only inches from his face. He looked up, took a moment to focus, and said hello. I said hi and asked him what he was reading.

"Karl Marx," he said.

I was impressed. I knew Marx was the father of Communism, an ideology that was still viewed as tantamount to Satanism in those days when the chill of the cold war could make you dive under a desk at the sound of the noon fire siren.

"Cool," I said.

"What have you got there?" he asked me.

I showed him what I was carrying. I think it was *Dandelion Wine* by Bradbury. He pushed those weighty glasses up on his nose and studied it. Then he closed his eyes for a moment, as if remembering, and when he opened them proceeded to rattle off the entire plot.

"Sounds like it would have been a good one," I said.

"Yeah," he told me, "it's alright – fantasy with a dash of horror meets the child of Kerouac and Norman Rockwell."

"Cool," I said, not knowing what he was talking about, but recalling him correcting the math teacher on more than one occasion.

"Hey, you want to read something really wild?" he asked.

"Sure," I said uncertainly, thinking about the first time I was dared into smoking weed.

He closed the book in his hand and walked to the end of the aisle. I followed. Three rows down, he turned left and went to the middle of one of the stacks. Moving his face up close to the titles, he scanned along the shelf as if sniffing out the volume he was searching for. Finally, he stepped back, reached out a hand and grabbed a thick, violet-covered book from the shelf. When he turned to me he was wearing a wide smile that allowed me to see through his strange exterior for a split second and genuinely like him.

"There's a story in here called "'The Metamorphosis,'" he said. "Just check it out." Then he laughed loudly and that pouch of flesh that caused the other kids to call him *The Sultan of Chin* jiggled like the math teacher's flabby ass when she ran out of the room, embarrassed at her own ignorance in the face of Bettleman's genius.

He handed it over to me and I said, "Thanks." I turned the book over to see the title and the author and when I looked up again, he was gone. So I spent that sunny winter afternoon in the West Islip public library reading Kafka for the first time. That story was profound in a way I couldn't put my finger on. I knew it was heavy, but its burden was invisible like that of gravity. There was also sadness in it that surfaced as an unfounded self-pity, and underneath it all, somehow, a sense of humor that elicited in me that feeling of trying not to laugh in church. I checked the book out, took it home, and read every word of every tale and parable between its covers.

It took me a long time to read them all, because after ingesting one, I'd chew on it, so to speak, for a week or two, attempting to identify the flavor of its absurdity, what spices were used to give it just that special tang of nightmare. Occasionally, I'd see Bettleman at school and run a title by him. He'd usually push his glasses up with the middle finger of his left hand, give me a one-line review of the story in question, and before scuttling hastily off to square the circle, he'd let loose one of his Sultanic laughs.

"Hey, Bettleman, 'The Imperial Message,'" I'd say.

"Waiting for a sign from God that validates the industrious drudgery of existence while God waits for a sign to validate his own industrious drudgery."

"Yo, Bettleman, what do you say to 'The Hunter Gracchus'?"

"Siamese twins, altogether stuck. One judgment, one guilt, both unable to see their likeness in the other which would allow them to transcend."

"Yeah, whatever."

Then in the first days of spring, I came across a story in the Kafka collection that I will admit did have a true influence on me. Wedged in between "The Bucket Rider" and "Josephine the Singer, or the Mouse Folk," I discovered an unusual piece that was longer than the parables but not quite the length of a full-fledged story. Its title was "Bright Morning," and for all intents and purposes it seemed to me to be a vampire story. I read it at least a half dozen times one weekend and afterward couldn't get its imagery out of my mind.

I went to school Wednesday, hoping to find Bettleman and get his cryptic lowdown on it. Bettleman, it seems, had his own plans for that day. He sailed into the parking lot in the rusty Palomino, three-door Buick Special, he'd inherited from his old man and didn't stop to park, but drove right up on the curb in front of the entrance to the school. When he got out of the car, he was wearing a Richard Nixon Halloween mask and lugging a huge basket of rotten apples. He climbed up on top of the hood of his car and then, laughing like a maniac behind the frozen leer of Tricky Dick, started beaning students and teachers with the apples.

Although Bettleman's genetic mishap of a body prevented him from being taken seriously by the sports coaches at school, those primate arms of his were famous for having the ability to hurl a baseball at Nolan Ryan speeds. He broke a few windows, nailed Romona Vacavage in the right breast, splattered a soft brown one against the back of Jake Harwood's head, and pelted the principal, No Foolin' Doolin', so badly he slipped and fell on the sauce that had dripped off his suit, dislocating his back. Everyone ran. Even the tough kids with the leather jackets and straight-pin-and-India-ink tattoos of the word SHIT on their ankles were afraid of his weirdness. Finally the cops came and took Bettleman away. He didn't come back to school. In the years that followed, I never heard anything more about him but half expected to discover his name on the Nobel lists when I'd run across them in the newspaper.

The Kafka collection didn't get returned to the library until the end of the summer. I'd run up a twenty-dollar late fee on it. In those days, twenty dollars was a lot of money, and my old man was pissed when he got the letter from the librarian. He paid for my book truancy, but I had to work off the debt by raking and burning leaves in the fall. Under those cold, violet-gray skies of autumn, the same color as the cover of the book, I gathered and incinerated the detritus of August and considered Kafka and the plight of Bettleman. I realized the last thing that poor bastard needed was Kafka, and so when my labor was completed I put the two of them out of my mind by picking up a book by Richard Brautigan, *In Watermelon Sugar*. The light confection of that work gave me a rush that set me off on another course of reading, like "The Hunter Gracchus," in frustrated search of transcendence.

The hunt lasted throughout most of my senior year of high school, taking me through the wilds of Burroughs and Kerouac and Miller, but near the end, when I was about to graduate, I found myself one day in the stacks of the public library, returning to the absurd son of Prague for a hit of real reality before I went forth into the world. To my disbelief and utter annoyance, I discovered the book had been removed as soon as I had returned it at the end of the summer and never brought back. In its place was a brand new edition of *The Collected Stories of Franz Kafka*. I paged through the crisp, clean book, but could not find the story "Bright Morning." The incompleteness of this new volume put me off and I just said, "The hell with it!" – much to the dismay of the librarian who was within easy earshot of my epithet.

I went to college and dropped out after one semester, bought a boat and became a clammer on the Great South Bay for two years. All this time, I continued to read, and occasionally Kafka would rear his thin head in a mention by another author. These were usually allusions to "The Metamorphosis," which seemed the only work of his anyone ever mentioned.

One night on Grass Island out in the middle of the bay, a place where clammers congregated on Saturday nights to party, I ran into a guy I knew from having spoken to him previously, when I'd be out of the boat, with a tube and basket, scratch raking in the flats. If we were both working the same area, he'd take a break around three o'clock when the south wind would invariably pick up, and wander over to talk with me for a while. He was also a big reader, but usually his tastes ran to massive tomes like the Gulag books, Mann's *The Magic Mountain*, Proust.

That night on Grass Island, in the gaze of Orion, with a warm breeze from off the mainland carrying the sounds of Lela Ritz getting laid by Shab Wellow down in the lean-to, we were sitting atop the highest dune, passing a joint back and forth, when the conversation turned to Kafka. This guy from the bay, I don't remember his name, said to me, "I really like that story, 'Bright Morning.'"

"You know it?" I said.

"Sure." Then he proceeded to tell the entire thing just as I remembered it.

"Do you have a copy of it?" I asked.

"Sure," he said. "I'll bring it out with me some day for you."

The discussion ended then because we spotted Lela in the moonlight, naked, down by the water's edge. Lela Ritz had the kind of body that made Kafka seem like a bad joke.

In the days that followed, I'd see that guy from time to time who owned the book, and he'd always promise to remember to bring it out with him. But at the end of summer, I'd heard that he'd raked up the beringed left hand of a woman who, in June, had been knocked out of a boat, caught in the propeller, and supposedly never found. The buyer at the dock told me the guy gave up clamming because of it. That fall I returned to college and never saw him again.

I went to school for my undergraduate and masters degrees at SUNY Binghamton, in upstate New York, where I studied literature and writing. It was there that I met and worked with novelist John Gardner, who did what he could to help me become a fiction writer. His knowledge of literature, short stories, and novels was encyclopedic, and when I was feeling mischievous, I would try to stump him by giving him merely a snippet of the plot of, what I considered to be, some obscure piece I had recently discovered: Bunin's "The Elaghin Affair," Blackwood's "The Willows," Collier's *His Monkey Wife*. He never failed to get them, and could discuss their merits as if he had read them but an hour earlier. Twice in conversation I brought up the story by Kafka, and on the first occasion he said he knew it. He even posited some interpretation of it, which I can't now remember. The second time I brought it up, in relation to having just read his own story, "Julius Caesar and the Werewolf," he shook his head and said that there was no such piece by Kafka, but if there was, with that title, it would have to be a horror story.

What was even more interesting concerning the story during my college years, and really the last time I would hear anything about it for a very long time, was an incident that transpired at the motel where I lived with my future wife, Lynn. The Colony Motor Inn on Vestal Parkway had a string of single rooms that sat up on a hill, separated from the main complex of the establishment. These rooms were reserved for students, long-time borders, and the illegal Chinese immigrants who worked at the motel restaurant, The House of Yu. It was a dreary setting in which to live on a daily basis – a heaping helping of

Susquehanna gothic. The maintenance guy had one arm and an eye patch, and two of the maids were mother and daughter *and* sisters, whose *other* job was slaughtering livestock.

Lynn was in nursing school and I was doing my literary thing, spending a lot of time writing crappy stories with pencil in composition books. The room we had was really small, and the bathroom doubled as a kitchen. We had a toaster oven in there on the counter, and we cooked our own food to save money. In the mornings I'd shave onto ketchup-puddled plates in the sink. The toilet was also the garbage disposal, and it wasn't unusual for me to try to hit the floating macaroni when I'd take a piss. That bathroom had no door, just a sliding curtain. Right next to the entrance, we kept an old Victrola, and if one of us was going in to do our thing, for a little privacy, we'd spin the "Blue Danube Waltz" at top volume.

When the weather was good and the temperature was still warm, we'd walk, in the mornings, down to the motel pool at the bottom of the hill. Lynn would swim laps, and I would sit at one of the tables and write. If we went early enough, we usually had the spot to ourselves.

On one typical day, while Lynn was swimming and I was hunched over my notebook, smoking a butt, trying to end a story without having the protagonist commit suicide or kill someone, I heard the little gate in the chain-link fence surrounding the pool open and close. I looked up and there stood this skinny guy dressed in a sailor's uniform, white gob hat tilted at an angle on his shaved head, holding a Polaroid camera. He said hello to me and I nodded, hoping he wasn't going to strike up a conversation. I watched his Adam's apple bob and his eyes shift back and forth and immediately knew I was in for it.

He came over and sat at my table and asked to bum a smoke. I gave him one and he lifted my matches and lit it.

"That your girl?" he asked, nodding toward Lynn as she passed by in the water.

"Yeah," I said.

"Nice hair," he said and grinned.

"You on leave?" I asked.

"Yeah," he said. "Got a big bunch of money and a week or so off. Bought this new camera."

"Where you staying?"

"Up on the hill," he said.

"They usually don't rent the places up on the hill unless you're staying for a long time," I said.

"I made it worth their while," he told me, flicking his ashes. "I wanted to be able to see everything."

I was going to tell him I had to get back to work, but just then Lynn got out of the pool and came over to the table.

"Ma'am," he said, and got up to let her sit down.

"Well, have a nice day," I told him, but he just stood there looking at us.

I was going to tell him to shove off, but finally he spoke. "Would you two like me to take your portrait?" he asked.

I shook my head no, and Lynn said yes. She made me get up and drew me over to stand against the chain-link fence with the Vestal Parkway in the background.

The sailor brought the Polaroid up to his eye and focused on us. "Let's have a kiss, now," he said, that Adam's apple bobbing like mad.

I put my arm around Lynn and kissed her for a long time. In the middle of it, I heard the pool gate open and close and saw the sailor running away across the parking lot toward the hill.

"Creep," said Lynn.

Then I read her my new story and she dozed off while sitting straight up.

That night, as we lay in bed on the verge of sleep, I heard a loud bang come from somewhere down the row of rooms. I knew immediately that it was a gunshot, so I grabbed Lynn and rolled onto the floor. We lay there breathing heavily from fear and she said to me, "What the hell was that?"

"Maybe Mrs. West's hair finally exploded," I said, and we laughed. Mrs. West was the maids' supervisor. She had a seven-story beehive hairdo she was constantly jabbing a sharpened pencil into to scratch her scalp.

About ten minutes later, I heard the police car pull up and saw the flashing red light through the split in the curtains. I hastily put my shorts and sneakers on and went outside. In the parking lot, I met Chester, our next-door neighbor.

"What's up?" I asked him.

He was shaking his head, and in that Horse Heads, New York, upstate drawl, said, "Man, that's gonna ruin my night."

"What happened?" I said.

"Admiral asshole blew his brains out down there in 268."

"The sailor?" I asked.

"Yeah, I heard the shot and went down to his room. The door was open part way. Jeez, there was a piece of jaw bone stuck in the wall and blood everywhere."

Two more cop cars pulled up and when the officers got out they told us to go back inside.

After I told Lynn what had happened, she didn't get much sleep, and I tossed and turned all night, falling in and out of dreams about that goofy sailor. I just remember one dream that showed him in a small boat in shark-infested waters, while in the background a volcano erupted. I awoke in the morning to the sound of someone knocking on the door; Lynn had already left for her shift at the hospital. I got out of bed and dressed quickly.

It was Mrs. West. She wanted to know if I wanted the room cleaned. I said no, and quickly shut the door. A second later, she knocked again. I opened up and she stood there, holding something out toward me. It was then that I noticed that her hands and arms were red.

"They had me here early this morning, cleaning the death," she said. "I found this amidst the fragments." She handed me what I took to be a square of paper. Only when I touched it did I realize it was a photograph – the picture of Lynn and me kissing, while all around us splattered flecks of red filled the sky like a blood rain.

That afternoon, I had the photo setting on the table next to where I was writing a story about a sailor who goes to a motel to commit suicide and falls in love with the maid. Every time I'd look up, there would be that picture. It gave me the willies, so eventually I turned it over. I hadn't noticed before, but written on the back in very light pencil were these words: *He stepped out into the bright morning and quietly evaporated...* I recognized it immediately as part of the last line of Kafka's elusive story. That photograph is still in my possession, at the bottom of a cardboard box, out in the garage or in the basement, I think.

Just when the synchronistic influence of that text seemed to be reaching a crescendo of revelation, it suddenly turned its back on me, and I heard nothing, saw nothing about it for years and years, until I could easily ignore my awareness of it. The avalanche of books and stories I read in the interim helped to bury it. Occasionally, when I was in a bookstore and would see some new edition of Kafka's stories, I would pick it up and scan the table of contents, hoping not to see the piece listed. I was never disappointed. So many other writers came to call, and their personalities and plots and words became ever so much more important to me than his.

Slowly, and I mean slowly, the stories I wrote became less and less crappy and I actually had a few published by small-press magazines. The amount of time it took me to become a professional writer is reminiscent of the adage of a hundred apes in a room with a hundred typewriters, at work for a hundred years, eventually producing Hamlet's soliloquy. From there, it was only a matter of more time, and then one day I sold a novel to a major publisher. I could less believe it than the fact that the sailor had known "Bright Morning" well enough to quote it. When my novel was published, the blurb the publisher had written for it mentioned Kafka twice. At the time, I wasn't thinking about all the incidents that had been related to the Kafka story; they seemed light-years away. All I thought was, "Hey, Kafka, it's better than Harold Robbins." Or was it? The book didn't sell all too well, but it got great reviews. Nearly every critic who wrote about it mentioned Kafka at least once, so that when the paperback edition came out, it carried all of the critical blurbs and the back cover was lousy with Kafka.

In four years, I'd published three fantasy novels, a dozen short stories also in the genre, and a couple of essays. The first novel won a World Fantasy Award, the first two were *New York Times* Notable Books of the Year; one of the stories was nominated for a Nebula Award, another appeared in *The Year's Best Fantasy and Horror*; there were starred reviews in *Publishers Weekly*, *Kirkus Review*, the *Library Journal*; three stories in one year made *Locus* magazine's recommended reading list. I tell you all of this not by way of bragging, because there are others who have written more and garnered more accolades, there are others who *are* better writers, but for me it was a goad. I thought that to stop for a moment would mean to let all I had worked for slip away. At the same time, I was teaching five classes, over a hundred writing students a semester, at a community college an hour and a half from my house, and I had two young sons with whom I needed to spend a considerable amount of time. So I slept no more than four hours a night, smoked like mad when writing, and lived on coffee and fast food. It was an insane period and it made me into a bloated zombie. Finally I hit an impasse and needed a break. I couldn't think of one more damn fantasy story I could write. And as it turned out, what stood between me and a vacation from it all was just one more story.

Like a good soldier, I had finished off all the pieces I had promised to editors, and then all that remained was a final story for a collection of short fiction I really wanted to see published. When the project had first presented itself I had, with reckless largesse, promised to write a piece for it that would appear nowhere else. My imagination, though, was emptier than the dark, abandoned railway station I visited every night in my dreams. In four years, I'd done just about everything *I* could possibly do in fantasy. I told you already about the flying head, the cloud city with attendant panopticon, but there was much more – demons, werewolves, men turned to blue stone, evil geniuses, postmodern fairy-tale kingdoms, giant moths, zombies, parodies of fantasy heroes, an interview with Jules Verne, big bug-aliens enamored of old movies, Lovecraft rip-offs, experimental hoodoo, and that's just for starters. The only fantasy I could now conceive of was sneaking in a nap on Saturday afternoon after the kids' basketball games and before the obligatory family trip to the mall. I was burnt crisper than a fucking cinder on the whole genre.

The deadline for the story collection was fast approaching, and all I had was a computer file full of aborted beginnings, all of which stunk. I was determined not to fail, so when the college I taught at closed for spring break and I had a week to write, I said to myself, "Okay, get a grip." Driving home the last night before the vacation, I had a brainstorm. Why reinvent the wheel? I decided I'd just take one of the old fantasy tropes and work it over a little – a ready-made theme. Upon arriving home, I went to my office and scanned the bookshelves for an idea, and that's when I came upon a book I had bought at a yard sale back when Lynn and I were still in college. I'd almost forgotten I'd owned the thing – an anthology of vampire stories. That night and the next day, I read almost all of the pieces in it. There was one great one, "Viy," by Gogol, that reinvigorated my imagination somewhat. As I sat down to compose, though, a memory of Kafka's "Bright Morning" came floating up from where it had been buried, and breached the surface of my consciousness like the hand of that corpse at the end of the movie *Deliverance*. I thought to myself, "If I could just read that story one more time, that would be all I'd need to get something good going."

Sitting back in my office chair, I lit a cigarette and tried to remember what I could about the piece. Bettleman and his apples; Gregor Samsa lying in bed on his back, six legs kicking; the sailor's hat; the worm-filled wound of the kid in "The Country Doctor" – all passed through my mind as I called forth the intricacies of the plot. Then I imagined I was back in the West Islip public library on a winter's afternoon, reading from the violet book. Ironically enough, it dawned on me that "Bright Morning" centered around a frustrated writer, F. – a young dilettante of literary aspirations, who feels he has all of the aesthetic acumen and an overabundance of style, but, for the life of him, cannot conceive of a story worth telling. It is intimated that the reason for this is that he has spent all of his days with his nose in a book and is devoid of life experience. There is more to it than that, but that's how the story begins. Somewhere along the way he hooks up with this haggard, bent, old man, a Mr. Krouch, whose face is "a mask of wrinkles." I think they meet at night on the bridge leading into the small town that is the story's setting. The old man offers his life story to the young writer in exchange for half the proceeds if the book is ever published. The writer is reticent, but then the old man tells him just one short tale about when he was a sailor, shipwrecked on a volcanic island in the Indian Ocean, south of Sumatra, and encountered a species of ferocious blue lizards as big as horses.

The young man is soon convinced he will become famous writing the old man's biography. Each night, after their initial meeting, the old man comes to F.'s house. On the first night, as a gift to the writer, the old man gives him, from his tattered traveling bag, a beautiful silver pen and a bottle of ink. The pen feels to the young man as if it has been specifically designed for his grip; the ink flows so smoothly it is as if the words are writing themselves. Then the old man begins to recount his long, long life, a chapter a night. In that wonderfully compressed style Kafka utilizes in his parables, he gives selections from the annals of Krouch. Years tending the tombs of monarchs in some distant eastern land, a career as a silhouette puppeteer in Venice, a love affair with a young woman half his age – these are a few I remember, but there were more and they were packed into the space of two or three modestly sized paragraphs.

At the end of each session, Krouch leaves just before dawn, and F. falls asleep to the sounds of bird song that accompanies the coming of the sun. The work has an exhausting effect upon him and he sleeps all day, until nightfall, when he wakes only an hour before the old man returns. The gist of the story is that, as the auto/biography grows, F. slowly wastes away while Krouch gets younger and more robust. It becomes evident as to how the old man has managed to fit so many adventures into one lifetime, and the reader begins to suspect that there have been other unsuspecting writers before F. By the time the young man places the last period at the end of the last sentence – a sentence about him placing the last period at the end of the last sentence – he is no longer young but has become shriveled and wrinkled and bent.

"Now off to the publisher with it," Krouch commands and gives a hearty laugh. F. can barely stand. He struggles to lift the pile of pages and then, knees creaking, altogether out of breath, he shuffles toward the door. "Allow me," says Krouch, and he leaps from his chair and moves to open the door.

It takes much of his remaining energy, but F. manages to whisper, "Thank you."

He steps out into the bright morning and quietly evaporates, the pages scattering on the wind like frightened ghosts.

It is one thing to vaguely remember a story by Kafka and quite another to actually have the book before you. There is that wonderfully idiosyncratic style: the meek authorial voice, the infrequent but strategically placed metaphor, a businesslike approach to plot, and those deceptive devices of craft, nearly as invisible as chameleons that make all the difference to the beauty of the imagery and the impact of the tale. I knew I needed that story in my hands, before my eyes, and that I would obsess over it, unable to write a word of my own, until I had it.

I enlisted the help of my older son, and together we scoured the Internet, made phone calls to antiquarian and used book shops as far away as Delaware; the western wilds of Pennsylvania; Watertown, New York, up by the Canadian border. Nothing. Most had never heard of the story. One or two said they had a very vague recollection of the violet edition but couldn't swear to it. The used book sites on the Web were crammed with copies of the more recent Schocken edition and some even had expensive originals from Europe, but none of the abstracts described the book I was searching for. I drove around one day to all the used bookstores I knew of and, in one, found the violet-covered book. I was so frantic to have my hands on it, I could hardly control my shaking as I forked over the $23.50 to the clerk. When I got out to my car and opened it, I discovered that it was really a copy of *Mansfield Park* by Jane Austen. I was livid, and on my way home as I drove across an overpass, I opened the window and tossed the damned thing out into the traffic below.

My week off was nearing its end and I was no closer to Kafka's story, no closer to my own. The frustration of the search, my fear of impending failure, finally peaked and then dropped me into a sullen depression. On Saturday afternoon, between basketball and the mall, I received a phone call. Lynn answered it and handed me the receiver.

"Hello?" I said.

"I understand you are looking for the violet Kafka," said the voice.

I was rendered speechless for a moment. Then I blurted out, "Who is this?"

"Am I correct?" asked the voice.

"Yes," I said. "The one with the story..."

"'Bright Morning,'" he said. "I know the story. Very rare."

"Supposedly it doesn't exist," I said.

"That's interesting," he said, "because I have a copy of the volume before me as we speak. I'm selling it."

"How much?" I inquired, too eagerly.

"That depends. I have another client also interested in it. I thought perhaps you and he would like to bid for it. The bidding starts at eighty dollars."

"That seems rather low," I said.

"Come tonight," he said, and gave me a set of directions to his place. The location was not too far from me, directly south, in the Pine Barrens. "Eight o'clock, and if you should decide to participate, I will explain more than the price."

"What is your name?" I asked.

He hung up on me.

I was altogether elated that this voice had validated the existence of the story, but at the same time I found the enigmatic nature of the call somewhat disturbing. The starting price was suspiciously low, and the fact that the caller would not give a name didn't bode well. I envisioned myself going to some darkened address and being murdered for my wallet. This alternated with a vision of discovering an abandoned railway station in the woods where the angry Kafka of my dreams would be waiting to bite my neck. At seven o'clock, though, I drove down to the money machine in town, withdrew five hundred dollars (more than I could afford), and then headed south on route 206.

My fears were allayed when, at precisely 7:45, I pulled up in front of a beautifully well-kept Victorian of near-mansion dimensions on a well-lit street in the small town of Pendricksburg. I parked in the long driveway and went to the front door. After knocking twice, a young woman answered and let me in.

"Mr. Deryn will see you. Come this way," she said.

I followed. The place was stunning, the woodwork and floors so highly polished, it was like walking through a hall of mirrors. There were chandeliers and Persian carpets and fresh flowers, like something from one of my wife's magazines. Classical music drifted through the house at low volume, and I felt as though I was touring a museum. We came to a door at the back of the house; she opened it and invited me to step inside.

The first thing I noticed were the bookcases lining the walls, and then I gave a start because sitting behind the desk was what I at first took to be a human frog, smoking a cigar. When I concentrated on the form it resolved its goggle eyes, hunch, and pouch into nothing more than an oddly put together person. But what was even more incredible, it was Bettleman. He was older, with a few days' growth of beard, but it was most definitely him. Not rising, he waved his hand to indicate one of the chairs facing his desk.

"Have a seat," he said.

I walked slowly forward and sat down, experiencing a twinge of déjà vu.

"Bettleman," I said.

He looked quizzically at me, and said, "I'm sorry, you must be mistaken. My name is John Deryn." Then he laughed and the pouch undulated, convincing me even more completely it was him.

"You're not Christian Bettleman?" I asked.

He shook his head and smiled.

I quickly decided that if he wanted to play-act it was fine by me; I was there for the book. "The violet Kafka," I said, "can I see it?"

He reached into a drawer in front of him and pulled out a thick volume. There it was, in seemingly pristine condition. Paging through it with his long graceful fingers, he stopped somewhere in the middle and then turned it around and laid it on the desk facing me. "Bright Morning," he said.

"My God," I said. "I was beginning to think it had merely been a delusion."

"Yes, I know exactly what you mean," he said. "I've spent a good portion of my life tracing the history of that story."

"Is it a forgery?" I asked.

"Nothing of the sort, though, in its style it is slightly unusual for Kafka, somewhat reminiscent of Hoffmann."

"What can you tell me about it?" I asked.

"I will try to keep this brief," he said, drawing on his cigar. His exposition came forth wrapped in a cloud. "In the words of Kafka's Czech translator and one-time girl friend, Milena Jesenska, Kafka 'saw the world as full of invisible demons, who tear apart and destroy defenseless people.' She was not speaking metaphorically. From the now expurgated portions of his diaries, we know that he had a recurring dream of one of these demons, who appeared to him as an old man named Krouch. Of course, knowing Kafka's problems with his father, the idea of it being an 'old man' admittedly has its psychological explanations.

"In 1921, when Franz was in the advanced stages of tuberculosis, he attests to his friend Max Brod, as evidenced in Brod's own journal, that this demon, Krouch, is responsible for his inability to write. He feels that every day that goes by that he does not write a new story, the disease becomes stronger. Being the mystic that he is, Kafka devises a plan to exorcise the demon. What he does is utterly brilliant. He writes a story about the vampiric Krouch, ensnaring him in the words. At the end of the tale, F., the figure who represents Kafka, disappears from the story back to the freedom of this reality. One believes upon reading it that the young writer is, himself, trapped, but not so, or at least not in Kafka's mind. This is all documented in a letter to the writer, Franz Werfel. Hence the non-indicative but promising title of the story, 'Bright Morning.'

"It becomes clear to Kafka soon after that, although he has effectively imprisoned the demon in the words of the story, Krouch still has a limited effect on him when the text is in close proximity. So what does he do? In 1922, at his last meeting with Milena, in a small town known as Gmünd, on the Czech-Austrian border, he gives her all of his diaries. Along with those notebooks and papers is 'Bright Morning.' How effective Kafka's plan was is open to question. He only lived until 1924, but consider the further life of poor Milena, now the owner of the possessed text: she nearly dies in childbirth; has an accident which causes a fracture of her right knee, leaving her partially crippled for the rest of her life; becomes addicted to morphine; is arrested in Prague for her pro-Jewish writing, and is sent, in 1940, to Ravensbrück concentration camp in Germany where she suffers poor health. A kidney is removed when it gets infected, and not too long afterward the other fails and she dies.

"Here, 'Bright Morning' seems to quietly evaporate for some time until 1959 when the Pearfield Publishing Company of Commack, Long Island, New York, publishes an edition of Kafka containing the story. At the time, the building that houses the small publisher catches fire, burns to the ground, and of the few boxes of books salvaged, one contains twelve copies of the violet edition. Six of them went to local libraries, six to the local USO."

"And so, it carries a curse," I said.

"That is for you to decide," he said. "I acquired this copy years ago from a shellfish harvester who worked the waters of the Great South Bay. He might have said something about a curse, but then people who make a living on the water are usually somewhat superstitious. Another might laugh at the idea. I will admit that I have had my own brushes with fate."

"You cannot deny that you are Bettleman," I said.

He stared at me and a moment later the young woman was at the door. "Mr. Deryn," she said, "the other gentleman is here. Shall I show him in?"

"Please do," he told her. When she left to carry out his wish, he turned back to me. "I have chosen to only tell you the story behind the story," said Deryn. "For old time's sake." Then he smiled and with his middle finger pushed his glasses up the bridge of his nose. By now, the cigar was a smoldering stub, and he laid it in the ashtray to extinguish itself.

I was, of course, about to make some inane exclamation, like "I knew it!" or "Did you think I could be so easily fooled?" but the other bidder entered the room and saved Bettleman and myself from the embarrassment.

Not only had I recognized Bettleman, but with one glance, I also knew my competition in the auction. I should have been more startled by the synchronicity of it all, but the events that preceded this fresh twist allowed me to take it in stride. He was another writer, working also in my genre, a big, oafish lout by the name of Jeffrey Ford. You might have heard of him, perhaps not. A few years ago he wrote a book called *The Physiognomy* which, by some bizarre fluke, perhaps the judges were drugged, won a World Fantasy Award. I'd met and spoken to him before on more than one occasion at various conferences. What the critics and editors saw in his work, I'll never know. Our brief careers, so far, had been very similar, but there was no question I was the better writer. He leaned over the desk and shook Bettleman's hand, and then he turned to me and, before sitting, nodded but said nothing.

Bettleman, in his affable Mr. Deryn guise, allowed Ford to inspect the book. Once that was finished, the bidding was to begin. Ford wanted to know why it was to start as low as eighty dollars, and Deryn told him only, "I have my reasons."

I had been slightly put off the book by what I had been told, but once Ford started making offers, I couldn't resist. I felt like if he were to win, he would be walking out of there with my best plot ever. We two cheapskate writers upped the ante at ten dollars an increment, but even at this laggardly pace, we were soon in the three-hundred-dollar range. Bettleman was smiling like Toad of Toad Hall, and when he stopped for a moment to light another cigar, my gaze moved around the room. Off in the corner, behind his desk, wedged into a row of books, I saw a large bell jar, and floating in it, a delicate, beringed hand. For some reason the sight of this horrid curio jogged my memory, and I recalled, perhaps for the first time something that I had wanted to suppress, that the woman who had fallen off the boat back in the bay and was lost those many years ago, was not a woman at all but a young girl, Lela Ritz. For a brief moment, I saw her naked in the moonlight. Then Bettleman croaked and the bidding resumed.

As we pushed onward, nickel-and-diming our way toward my magic number, five hundred dollars, I could not dismiss all of the tragedy left in the wake of "Bright Morning." I thought about Lynn and the kids and how I might be jeopardizing their safety or maybe their lives by this foolish desire. Still my mouth worked, and I let the prices roll off my tongue. By the time I took control of myself and fully awoke to the auction, my counterpart had just proposed four hundred and fifty.

He added, "And I mean it. It is my absolute final offer."

Ford now turned to look at me, and I knew I had him. By a good fifty dollars, I had him.

"Your apple," said Bettleman, looking at me from behind his thick lenses. Now he was no longer smiling, but I saw a look of sadness on his face.

That long second of my decision was like a year scratch raking for hands in the pool of the Colony Inn. The truth was, I didn't know what I wanted. I felt the margins of the story closing in, the sentences wrapping around my wrists and ankles, the dots of i's swimming in schools across my field of vision. Experiencing now the full weight of my weariness, I finally said, "I pass."

"Very well," said Bettleman.

I rose and shook his hand, nodded to Ford, who was already reaching into the pocket of his two-sizes-too-small jeans to retrieve a crumpled wad of money, and left.

Call me a superstitious fool if you like, I might very well deserve the appellation. As it turned out, I never finished the promised story, and the publisher of the collection, Golden Gryphon Press, retracted their offer to do the book. Of all the ironies, they filled my spot on their list with a collection by Ford. He even wrote, especially for it, a story entitled "Bright Morning," making no attempt to disguise his swiping of Kafka's material. One of the early, prepublication critics of the book wrote in a scathing review, "Ford is Kafka's monkey." Nothing could have interested me less. I returned to my teaching job. I spent time with my family. I slept at night with no frightening visits from old or thin demons. In the mornings I woke to the beauty of the sun.

A year later, after retiring from my brief career as a fantasy writer, I read that Ford, two weeks prior to the publication of his collection, had given a reading from his manuscript of "Bright Morning" at one of the conventions (I believe in Massachusetts). According to the article, which appeared in a reputable newspaper, after receiving a modest round of applause from the six or seven people in attendance, he stepped out into the bright morning and quietly evaporated, the pages scattering on the wind like frightened ghosts.

I Want My 20th-Century Schizoid Art, III

I THINK there's so much ambivalence around the category of *slipstream* because *strange* or *genre-straddling* are inadequate descriptions of what's going on. Namely, what often gets called slipstream in the genre seems to me to be work that is not just situated in, or straddling genre. It's work that's also about the genre in a certain way. I hate talk of postmodern self-awareness because I'm a postmodern baby, and I think the term implies a callousness that is rarely present, but I think there is an astounding amount of play with conventions going on, especially in the work of younger writers. In a quest to make something new, something distinctive, people are writing stories that on one level or another want you to notice the ideas they're shuffling together, the conventions and traditions that are colliding.

When it's only that shuffling, it tends towards the merely strange or even boring, because the only pleasure is intellectual, to see the pieces moving. And in general, because it's a technique about play, and about the joy of playing, it often rings false when it takes itself too seriously. But when the juxtapositions become emotional, when the joy and the trickiness come through, it rocks my socks.

MEGHAN MCCARRON, 9:32 PM, WEDNESDAY, MAY 4, 2005

I think from the very start, the pun underlying the term collapsed the meaning of *slipstream* into something defined not so much by content, process or effect but by a spatial metaphor of location – as a sort of stream of fiction that sheers off at the margins of the mainstream and picks up and drags along whatever genre material is in its path. Arguably, you can invert the imagery and see slipstream as the stream of fiction that sheers off at the margins of the *genre* and picks up and drags along whatever *mainstream* material is in its path – but either way the idea of a turbulent area between mainstream and genre is at the heart of the term as an image. And in terms of overlap and perturbation, Horton's idea of "taking a familiar context and disturbing it with SFnal/fantastical intrusions" makes perfect sense to me.

I've grown uncomfortable with the term *slipstream* over the years because I think such definitions-by-location, while they fairly accurately place this form of fabulation in a metaphoric interzone where mainstream and genre tropes and techniques commingle, tend to do so from the genre ghetto perspective. Sterling recognizes this limitation when he says, "nobody calls mainstream 'mainstream' except for us skiffy trolls." I suspect the end result is actually to focus slipstream simply on a subset of SF/F writers and readers who frequent that interzone and know it like the back of their hands; they understand what the term is labeling even if they don't agree on the fuzzy boundaries. The subset of *non-SF/F* writers and readers who might also belong in that metaphoric zone, meanwhile, don't think in terms of mainstream, so this definition-by-location is sort of like giving them meaningless directions – pointing them towards an area between somewhere they're wary of and somewhere they've never heard of. The theoretical interzone thus ends up, practically speaking, as just another wee corner of the ghetto, a café where the cool kids hang out and play their music, which those who live uptown know next to nothing of.

I actually wonder if that's part of the reason behind Sterling's obvious reticence with regard to the term.

HAL DUNCAN, 4:43 AM, THURSDAY, MAY 5, 2005

Wow. Seventeen years of arguing about what slipstream is? How the time flies!

From my POV, Horton's definition of slipstream – genre intrusion on normal events – is a clear example of the genre attempting to digest slipstream into itself, which, by definition, it simply has to do.

Because SF/F/H defines itself by the presence of magical elements or fantastic occurrences, genre readers and critics discovering these traits in other literatures by definition have to view these literatures as extensions or examples of genre fiction. Magic *can't* occur in writing outside the genre without it also being considered *of* the genre. That, or the genre must contemplate the irrelevance of itself – and that's too damn scary. Consequently, seventeen years after Sterling defined slipstream as being beyond genre, you get *definition creep,* where a magical lit like slipstream is now defined in genre terms.

Can magic intrude on a realist story without it being a genre story? Personally, I think so, and Sterling, even if he was being ironic, seems to suggest at least that much in his definition of slipstream.

BARTH ANDERSON, 6:18 AM, THURSDAY, MAY 5, 2005

Meghan, thank you for pulling away from the between genres business and pointing toward the "playing with tropes such that the reader's awareness that you are playing, but playing seriously, is part of the story's joy." Yes. And, of course, as well as being a fun thing we like to do hereabouts, that is a very old thing. John Gardner, I believe in *On Becoming a Novelist,* calls it "deconstructionist" fiction and gives the example of Shakespeare. Shakespeare was all about the deconstruction – a ghost/revenge tragedy with an indecisive hero? A sonnet making fun of sonnets – "My mistress' eyes are nothing like the sun." The earliest one I can think of is the Book of Jonah, a comic send-up of the prophetic tradition. And you point, rightly, to the sweet spot, where this isn't mere satire, but where it can actually heighten rather than deflate the emotional effect.

Hannah, I don't know what Sterling meant by the essay, but I read it as a provocative wake-up call to SF. I reckon he did think there was something going on in the works he cited. I surely don't think he meant to start a new genre, and he must be appalled that the stupid name *slipstream* has stuck.

Hal, you pinpoint precisely what's wrong with the term *slipstream* and why we'd really be best off abandoning it. Probably it has too much momentum, alas. But I'd much rather regard someone saying the word *slipstream* as a jumping-off point for a discussion. I'd like to steer them away from the skiffy-troll conversation about the mainstream mixing with genre and towards the idea of the irrealist literary traditions and their intrusions into the popular literatures of the fantastic.

No genres really have if-and-only-if borders, other than very contrived ones. More useful than looking at recipes is looking at sources of reader pleasure, and the constructions and moves that mediate and produce it. And looking at traditions, which are not if-and-only-if boxes, but things that are handed down, changed by each pair of hands.

Don't believe me? Try to come up with an if-and-if border for Southern Gothic fiction.

BENJAMIN ROSENBAUM, 8:04 AM, THURSDAY, MAY 5, 2005

Biographical Notes to "A Discourse on the Nature of Causality, with Air-Planes," by Benjamin Rosenbaum

Benjamin Rosenbaum

ON MY RETURN from PlausFab-Wisconsin (a delightful festival of art and inquiry, which styles itself "the World's Only Gynarchist Plausible-Fable Assembly") aboard the *P.R.G.B. Śri George Bernard Shaw*, I happened to share a compartment with Prem Ramasson, Raja of Outermost Thule, and his consort, a dour but beautiful woman whose name I did not know.

Two great blond barbarians bearing the livery of Outermost Thule (an elephant astride an iceberg and a volcano) stood in the hallway outside, armed with sabres and needlethrowers. Politely they asked if they might frisk me, then allowed me in. They ignored the short dagger at my belt – presumably accounting their liege's skill at arms more than sufficient to equal mine.

I took my place on the embroidered divan. "Good evening," I said.

The Raja flashed me a white-toothed smile and inclined his head. His consort pulled a wisp of blue veil across her lips, and looked out the porthole.

I took my notebook, pen, and inkwell from my valise, set the inkwell into the port provided in the white pine table set in the wall, and slid aside the strings that bound the notebook. The inkwell lit with a faint blue glow.

The Raja was shuffling through a Wisdom Deck, pausing to look at the incandescent faces of the cards, then up at me. "You are the plausible-fabulist, Benjamin Rosenbaum," he said at length.

I bowed stiffly. "A pen name, of course," I said.

"Taken from *The Scarlet Pimpernel?*" he asked, cocking one eyebrow curiously.

"My lord is very quick," I said mildly.

The Raja laughed, indicating the Wisdom Deck with a wave. "He isn't the most heroic or sympathetic character in that book, however."

"Indeed not, my lord," I said with polite restraint. "The name is chosen ironically. As a sort of challenge to myself, if you will. Bearing the name of a notorious anti-Hebraic caricature, I must needs be all the prouder and more subtle in my own literary endeavors."

"You are a Karaite, then?" he asked.

"I am an Israelite, at any rate," I said. "If not an orthodox follower of my people's traditional religion of despair."

The prince's eyes glittered with interest, so – despite my reservations – I explained my researches into the Rabbinical Heresy which had briefly flourished in Palestine and Babylon at the time of Ashoka, and its lost Talmud.

"Fascinating," said the Raja. "Do you return now to your family?"

"I am altogether without attachments, my liege," I said, my face darkening with shame.

Excusing myself, I delved once again into my writing, pausing now and then to let my Wisdom Ants scurry from the inkwell to taste the ink with their antennae, committing it to memory for later editing. At PlausFab-Wisconsin, I had received an assignment – to construct a plausible-fable of a world without zeppelins – and I was trying to imagine some alternative air conveyance for my characters when the Prince spoke again.

"I am an enthusiast for plausible-fables myself," he said. "I enjoyed your 'Droplet' greatly."

"Thank you, Your Highness."

"Are you writing such a grand extrapolation now?"

"I am trying my hand at a shadow history," I said.

The prince laughed gleefully. His consort had nestled herself against the bulkhead and fallen asleep, the blue gauze of her veil obscuring her features. "I adore shadow history," he said.

"Most shadow history proceeds with the logic of dream, full of odd echoes and distorted resonances of our world," I said. "I am experimenting with a new form, in which a single point of divergence in history leads to a new causal chain of events, and thus a different present."

"But the world *is* a dream," he said excitedly. "Your idea smacks of Democritan materialism – as if the events of the world were produced purely by linear cause and effect, the simplest of the Five Forms of causality."

"Indeed," I said.

"How fanciful!" he cried.

I was about to turn again to my work, but the prince clapped his hands thrice. From his baggage, a birdlike Wisdom Servant unfolded itself and stepped agilely onto the floor. Fully unfolded, it was three cubits tall, with a trapezoidal head and incandescent blue eyes. It took a silver tea service from an alcove in the wall, set the tray on the table between us, and began to pour.

"Wake up, Sarasvati Sitasdottir," the prince said to his consort, stroking her shoulder. "We are celebrating."

The servitor placed a steaming teacup before me. I capped my pen and shooed my Ants back into their inkwell, though one crawled stubbornly towards the tea. "What are we celebrating?" I asked.

"You shall come with me to Outermost Thule," he said. "It is a magical place – all fire and ice, except where it is greensward and sheep. Home once of epic heroes, Rama's cousins." His consort took a sleepy sip of her tea. "I have need of a plausible-fabulist. You can write the history of the Thule that might have been, to inspire and quell my restive subjects."

"Why me, Your Highness? I am hardly a fabulist of great renown. Perhaps I could help you contact someone more suitable – Karen Despair Robinson, say, or Howi Qomr Faukota."

"Nonsense," laughed the Raja, "for I have met none of them by chance in an airship compartment."

"But yet...," I said, discomfited.

"You speak again like a materialist! This is why the East, once it was awakened, was able to conquer the West – we understand how to read the dream that the world is. Come, no more fuss."

I lifted my teacup. The stray Wisdom Ant was crawling along its rim;

I positioned my forefinger before her, that she might climb onto it.

Just then there was a scuffle at the door, and Prem Ramasson set his teacup down and rose. He said something admonitory in the harsh Nordic tongue of his adopted country, something I imagined to mean "come now, boys, let the conductor through." The scuffle ceased, and the Raja slid the door of the compartment open, one hand on the hilt of his sword. There was the sharp hiss of a needlethrower, and he staggered backward, collapsing into the arms of his consort, who cried out.

The thin and angular Wisdom Servant plucked the dart from its master's neck. "Poison," it said, its voice a tangle of flutelike harmonics. "The assassin will possess its antidote."

Sarasvati Sitasdottir began to scream.

It is true that I had not accepted Prem Ramasson's offer of employment – indeed, that he had not seemed to find it necessary to actually ask. It is true also that I am a man of letters, neither spy nor bodyguard. It is furthermore true that I was unarmed, save for the ceremonial dagger at my belt, which had thus far seen employment only in the slicing of bread, cheese, and tomatoes.

Thus, the fact that I leapt through the doorway, over the fallen bodies of the prince's bodyguard, and pursued the fleeting form of the assassin down the long and curving corridor, cannot be reckoned as a habitual or forthright action. Nor, in truth, was it a considered one. In Śri Grigory Guptanovich Karthaganov's typology of action and motive, it must be accounted an impulsive-transformative action: the unreflective moment which changes forever the path of events.

Causes buzz around any such moment like bees around a hive, returning with pollen and information, exiting with hunger and ambition. The assassin's strike was the proximate cause. The prince's kind manner, his enthusiasm for plausible-fables (and my work in particular), his apparent sympathy for my people, the dark eyes of his consort – all these were inciting causes.

The psychological cause, surely, can be found in this name that I have chosen – "Benjamin Rosenbaum" – the fat and cowardly merchant of *The Scarlet Pimpernel* who is beaten and raises no hand to defend himself; just as we, deprived of our Temple, found refuge in endless, beautiful elegies of despair, turning our backs on the Rabbis and their dreams of a new beginning. I have always seethed against this passivity. Perhaps, then, I was waiting – my whole life – for such a chance at rash and violent action.

The figure – clothed head to toe in a dull gray that matched the airship's hull – raced ahead of me down the deserted corridor, and descended through a maintenance hatch set in the floor. I reached it, and paused for breath, thankful my enthusiasm for the favorite sport of my continent – the exalted Lacrosse – had prepared me somewhat for the chase. I did not imagine, though, that I could overpower an armed and trained assassin. Yet, the weave of the world had brought me here – surely to some purpose. How could I do aught but follow?

Beyond the proximate, inciting, and psychological causes, there are the more fundamental causes of an action. These address how the action embeds itself into the weave of the world, like a nettle in cloth. They rely on cosmology and epistemology. If the world is a dream, what caused the dreamer to dream that I chased the assassin? If the world is a lesson, what should this action teach? If the world is a gift, a wild and mindless rush of beauty, riven of logic or purpose – as it sometimes seems – still, seen from above, it must possess its own aesthetic harmony. The spectacle, then, of a ludicrously named practitioner of a half-despised art (bastard child of literature and philosophy), clumsily attempting the role of hero on the middledeck of the *P.R.G.B. Śri George Bernard Shaw*, must surely have some part in the pattern – chord or discord, tragic or comic.

Hesitantly, I poked my head down through the hatch. Beneath, a spiral staircase descended through a workroom cluttered with tools. I could hear the faint hum of engines nearby. There, in the canvas of the outer hull, between the Shaw's great aluminum ribs, a door to the sky was open.

From a workbench, I took and donned an airman's vest, supple leather gloves, and a visored mask, to shield me somewhat from the assassin's needle. I leaned my head out the door.

A brisk wind whipped across the skin of the ship. I took a tether from a nearby anchor and hooked it to my vest. The assassin was untethered. He crawled along a line of handholds and footholds set in the airship's gently curving surface. Many cubits beyond him, a small and brightly colored glider clung to the *Shaw* – like a dragonfly splayed upon a watermelon.

It was the first time I had seen a glider put to any utilitarian purpose – espionage rather than sport – and immediately I was seized by the longing to return to my notebook. Gliders! In a world without dirigibles, my heroes could travel in some kind of immense, powered gliders! Of course, they would be forced to land whenever winds were unfavorable.

Or would they? I recalled that my purpose was not to repaint our world anew, but to speculate rigorously according to Democritan logic. Each new cause could lead to some wholly new effect, causing in turn some unimagined consequence. Given different economic incentives, then, and with no overriding, higher pattern to dictate the results, who knew what advances a glider-based science of aeronautics might achieve? Exhilarating speculation!

I glanced down, and the sight below wrenched me from my reverie:

The immense panoply of the Great Lakes –

– their dark green wave-wrinkled water –

– the paler green and tawny yellow fingers of land reaching in among them –

– puffs of cloud gamboling in the bulk of air between –

– and beyond, the vault of sky presiding over the Frankish and Athapascan Moeity.

It was a long way down.

"Malkat Ha-Shamayim," I murmured aloud. "What am I doing?"

"I was wondering that myself," said a high and glittering timbrel of chords and discords by my ear. It was the recalcitrant, tea-seeking Wisdom Ant, now perched on my shoulder.

"Well," I said crossly, "do you have any suggestions?"

"My sisters have tasted the neurotoxin coursing the through the prince's blood," the Ant said. "We do not recognize it. His servant has kept him alive so far, but an antidote is beyond us." She gestured towards the fleeing villain with one delicate antenna. "The assassin will likely carry an antidote to his venom. If you can place me on his body, I can find it. I will then transmit the recipe to my sisters through the Brahmanic field. Perhaps they can formulate a close analogue in our inkwell."

"It is a chance," I agreed. "But the assassin is half-way to his craft."

"True," said the Ant pensively.

"I have an idea for getting there," I said. "But you will have to do the math."

The tether which bound me to the *Shaw* was fastened high above us. I crawled upwards and away from the glider, to a point the Ant calculated. The handholds ceased, but I improvised with the letters of the airship's name, raised in decoration from its side.

From the top of an *R*, I leapt into the air – struck with my heels against the resilient canvas – and rebounded, sailing outwards, snapping the tether taut.

The Ant took shelter in my collar as the air roared around us. We described a long arc, swinging past the surprised assassin to the brightly colored glider; I was able to seize its aluminum frame.

I hooked my feet onto its seat, and hung there, my heart racing. The glider creaked, but held.

"Disembark," I panted to the Ant. "When the assassin gains the craft, you can search him."

"Her," said the Ant, crawling down my shoulder. "She has removed her mask, and in our passing I was able to observe her striking resemblance to Sarasvati Sitasdottir, the prince's consort. She is clearly her sister."

I glanced at the assassin. Her long black hair now whipped in the wind. She was braced against the airship's hull with one hand and one foot; with the other hand she had drawn her needlethrower.

"That is interesting information," I said as the Ant crawled off my hand and onto the glider. "Good luck."

"Good-bye," said the Ant.

A needle whizzed by my cheek. I released the glider and swung once more into the cerulean sphere.

Once again I passed the killer, covering my face with my leather gloves – a dart glanced off my visor. Once again I swung beyond the door to the maintenance room and towards the hull.

Predictably, however, my momentum was insufficient to attain it. I described a few more dizzying swings of decreasing arc-length until I hung, nauseous, terrified, and gently swaying, at the end of the tether, amidst the sky.

To discourage further needles, I protected the back of my head with my arms, and faced downwards. That is when I noticed the pirate ship.

It was sleek and narrow and black, designed for maneuverability. Like the *Shaw*, it had a battery of sails for fair winds, and propellers in an aft assemblage. But the *Shaw* traveled in a predictable course and carried a fixed set of coiled tensors, whose millions of microsprings gradually relaxed to produce its motive force. The new craft spouted clouds of white steam; carrying its own generatory, it could rewind its tensor batteries while underway. And, unlike the *Shaw*, it was armed – a cruel array of arbalest-harpoons was mounted at either side. It carried its sails below, sporting at its top two razor-sharp saw-ridges with which it could gut recalcitrant prey.

All this would have been enough to recognize the craft as a pirate – but it displayed the universal device of pirates as well, that parody of the Yin-Yang: all Yang, declaring allegiance to imbalance. In a yellow circle, two round black dots stared like unblinking demonic eyes; beneath, a black semicircle leered with empty, ravenous bonhomie.

I dared a glance upward in time to see the glider launch from the *Shaw*'s side. Whoever the mysterious assassin-sister was, whatever her purpose (political symbolism? personal revenge? dynastic ambition? anarchic mania?), she was a fantastic glider pilot. She gained the air with a single, supple back-flip, twirled the glider once, then hung deftly in the sky, considering.

Most people, surely, would have wondered at the meaning of a pirate and an assassin showing up together – what resonance, what symbolism, what hortatory or aesthetic purpose did the world intend thereby? But my mind was still with my thought-experiment.

Imagine there are no causes but mechanical ones – that the world is nothing but a chain of dominoes! Every plausible-fabulist spends long hours teasing apart fictional plots, imagining consequences, conjuring and discarding the antecedents of desired events. We dirty our hands daily with the simplest and grubbiest of the Five Forms. Now I tried to reason thus about life.

Were the pirate and the assassin in league? It seemed unlikely. If the assassin intended to trigger political upheaval and turmoil, pirates surely spoiled the attempt. A death at the hands of pirates while traveling in a foreign land is not the stuff of which revolutions are made. If the intent was merely to kill Ramasson, surely one or the other would suffice.

Yet was I to credit chance, then, with the intrusion of two violent enemies, in the same hour, into my hitherto tranquil existence?

Absurd! Yet the idea had an odd attractiveness. If the world was a blind machine, surely such clumsy coincidences would be common!

The assassin saw the pirate ship; yet, with an admirable consistency, she seemed resolved to finish what she had started. She came for me.

I drew my dagger from its sheath. Perhaps, at first, I had some wild idea of throwing it, or parrying her needles, though I had the skill for neither.

She advanced to a point some fifteen cubits away; from there, her spring-fired darts had more than enough power to pierce my clothing. I could see her face now, a choleric, wild-eyed homunculus of her phlegmatic sister's.

The smooth black canvas of the pirate ship was now thirty cubits below me.

The assassin banked her glider's wings against the wind, hanging like a kite. She let go its aluminum frame with her right hand, and drew her needlethrower.

Summoning all my strength, I struck the tether that held me with my dagger's blade.

My strength, as it happened, was extremely insufficient. The tether twanged like a harp-string, but was otherwise unharmed, and the dagger was knocked from my grasp by the recoil.

The assassin burst out laughing, and covered her eyes. Feeling foolish, I seized the tether in one hand and unhooked it from my vest with the other.

Then I let go.

Since that time, I have on various occasions enumerated to myself, with a mixture of wonder and chagrin, the various ways I might have died. I might have snapped my neck, or, landing on my stomach, folded in a V and broken my spine like a twig. If I had struck one of the craft's aluminum ribs, I should certainly have shattered bones.

What is chance? Is it best to liken it to the whim of some being of another scale or scope, the dreamer of our dream? Or to regard the world as having an inherent pattern, mirroring itself at every stage and scale?

Or *could* our world arise, as Democritus held, willy-nilly, of the couplings and patternings of endless dumb particulates?

While hanging from the *Shaw,* I had decided that the protagonist of my Democritan shadow-history (should I live to write it) would be a man of letters, a dabbler in philosophy like myself, who lived in an advanced society committed to philosophical materialism. I relished the apparent paradox – an intelligent man, in a sophisticated nation, forced to account for all events purely within the rubric of overt mechanical causation!

Yet those who today, complacently, regard the materialist hypothesis as dead – pointing to the Brahmanic field and its Wisdom Creatures, to the predictive successes, from weather to history, of the Theory of Five Causal Forms – forget that the question is, at bottom, axiomatic. The materialist hypothesis – the primacy of Matter over Mind – is undisprovable. What successes might some other science, in another history, have built, upon its bulwark?

So I cannot say – I cannot say! – if it is meaningful or meaningless, the fact that I struck the pirate vessel's resilient canvas with my legs and buttocks, was flung upwards again, to bounce and roll until I fetched up against the wall of the airship's dorsal razor-weapon. I cannot say if some Preserver spared my life through will, if some Pattern needed me for the skein it wove – or if a patternless and unforetellable Chance spared me all unknowing.

There was a small closed hatchway in the razor-spine nearby, whose overhanging ridge provided some protection against my adversary. Bruised and weary, groping inchoately among theories of chance and purpose, I scrambled for it as the boarding gongs and klaxons began.

The *Shaw* knew it could neither outrun nor outfight the swift and dangerous corsair – it idled above me, awaiting rapine. The brigand's longboats launched – lean and maneuverable black dirigibles the size of killer whales, with parties of armed sky-bandits clinging to their sides.

The glider turned and dove, a blur of gold and crimson and verdant blue disappearing over the pirate zeppelin's side – abandoning our duel, I imagined, for some redoubt many leagues below us.

Oddly, I was sad to see her go. True, I had known from her only wanton violence; she had almost killed me; I crouched battered, terrified, and nauseous on the summit of a pirate corsair on her account; and the kind Raja, my almost-employer, might be dead. Yet I felt our relations had reached as yet no satisfactory conclusion.

It is said that we fabulists live two lives at once. First we live as others do: seeking to feed and clothe ourselves, earn the respect and affection of our fellows, fly from danger, entertain and satiate ourselves on the things of this world. But then, too, we live a second life, pawing through the moments of the first, even as they happen, like a market-woman of the bazaar sifting trash for treasures. Every agony we endure, we also hold up to the light with great excitement, expecting it will be of use; every simple joy, we regard with a critical eye, wondering how it could be changed, honed, tightened, to fit inside a fable's walls.

The hatch was locked. I removed my mask and visor and lay on the canvas, basking in the afternoon sun, hoping my Ants had met success in their apothecary and saved the Prince; watching the pirate longboats sack the unresisting *P.R.G.B. Śri George Bernard Shaw* and return laden with valuables and – perhaps – hostages.

I was beginning to wonder if they would ever notice me – if, perhaps, I should signal them – when the cacophony of gongs and klaxons resumed – louder, insistent, angry – and the longboats raced back down to anchor beneath the pirate ship.

Curious, I found a ladder set in the razor-ridge's metal wall that led to a lookout platform.

A war-city was emerging from a cloudbank some leagues away.

I had never seen any work of man so vast. Fully twelve great dirigible hulls, each dwarfing the *Shaw,* were bound together in a constellation of outbuildings and propeller assemblies. Near the center, a great plume of white steam rose from a pillar; a Heart-of-the-Sun reactor, where the dull yellow ore called Yama's-flesh is driven to realize enlightenment through the ministrations of Wisdom-Sadhus.

There was a spyglass set in the railing by my side; I peered through, scanning the features of this new apparition.

None of the squabbling statelets of my continent could muster such a vessel, certainly; and only the Powers – Cathay, Gabon, the Aryan Raj – could afford to fly one so far afield, though the Khmer and Malay might have the capacity to build them.

There is little enough to choose between the meddling Powers, though Gabon makes the most pretense of investing in its colonies and believing in its supposed civilizing mission. This craft, though, was clearly Hindu. Every cubit of its surface was bedecked with a façade of cytoceramic statuary – couples coupling in five thousand erotic poses; theromorphic gods gesturing to soothe or menace; Rama in his chariot; heroes riddled with arrows and fighting on; saints undergoing martyrdom. In one corner, I spotted the Israelite avatar of Vishnu, hanging on his cross between Shiva and Ganesh.

Then I felt rough hands on my shoulders.

Five pirates had emerged from the hatch, cutlasses drawn. Their dress was motley and ragged, their features varied – Sikh, Xhosan, Baltic, Frankish, and Aztec, I surmised. None of us spoke as they led me through the rat's maze of catwalks and ladders set between the ship's inner and outer hulls.

I was queasy and light-headed with bruises, hunger, and the aftermath of rash and strenuous action; it seemed odd indeed that the day before, I had been celebrating and debating with the plausible-fabulists gathered at Wisconsin. I recalled that there had been a fancy-dress ball there, with a pirate theme; and the images of yesterday's festive, well-groomed pirates of fancy interleaved with those of today's grim and unwashed captors on the long climb down to the bridge.

The bridge was in the gondola that hung beneath the pirate airship's bulk, forwards of the rigging. It was crowded with lean and dangerous men in pantaloons, sarongs and leather trousers. They consulted paper charts and the liquid, glowing forms swimming in Wisdom Tanks, spoke through bronze tubes set in the walls, barked orders to cabin boys who raced away across the airship's webwork of spars.

At the great window that occupied the whole of the forward wall, watching the clouds part as we plunged into them, stood the captain.

I had suspected whose ship this might be upon seeing it; now I was sure. A giant of a man, dressed in buckskin and adorned with feathers, his braided red hair and bristling beard proclaimed him the scion of those who had fled the destruction of Viking Eire to settle on the banks of the Father-of-Waters.

This ship, then, was the *Hiawatha MacCool,* and this the man who terrorized commerce from the shores of Lake Erie to the border of Texas.

"Chippewa Melko," I said.

He turned, raising an eyebrow.

"Found him sightseeing on the starboard spine," one of my captors said.

"Indeed?" said Melko. "Did you fall off the *Shaw*?"

"I jumped, after a fashion," I said. "The reason thereof is a tale that strains my own credibility, although I lived it."

Sadly, this quip was lost on Melko, as he was distracted by some pressing bit of martial business.

We were descending at a precipitous rate; the water of Lake Erie loomed before us, filling the window. Individual whitecaps were discernable upon its surface.

When I glanced away from the window, the bridge had darkened – every Wisdom Tank was gray and lifeless.

"You there! Spy!" Melko barked. I noted with discomfiture that he addressed me. "Why would they disrupt our communications?"

"What?" I said.

The pirate captain gestured at the muddy tanks. "The Aryan war-city – they've disrupted the Brahmanic field with some damned device. They mean to cripple us, I suppose – ships like theirs are dependent on it. Won't work. But how do they expect to get their hostages back alive if they refuse to parley?"

"Perhaps they mean to board and take them," I offered.

"We'll see about that," he said grimly. "Listen up, boys – we hauled ass to avoid a trap, but the trap found us anyway. But we can outrun this bastard in the high airstreams if we lose all extra weight. Dinky – run and tell Max to drop the steamer. Red, Ali – mark the aft, fore, and starboard harpoons with buoys and let 'em go. Grig, Ngube – same with the spent tensors. Fast!"

He turned to me as his minions scurried to their tasks. "We're throwing all dead weight over the side. That includes you, unless I'm swiftly convinced otherwise. Who are you?"

"Gabriel Goodman," I said truthfully, "but better known by my quill-name – 'Benjamin Rosenbaum.'"

"Benjamin Rosenbaum?" the pirate cried. "The great Iowa poet, author of 'Green Nakedness' and 'Broken Lines'? You are a hero of our land, sir! Fear not, I shall – "

"No," I interrupted crossly. "Not that Benjamin Rosenbaum."

The pirate reddened, and tapped his teeth, frowning. "Aha, hold then, I have heard of you – the children's tale-scribe, I take it? 'Legs the Caterpillar'? I'll spare you, then, for the sake of my son Timmy, who – "

"No," I said again, through gritted teeth. "I am an author of plausible-fables, sir, not picture-books."

"Never read the stuff," said Melko. There was a great shudder, and the steel bulk of the steam generatory, billowing white clouds, fell past us. It struck the lake, raising a plume of spray that spotted the window with droplets. The forward harpoon assembly followed, trailing a red buoy on a line.

"Right then," said Melko. "Over you go."

"You spoke of Aryan hostages," I said hastily, thinking it wise now to mention the position I seemed to have accepted *de facto*, if not yet *de jure*. "Do you by any chance refer to my employer, Prem Ramasson, and his consort?"

Melko spat on the floor, causing a cabin boy to rush forward with a mop. "So you're one of those quislings who serves Hindoo royalty even as they divide up the land of your fathers, are you?" He advanced towards me menacingly.

"Outer Thule is a minor province of the Raj, sir," I said. "It is absurd to blame Ramasson for the war in Texas."

"Ready to rise, sir," came the cry.

"Rise then!" Melko ordered. "And throw this dog in the brig with its master. If we can't ransom them, we'll throw them off at the top." He glowered at me. "That will give you a nice long while to salve your conscience with making fine distinctions among Hindoos. What do you think he's doing here in our lands, if not plotting with his brothers to steal more of our gold and helium?"

I was unable to further pursue my political debate with Chippewa Melko, as his henchmen dragged me at once to cramped quarters between the inner and outer hulls. The prince lay on the single bunk, ashen and unmoving. His consort knelt at his side, weeping silently. The Wisdom Servant, deprived of its animating field, had collapsed into a tangle of reedlike protuberances.

My valise was there; I opened it and took out my inkwell. The Wisdom Ants lay within, tiny crumpled blobs of brassy metal. I put the inkwell in my pocket.

"Thank you for trying," Sarasvati Sitasdottir said hoarsely. "Alas, luck has turned against us."

"All may not be lost," I said. "An Aryan war-city pursues the pirates, and may yet buy our ransom; although, strangely, they have damped the Brahmanic field and so cannot hear the pirates' offer of parley."

"If they were going to parley, they would have done so by now," she said dully. "They will burn the pirate from the sky. They do not know we are aboard."

"Then our bad luck comes in threes." It is an old rule of thumb, derided as superstition by professional causalists. But they, like all professionals, like to obfuscate their science, rendering it inaccessible to the layman; in truth, the old rule holds a glimmer of the workings of the third form of causality.

"A swift death is no bad luck for me," Sarasvati Sitasdottir said. "Not when he is gone." She choked a sob, and turned away.

I felt for the Raja's pulse; his blood was still beneath his amber skin. His face was turned towards the metal bulkhead; droplets of moisture there told of his last breath, not long ago. I wiped them away, and closed his eyes.

We waited, for one doom or another. I could feel the zeppelin rising swiftly; the *Hiawatha* was unheated, and the air turned cold. The princess did not speak.

My mind turned again to the fable I had been commissioned to write, the materialist shadow-history of a world without zeppelins. If by some unlikely chance I should live to finish it, I resolved to make do without the extravagant perils, ironic coincidences, sudden bursts of insight, death-defying escapades and beautiful villainesses that litter our genre and cheapen its high philosophical concerns. Why must every protagonist be doomed, daring, lonely, and overly proud? No, my philosopher-hero would enjoy precisely those goods of which I was deprived – a happy family, a secure situation, a prosperous and powerful nation, a conciliatory nature; above all, an absence of immediate physical peril. Of course, there must be conflict, worry, sorrow – but, I vowed, of a rich and subtle kind!

I wondered how my hero would view the chain of events in which I was embroiled. With derision? With compassion? I loved him, after a fashion, for he was my creation. How would he regard me?

If only the first and simplest form of causality had earned his allegiance, he would not be placated by such easy saws as "bad things come in threes." An assassin, *and* a pirate, *and* an uncommunicative war-city, he would ask? All within the space of an hour?

Would he simply accept the absurd and improbable results of living within a blind and random machine? Yet his society could not have advanced far, mired in such fatalism!

Would he not doggedly seek meaning, despite the limitations of his framework?

What if our bad luck were no coincidence at all, he would ask. What if all three misfortunes had a single, linear, proximate cause, intelligible to reason?

"My lady," I said, "I do not wish to cause you further pain. Yet I find I must speak. I saw the face of the prince's killer – it was a young woman's face, in lineament much like your own."

"Shakuntala!" the princess cried. "My sister! No! It cannot be! She would never do this – " she curled her hands into fists. "No!"

"And yet," I said gently, "it seems you regard the assertion as not utterly implausible."

"She is banished," Sarasvati Sitasdottir said. "She has gone over to the Thanes – the Nordic Liberation Army – the anarcho-gynarchist insurgents in our land. It is like her to seek danger and glory. But she would not kill Prem! She loved him before I!"

To that, I could find no response. The *Hiawatha* shuddered around us – some battle had been joined. We heard shouts and running footsteps.

Sarasvati, the prince, the pirates – any of them would have had a thousand gods to pray to, convenient gods for any occasion. Such solace I could sorely have used. But I was raised a Karaite. We acknowledge only one God, austere and magnificent; the One God of All Things, attended by His angels and His consort, the Queen of Heaven. The only way to speak to Him, we are taught, is in His Holy Temple; and it lies in ruins these two thousand years. In times like these, we are told to meditate on the contrast between His imperturbable magnificence and our own abandoned and abject vulnerability, and to be certain that He watches us with immeasurable compassion, though He will not act. I have never found this much comfort.

Instead, I turned to the prince, curious what in his visage might have inspired the passions of the two sisters.

On the bulkhead just before his lips – where, before, I had wiped away the sign of his last breath – a tracery of condensation stood.

Was this some effluvium issued by the organs of a decaying corpse?

I bent, and delicately sniffed – detecting no corruption.

"My lady," I said, indicating the droplets on the cool metal, "he lives."

"What?" the princess cried. "But how?"

"A diguanidinium compound produced by certain marine dinoflagellates," I said, "can induce a deathlike coma, in which the subject breathes but thrice an hour; the heartbeat is similarly undetectable."

Delicately, she felt his face. "Can he hear us?"

"Perhaps."

"Why would she do this?"

"The body would be rushed back to Thule, would it not? Perhaps the revolutionaries meant to steal it and revive him as a hostage?"

A tremendous thunderclap shook the *Hiawatha MacCool,* and I noticed we were listing to one side. There was a commotion in the gangway; then Chippewa Melko entered. Several guards stood behind him.

"Damned tenacious," he spat. "If they want you so badly, why won't they parley? We're still out of range of the war-city itself and its big guns, thank Buddha, Thor, and Darwin. We burned one of their launches, at the cost of many of my men. But the other launch is gaining."

"Perhaps they don't know the hostages are aboard?" I asked.

"Then why pursue me this distance? I'm no fool – I know what it costs them to detour that monster. They don't do it for sport, and I don't flatter myself I'm worth that much to them. No, it's you they want. So they can have you – I've no more stomach for this chase." He gestured at the prince with his chin. "Is he dead?"

"No," I said.

"Doesn't look well. No matter – come along. I'm putting you all in a launch with a flag of parley on it. Their war-boat will have to stop for you, and that will give us the time we need."

So it was that we found ourselves in the freezing, cramped bay of a pirate longboat. Three of Melko's crewmen accompanied us – one at the controls, the other two clinging to the longboat's sides. Sarasvati and I huddled on the aluminum deck beside the pilot, the prince's body held between us. All three of Melko's men had parachutes – they planned to escape as soon as we docked. Our longboat flew the white flag of parley, and – taken from the prince's luggage – the royal standard of Outermost Thule.

All the others were gazing tensely at our target – the war-city's fighter launch, which climbed toward us from below. It was almost as big as Melko's flagship. I, alone, glanced back out the open doorway as we swung away from the *Hiawatha*.

So only I saw a brightly colored glider detach itself from the *Hiawatha*'s side and swoop to follow us.

Why would Shakuntala have lingered with the pirates thus far? Once the rebels' plan to abduct the prince was foiled by Melko's arrival, why not simply abandon it and await a fairer chance?

Unless the intent was not to abduct – but to protect.

"My lady," I said in my halting middle-school Sanskrit, "your sister is here."

Sarasvati gasped, following my gaze.

"Madam – your husband was aiding the rebels."

"How dare you?" she hissed in the same tongue, much more fluently.

"It is the only – " I struggled for the Sanskrit word for 'hypothesis,' then abandoned the attempt, leaning over to whisper in English. "Why else did the pirates and the war-city arrive together? Consider: the prince's collusion with the Thanes was discovered by the Aryan Raj. But to try him for treason would provoke great scandal and stir sympathy for the insurgents. Instead, they made sure rumor of a valuable hostage reached Melko. With the prince in the hands of the pirates, his death would simply be a regrettable calamity."

Her eyes widened. "Those monsters!" she hissed.

"Your sister aimed to save him, but Melko arrived too soon – before news of the prince's death could discourage his brigandy. My lady, I fear that if we reach that launch, they will discover that the Prince lives. Then some accident will befall us all."

There were shouts from outside. Melko's crewmen drew their needlethrowers and fired at the advancing glider.

With a shriek, Sarasvati flung herself upon the pilot, knocking the controls from his hands.

The longboat lurched sickeningly.

I gained my feet, then fell against the prince. I saw a flash of orange and gold – the glider, swooping by us.

I struggled to stand. The pilot drew his cutlass. He seized Sarasvati by the hair and spun her away from the controls.

Just then, one of the men clinging to the outside, pricked by Shakuntala's needle, fell. His tether caught him, and the floor jerked beneath us.

The pilot staggered back. Sarasvati Sitasdottir punched him in the throat. They stumbled towards the door.

I started forward. The other pirate on the outside fell, untethered, and the longboat lurched again. Unbalanced, our craft drove in a tight circle, listing dangerously.

Sarasvati fought with uncommon ferocity, forcing the pirate towards the open hatch. Fearing they would both tumble through, I seized the controls.

Regrettably, I knew nothing of flying airship-longboats, whose controls, it happens, are of a remarkably poor design.

One would imagine that the principal steering element could be moved in the direction that one wishes the craft to go; instead, just the opposite is the case. Then, too, one would expect these brawny and unrefined air-men to use controls lending themselves to rough usage; instead, it seems an exceedingly fine hand is required.

Thus, rather than steadying the craft, I achieved the opposite.

Not only were Sarasvati and the pilot flung out the cabin door, but I myself was thrown through it, just managing to catch with both hands a metal protuberance in the hatchway's base. My feet swung freely over the void.

I looked up in time to see the Raja's limp body come sliding towards me like a missile.

I fear that I hesitated too long in deciding whether to dodge or catch my almost-employer. At the last minute courage won out, and I flung one arm around his chest as he struck me.

This dislodged my grip, and the two of us fell from the airship.

In an extremity of terror, I let go the prince, and clawed wildly at nothing.

I slammed into the body of the pirate who hung, poisoned by Shakuntala's needle, from the airship's tether. I slid along him, and finally caught myself at his feet.

As I clung there, shaking miserably, I watched Prem Ramasson tumble through the air, and I cursed myself for having caused the very tragedies I had endeavored to avoid, like a figure in an Athenian tragedy. But such tragedies proceed from some essential flaw in their heroes – some illustrative hubris, some damning vice. Searching my own character and actions, I could find only that I had endeavored to make do, as well as I could, in situations for which I was ill-prepared. Is that not the fate of any of us, confronting life and its vagaries?

Was my tale, then, an absurd and tragic farce? Was its lesson one merely of ignominy and despair?

Or perhaps – as my shadow-protagonist might imagine – there was no tale, no teller – perhaps the dramatic and sensational events I had endured were part of no story at all, but brute and silent facts of Matter.

From above, Shakuntala Sitasdottir dove in her glider. It was folded like a spear, and she swept past the prince in seconds. Nimbly, she flung open the glider's wings, sweeping up to the falling Raja, and rolling the glider, took him into her embrace.

Thus encumbered – she must have secured him somehow – she dove again (chasing her sister, I imagine) and disappeared in a bank of cloud.

A flock of brass-colored Wisdom Gulls, arriving from the Aryan war-city, flew around the pirates' launch. They entered its empty cabin, glanced at me and the poisoned pirate to whom I clung, and departed.

I climbed up the body to sit upon its shoulders, a much more comfortable position. There, clinging to the tether and shivering, I rested.

The *Hiawatha MacCool*, black smoke guttering from one side of her, climbed higher and higher into the sky, pursued by the Aryan war-boat. The sun was setting, limning the clouds with gold and pink and violet. The war-city, terrible and glorious, sailed slowly by, under my feet, its shadow an island of darkness in the sunset's gold-glitter, on the waters of the lake beneath.

Some distance to the east, where the sky was already darkening to a rich cobalt, the Aryan war-boat which Melko had successfully struck was bathed in white fire. After a while, the inner hull must have been breached, for the fire went out, extinguished by escaping helium, and the zeppelin plummeted.

Above me, the propeller hummed, driving my launch in the same small circle again and again.

I hoped that I had saved the prince after all. I hoped Shakuntala had saved her sister, and that the three of them would find refuge with the Thanes.

My shadow-protagonist had given me a gift; it was the logic of his world that had led me to discover the war-city's threat. Did this mean his philosophy was the correct one?

Yet the events that followed were so dramatic and contrived – precisely as if I inhabited a pulp romance. Perhaps he was writing my story, as I wrote his; perhaps, with the comfortable life I had given him, he longed to lose himself in uncomfortable escapades of this sort. In that case, we both of us lived in a world designed, a world of story, full of meaning.

But perhaps I had framed the question wrong. Perhaps the division between Mind and Matter is itself illusory; perhaps Randomness, Pattern, and Plan are all but stories we tell about the inchoate and unknowable world which fills the darkness beyond the thin circle illumed by reason's light. Perhaps it is foolish to ask if I or the protagonist of my world-without-zeppelins story is the more real. Each of us is flesh, a buzzing swarm of atoms; yet each of us also a tale contained in the pages of the other's notebook. We are bodies. But we are also the stories we tell about each other. Perhaps not knowing is enough.

Maybe it is not a matter of discovering the correct philosophy. Maybe the desire that burns behind this question is the desire to be real. And which is more real – a clod of dirt unnoticed at your feet, or a hero in a legend?

And maybe behind the desire to be real is simply wanting to be known.

To be held.

The first stars glittered against the fading blue. I was in the bosom of the Queen of Heaven. My fingers and toes were getting numb – soon frostbite would set in. I recited the prayer the ancient heretical Rabbis would say before death, which begins, "Hear O Israel, the Lord is Our God, the Lord is One."

Then I began to climb the tether.

The God of Dark Laughter

Michael Chabon

THIRTEEN DAYS after the Entwhistle-Ealing Bros. circus left Ashtown, beating a long retreat toward its winter headquarters in Peru, Indiana, two boys out hunting squirrels in the woods along Portwine Road stumbled on a body that was dressed in a mad suit of purple and orange velour. They found it at the end of a muddy strip of gravel that began, five miles to the west, as Yuggogheny County Road 22A. Another half mile farther to the east and it would have been left to my colleagues over in Fayette County to puzzle out the question of who had shot the man and skinned his head from chin to crown and clavicle to clavicle, taking ears, eyelids, lips, and scalp in a single grisly flap, like the cupped husk of a peeled orange. My name is Edward D. Satterlee, and for the last twelve years I have faithfully served Yuggogheny County as its district attorney, in cases that have all too often run to the outrageous and bizarre. I make the following report in no confidence that it, or I, will be believed, and beg the reader to consider this, at least in part, my letter of resignation.

The boys who found the body were themselves fresh from several hours' worth of bloody amusement with long knives and dead squirrels, and at first the investigating officers took them for the perpetrators of the crime. There was blood on the boys' cuffs, their shirttails, and the bills of their gray twill caps. But the county detectives and I quickly moved beyond Joey Matuszak and Frankie Corro. For all their familiarity with gristle and sinew and the bright-purple discovered interior of a body, the boys had come into the station looking pale and bewildered, and we found ample evidence at the crime scene of their having lost the contents of their stomachs when confronted with the corpse.

Now, I have every intention of setting down the facts of this case as I understand and experienced them, without fear of the reader's doubting them (or my own sanity), but I see no point in mentioning any further *anatomical* details of the crime, except to say that our coroner, Dr. Sauer, though he labored at the problem with a sad fervor, was hard put to establish conclusively that the victim had been dead before his killer went to work on him with a very long, very sharp knife.

The dead man, as I have already mentioned, was attired in a curious suit – the trousers and jacket of threadbare purple velour, the waistcoat bright orange, the whole thing patched with outsized squares of fabric cut from a variety of loudly clashing plaids. It was on account of the patches, along with the victim's cracked and split-soled shoes and a certain undeniable shabbiness in the stuff of the suit, that the primary detective – a man not apt to see deeper than the outermost wrapper of the world (we do not attract, I must confess, the finest police talent in this doleful little corner of western Pennsylvania) – had already figured the victim for a vagrant, albeit one with extraordinarily big feet.

"Those cannot possibly be his real shoes, Ganz, you idiot," I gently suggested. The call, patched through to my boarding house from that gruesome clearing in the woods, had interrupted my supper, which by a grim coincidence had been a Brunswick stew (the specialty of my Virginia-born landlady) of pork and *squirrel*. "They're supposed to make you laugh."

"They *are* pretty funny," said Ganz. "Come to think of it." Detective John Ganz was a large-boned fellow, upholstered in a layer of ruddy flesh. He breathed through his mouth, and walked with a tall man's defeated stoop, and five times a day he took out his comb and ritually plastered his thinning blond hair to the top of his head with a dime-size dab of Tres Flores.

When I arrived at the clearing, having abandoned my solitary dinner, I found the corpse lying just as the young hunters had come upon it, supine, arms thrown up and to either side of the flayed face in a startled attitude that fuelled the hopes of poor Dr. Sauer that the victim's death by gunshot had preceded his mutilation. Ganz or one of the other investigators had kindly thrown a chamois cloth over the vandalized head. I took enough of a peek beneath it to provide me with everything that I or the reader could possibly need to know about the condition of the head – I will never forget the sight of that monstrous, fleshless grin – and to remark the dead man's unusual choice of cravat. It was a giant, floppy bow tie, white with orange and purple polka dots.

"Damn you, Ganz," I said, though I was not in truth addressing the poor fellow, who, I knew, would not be able to answer my question anytime soon. "What's a dead clown doing in my woods?"

We found no wallet on the corpse, nor any kind of identifying objects. My men, along with the better part of the Ashtown Police Department, went over and over the woods east of town, hourly widening the radius of their search. That day, when not attending to my other duties (I was then in the process of breaking up the Dushnyk cigarette-smuggling ring), I managed to work my way back along a chain of inferences to the Entwhistle-Ealing Bros. Circus, which, as I eventually recalled, had recently stayed on the eastern outskirts of Ashtown, at the fringe of the woods where the body was found.

The following day, I succeeded in reaching the circus's general manager, a man named Onheuser, at their winter headquarters in Peru. He informed me over the phone that the company had left Pennsylvania and was now en route to Peru, and I asked him if he had received any reports from the road manager of a clown's having suddenly gone missing.

"Missing?" he said. I wished that I could see his face, for I thought I heard the flatted note of something false in his tone. Perhaps he was merely nervous about talking to a county district attorney. The Entwhistle-Ealing Bros. Circus was a mangy affair, by all accounts, and probably no stranger to pursuit by officers of the court. "Why, I don't believe so, no."

I explained to him that a man who gave every indication of having once been a circus clown had turned up dead in a pinewood outside Ashtown, Pennsylvania.

"Oh, no," Onheuser said. "I truly hope he wasn't one of mine, Mr. Satterlee."

"Is it possible you might have left one of your clowns behind, Mr. Onheuser?"

"Clowns are special people," Onheuser replied, sounding a touch on the defensive. "They love their work, but sometimes it can get to be a little, well, too much for them." It developed that Mr. Onheuser had, in his younger days, performed as a clown, under the name of Mr. Wingo, in the circus of which he was now the general manager. "It's not unusual for a clown to drop out for a little while, cool his heels, you know, in some town where he can get a few months of well-earned rest. It isn't *common,* I wouldn't say, but it's not unusual. I will wire my road manager – they're in Canton, Ohio – and see what I can find out."

I gathered, reading between the lines, that clowns were high-strung types, and not above going off on the occasional bender. This poor fellow had probably jumped ship here two weeks ago, holing up somewhere with a case of rye, only to run afoul of a very nasty person, possibly one who harbored no great love of clowns. In fact, I had an odd feeling, nothing more than a hunch, really, that the ordinary citizens of Ashtown and its environs were safe, even though the killer was still at large. Once more, I picked up a slip of paper that I had tucked into my desk blotter that morning. It was something that Dr. Sauer had clipped from his files and passed along to me. *Coulrophobia: morbid, irrational fear of or aversion to clowns.*

"Er, listen, Mr. Satterlee," Onheuser went on. "I hope you won't mind my asking. That is, I hope it's not a, well, a confidential police matter, or something of the sort. But I know that when I do get through to them, out in Canton, they're going to want to know."

I guessed, somehow, what he was about to ask me. I could hear the prickling fear behind his curiosity, the note of dread in his voice. I waited him out.

"Did they – was there any – how did he die?"

"He was shot," I said, for the moment supplying only the least interesting part of the answer, tugging on that loose thread of fear. "In the head."

"And there was...forgive me. No...no harm done? To the body? Other than the gunshot wound, I mean to say."

"Well, yes, his head was rather savagely mutilated," I said brightly.

"Is that what you mean to say?"

"Ah! No, no, I don't – "

"The killer or killers removed all the skin from the cranium. It was very skillfully done. Now, suppose you tell me what you know about it."

There was another pause, and a stream of agitated electrons burbled along between us.

"I don't know anything, Mr. District Attorney. I'm sorry. I really must go I'll wire you when I have some – "

The line went dead. He was so keen to hang up on me that he could not even wait to finish his sentence. I got up and went to the shelf where, in recent months, I had taken to keeping a bottle of whiskey tucked behind my bust of Daniel Webster. Carrying the bottle and a dusty glass back to my desk, I sat down and tried to reconcile myself to the thought that I was confronted – not, alas, for the first time in my tenure as chief law-enforcement officer of Yuggogheny County – with a crime whose explanation was going to involve not the usual amalgam of stupidity, meanness, and singularly poor judgment but the incalculable intentions of a being who was genuinely evil. What disheartened me was not that I viewed a crime committed out of the promptings of an evil nature as inherently less liable to solution than the misdeeds of the foolish, the unlucky, or the habitually cruel. On the contrary, evil often expresses itself through refreshingly discernible patterns, through schedules and syllogisms. But the presence of evil, once scented, tends to bring out all that is most irrational and uncontrollable in the public imagination. It is a catalyst for pea-brained theories, gimcrack scholarship, and the credulous cosmologies of hysteria.

At that moment, there was a knock on the door to my office, and Detective Ganz came in. At one time I would have tried to hide the glass of whiskey, behind the typewriter or the photo of my wife and son, but now it did not seem to be worth the effort. I was not fooling anyone. Ganz took note of the glass in my hand with a raised eyebrow and a schoolmarmish pursing of his lips.

"Well?" I said. There had been a brief period, following my son's death and the subsequent suicide of my dear wife, Mary, when I had indulged the pitying regard of my staff. I now found that I regretted having shown such weakness. "What is it, then? Has something turned up?"

"A cave," Ganz said. "The poor bastard was living in a cave."

The range of low hills and hollows separating lower Yuggogheny from Fayette County is rotten with caves. For many years, when I was a boy, a man named Colonel Earnshawe operated penny tours of the iridescent organ pipes and jagged stone teeth of Neighborsburg Caverns, before they collapsed in the mysterious earthquake of 1919, killing the Colonel and his sister Irene, and putting to rest many strange rumors about that eccentric old pair. My childhood friends and I, ranging in the woods, would from time to time come upon the root-choked mouth of a cave exhaling its cool plutonic breath, and dare one another to leave the sunshine and enter that world of shadow – the entrance, as it always seemed to me, to the legendary past itself, where the bones of Indians and Frenchmen might be moldering. It was in one of these anterooms of buried history that the beam of a flashlight, wielded by a deputy sheriff from Plunkettsburg, had struck the silvery lip of a can of pork and beans. Calling to his companions, the deputy plunged through a curtain of spiderweb and found himself in the parlor, bedroom, and kitchen of the dead man.

There were some cans of chili and hash, a Primus stove, a lantern, a bedroll, a mess kit, and an old Colt revolver, Army issue, loaded and apparently not fired for some time. And there were also books – a Scout guide to roughing it, a collected Blake, and a couple of odd texts, elderly and tattered: one in German called *Über das Finstere Lachen,* by a man named Friedrich von Junzt, which appeared to be religious or philosophical in nature, and one a small volume bound in black leather and printed in no alphabet known to me, the letters sinuous and furred with wild diacritical marks.

"Pretty heavy reading for a clown," Ganz said.

"It's not all rubber chickens and hosing each other down with seltzer bottles, Jack."

"Oh, no?"

"No, sir. Clowns have unsuspected depths."

"I'm starting to get that impression, sir."

Propped against the straightest wall of the cave, just beside the lantern, there was a large mirror, still bearing the bent clasps and sheared bolts that had once, I inferred, held it to the wall of a filling-station men's room. At its foot was the item that had earlier confirmed to Detective Ganz – and now confirmed to me as I went to inspect it – the recent habitation of the cave by a painted circus clown: a large, padlocked wooden makeup kit, of heavy and rather elaborate construction. I directed Ganz to send for a Pittsburgh criminalist who had served us with discretion in the horrific Primm case, reminding him that nothing must be touched until this Mr. Espy and his black bag of dusts and luminous powders arrived.

The air in the cave had a sharp, briny tinge; beneath it there was a stale animal musk that reminded me, absurdly, of the smell inside a circus tent.

"Why was he living in a cave?" I said to Ganz. "We have a perfectly nice hotel in town."

"Maybe he was broke."

"Or maybe he thought that a hotel was the first place they would look for him."

Ganz looked confused, and a little annoyed, as if he thought I were being deliberately mysterious.

"*Who* was looking for him?"

"I don't know, Detective. Maybe no one. I'm just thinking out loud."

Impatience marred Ganz's fair, bland features. He could tell that I was in the grip of a hunch, and hunches were always among the first considerations ruled out by the procedural practices of Detective John Ganz. My hunches had, admittedly, an uneven record. In the Primm business, one had very nearly got both Ganz and me killed. As for the wayward hunch about my mother's old crony Thaddeus Craven and the strength of his will to quit drinking – I suppose I shall regret indulging that one for the rest of my life.

"If you'll excuse me, Jack..." I said. "I'm having a bit of a hard time with the stench in here."

"I was thinking he might have been keeping a pig." Ganz inclined his head to one side and gave an empirical sniff. "It smells like pig to me."

I covered my mouth and hurried outside into the cool, dank pinewood. I gathered in great lungfuls of air. The nausea passed, and I filled my pipe, walking up and down outside the mouth of the cave and trying to connect this new discovery to my talk with the circus man, Onheuser. Clearly, he had suspected that this clown might have met with a grisly end. Not only that, he had known that his fellow circus people would fear the very same thing – as if there were some coulrophobic madman with a knife who was as much a part of circus lore as the prohibition on whistling in the dressing room or on looking over your shoulder when you marched in the circus parade.

I got my pipe lit, and wandered down into the woods, toward the clearing where the boys had stumbled over the dead man, following a rough trail that the police had found. Really, it was not a trail so much as an impromptu alley of broken saplings and trampled ground that wound a convoluted course down the hill from the cave to the clearing. It appeared to have been blazed a few days before by the victim and his pursuer; near the bottom, where the trees gave way to open sky, there were grooves of plowed earth that corresponded neatly with encrustations on the heels of the clown's giant brogues. The killer must have caught the clown at the edge of the clearing, and then dragged him along by the hair, or by the collar of his shirt, for the last twenty-five yards, leaving this furrowed record of the panicked, slipping flight of the clown. The presumed killer's footprints were everywhere in evidence, and appeared to have been made by a pair of long and pointed boots. But the really puzzling thing was a third set of prints, which Ganz had noticed and mentioned to me, scattered here and there along the cold black mud of the path. They seemed to have been made by a barefoot child of eight or nine years. And damned, as Ganz had concluded his report to me, if that barefoot child did not appear to have been dancing!

I came into the clearing, a little short of breath, and stood listening to the wind in the pines and the distant rumble of the state highway, until my pipe went out. It was a cool afternoon, but the sky had been blue all day and the woods were peaceful and fragrant. Nevertheless, I was conscious of a mounting sense of disquiet as I stood over the bed of sodden leaves where the body had been found. I did not then, nor do I now, believe in ghosts, but as the sun dipped down behind the tops of the trees, lengthening the long shadows encompassing me, I became aware of an irresistible feeling that somebody was watching me. After a moment, the feeling intensified, and localized, as it were, so I was certain that to see who it was I need only turn around. Bravely – meaning not that I am a brave man but that I behaved as if I were – I took my matches from my jacket pocket and relit my pipe. Then I turned. I knew that when I glanced behind me I would not see Jack Ganz or one of the other policemen standing there; any of them would have said something to me by now. No, it was either going to be nothing at all or something that I could not even allow myself to imagine.

It was, in fact, a baboon, crouching on its hind legs in the middle of the trail, regarding me with close-set orange eyes, one hand cupped at its side. It had great puffed whiskers and a long canine snout. There was something in the barrel chest and the muttonchop sideburns that led me to conclude, correctly, as it turned out, that the specimen was male. For all his majestic bulk, the old fellow presented a rather sad spectacle. His fur was matted and caked with mud, and a sticky coating of pine needles clung to his feet. The expression in his eyes was unsettlingly forlorn, almost pleading, I would have said, and in his mute gaze I imagined I detected a hint of outraged dignity. This might, of course, have been due to the hat he was wearing. It was conical, particolored with orange and purple lozenges, and ornamented at the tip with a bright-orange pompom. Tied under his chin with a length of black ribbon, it hung from the side of his head at a humorous angle. I myself might have been tempted to kill the man who had tied it to my head.

"Was it you?" I said, thinking of Poe's story of the rampaging orang swinging a razor in a Parisian apartment. Had that story had any basis in fact? Could the dead clown have been killed by the pet or sidekick with whom, as the mystery of the animal smell in the cave now resolved itself, he had shared his fugitive existence?

The baboon declined to answer my question. After a moment, though, he raised his long crooked left arm and gestured vaguely toward his belly. The import of this message was unmistakable, and thus I had the answer to my question – if he could not open a can of franks and beans, he would not have been able to perform that awful surgery on his owner or partner.

"All right, old boy," I said. "Let's get you something to eat." I took a step toward him, watching for signs that he might bolt or, worse, throw himself at me. But he sat, looking miserable, clenching something in his right paw. I crossed the distance between us. His rancid-hair smell was unbearable. "You need a bath, don't you?" I spoke, by reflex, as if I were talking to somebody's tired old dog. "Were you and your friend in the habit of bathing together? Were you there when it happened, old boy? Any idea who did it?"

The animal gazed up at me, its eyes kindled with that luminous and sagacious sorrow that lends to the faces of apes and mandrills an air of cousinly reproach, as if we humans have betrayed the principles of our kind. Tentatively, I reached out to him with one hand. He grasped my fingers in his dry leather paw, and then the next instant he had leapt bodily into my arms, like a child seeking solace. The garbage-and-skunk stench of him burned my nose. I gagged and stumbled backward as the baboon scrambled to wrap his arms and legs around me. I must have cried out; a moment later a pair of iron lids seemed to slam against my skull, and the animal went slack, sliding, with a horrible, human sigh of disappointment, to the ground at my feet.

Ganz and two Ashtown policemen came running over and dragged the dead baboon away from me.

"He wasn't – he was just – " I was too outraged to form a coherent expression of my anger. "You could have hit *me!*"

Ganz closed the animal's eyes, and laid its arms out at its sides. The right paw was still clenched in a shaggy fist. Ganz, not without some difficulty, managed to pry it open. He uttered an unprintable oath.

In the baboon's palm lay a human finger. Ganz and I looked at each other, wordlessly confirming that the dead clown had been in possession of a full complement of digits.

"See that Espy gets that finger," I said. "Maybe we can find out whose it was."

"It's a woman's," Ganz said. "Look at that nail."

I took it from him, holding it by the chewed and bloody end so as not to dislodge any evidence that might be trapped under the long nail. Though rigid, it was strangely warm, perhaps from having spent a few days in the vengeful grip of the animal who had claimed it from his master's murderer. It appeared to be an index finger, with a manicured, pointed nail nearly three-quarters of an inch long. I shook my head.

"It isn't painted," I said. "Not even varnished. How many women wear their nails like that?"

"Maybe the paint rubbed off," one of the policemen suggested.

"Maybe," I said. I knelt on the ground beside the body of the baboon. There was, I noted, a wound on the back of his neck, long and deep and crusted over with dirt and dried blood. I now saw him in my mind's eye, dancing like a barefoot child around the murderer and the victim as they struggled down the path to the clearing. It would take a powerful man to fight such an animal off. "I can't believe you killed our only witness, Detective Ganz. The poor bastard was just giving me a hug."

This information seemed to amuse Ganz nearly as much as it puzzled him.

"He was a monkey, sir," Ganz said. "I doubt he – "

"He could make signs, you fool! He told me he was *hungry*."

Ganz blinked, trying, I supposed, to append to his personal operations manual this evidence of the potential usefulness of circus apes to police inquiries.

"If I had a dozen baboons like that one on my staff," I said, "I would never have to leave the office."

That evening, before going home, I stopped by the evidence room in the High Street annex and signed out the two books that had been found in the cave that morning. As I walked back into the corridor, I thought I detected an odd odor – odd, at any rate, for that dull expanse of linoleum and buzzing fluorescent tubes – of the sea: a sharp, salty, briny smell. I decided that it must be some new disinfectant being used by the custodian, but it reminded me of the smell of blood from the specimen bags and sealed containers in the evidence room. I turned the lock on the room's door and slipped the books, in their waxy protective envelopes, into my briefcase, and walked down High Street to Dennistoun Road, where the public library was. It stayed open late on Wednesday nights, and I would need a German–English dictionary if my college German and I were going to get anywhere with Herr von Junzt.

The librarian, Lucy Brand, returned my greeting with the circumspect air of one who hopes to be rewarded for her forbearance with a wealth of juicy tidbits. Word of the murder, denuded of most of the relevant details, had made the Ashtown *Ambler* yesterday morning, and though I had cautioned the unlucky young squirrel hunters against talking about the case, already conjectures, misprisions, and outright lies had begun wildly to coalesce; I knew the temper of my home town well enough to realize that if I did not close this case soon things might get out of hand. Ashtown, as the events surrounding the appearance of the so-called Green Man, in 1932, amply demonstrated, has a lamentable tendency toward municipal panic.

Having secured a copy of Köhler's Dictionary of the English and German Languages, I went, on an impulse, to the card catalogue and looked up von Junzt, Friedrich. There was no card for any work by this author – hardly surprising, perhaps, in a small-town library like ours. I returned to the reference shelf, and consulted an encyclopedia of philosophical biography and comparable volumes of philologic reference, but found no entry for any von Junzt – a diplomate, by the testimony of his title page, of the University of Tübingen and of the Sorbonne. It seemed that von Junzt had been dismissed, or expunged, from the dusty memory of his discipline.

It was as I was closing the Encyclopedia of Archaeo-Anthropological Research that a name suddenly leapt out at me, catching my eye just before the pages slammed together. It was a word that I had noticed in von Junzt's book: "Urartu." I barely managed to slip the edge of my thumb into the encyclopedia to mark the place; half a second later and the reference might have been lost to me. As it turned out, the name of von Junzt itself was also contained – sealed up – in the sarcophagus of this entry, a long and tedious one devoted to the work of an Oxford man by the name of St. Dennis T. R. Gladfellow, "a noted scholar," as the entry had it, "in the field of inquiry into the belief of the ancient, largely unknown peoples referred to conjecturally today as proto-Urartians." The reference lay buried in a column dense with comparisons among various bits of obsidian and broken bronze:

> G.'s analysis of the meaning of such ceremonial blades admittedly was aided by the earlier discoveries of Friedrich von Junzt, at the site of the former Temple of Yrrh, in north central Armenia, among them certain sacrificial artifacts pertaining to the worship of the proto-Urartian deity Yê-Heh, rather grandly (though regrettably without credible evidence) styled "the god of dark or mocking laughter" by the German, a notorious adventurer and fake whose work, nevertheless, in this instance, has managed to prove useful to science.

The prospect of spending the evening in the company of Herr von Junzt began to seem even less appealing. One of the most tedious human beings I have ever known was my own mother, who, early in my childhood, fell under the spell of Madame Blavatsky and her followers and proceeded to weary my youth and deplete my patrimony with her devotion to that indigestible caseation of balderdash and lies. Mother drew a number of local simpletons into her orbit, among them poor old drunken Thaddeus Craven, and burnt them up as thoroughly as the earth's atmosphere consumes asteroids. The most satisfying episodes of my career have been those which afforded me the opportunity to prosecute charlatans and frauds and those who preyed on the credulous; I did not now relish the thought of sitting at home with such a man all evening, in particular one who spoke only German.

Nevertheless, I could not ignore the undeniable novelty of a murdered circus clown who was familiar with scholarship – however spurious or misguided – concerning the religious beliefs of proto-Urartians. I carried the Köhler's over to the counter, where Lucy Brand waited eagerly for me to spill some small ration of beans. When I offered nothing for her delectation, she finally spoke.

"Was he a German?" she said, showing unaccustomed boldness, it seemed to me.

"Was *who* a German, my dear Miss Brand?"

"The victim." She lowered her voice to a textbook librarian's whisper, though there was no one in the building but old Bob Spherakis, asleep and snoring in the periodicals room over a copy of *Grit*.

"I – I don't know," I said, taken aback by the simplicity of her inference, or rather by its having escaped me. "I suppose he may have been, yes."

She slid the book across the counter toward me.

"There was another one of them in here this afternoon," she said. "At least, I think he was a German. A Jew, come to think of it. Somehow he managed to find the only book in Hebrew we have in our collection. It's one of the books old Mr. Vorzeichen donated when he died. A prayer book, I think it is. Tiny little thing. Black leather."

This information ought to have struck a chord in my memory, of course, but it did not. I settled my hat on my head, bid Miss Brand good night, and walked slowly home, with the dictionary under my arm, and, in my briefcase, von Junzt's stout tome and the little black leather volume filled with sinuous mysterious script.

I will not tax the reader with an account of my struggles with Köhler's dictionary and the thorny bramble of von Junzt's overheated German prose. Suffice to say that it took me the better part of the evening to make my way through the introduction. It was well past midnight by the time I arrived at the first chapter, and nearing two o'clock before I had amassed the information that I will now pass along to the reader, with no endorsement beyond the testimony of these pages, nor any hope of its being believed.

It was a blustery night; I sat in the study on the top floor of my old house's round tower, listening to the windows rattle in their casements, as if a gang of intruders were seeking a way in. In this high room, in 1885, it was said, Howard Ash, the last living descendant of our town's founder, General Hannaniah Ash, had sealed the blank note of his life and dispatched himself, with postage due, to his Creator. A fugitive draft blew from time to time across my desk and stirred the pages of the dictionary by my left hand. I felt, as I read, as if the whole world were asleep – benighted, ignorant, and dreaming – while I had been left to man the crow's nest, standing lonely vigil in the teeth of a storm that was blowing in from a tropic of dread.

According to the scholar or charlatan Friedrich von Junzt, the regions around what is now northern Armenia had spawned, along with an entire cosmology, two competing cults of incalculable antiquity, which survived to the present day: that of Yê-Heh, the God of Dark Laughter, and that of Ai, the God of Unbearable and Ubiquitous Sorrow. The Yê-Hehists viewed the universe as a cosmic hoax, perpetrated by the father-god Yrrh for unknowable purposes: a place of calamity and cruel irony so overwhelming that the only possible response was a malevolent laughter like that, presumably, of Yrrh himself. The laughing followers of baboon-headed Yê-Heh created a sacred burlesque, mentioned by Pausanias and by one of the travellers in Plutarch's dialogue "On the Passing of the Oracles," to express their mockery of life, death, and all human aspirations. The rite involved the flaying of a human head, severed from the shoulders of one who had died in battle or in the course of some other supposedly exalted endeavor. The clown-priest would don the bloodless mask and then dance, making a public travesty of the noble dead. Through generations of inbreeding, the worshippers of Yê-Heh had evolved into a virtual subspecies of humanity, characterized by distended grins and skin as white as chalk. Von Junzt even claimed that the tradition of painted circus clowns derived from the clumsy imitation, by noninitiates, of these ancient kooks.

The "immemorial foes" of the baboon boys, as the reader may have surmised, were the followers of Ai, the God Who Mourns. These gloomy fanatics saw the world as no less horrifying and cruel than did their archenemies, but their response to the whole mess was a more or less permanent wailing. Over the long millennia since the heyday of ancient Urartu, the Aiites had developed a complicated physical discipline, a sort of jujitsu or calisthenics of murder, which they chiefly employed in a ruthless hunt of followers of Yê-Heh. For they believed that Yrrh, the Absent One, the Silent Devisor who, an eternity ago, tossed the cosmos over his shoulder like a sheet of fish wrap and wandered away leaving not a clue as to his intentions, would not return to explain the meaning of his inexplicable and tragic creation until the progeny of Yê-Heh, along with all copies of the Yê-Hehist sacred book, "Khndzut Dzul," or "The Unfathomable Ruse," had been expunged from the face of the earth. Only then would Yrrh return from his primeval hiatus – bringing what new horror or redemption," as the German intoned, "none can say."

All this struck me as a gamier variety of the same loony, Zoroastrian plonk that my mother had spent her life decanting, and I might have been inclined to set the whole business aside and leave the case to be swept under the administrative rug by Jack Ganz had it not been for the words with which Herr von Junzt concluded the second chapter of his tedious work:

> While the Yê-Hehist gospel of cynicism and ridicule has, quite obviously, spread around the world, the cult itself has largely died out, in part through the predations of foes and in part through chronic health problems brought about by inbreeding. Today [von Junzt's book carried a date of 1849] it is reported that there may be fewer than 150 of the Yê-Hehists left in the world. They have survived, for the most part, by taking on work in travelling circuses. While their existence is known to ordinary members of the circus world, their secret has, by and large, been kept. And in the sideshows they have gone to ground, awaiting the tread outside the wagon, the shadow on the tent-flap, the cruel knife that will, in a mockery of their own long-abandoned ritual of mockery, deprive them of the lily-white flesh of their skulls.

Here I put down the book, my hands trembling from fatigue, and took up the other one, printed in an unknown tongue. "The Unfathomable Ruse"? I hardly thought so; I was inclined to give as little credit as I reasonably could to Herr von Junzt's account. More than likely the small black volume was some inspirational text in the mother tongue of the dead man, a translation of the Gospels, perhaps. And yet I must confess that there were a few tangential points in von Junzt's account that caused me some misgiving.

There was a scrape then just outside my window, as if a finger with a very long nail were being drawn almost lovingly along the glass. But the finger turned out to be one of the branches of a fine old horse-chestnut tree that stood outside the tower, scratching at the window in the wind. I was relieved and humiliated. Time to go to bed, I said to myself. Before I turned in, I went to the shelf and moved to one side the bust of Galen that I had inherited from my father, a country doctor. I took a quick snort of good Tennessee whiskey, a taste for which I had also inherited from the old man. Thus emboldened, I went over to the desk and picked up the books. To be frank, I would have preferred to leave them there – I would have preferred to burn them, to be really frank – but I felt that it was my duty to keep them about me while they were under my watch. So I slept with the books beneath my pillow, in their wax envelopes, and I had the worst dream of my life.

It was one of those dreams where you are a fly on the wall, a phantom bystander, disembodied, unable to speak or intervene. In it, I was treated to the spectacle of a man whose young son was going to die. The man lived in a corner of the world where, from time to time, evil seemed to bubble up from the rusty red earth like a black combustible compound of ancient things long dead. And yet, year after year, this man met each new outburst of horror, true to his code, with nothing but law books, statutes, and county ordinances, as if sheltering with only a sheet of newspaper those he had sworn to protect, insisting that the steaming black geyser pouring down on them was nothing but a light spring rain. That vision started me laughing, but the cream of the jest came when, seized by a spasm of forgiveness toward his late, mad mother, the man decided not to prosecute one of her old paramours, a rummy by the name of Craven, for driving under the influence. Shortly thereafter, Craven steered his old Hudson Terraplane the wrong way down a one-way street, where it encountered, with appropriate cartoon sound effects, an oncoming bicycle ridden by the man's heedless, darling, wildly pedalling son. That was the funniest thing of all, funnier than the amusing ironies of the man's profession, than his furtive drinking and his wordless, solitary suppers, funnier even than his having been widowed by suicide: the joke of a father's outliving his boy. It was so funny that watching this ridiculous man in my dream, I could not catch my breath for laughing. I laughed so hard that my eyes popped from their sockets, and my smile stretched until it broke my aching jaw. I laughed until the husk of my head burst like a pod and fell away, and my skull and brains went floating off into the sky, white dandelion fluff, a cloud of fairy parasols.

Around four o'clock in the morning, I woke and was conscious of someone in the room with me. There was an unmistakable tang of the sea in the air. My eyesight is poor and it took me a while to make him out in the darkness, though he was standing just beside my bed, with his long thin arm snaked under my pillow, creeping around. I lay perfectly still, aware of the tips of this slender shadow's fingernails and the scrape of his scaly knuckles, as he rifled the contents of my head and absconded with them through the bedroom window, which was somehow also the mouth of the Neighborsburg Caverns, with tiny old Colonel Earnshaw taking tickets in the booth.

I awakened now in truth, and reached immediately under the pillow. The books were still there. I returned them to the evidence room at eight o'clock this morning. At nine, there was a call from Dolores and Victor Abbott, at their motor lodge out on the Plunkettsburgh Pike. A guest had made an abrupt departure, leaving a mess. I got into a car with Ganz and we drove out to get a look. The Ashtown police were already there, going over the buildings and grounds of the Vista Dolores Lodge. The bathroom wastebasket of Room 201 was overflowing with blood-soaked bandages. There was evidence that the guest had been keeping some kind of live bird in the room; one of the neighboring guests reported that it had sounded like a crow. And over the whole room there hung a salt smell that I recognized immediately, a smell that some compared to the smell of the ocean, and others to that of blood. When the pillow, wringing wet, was sent up to Pittsburgh for analysis by Mr. Espy, it was found to have been saturated with human tears.

When I returned from court, late this afternoon, there was a message from Dr. Sauer. He had completed his postmortem and wondered if I would drop by. I took the bottle from behind Daniel Webster and headed on down to the county morgue.

"He was already dead, the poor son of a biscuit eater," Dr. Sauer said, looking less morose than he had the last time we spoke. Sauer was a gaunt old Methodist who avoided strong language but never, so long as I had known him, strong drink. I poured us each a tumbler, and then a second. "It took me a while to establish it because there was something about the fellow that I was missing."

"What was that?"

"Well, I'm reasonably sure that he was a hemophiliac. So my reckoning time of death by coagulation of the blood was all thrown off."

"Hemophilia," I said.

"Yes," Dr. Sauer said. "It is associated sometimes with inbreeding, as in the case of royal families of Europe."

Inbreeding. We stood there for a while, looking at the sad bulk of the dead man under the sheet.

"I also found a tattoo," Dr. Sauer added. "The head of a grinning baboon. On his left forearm. Oh, and one other thing. He suffered from some kind of vitiligo. There are white patches on his nape and throat."

Let the record show that the contents of the victim's makeup kit, when it was inventoried, included cold cream, rouge, red greasepaint, a powder puff, some brushes, cotton swabs, and five cans of foundation in a tint the label described as "Olive Male." There was no trace, however, of the white greasepaint with which clowns daub their grinning faces.

Here I conclude my report, and with it my tenure as district attorney for this blighted and unfortunate county. I have staked my career – my life itself – on the things I could see, on the stories I could credit, and on the eventual vindication, when the book was closed, of the reasonable and skeptical approach. In the face of twenty-five years of bloodshed, mayhem, criminality, and the universal human pastime of ruination, I have clung fiercely to Occam's razor, seeking always to keep my solutions unadorned and free of conjecture, and never to resort to conspiracy or any kind of prosecutorial woolgathering. My mother, whenever she was confronted by calamity or personal sorrow, invoked cosmic emanations, invisible empires, ancient prophecies, and intrigues; it has been the business of my life to reject such folderol and seek the simpler explanation. But we were fools, she and I, arrant blockheads, each of us blind to or heedless of the readiest explanation: that the world is an ungettable joke, and our human need to explain its wonders and horrors, our appalling genius for devising such explanations, is nothing more than the rim shot that accompanies the punch line.

I do not know if that nameless clown was the last, but in any case, with such pursuers, there can be few of his kind left. And if there is any truth in the grim doctrine of those hunters, then the return of our father Yrrh, with his inscrutable intentions, cannot be far off. But I fear that, in spite of their efforts over the last ten thousand years, the followers of Ai are going to be gravely disappointed when, at the end of all we know and everything we have ever lost or imagined, the rafters of the world are shaken by a single, a terrible guffaw.

The Rose in Twelve Petals

Theodora Goss

I. *The Witch*

THIS ROSE has twelve petals. Let the first one fall: Madeleine taps the glass bottle, and out tumbles a bit of pink silk that clinks on the table – a chip of tinted glass – no, look closer, a crystallized rose petal. She lifts it into a saucer and crushes it with the back of a spoon until it is reduced to lumpy powder and a puff of fragrance.

She looks at the book again. "Petal of one rose crushed, dung of small bat soaked in vinegar." Not enough light comes through the cottage's small-paned windows, and besides she is growing nearsighted, although she is only thirty-two. She leans closer to the page. He should have given her spectacles rather than pearls. She wrinkles her forehead to focus her eyes, which makes her look prematurely old, as in a few years she no doubt will be.

Bat dung has a dank, uncomfortable smell, like earth in caves that has never seen sunlight.

Can she trust it, this book? Two pounds ten shillings it cost her, including postage. She remembers the notice in *The Gentlewoman's Companion*: "Every lady her own magician. Confound your enemies, astonish your friends! As simple as a cookery manual." It looks magical enough, with *Compendium Magicarum* stamped on its spine and gilt pentagrams on its red leather cover.

But the back pages advertise "a most miraculous lotion, that will make any lady's skin as smooth as an infant's bottom" and the collected works of Scott.

Not easy to spare ten shillings, not to mention two pounds, now that the King has cut off her income. Rather lucky, this cottage coming so cheap, although it has no proper plumbing, just a privy out back among the honeysuckle.

Madeleine crumbles a pair of dragonfly wings into the bowl, which is already half full: orris root; cat's bones found on the village dust heap; oak gall from a branch fallen into a fairy ring; madder, presumably for its color; crushed rose petal; bat dung.

And the magical words, are they quite correct? She knows a little Latin, learned from her brother. After her mother's death, when her father began spending days in his bedroom with a bottle of beer, she tended the shop, selling flour and printed cloth to the village women, scythes and tobacco to the men, sweets to children on their way to school. When her brother came home, he would sit at the counter beside her, saying his amo, amas. The silver cross he earned by taking a Hibernian bayonet in the throat is the only necklace she now wears.

She binds the mixture with water from a hollow stone and her own saliva. Not pleasant this, she was brought up not to spit, but she imagines she is spitting into the King's face, that first time when he came into the shop, and leaned on the counter, and smiled through his golden beard. "If I had known there was such a pretty shopkeeper in this village, I would have done my own shopping long ago."

She remembers: buttocks covered with golden hair among folds of white linen, like twin halves of a peach on a napkin. "Come here, Madeleine." The sounds of the palace, horses clopping, pageboys shouting to one another in the early morning air. "You'll never want for anything, haven't I told you that?" A string of pearls, each as large as her smallest fingernail, with a clasp of gold filigree. "Like it? That's Hibernian work, taken in the siege of London." Only later does she notice that between two pearls, the knotted silk is stained with blood.

She leaves the mixture under cheesecloth, to dry overnight.

Madeleine walks into the other room, the only other room of the cottage, and sits at the table that serves as her writing desk. She picks up a tin of throat lozenges. How it rattles. She knows, without opening it, that there are five pearls left, and that after next month's rent there will only be four.

Confound your enemies, she thinks, peering through the inadequate light, and the wrinkles on her forehead make her look prematurely old, as in a few years she certainly will be.

II. *The Queen*

Petals fall from the roses that hang over the stream, Empress Josephine and Gloire de Dijon, which dislike growing so close to the water. This corner of the garden has been planted to resemble a country landscape in miniature: artificial stream with ornamental fish, a pear tree that has never yet bloomed, bluebells that the gardener plants out every spring. This is the Queen's favorite part of the garden, although the roses dislike her as well, with her romantically diaphanous gowns, her lisping voice, her poetry.

Here she comes, reciting Tennyson.

She holds her arms out, allowing her sleeves to drift on the slight breeze, imagining she is Elaine the lovable, floating on a river down to Camelot. Hard, being a lily maid now her belly is swelling.

She remembers her belly reluctantly, not wanting to touch it, unwilling to acknowledge that it exists. Elaine the lily maid had no belly, surely, she thinks, forgetting that Galahad must have been born somehow. (Perhaps he rose out of the lake?) She imagines her belly as a sort of cavern, where something is growing in the darkness, something that is not hers, alien and unwelcome.

Only twelve months ago (fourteen, actually, but she is bad at numbers), she was Princess Elizabeth of Hibernia, dressed in pink satin, gossiping about the riding master with her friends, dancing with her brothers through the ruined arches of Westminster Cathedral, and eating too much cake at her seventeenth birthday party. Now, and she does not want to think about this so it remains at the edges of her mind, where unpleasant things, frogs and slugs, reside, she is a cavern with something growing inside her, something repugnant, something that is not hers, not the lily maid of Astolat's.

She reaches for a rose, an overblown Gloire de Dijon that, in a fit of temper, pierces her finger with its thorns. She cries out, sucks the blood from her finger, and flops down on the bank like a miserable child. The hem of her diaphanous dress begins to absorb the mud at the edge of the water.

III. *The Magician*

Wolfgang Magus places the rose he picked that morning in his buttonhole and looks at his reflection in the glass. He frowns, as his master Herr Doktor Ambrosius would have frowned, at the scarecrow in faded wool with a drooping gray mustache. A sad figure for a court magician.

"Gott in Himmel," he says to himself, a childhood habit he has kept from nostalgia, for Wolfgang Magus is a reluctant atheist. He knows it is not God's fault but the King's, who pays him so little. If the King were to pay him, say, another shilling per week – but no, that too he would send to his sister, dying of consumption at a spa in Berne. His mind turns, painfully, from the memory of her face, white and drained, which already haunts him like a ghost.

He picks up a volume of Goethe's poems that he has carefully tied with a bit of pink ribbon and sighs. What sort of present is this, for the Princess' christening?

He enters the chapel with shy, stooping movements. It is full, and noisy with court gossip. As he proceeds up the aisle, he is swept by a Duchess' train of peau de soie, poked by a Viscountess' aigrette. The sword of a Marquis smelling of Napoleon-water tangles in his legs, and he almost falls on a Baroness, who stares at him through her lorgnette. He sidles through the crush until he comes to a corner of the chapel wall, where he takes refuge.

The christening has begun, he supposes, for he can hear the Archbishop droning in bad Latin, although he can see nothing from his corner but taxidermed birds and heads slick with macassar oil. Ah, if the Archbishop could have learned from Herr Doktor Ambrosius! His mind wanders, as it often does, to a house in Berlin and a laboratory smelling of strong soap, filled with braziers and alembics, books whose covers have been half-eaten by moths, a stuffed basilisk. He remembers his bed in the attic, and his sister, who worked as the Herr Doktor's housemaid so he could learn to be a magician. He sees her face on her pillow at the spa in Berne and thinks of her expensive medications.

What has he missed? The crowd is moving forward, and presents are being given: a rocking horse with a red leather saddle, a silver tumbler, a cap embroidered by the nuns of Iona. He hides the volume of Goethe behind his back.

Suddenly, he sees a face he recognizes. One day she came and sat beside him in the garden, and asked him about his sister. Her brother had died, he remembers, not long before, and as he described his loneliness, her eyes glazed over with tears. Even he, who understands little about court politics, knew she was the King's mistress.

She disappears behind the scented Marquis, then appears again, close to the altar where the Queen, awkwardly holding a linen bundle, is receiving the Princess' presents. The King has seen her, and frowns through his golden beard. Wolfgang Magus, who knows nothing about the feelings of a king toward his former mistress, wonders why he is angry.

She lifts her hand in a gesture that reminds him of the Archbishop. What fragrance is this, so sweet, so dark, that makes the brain clear, that makes the nostrils water? He instinctively tabulates: orris-root, oak gall, rose petal, dung of bat with a hint of vinegar.

Conversations hush, until even the Baronets, clustered in a rustic clump at the back of the chapel, are silent.

She speaks: "This is the gift I give the Princess. On her seventeenth birthday she will prick her finger on the spindle of a spinning wheel and die."

Needless to describe the confusion that follows. Wolfgang Magus watches from its edge, chewing his mustache, worried, unhappy. How her eyes glazed, that day in the garden. Someone treads on his toes.

Then, unexpectedly, he is summoned. "Where is that blasted magician!" Gloved hands push him forward. He stands before the King, whose face has turned unattractively red. The Queen has fainted and a bottle of salts is waved under her nose. The Archbishop is holding the Princess, like a sack of barley he has accidentally caught.

"Is this magic, Magus, or just some bloody trick?"

Wolfgang Magus rubs his hands together. He has not stuttered since he was a child, but he answers, "Y-yes, your Majesty. Magic." Sweet, dark, utterly magic. He can smell its power.

"Then get rid of it. Un-magic it. Do whatever you bloody well have to. Make it not be!"

Wolfgang Magus already knows that he will not be able to do so, but he says, without realizing that he is chewing his mustache in front of the King, "O-of course, your Majesty!"

IV. *The King*

What would you do, if you were James IV of Britannia, pacing across your council chamber floor before your councilors: the Count of Edinburgh, whose estates are larger than yours and include hillsides of uncut wood for which the French Emperor, who needs to refurbish his navy after the disastrous Indian campaign, would pay handsomely; the Earl of York, who can trace descent, albeit in the female line, from the Tudors; and the Archbishop, who has preached against marital infidelity in his cathedral at Aberdeen? The banner over your head, embroidered with the twelve-petaled rose of Britannia, reminds you that your claim to the throne rests tenuously on a former James' dalliance, Edinburgh's thinning hair, York's hanging jowl, the seams, edged with gold thread, where the Archbishop's robe has been let out, warn you, young as you are, with a beard that shines like a tangle of golden wires in the afternoon light, of your gouty future.

Britannia's economy depends on the wool trade, and spun wool sells for twice as much as unspun. Your income depends on the wool tax. The Queen, whom you seldom think of as Elizabeth, is young. You calculate: three months before she recovers from the birth, nine months before she can deliver another child. You might have an heir by next autumn.

"Well?" Edinburgh leans back in his chair, and you wish you could strangle his wrinkled neck.

You say, "I see no reason to destroy a thousand spinning wheels for one madwoman." Madeleine, her face puffed with sleep, her neck covered with a line of red spots where she lay on the pearl necklace you gave her the night before, one black hair tickling your ear. Clever of her, to choose a spinning wheel. "I rely entirely on Wolfgang Magus," whom you believe is a fraud. "Gentlemen, your fairy tales will have taught you that magic must be met with magic. One cannot fight a spell by altering material conditions."

Guffaws from the Archbishop, who is amused to think that he once read fairy tales.

You are a selfish man, James IV, and this is essentially your fault, but you have spoken the truth. Which, I suppose, is why you are the King.

v. *The Queen Dowager*

What is the girl doing? Playing at tug-of-war, evidently, and far too close to the stream. She'll tear her dress on the rosebushes. Careless, these young people, thinks the Queen Dowager. And who is she playing with? Young Lord Harry, who will one day be Count of Edinburgh. The Queen Dowager is proud of her keen eyesight and will not wear spectacles, although she is almost sixty-three.

What a pity the girl is so plain. The Queen Dowager jabs her needle into a black velvet slipper. Eyes like boiled gooseberries that always seem to be staring at you, and no discipline. Now in her day, thinks the Queen Dowager, remembering backboards and nuns who rapped your fingers with canes, in her day girls had discipline. Just look at the Queen: no discipline. Two miscarriages in ten years, and dead before her thirtieth birthday. Of course linen is so much cheaper now that the kingdoms are united. But if only her Jims (which is how she thinks of the King) could have married that nice German princess.

She jabs the needle again, pulls it out, jabs, knots. She holds up the slipper and then its pair, comparing the roses embroidered on each toe in stitches so even they seem to have been made by a machine. Quite perfect for her Jims, to keep his feet warm on the drafty palace floors.

A tearing sound, and a splash. The girl, of course, as the Queen Dowager could have warned you. Just look at her, with her skirt ripped up one side and her petticoat muddy to the knees.

"I do apologize, Madam. I assure you it's entirely my fault," says Lord Harry, bowing with the superfluous grace of a dancing master.

"It *is* all your fault," says the girl, trying to kick him.

"Alice!" says the Queen Dowager. Imagine the Queen wanting to name the girl Elaine. What a name, for a Princess of Britannia.

"But he took my book of poems and said he was going to throw it into the stream!"

"I'm perfectly sure he did no such thing. Go to your room at once. This is the sort of behavior I would expect from a chimney sweep."

"Then tell him to give my book back!"

Lord Harry bows again and holds out the battered volume. "It was always yours for the asking, your Highness."

Alice turns away, and you see what the Queen Dowager cannot, despite her keen vision: Alice's eyes, slightly prominent, with irises that are indeed the color of gooseberries, have turned red at the corners, and her nose has begun to drip.

VI. *The Spinning Wheel*

It has never wanted to be an assassin. It remembers the cottage on the Isles where it was first made: the warmth of the hearth and the feel of its maker's hands, worn smooth from rubbing and lanolin.

It remembers the first words it heard: "And why are you carving roses on it, then?"

"This one's for a lady. Look how slender it is. It won't take your upland ram's wool. Yearling it'll have to be, for this one."

At night it heard the waves crashing on the rocks, and it listened as their sound mingled with the snoring of its maker and his wife. By day it heard the crying of the sea birds. But it remembered, as in a dream, the songs of inland birds and sunlight on a stone wall. Then the fishermen would come, and one would say, "What's that you're making there, Enoch? Is it for a midget, then?"

Its maker would stroke it with the tips of his fingers and answer, "Silent, lads. This one's for a lady. It'll spin yarn so fine that a shawl of it will slip through a wedding ring."

It has never wanted to be an assassin, and as it sits in a cottage to the south, listening as Madeleine mutters to herself, it remembers the sounds of seabirds and tries to forget that it was made, not to spin yarn so fine that a shawl of it will slip through a wedding ring, but to kill the King's daughter.

VII. *The Princess*

Alice climbs the tower stairs. She could avoid this perhaps, disguise herself as a peasant woman and beg her way to the Highlands, like a heroine in Scott's novels. But she does not want to avoid this, so she is climbing up the tower stairs on the morning of her seventeenth birthday, still in her nightgown and clutching a battered copy of Goethe's poems whose binding is so torn that the book is tied with pink ribbon to keep the pages together. Her feet are bare, because opening the shoe closet might have woken the Baroness, who has slept in her room since she was a child. Barefoot, she has walked silently past the sleeping guards, who are supposed to guard her today with particular care. She has walked past the Queen Dowager's drawing room thinking: if anyone hears me, I will be in disgrace. She has spent a larger portion of her life in disgrace than out of it, and she remembers that she once thought of it as an imaginary country, Disgrace, with its own rivers and towns and trade routes. Would it be different if her mother were alive? She remembers a face creased from the folds of the pillow, and pale lips whispering to her about the lily maid of Astolat. It would, she supposes, have made no difference. She trips on a step and almost drops the book.

She has no reason to suppose, of course, that the Witch will be there, so early in the morning. But somehow, Alice hopes she will be.

She is, sitting on a low stool with a spinning wheel in front of her.

"Were you waiting for me?" asks Alice. It sounds silly – who else would the Witch be waiting for? But she can think of nothing else to say.

"I was." The Witch's voice is low and cadenced, and although she has wrinkles at the corners of her mouth and her hair has turned gray, she is still rather beautiful. She is not, exactly, what Alice expected.

"How did you know I was coming so early?"

The Witch smiles. "I've gotten rather good at magic. I sell fortunes for my living, you see. It's not much, just enough to buy bread and butter, and to rent a small cottage. But it amuses me, knowing things about people – their lives and their future."

"Do you know anything – about me?" Alice looks down at the book. What idiotic questions to be asking. Surely a heroine from Scott's novels would think of better.

The Witch nods, and sunlight catches the silver cross suspended from a chain around her neck. She says, "I'm sorry."

Alice understands, and her face flushes. "You mean that you've been watching all along. That you've known what it's been like, being the cursed princess." She turns and walks to the tower window, so the Witch will not see how her hands are shaking. "You know the other girls wouldn't play with me or touch my toys, that the boys would spit over their shoulder, to break the curse they said. Even the chambermaids would make the sign of the cross when I wasn't looking." She can feel tears where they always begin, at the corners of her eyes, and she leans out the window to cool her face. Far below, a gardener is crossing the courtyard, carrying a pair of pruning shears. She says, "Why didn't you remove the curse, then?"

"Magic doesn't work that way." The Witch's voice is sad. Alice turns around and sees that her cheeks are wet with tears. Alice steps toward her, trips again, and drops the book, which falls under the spinning wheel.

The Witch picks it up and smiles as she examines the cover. "Of course, your Goethe. I always wondered what happened to Wolfgang Magus."

Alice thinks with relief: I'm not going to cry after all. "He went away, after his sister died. She had consumption, you know, for years and years. He was always sending her money for medicine. He wrote to me once after he left, from Berlin, to say that he had bought his old master's house. But I never heard from him again."

The Witch wipes her cheeks with the back of one hand. "I didn't know about his sister. I spoke to him once. He was a kind man."

Alice takes the book from her, then says, carefully, as though each word has to be placed in the correct order, "Do you think his spell will work? I mean, do you think I'll really sleep for a hundred years, rather than – you know?"

The Witch looks up, her cheeks still damp, but her face composed. "I can't answer that for you. You may simply be – preserved. In a pocket of time, as it were."

Alice tugs at the ribbon that binds the book together. "It doesn't matter, really. I don't think I care either way." She strokes the spinning wheel, which turns as she touches it. "How beautiful, as though it had been made just for me."

The Witch raises a hand, to stop her perhaps, or arrest time itself, but Alice places her finger on the spindle and presses until a drop of blood blossoms, as dark as the petal of a Cardinal de Richelieu, and runs into her palm.

Before she falls, she sees the Witch with her head bowed and her shoulders shaking. She thinks, for no reason she can remember, Elaine the fair, Elaine the lovable...

VIII. *The Gardener*

Long after, when the gardener has grown into an old man, he will tell his grandchildren about that day: skittish horses being harnessed by panicked grooms, nobles struggling with boxes while their valets carry armchairs and even bedsteads through the palace halls, the King in a pair of black velvet slippers shouting directions. The cooks leave the kettles whistling in the kitchen, the Queen Dowager leaves her jewels lying where she has dropped them while tripping over the hem of her nightgown. Everyone runs to escape the spreading lethargy that has already caught a canary in his cage, who makes soft noises as he settles into his feathers. The flowers are closing in the garden, and even the lobsters that the chef was planning to serve with melted butter for lunch have lain down in a corner of their tank.

In a few hours, the palace is left to the canary, and the lobsters, and the Princess lying on the floor of the tower.

He will say, "I was pruning a rosebush at the bottom of the tower that day. Look what I took away with me!" Then he will display a rose of the variety called Britannia, with its twelve petals half-open, still fresh and moist with dew. His granddaughter will say, "Oh, grandpa, you picked that in the garden just this morning!" His grandson, who is practical and wants to be an engineer, will say, "Grandpa, people can't sleep for a hundred years."

IX. *The Tower*

Let us get a historical perspective. When the tower was quite young, only a hovel really, a child knocked a stone out of its wall, and it gained an eye. With that eye it watched as the child's father, a chieftain, led his tribe against soldiers with metal breastplates and plumed helmets. Two lines met on the plain below: one regular, gleaming in the morning sun like the edge of a sword, the other ragged and blue like the crest of a wave. The wave washed over the sword, which splintered into a hundred pieces.

Time passed, and the tower gained a second story with a vertical eye as narrow as a staff. It watched a wooden structure grow beside it, in which men and cattle mingled indiscriminately. One morning it felt a prick, the point of an arrow. A bright flame blossomed from the beams of the wooden structure, men scattered, cattle screamed. One of its walls was singed, and it felt the wound as a distant heat. A castle rose, commanded by a man with eyebrows so blond that they were almost white, who caused the name Aelfric to be carved on the lintel of the tower. The castle's stone walls, pummeled with catapults, battered by rams, fell into fragments. From the hilltop a man watched, whose nose had been broken in childhood and remained perpetually crooked. When a palace rose from the broken rock, he caused the name D'Arblay to be carved on the lintel of the tower, beside a boar rampant.

Time passed, and a woman on a white horse rode through the village that had grown around the palace walls, followed by a retinue that stretched behind her like a scarf. At the palace gates, a Darbley grown rich on tobacco plantations in the New World presented her with the palace, in honor of her marriage to the Earl of Essex. The lintel of the tower was carved with the name Elizabeth I, and it gained a third story with a lead-paned window, through which it saw in facets like a fly. One morning it watched the Queen's son, who had been playing ball in the courtyard, fall to the ground with blood dripping from his nostrils. The windows of the palace were draped in black velvet, the Queen and her consort rode away with their retinue, and the village was deserted.

Time passed. Leaves turned red or gold, snow fell and melted into rivulets, young hawks took their first flight from the battlements. A rosebush grew at the foot of the tower: a hybrid, half wild rose, half Cuisse de Nymphe, with twelve petals and briary canes. One morning men rode up to the tower on horses whose hides were mottled with sweat. In its first story, where the chieftain's son had played, they talked of James III. Troops were coming from France, and the password was Britannia. As they left the tower, one of them plucked a flower from the rosebush. "Let this be our symbol," he said in the self-conscious voice of a man who thinks that his words will be recorded in history books. The tower thought it would be alone again, but by the time the leaves had turned, a procession rode up to the palace gates, waving banners embroidered with a twelve-petaled rose. Furniture arrived from France, fruit trees were planted, and the village streets were paved so that the hooves of cattle clopped on the stones.

It has stood a long time, that tower, watching the life around it shift and alter, like eddies in a stream. It looks down once again on a deserted village – but no, not entirely deserted. A woman still lives in a cottage at its edge. Her hair has turned white, but she works every day in her garden, gathering tomatoes and cutting back the mint. When the day is particularly warm, she brings out a spinning wheel and sits in the garden, spinning yarn so fine that a shawl of it will slip through a wedding ring. If the breezes come from the west, the tower can hear her humming, just above the humming that the wheel makes as it spins. Time passes, and she sits out in the garden less often, until one day it realizes that it has not seen her for many days, or perhaps years.

Sometimes at night it thinks it can hear the Princess breathing in her sleep.

x. *The Hound*

In a hundred years, only one creature comes to the palace: a hound whose coat is matted with dust. Along his back the hair has come out in tufts, exposing a mass of sores. He lopes unevenly: on one of his forepaws, the inner toes have been crushed.

He has run from a city reduced to stone skeletons and drifting piles of ash, dodging tanks, mortar fire, the rifles of farmers desperate for food. For weeks now, he has been loping along the dusty roads. When rain comes, he has curled himself under a tree. Afterward, he has drunk from puddles, then loped along again with mud drying in the hollows of his paws. Sometimes he has left the road and tried to catch rabbits in the fields, but his damaged paw prevents him from running quickly enough. He has smelled them in their burrows beneath the summer grasses, beneath the poppies and cornflowers, tantalizing, inaccessible.

This morning he has smelled something different, pungent, like spoiled meat: the smell of enchantment. He has left the road and entered the forest, finding his way through a tangle of briars. He has come to the village, loped up its cobbled streets and through the gates of the palace. His claws click on its stone floor.

What does he smell? A fragrance, drifting, indistinct, remembered from when he was a pup: bacon. There, through that doorway. He lopes into the Great Hall, where breakfast waits in chafing dishes. The eggs are still firm, their yolks plump and yellow, their whites delicately fried. Sausages sit in their own grease. The toast is crisp.

He leaves a streak of egg yolk and sausage grease on the tablecloth, which has remained pristine for half a century, and falls asleep in the Queen Dowager's drawing room, in a square of sunlight that has not faded the baroque carpet.

He lives happily ever after. Someone has to. As summer passes, he wanders through the palace gardens, digging in the flower beds and trying to catch the sleeping fish that float in the ornamental pools. One day he urinates on the side of the tower, from which the dark smell emanates, to show his disapproval. When he is hungry he eats from the side of beef hanging in the larder, the sausage and eggs remaining on the breakfast table, or the mice sleeping beneath the harpsichord. In autumn, he chases the leaves falling red and yellow over the lawns and manages to pull a lobster from the kitchen tank, although his teeth can barely crack its hard shell. He never figures out how to extract the canary from its cage. When winter comes, the stone floor sends an ache through his damaged paw, and he sleeps in the King's bed, under velvet covers.

When summer comes again, he is too old to run about the garden. He lies in the Queen Dowager's drawing room and dreams of being a pup, of warm hands and a voice that whispered "What a beautiful dog," and that magical thing called a ball. He dies, his stomach still full with the last of the poached eggs. A proper fairy tale should, perhaps, end here.

XI. *The Prince*

Here comes the Prince on a bulldozer. What did you expect? Things change in a hundred years.

Harry pulls back the brake and wipes his forehead, which is glistening with sweat. He runs his fingers through blond hair that stands up like a shock of corn. It is just past noon, and the skin on his nose is already red and peeling.

Two acres, and he'll knock off for some beer and that liver and onion sandwich Madge made him this morning, whose grease, together with the juice of a large gherkin, is soaking its way through a brown paper wrapper and will soon stain the leather of his satchel. He leans back, looks at the tangle of briars that form the undergrowth in this part of the forest, and chews on the knuckle of his thumb.

Two acres in the middle of the forest, enough for some barley and a still. Hell of a good idea, he thinks, already imagining the bottles on their way to Amsterdam, already imagining his pals Mike and Steve watching football on a color telly. Linoleum on the kitchen floor, like Madge always wanted, and cigarettes from America. "Not that damn rationed stuff," he says out loud, then looks around startled. What kind of fool idiot talks to himself? He chews on the knuckle of his thumb again. Twenty pounds to make the Police Commissioner look the other way. Damn lucky Madge could lend them the money. The bulldozer starts up again with a roar and the smell of diesel.

You don't like where this is going. What sort of Prince is this, with his liver and onion sandwich, his gherkin and beer? Forgive me, I give you the only Prince I can find, a direct descendant of the Count of Edinburgh, himself descended from the Tudors, albeit in the female line. Of course, all such titles have been abolished. This is, after all, the Socialist Union of Britannia. If Harry knows he is a Prince, he certainly isn't telling Mike or Steve, who might sell him out for a pack of American cigarettes. Even Madge can't be trusted, though they've been sharing a flat in the commune's apartment building for three years.

Hell, she made a big enough fuss about the distillery business.

The bulldozer's roar grows louder, then turns into a whine. The front wheel is stuck in a ditch. Harry climbs down and looks at the wheel. Damn, he'll have to get Mike and Steve. He kicks the wheel, kicks a tree trunk and almost gets his foot caught in a briar, kicks the wheel again.

Something flashes in the forest. Now what the hell is that? (You and I know it is sunlight flashing from the faceted upper window of the tower.) Harry opens his beer and swallows a mouthful of its warm bitterness. Some damn poacher, walking around on his land. (You and I remember that it belongs to the Socialist Union of Britannia.) He takes a bite of his liver and onion sandwich. Madge shouldn't frown so much, he thinks, remembering her in her housecoat, standing by the kitchen sink. She's getting wrinkles on her forehead. Should he fetch Mike and Steve? But the beer in his stomach, warm, bitter, tells him that he doesn't need Mike and Steve, because he can damn well handle any damn poacher himself. He bites into the gherkin.

Stay away, Prince Harry. Stay away from the forest full of briars. The Princess is not for you. You will never stumble up the tower stairs, smelling of beer; never leave a smear of mingled grease and sweat on her mouth; never take her away (thinking, Madge's rump is getting too damn broad) to fry your liver and onions and empty your ashtray of cigarette butts and iron your briefs.

At least, I hope not.

XII. *The Rose*

Let us go back to the beginning: petals fall. Unpruned for a hundred years, the rosebush has climbed to the top of the tower. A cane of it has found a chink in the tower window, and it has grown into the room where the Princess lies. It has formed a canopy over her, a network of canes now covered with blossoms, and their petals fall slowly in the still air. Her nightgown is covered with petals: this summer's, pink and fragrant, and those of summers past, like bits of torn parchment curling at the edges.

While everything in the palace has been suspended in a pool of time without ripples or eddies, it has responded to the seasons. Its roots go down to dark caverns which are the homes of moles and worms, and curl around a bronze helmet that is now little more than rust. More than two hundred years ago, it was rather carelessly chosen as the emblem of a nation. Almost a hundred years ago, Madeleine plucked a petal of it for her magic spell. Wolfgang Magus picked a blossom of it for his buttonhole, which fell in the chapel and was trampled under a succession of court heels and cavalry boots. A spindle was carved from its dead and hardened wood. Half a century ago, a dusty hound urinated on its roots. From its seeds, dispersed by birds who have eaten its orange hips, has grown the tangle of briars that surround the palace, which have already torn the Prince's work pants and left a gash on his right shoulder. If you listen, you can hear him cursing.

It can tell us how the story ends. Does the Prince emerge from the forest, his shirtsleeve stained with blood? The briars of the forest know. Does the Witch lie dead, or does she still sit by the small-paned window of her cottage, contemplating a solitary pearl that glows in the wrinkled palm of her hand like a miniature moon? The spinning wheel knows, and surely its wood will speak to the wood from which it was made. Is the Princess breathing? Perhaps she has been sleeping for a hundred years, and the petals that have settled under her nostrils flutter each time she exhales. Perhaps she has not been sleeping, perhaps she is an exquisitely preserved corpse, and the petals under her nostrils never quiver. The rose can tell us, but it will not. The wind sets its leaves stirring, and petals fall, and it whispers to us: you must find your own ending.

This is mine. The Prince trips over an oak log, falls into a fairy ring, and disappears. (He is forced to wash miniature clothes, and pinched when he complains.) Alice stretches and brushes the rose petals from her nightgown. She makes her way to the Great Hall and eats what is left in the breakfast dishes: porridge with brown sugar. She walks through the streets of the village, wondering at the silence, then hears a humming. Following it, she comes to a cottage at the village edge where Madeleine, her hair now completely white, sits and spins in her garden. Witches, you know, are extraordinarily long-lived. Alice says, "Good morning," and Madeleine asks, "Would you like some breakfast?" Alice says, "I've had some, thank you." Then the Witch spins while the Princess reads Goethe, and the spinning wheel produces yarn so fine that a shawl of it will slip through a wedding ring.

Will it come to pass? I do not know. I am waiting, like you, for the canary to lift its head from under its wing, for the Empress Josephine to open in the garden, for a sound that will tell us someone, somewhere, is awake.

I Want My 20th-Century Schizoid Art, IV

I GUESS my question is, is the whole point of blending two genres, or even just smushing them together, an attempt to get out of genre all together? Is slipstream ultimately about being Margaret Atwood?

And if that argument is true, then slipstream is not just diluting the genre – it's trying desperately to escape it.

I'm highly dubious that that is the case. If slipstream writers wanted out of SF, they wouldn't be publishing in the places they do. And moreover, for someone who wants to push the bounds of science fiction and the fantastic, identifying with a genre offers them the huge benefits of a history to push against and a tradition of that same kind of pushing.

MEGHAN MCCARRON, 8:22 AM, THURSDAY, MAY 5, 2005

Yup. People with content-based definitions of genres are going to find themselves increasingly bewildered. It's all about traditions and communities.

And, who the hell would want to get out of the SF/F genre? For me, if I have any selfish, ulterior motive behind my arguments for how "slipstream" gets constructed and construed, it's that I want to be able to write literary-influenced experimentalist fiction and talk about it at cons.

BENJAMIN ROSENBAUM, 8:36 AM, THURSDAY, MAY 5, 2005

Damn, you people are prolific.

I'm going to jump way back to David's original posting and respond belatedly to it even though the conversation has long since moved on:

I would argue that *slipstream* has been an ill-defined hodgepodge of several overlapping concepts ever since Sterling's essay; if you look at his booklist, it includes plenty of stuff that has nothing to do with that 20th-century-weirdness definition, and in fact I would argue that the essay itself provides multiple definitions. In my 2001 editorial "Where Does Genre Come From?" I noted that I thought "fiction with fantastical elements that's published in a marketing category other than speculative fiction" was fairly close to one of Sterling's definitions. I added: "Sterling says that on being given a vague definition of the term, any SF reader can immediately add books to the slipstream reading list, but I think that's partly because there are several overlapping definitions, some of which are very vague."

JED HARTMAN, 11:44 AM, THURSDAY, MAY 5, 2005

Yes to *slipstream* as a mess of incompatible definitions, from the moment Sterling spawned it.

BENJAMIN ROSENBAUM, 12:25 PM, THURSDAY, MAY 5, 2005

Slipstream, ultimately, is just a wussy term. We should be drawing names less from wishy-washy words (slip, stream) and more from monster trucks (krusher, inferno).

MEGHAN MCCARRON, 12:44 PM, THURSDAY, MAY 5, 2005

I hereby rebaptize *slipstream* fiction *infernocrusher* fiction, per Ms. McCarron.

DAVE SCHWARTZ, 12:49 PM, THURSDAY, MAY 5, 2005

There's a market I'd like to see: *The Magazine of Infernocrusher Fiction.* Probably have one interesting slush pile.

JON HANSEN, 1:12 PM, THURSDAY, MAY 5, 2005

My favorite thing about this *infernokrusher* concept is now there are all sorts of new debates to be had. Instead of, "Well, where are we slipping? Are we beaver-like dam builders, or just clumsy waders?" we can now ask "Are we glad things are on fire? Do we like to Krush?"

MEGHAN MCCARRON, 2:36 PM, THURSDAY, MAY 5, 2005

We must now all swear a solemn vow to say everywhere with a straight face, "Slipstream? Never heard of it. Do you know about infernokrusher fiction, though? Exciting new movement."

We can do this, people.

BENJAMIN ROSENBAUM, 7:09 AM, FRIDAY, MAY 6, 2005

I had been intending to start throwing the term *Indie Fiction* around as my own way of referring to slipstream by analogy to music and movies. Indie Fiction is to Genre SF or Fantasy as Indie Music is to Stadium Rock or Heavy Metal. Indie Fiction is to mainstream as Indie cinema is to Art House. And so on. Largely, though, I like the term because it sounds vaguely hip and means very little.

Now, though, *Infernokrusher* is clearly the way to go. Burn, baby, burn! Genre inferno!

HAL DUNCAN, 5:57 AM, SATURDAY, MAY 7, 2005

Look, young, dewy-eyed, infernokrusher people: if you coin some neologism as a critic, and people still cite that *seventeen years later,* you don't rue the damn day! That means you've *become canonical.* You're a classic, a definitive figure! You should live so long. Really.

Infernokrusher sounds to me like a coinage with 21st-Century legs. It's got that fierce Moslem fundie with a dynamite beltpack thing going on, so it's very of-the-moment. Not that I'd want to confusingly conflate genre tropes with the underlying motifs of global culture – heaven forbid that I should imply that there's even more going on than you suspect – but, well, if you want to get cited in seventeen years, that's kind of the trick of it, really.

9/11, WTC, Shock and Awe, Infernokrusher: hey, it's your world: run with it.

BRUCE STERLING, 10:45 AM, WEDNESDAY, JUNE 1, 2005

[*Here is what our bloggers had to say about themselves:*]

BARTH ANDERSON's fiction has appeared in *Asimov's, Strange Horizons, Polyphony,* among others. His first novel, *The Patron Saint of Plagues* from Bantam Spectra, is currently available.

CHRISTOPHER BARZAK grew up in Ohio, but currently lives in Japan. His strange stories have appeared in *Nerve, Realms of Fantasy, Trampoline,* and various Year's Best anthologies.

HANNAH WOLF BOWEN has moved to Boston and discovered a whole new kind of strange. Her stories have appeared in *Strange Horizons, ChiZine,* and others.

HAL DUNCAN'S first novel, *Vellum,* is available in the U.K. from Macmillan and from Del Rey in the United States.

JON HANSEN is a writer, librarian, and occasional blood donor. His wife Lisa and their four cats all think he's adorable. No, really.

JED HARTMAN is a fiction editor for the quasi-slipstreamesque online magazine *Strange Horizons.* He's also a founding member of Daisy-Sunshine, the literary movement for overly cheerful people.

MEGHAN MCCARRON was called "Bucky" in the womb (after R. Buckminster Fuller). She lives in Los Angeles. She likes hamburgers, high heels, and science fiction.

DAVID MOLES has lived in six time zones on three continents, and hopes some day to collect the set. Some of his work is slipstream-ish.

BENJAMIN ROSENBAUM is a person of a certain sensibility. His stories have appeared in *Harper's, Asimov's, McSweeney's, F&SF, Strange Horizons,* and *Nature.*

CHRISTOPHER ROWE has been nominated for the Nebula, Hugo, and Theodore Sturgeon Awards. He lives in Lexington, Kentucky.

DAVID J. SCHWARTZ'S fiction has or will soon appear in such venues as *Strange Horizons, The Third Alternative, Twenty Epics,* and *Spicy Slipstream Stories.*

The Lions Are Asleep This Night

Howard Waldrop

THE WHITE MAN was drunk again. Robert Oinenke crossed the narrow, graveled street and stepped up on the boardwalk at the other side. Out of the corner of his eyes he saw the white man raving. The man sat, feet out, back against a wall, shaking his head, punctuating his monologue with cursing words.

Some said he had been a mercenary in one of the border wars up the coast, one of those conflicts in which two countries had become one; or one country, three. Robert could not remember which. Mr Lemuel, his history teacher, had mentioned it only in passing.

Since showing up in Onitsha town the white man had worn the same khaki pants. They were of a military cut, now torn and stained. The shirt he wore today was a dashiki, perhaps variegated bright blue and red when made, now faded purple. He wore a cap with a foreign insignia. Some said he had been a general; others, a sergeant. His loud harangues terrified schoolchildren. Robert's classmates looked on the man as a forest demon. Sometimes the constables came and took him away; sometimes they only asked him to be quiet, and he would subside.

Mostly he could be seen propped against a building, talking to himself. Occasionally somebody would give him money. Then he would make his way to the nearest store or market stall that sold palm wine.

He had been in Robert's neighborhood for a few months. Before that he had stayed near the marketplace.

Robert did not look at him. Thinking of the marketplace, he hurried his steps. The first school bell rang.

"You will not be dawdling at the market," his mother had said as he readied himself for school. "Miss Mbene spoke to me of your tardiness yesterday."

She took the first of many piles of laundry from her wash baskets and placed them near the ironing board. There was a roaring fire in the hearth, and her irons were lined up in the racks over it. The house was already hot as an oven and would soon be as damp as the monsoon season.

His mother was still young and pretty but worn. She had supported them since Robert's father had been killed in an accident while damming a tributary of the Niger. He and forty other men had been swept away when a cofferdam burst. Only two of the bodies had ever been found. There was a small monthly check from the company her husband had worked for, and the government check for single mothers.

Her neighbor Mrs Yortebe washed, and she ironed. They took washing from the well-to-do government workers and business people in the better section.

"I shan't be late," said Robert, torn with emotions. He knew he wouldn't spend a long time there this morning and be late for school, but he did know that he would take the long route that led through the marketplace.

He put his schoolbooks and supplies in his satchel. His mother turned to pick up somebody's shirt from the pile. She stopped, looking at Robert.

"What are you going to do with *two* copybooks?" she asked.

Robert froze. His mind tried out ten lies. His mother started toward him.

"I'm nearly out of pages," he said. She stopped. "If we do much work today, I shall have to borrow."

"I buy you ten copybooks at the start of each school year and then again at the start of the second semester. Money does not grow on the breadfruit trees, you know?"

"Yes, Mother," he said. He hoped she would not look in the copybooks, see that one was not yet half-filled with schoolwork and that the other was still clean and empty. His mother referred to all extravagance as "a heart-tearing waste of time and money."

"You have told me not to borrow from others. I thought I was using foresight."

"Well," said his mother, "see you don't go to the marketplace. It will only make you envious of all the things you can't have. And do not be late to school one more time this term, or I shall have you ever ironing."

"Yes, Mother," he said. Running to her, he rubbed his nose against her cheek. "Good-bye."

"Good day. And don't go near that marketplace!"

"Yes, Mother."

The market! Bright, pavilioned stalls covered a square Congo mile of ground filled with gaudy objects, goods, animals, and people. The Onitsha market was a crossroads of the trade routes, near the river and the railway station. Here a thousand vendors sold their wares on weekdays, many times that on weekends and holidays.

Robert passed the great piles of melons, guinea fowl in cages, tables of toys and geegaws, all bright and shiny in the morning light.

People talked in five languages, haggling with each other, calling back and forth, joking. Here men from Senegal stood in their bright red hats and robes. Robert saw a tall Waziri, silent and regal, indicating the prices he would pay with quick movements of his long fingers, while the merchant he stood before added two more each time. A few people with raised tattoos on their faces, backcountry people, wandered wide-eyed from table to table, talking quietly among themselves.

Scales clattered, food got weighed, chickens and ducks rattled, a donkey brayed near the big corral where larger livestock was sold. A goat wagon delivered yams to a merchant, who began yelling because they were still too hard. The teamster shrugged his shoulders and pointed to his bill of lading. The merchant threw down his apron and headed toward Onitsha's downtown, cursing the harvest, the wagoners, and the food cooperatives.

Robert passed by the food stalls, though the smell of ripe mangoes made his mouth water. He had been skipping lunch for three weeks, saving his Friday pennies. At the schoolhouse far away the ten-minute bell rang. He would have to hurry.

> As for his chiefs, they are now sent to grub ore and yams in the New Lands, no trouble to you forevermore. Of his cattle we made great feast, his sheep drove we all to the four winds.

This would be important to the playgoer. King Motofuko had escaped, but he had also taken his four-year-old-son, Motofene, and tied him under the bellwether just before the soldiers attacked in the big battle of Yotele. When the soldiers drove off the sheep, they sent his son to safety, where the shepherds would send him far away, where he could grow up and plot revenge.

The story of King Motofuko was an old one any Onitsha theatergoer would know. Robert was taking liberties with it – the story of the sheep was from one of his favorite parts of the *Odyssey,* where the Greeks were in the cave of Polyphemus. (The real Motofene had been sent away to live as hostage-son to the chief of the neighboring state long before the attack by Chief Renebe.) And Robert was going to change some other things, too. The trouble with real life, Robert thought, was that it was usually dull and full of people like Mr Yotofeka and Mr Labuba. Not like the story of King Motofuko should be at all.

Robert had his copy of *Clio's Whips* inside his Egyptian grammar book. He read:

> "Soon all the countries of Europe that could sent expeditions to the New Lands. There were riches in its islands and vast spaces, but the White Man had to bring others to dig them out and cut down the mighty trees for ships. That is when the White Europeans really began to buy slaves from Arab merchants, and to send them across to the Warm Sea to skin animals, build houses, and to serve them in all ways.
>
> "Africa was raided over. Whole tribes were sold to slavery and degradation; worse, wars were fought between black and black to make slaves to sell to the Europeans. Mother Africa was raped again and again, but she was also traveled over and mapped: Big areas marked 'unexplored' on the White Man's charts shrank and shrank so that by 1700 there were very few such places left."

Miss Mbene came in from the play yard, cocked an eye at Robert, then went to the slateboard and wrote mathematical problems on it. With a groan, Robert closed the Egyptian grammar book and took out his sums and ciphers.

Mr Labuba spat a stream of yohimbe-bark snuff into the weeds at the edge of the playground. His eyes were red and the pupils more open than they should have been in the bright afternoon sun.

"We be pulling at grasses," he said to Robert. He handed him a big pair of gloves, which came up to Robert's elbows. "Pull steady. These plants be cutting all the way through the gloves if you jerk."

In a few moments Robert was sweating. A smell of desk polish and eraser rubbings came off Mr Labuba's shirt as he knelt beside him. They soon had cleared all along the back fence.

Robert got into the rhythm of the work, taking pleasure when the cutter weeds came out of the ground with a tearing pop and a burst of dirt from the tenacious, octopuslike roots. Then they would cut away the runners with trowels. Soon they made quite a pile near the teeter-totters.

Robert was still writing his play in his head; he had stopped in the second act when Motofuko, in disguise, had come to the forgiveness-audience with the new King Renebe. Unbeknownst to him, Renebe, fearing revenge all out of keeping with custom, had persuaded his stupid brother Guba to sit on the throne for the one day when anyone could come to the new king and be absolved of crimes.

"Is he giving you any trouble?" asked the intrusive voice of Mr Yotofeka. He had come up and was standing behind Robert.

Mr Labuba swallowed hard, the yohimbe lump going down chokingly.

"No complaints, Mr Yotofeka," he said, looking up.

"Very good, Robert, you can go home when the tower bell rings at three o'clock."

"Yes, sir."

Mr Yotofeka went back inside.

Mr Labuba looked at Robert and winked.

MOTOFUKO: Many, many wrongs in my time. I pray you, king, forgive me. I let my wives, faithful all, be torn from me, watched my children die, while I stood by, believing them proof from death. My village dead, all friends slaves. Reason twisted like hemp.

GUBA: From what mad place came you where such happens?

MOTOFUKO: (*Aside*) Name a country where this is not the standard of normalcy. (*To Guba*) Aye, all these I have done. Blinded, I went to worse. Pray you, forgive my sin.

GUBA: What could that be?

MOTOFUKO: (*Uncovering himself*) Murdering a king. (*Stabs him*)

GUBA: Mother of gods! Avenge my death. You kill the wrong man. Yonder – (*Dies*)

(*Guards advance, weapons out.*)

MOTOFUKO: Wrong man, when all men are wrong? Come, dogs, crows, buzzards, tigers. I welcome barks, beaks, claws, and teeth. Make the earth one howl. Damned, damned world where men fight like jackals over the carrion of states! Bare my bones then; they call for rest.

(*Exeunt, fighting. Terrible screams off. Blood flows in from the wings in a river.*)

SOLDIER: (*Aghast*) Horror to report. They flay the ragged skin from him whole!

"But the hide and fishing stations were hard to run with just slave labor. Not enough criminals could be brought from the White Man's countries to fill all the needs.

"Gold was more and more precious, in the hands of fewer and fewer people in Europe. There was some, true, in the Southern New Lands, but it was high in the great mountain ranges and very hard to dig out. The slaves worked underground till they went blind. There were revolts under those cruel conditions.

"One of the first new nations was set up by slaves who threw off their chains. They called their land Freedom, which was the thing they had most longed for since being dragged from Mother Africa. All the armies of the White Man's trading stations could not overthrow them. The people of Freedom slowly dug gold out of the mountains and became rich and set out to free others, in the Southern New Land and in Africa itself...

"Rebellion followed rebellion. Mother Africa rose up. There were too few white men, and the slave armies they sent soon joined their brothers and sisters against the White Man.

"First to go were the impoverished French and Spanish dominions, then the richer Italian ones, and those of the British. Last of all were the colonies of the great German banking families. Then the wrath of Mother Africa turned on those Arabs and Egyptians who had helped the White Man in his enslavement of the black.

"Now they are all gone as powers from our continent and only carry on the kinds of commerce with us which put all the advantages to Africa."

ASHINGO: The ghost! The ghost of the dead king!

RENEBE: What! What madness this? Guards, your places! What mean you, man?

ASHINGO: He came, I swear, his skin all strings, his brain a red cawleyflower, his eyes empty holes!

RENEBE: What portent this? The old astrologer, quick. To find what means to turn out this being like a goat from our crops.

(*Alarums without. Enter Astrologer.*)

ASTROLOGER: Your men just now waked me from a mighty dream. Your majesty was in some high place, looking over the courtyard at all his friends and family. You were dressed in regal armor all of brass and iron. Bonfires of victory burned all around, and not a word of dissent was heard anywhere in the land. All was peace and calm.

RENEBE: Is this then a portent of continued long reign?

ASTROLOGER: I do not know, sire. It was *my* dream.

His mother was standing behind him, looking over his shoulder. Robert jerked, trying to close the copybook. His glasses flew off.

"What is that?" She reached forward and pulled the workbook from his hands.

"It is extra work for school," he said. He picked up his glasses.

"No, it is not." She looked over his last page. "It is wasting your paper. Do you think we have money to burn away?"

"No, Mother. Please..." He reached for the copybook.

"First you are tardy. Then you stay detention after school. You waste your school notebooks. Now you have *lied* to me."

"I'm sorry. I..."

"What is this?"

"It is a play, a historical play."

"What are you going to do with a play?"

Robert lowered his eyes. "I want to take to Mr Fred's Printers and have it published. I want it acted in the Niger Culture Hall. I want it to be sold all over Niger."

His mother walked over to the fireplace, where her irons were cooling on the racks away from the hearth.

"What are you going to *do!!?*" he yelled.

His mother flinched in surprise. She looked down at the notebook, then back at Robert. Her eyes narrowed.

"I was going to get my spectacles."

Robert began to cry.

She came back to him and put her arms around him. She smelled of the marketplace, of steam and cinnamon. He buried his head against her side.

"I will make you proud of me, Mother. I am sorry I used the copybook, but I *had* to write this play."

She pulled away from him. "I ought to beat you within the inch of your life, for ruining a copybook. You are going to have to help me for the rest of the week. You are not to work on this until you have finished every bit of your schoolwork. You should know Mr Fred nor nobody is going to publish anything written by a schoolboy."

She handed him the notebook. "Put it away. Then go out on the porch and bring in those piles of mending. I am going to sweat a copybook out of your brow before I am through."

Robert clutched the book to him as if it were his soul.

RENEBE: O rack, ruin, and pain! Falling stars and the winds do shake the foundations of night itself! Where my soldiers, my strength? What use taxes, tribute if they buy not strong men to die for me?

(*Off*): Gone. All Fled.

RENEBE: Hold! Who is there? (*Draws*)

MOTOFENE: (*Entering*) He whose name will freeze your blood's roots.

RENEBE: The son of that dead king!

MOTOFENE: Aye, dead to you and all the world else, but alive to me and as constant as that star about which the groaning axletree of the earth does spin.

(*Alarums and excursions off.*)

Now hear you the screams of your flesh and blood and friendship, such screams as those I have heard awake and fitfully asleep these fourteen years. Now hear them for all time.

RENEBE: Guards! To me!

MOTOFENE: To you? See those stars which shower to earth out your fine window? At each a wife, child, friend does die. You watched my father cut away to bone and blood and gore and called not for the death stroke! For you I have had my Vulcans make you a fine suit. All iron and brass, as befits a king! It you will wear, to look out over the palace yard of your dead, citizens and friends. You will have a good high view, for it is situate on cords of finest woods. (*Enter Motofene's soldiers.*) Seize him gently. (*Disarm*) And now, my former king, outside. Though full of hot stars, the night is cold. Fear not the touch of the brass. Anon you are garmented, my men will warm the suit for you.

(*Exeunt and curtain.*)

Robert passed the moaning white man and made his way down the street, beyond the market. He was going to Mr Fred's Printers in downtown Onitsha. He followed broad New Market Street, being careful to stay out of the way of the noisy streetcars that steamed on their rails toward the center of town.

He wore his best clothes, though it was Saturday morning. In his hands he carried his play, recopied in ink in yet another notebook. He had learned from the clerk at the market bookstall that the one sure way to find Mr Fred was at his office on Saturday forenoon, when the Onitsha *Weekly Volcano* was being put to bed.

Robert saw two *wayway* birds sitting on the single telegraph wire leading to the relay station downtown. In the old superstitions one *wayway* was a bad omen, two were good, three a surprise.

"Mr Fred is busy," said the woman in the *Weekly Volcano* office. Her desk was surrounded by copies of all the pamphlets printed by Mr Fred's bookstore, past headlines from the *Volcano*, and a big picture of Mr Fred, looking severe in his morning coat, under the giant clock, on whose face was engraved the motto in Egyptian: TIME IS BUSINESS.

The calendar on her desk, with the picture of a Niger author for each month, was open to October 1894. A listing of that author's books published by Mr Fred was appended at the bottom of each page.

"I should like to see Mr Fred about my play," said Robert.

"Your play?"

"Yes. A rousing historical play. It is called *Motofuko's Revenge*."

"Is your play in proper form?"

"Following the best rules of dramaturgy," said Robert.

"Let me see it a moment."

Robert hesitated.

"Is it papertypered?" she asked.

A cold chill ran down Robert's spine.

"All manuscripts must be papertypered, two spaces between lines, with wide margins," she said.

There was a lump in Robert's throat. "But it is in my very finest book-hand," he said.

"I'm sure it is. Mr Fred reads everything himself, is a very busy man, and insists on papertypered manuscripts."

The last three weeks came crashing down on Robert like a mud-wattle wall.

"Perhaps if I spoke to Mr Fred..."

"It will do you no good if your manuscript isn't papertypered."

"Please. I..."

"Very well. You shall have to wait until after one. Mr Fred has to put the *Volcano* in final form and cannot be disturbed."

It was ten-thirty.

"I'll wait," said Robert.

At noon the lady left, and a young man in a vest sat down in her chair.

Other people came, were waited on by the man or sent into another office to the left. From the other side of the shop door, behind the desk, came the sound of clanking, carts rolling, thumps, and bells. Robert imagined great machines, huge sweating men wrestling with cogs and gears, books stacked to the ceiling.

It got quieter as the morning turned to afternoon. Robert stood, stretched, and walked around the reception area again, reading the newspapers on the walls with their stories five, ten, fifteen years old, some printed before he was born.

Usually they were stories of rebellions, wars, floods, and fears. Robert did not see one about the burst dam that had killed his father, a yellowed clipping of which was in the Coptic Bible at home.

There was a poster on one wall advertising the fishing resort on Lake Sahara South, with pictures of trout and catfish caught by anglers.

At two o'clock the man behind the desk got up and pulled down the windowshade at the office. "You shall have to wait outside for your father," he said. "We're closing for the day."

"Wait for my father?"

"Aren't you Meletule's boy?"

"No. I have come to see Mr Fred about my play. The lady..."

"She told me nothing. I thought you were the printer's devil's boy. You say you want to see Mr Fred about a play?"

"Yes. I..."

"Is it papertypered?" asked the man.

Robert began to cry.

"Mr Fred will see you now," said the young man, coming back in the office and taking his handkerchief back.

"I'm sorry," said Robert.

"Mr Fred only knows you are here about a play," he said. He opened the door to the shop. There were no mighty machines there, only a few small ones in a dark, two story area, several worktables, boxes of type and lead. Everything was dusty and smelled of metal and thick ink.

A short man in his shirtsleeves leaned against a workbench reading a long, thin strip of paper while a boy Robert's age waited. Mr Fred scribbled something on the paper, and the boy took it back into the other room, where several men bent quietly over boxes and tables filled with type.

"Yes," said Mr Fred, looking up.

"I have come here about my play."

"Your play?"

"I have written a play, about King Motofuko. I wish you to publish it."

Mr Fred laughed. "Well, we shall have to see about that. Is it papertypered?"

Robert wanted to cry again.

"No, I am sorry to say, it is not. I didn't know..."

"We do not take manuscripts for publication unless..."

"It is my very best book-hand, sir. Had I known, I would have tried to get it papertypered."

"Is your name and address on the manuscript?"

"Only my name. I..."

Mr Fred took a pencil out from behind his ear. "What is your house number?"

Robert told him his address, and he wrote it down on the copybook.

"Well, Mr – Robert Oinenke. I shall read this, but not before Thursday after next. You are to come back to the shop at ten a.m. on Saturday the nineteenth for the manuscript and our decision on it."

"But..."

"What?"

"I really like the books you publish, Mr Fred, sir. I especially liked *Clio's Whips* by Mr Oskar Oshwenke."

"Always happy to meet a satisfied customer. We published that book five years ago. Tastes have changed. The public seems tired of history books now."

"That is why I am hoping you will like my play," said Robert.

"I will see you in two weeks," said Mr Fred. He tossed the book into a pile of manuscripts on the workbench.

"Because of the legacy of the White Man, we have many problems in Africa today. He destroyed much of what he could not take with him. Many areas are without telegraphy; many smaller towns have only primitive direct current power. More needs to be done with health and sanitation, but we are not as badly off as the most primitive of the White Europeans in their war-ravaged countries or in the few scattered enclaves in the plantations and timber forests of the New Lands.

"It is up to you, the youth of Africa of today, to take our message of prosperity and goodwill to these people, who have now been as abused by history as we Africans once were by them. I wish you good luck."

Oskar Oshwenke, Onitsha, Niger, 1889

Robert put off going to the market stall of Mr Fred's bookstore as long as he could. It was publication day.

He saw that the nice young clerk was there. (He had paid him back out of the ten Niger dollar advance Mr Fred had had his mother sign for two weeks before. His mother still could not believe it.)

"Ho, there, Mr Author!" said the clerk. "I have your three copies for you. Mr Fred wishes you every success."

The clerk was arranging his book and John-John Motulla's *Game Warden Bob and the Mad Ivory Hunter* on the counter with the big starburst saying: Just published!

His book would be on sale throughout the city. He looked at the covers of the copies in his hands:

The TRAGICALL DEATH OF KING MOTOFUKO
and HOW THEY WERE SORRY
a drama by Robert Oinenke
abetted by
MR FRED OLUNGENE
"The Mighty Man of the Press"

for sale at Mr Fred's High-Class Bookstore
300 Market, and the *Weekly Volcano*
Office, 12 New Market Road
ONITHSA, NIGER
price 10¢ N.

On his way home he came around the corner where a group of boys was taunting the white man. The man was drunk and had just vomited on the foundation post of a store. They were laughing at him.

"Kill you all. Kill you all. No shame," he mumbled, trying to stand.

The words of *Clio's Whips* came to Robert's ears. He walked between the older boys and handed the white man three Niger cents. The white man looked up at him with sick, grey eyes.

"Thank you, young sir," he said, closing his hand tightly.

Robert hurried home to show his mother and the neighbors his books.

You Have Never Been Here

M. Rickert

YOU ARE ON THE TRAIN, considering the tips of your clean fingers against the dirty glass through which you watch the small shapes of bodies, the silhouettes on the street, hurrying past in long coats, clutching briefcases, or there, that one in jeans and a sweater, hunched shoulders beneath a backpack. Any one of them would do. You resist the temptation to look at faces because faces can be deceiving, faces can make you think there is such a thing as a person, the mass illusion everyone falls for until they learn what you have come to learn (too young, you are too young for such terrible knowledge) there are no people here, there are only bodies, separate from what they contain, husks. Useless, eventually.

Yours is useless now, or most nearly, though it doesn't feel like it, the Doctors have assured you it is true, your body is moving towards disintegration even as it sits here with you on this train, behaving normally, moving with your breath and at your will. See, there, you move your hand against the glass *because you decided to,* you wipe your eyes *because you wanted to* (and your eyes are tired, but that is not a matter of alarm, you were up all night, so of course your eyes are tired), you sink further into the vague cushion of the seat, you do that, or your body does that because you tell it to, so no wonder you fell for the illusion of a body that belongs to you, no wonder you believed it, no wonder you loved it. Oh! How you love it still!

You look out the dirty window, blinking away the tears that have so quickly formed. You are leaving the city now. What city is this anyways? You have lost track. Later, you'll ask someone. Where are we? And, not understanding, he will say, "We're on a train." The edge of the city is littered with trash, the sharp scrawls of bright graffiti, houses with tiny lawns, laundry hanging on the line, Christmas lights strung across a porch, though it is too late or too early for that. You close your eyes. Let me sleep, you say to your body. Right? But no, you must admit, your body needs sleep so the body's eyes close and it swallows you, the way it's always done, the body says sleep so you sleep, just like that, you are gone.

The hospital, the Doctors say, has been here for a long time. It's one of those wonderful secrets, like the tiny, still undiscovered insects, like several sea creatures, like the rumored, but not proven aliens from other planets, like angels, like God, the hospital is one of the mysteries, something many people know for a fact which others discount variously as illusion, indigestion, dreams, spiritual hunger, fantasy, science fiction, rumor, lies, insanity.

It is made of brick and stucco (architecturally unfortunate but a reflection of the need for expansion) and it has a staff of a hundred and fifty. With a population that large, the rotating roster of patients, the salespeople who wander in offering medical supplies (not understanding what they do to sick bodies here), the food vendors, the occasional lost traveler (never returned to the world in quite the same way) it is remarkable that the hospital remains a secret.

The patients come to the auditorium for an orientation. Some, naively, bring suitcases. The Doctors do nothing about this. There is a point in the process when the familiar clothes are discarded. It's not the same for everyone and the Doctors have learned that it's best not to rush things.

The Doctors appear to be watching with bored disinterest as the patients file in. But this is not, in fact, the case. The Doctors are taking notes. They don't need pen and paper to do this, of course. They have developed their skills of observation quite keenly. They remember you, when you come in, skulking at the back of the room, like the teenager you so recently were, sliding into the auditorium chair, and crouching over as though afraid you will be singled out as being too young to be here, but that is ridiculous as there are several children in the group flocking around that lady, the one with orangey-red hair and the red and yellow kimono draped loosely over purple blouse and pants, a long purple scarf wrapped around her bloody neck. For some reason she is laughing while everyone else is solemn, even the Doctors standing there in their white lab coats, their eyes hooded as though supremely bored. (Though you are wrong about this. The Doctors are never bored.)

The Doctors introduce themselves. They hope everyone had a good trip. They know there is some confusion and fear. That's OK. It's normal. It's OK if there is none as well. That's normal too. All the feelings are normal and no one should worry about them.

The Doctors explain that the doors are locked but anyone can leave at any time. Just ring the bell and we will let you out.

The orangey-red-haired lady with the bloody neck raises her hand and the Doctors nod. You have to lean over to hear her raspy voice.

How often does that happen? How often does someone leave without going through with the procedure?

The Doctors confer amongst themselves. Never, they say in unison. It never happens.

The Doctors pass out room assignments and a folder that contains information about the dining hall (open for breakfast from six to nine, lunch from eleven-thirty to two, and dinner from five-thirty to eight), the swimming pool (towels and suits provided), the chapel (various denominational services offered throughout the week). The folder contains a map that designates these areas as well as the site of the operating rooms (marked with giant red smiley faces) and the areas that house the Doctors which are marked Private, though, the Doctors say, if there is an emergency it would be all right to enter the halls which, on the map have thick black lines across them.

Finally, the Doctors say, there is an assignment. This is the first step in the operation. The procedure cannot go any further until the first step is complete. The Doctors glance at each other and nod. Don't be afraid, they say. Things are different here. Everything will be all right, and then, as an afterthought, almost as though they'd forgotten what they had been talking about, they say, find someone to love.

The auditorium is suddenly weirdly silent. As though the bodies have forgotten to breathe.

It's simple really, the Doctors say. Love someone.

You look around. Are they nuts?

At the front of the room the Doctors are laughing. No one is sure what to do. You see everyone looking around nervously, you catch a couple of people looking at you but they look away immediately. You're not insulted by this. You expect it even.

The bloody neck lady raises her hand again. The Doctors nod.

Just one? she rasps.

The Doctors say, no, no, it can be one. It can be many.

And what happens next?

The Doctors shrug. They are organizing their papers and making their own plans for the evening. Apparently the meeting is over. Several patients stand, staring at the map in their hands, squinting at the exit signs.

Excuse me? the lady says again.

You can't decide if you admire her persistence or find it annoying but you wish she'd do something about her throat, suck on a lozenge maybe.

The Doctors nod.

After we find people to love, what do we do?

The Doctors shrug. Love them, they say.

This seems to make perfect sense to her. She stands up. The children stand too. They leave in a group, like a kindergarten class. Actually, you kind of want to go with them. But you can't. You look at the map in your hand. You find your exit and you walk towards it, only glancing up to avoid colliding with the others. Love someone? What's this shit all about? Love someone? Let someone love me, you think, angry at first and then, sadly. Let someone love me.

The bodies move down the long hallways, weaving around each other, pausing at doors with numbers and pictures on them. (Later, you find out the pictures are for the children who are too young to know their numbers.) The bodies open unlocked doors and the bodies see pleasant rooms painted yellow, wallpapered with roses, cream colored, pale blue, soft green, furnished with antiques and wicker. The bodies walk to the locked windows and stare out at the courtyard, a pleasant scene of grass and fountain, flowering fruit trees. The bodies open the closets filled with an odd assortment of clothes, plaid pants, striped shirts, flowery dresses, A-line skirts, knickers, hand-knit sweaters, and rain coats, all in various sizes. The bodies flick on the bathroom lights, which reveal toilets, sinks, tubs and showers, large white towels hanging from heated towel racks. The bodies look at the beds with feather pillows and down comforters. The bodies breathe, the bodies breathe, the bodies breathe. The bodies are perfect breathers. For now.

What if this is the strangest dream you ever had? What if none of this is true? The Doctors have not told you that your body has its own agenda, your mother has not held your hand and squeezed it tight, tears in her eyes, your father has never hugged you as though he thought you might suddenly float away, your hair has not fallen out, your skin become so dry it hurts, your swallowing blistered? What if all of this is only that you are having a strange dream? What if you aren't sick at all, only sleeping?

The Doctors eat pepperoni and discuss astronomy, bowling, liposuction, and who has been seen kissing when someone's spouse was away at a seminar. The Doctors drink red wine and eat pheasant stuffed with gooseberries and cornbread, a side of golden-hashed potatoes, green beans with slivered almonds and too much butter. They discuss spectral philosophy, spiritual monasticy, and biological relativism. They lean back in their chairs and loosen belts and buttons surreptitiously, burping behind hands or into napkins. Dessert is served on pink plates, chocolate cake with raspberry filling and chocolate frosting. Coffee and tea are served in individual pots. The Doctors say they couldn't possibly and then they pick up thin silver forks and slice into the cake, the raspberry gooing out. What do you think they are doing now? someone asks.

Oh, they are crying, several of the Doctors respond. The Doctors nod their knowledgeable heads. Yes. On this first night, the bodies are crying.

That first night is followed by other days and other nights and all around you life happens. There are barbecues, movies, tea parties, and dances. The scent of seared meat, popcorn, and Earl Grey tea wafts through the halls. You are amazed to observe everyone behaving as if this is all just the usual thing. Even the children, sickly pale, more ears and feet than anything, seem to have relaxed into the spirit of their surroundings. They ride bicycles, scooters, and skateboards down the hall, shouting, Excuse me, mister! Excuse me! You can never walk in a line from one end to the other and this is how, distracted and mumbling under your breath, you come face to face with the strange orange-haired woman. She no longer wears the kimono but the scarf remains around her throat, bloodied purple silk trailing down a black, white, and yellow daisy dress. Her head, topped with a paper crown, is haloed with orange feathers, downy as those from a pillow.

Where you going in such a hurry? she wheezes.

Upon closer inspection you see they are not feathers at all, but wisps of hair, her scalp spotted with drops of blood.

Name's Renata, she thrusts her freckled fleshy hand towards you.

Excuse me! Excuse me!

You step aside to let a girl on a bicycle and a boy on roller skates pass. When you turn back, Renata is running after them, her bloodied scarf dangling down her back, feathers of orangey-red hair floating through the air behind her.

She's as loony as a tune, wouldn't you say?

You hadn't seen the young man approaching behind the bicycle child and the roller-skating one. You haven't seen him before at all. He stares at you with blue eyes.

You don't got a cigarette, do you?

You shake your head, vigorously. No. Of course not. It goes without saying.

In spite of his stunning white hair, he's no more than five years older than you. He leans closer. I do, he says. Come on.

He doesn't look back. You follow him, stepping aside occasionally for the racing children. You follow him through a labyrinth of halls. After a while he begins to walk slowly, slinking almost. There are no children here, no noise at all. You follow his cue, pressing against the walls. You have an idea you have entered the forbidden area but what are they going to do anyway. Kill you? You snort and he turns those ghost-blue eyes on you.

You are a body following another body. Your heart is beating against your chest. Hard. Like the fist of a dying man. Let me out, let me out, let me out. You are a body and you are breathing but your breath is not your own.

The body in front of you quickly turns his head, left, right, looking down the long white hall. The body runs, and your body follows. Because he has your breath now.

What is love? The Doctors ponder this question in various meetings throughout the week. We have been discussing this for years, one of them points out, and still have come to no conclusion. The Doctors agree. There is no formula. No chemical examination. No certainty.

There's been a breech, the Doctor in charge of such matters reports.

The Doctors smile. Let me guess, one of them says, Farino?

But the others don't wait for a confirmation. They know it's Farino.

Who's he with?

They are surprised that it is you. Several of them say this.

The Doctors have a big debate. It lasts for several hours, but in the end, the pragmatists win out. They will not interfere. They must let things run their course. They end with the same question they began with. What is love?

It's quick as the strike of a match to flame. One minute you are a dying body, alone in all the world, and the next you are crouched in a small windowless room beside a boy whose blue eyes make you tremble, whose breathing, somehow, involves your own. Of course it isn't love. How could it be, so soon? But the possibility exists. He passes the cigarette to you and you hesitate but he says, Whatsa matter? Afraid you're going to get cancer? You place the cigarette between your lips, you draw breath. You do that. He watches you, his blue eyes clouded with smoke.

Thanks. You hand the cigarette back. He flicks the ash onto the floor. The floor is covered with ash. From wall to wall there is ash.

This isn't all mine, you know.

You nod. You don't want to look stupid so you nod. He hands the cigarette to you and your fingers touch momentarily. You are surprised by the thrill this sends through your body. I sing the body electric.

What's that?

You hadn't realized you'd spoken out loud. I sing the body electric, you say. It's from a poem.

You a fucking poet? he says.

You hand the cigarette back to him. Any moment now the Doctors could come and take you away. Any breath could be the last breath. His blue eyes remain locked on yours.

I mean, are you? A fucking poet? He doesn't look away, and you don't either.

You nod.

He grins. He crushes the precious cigarette into the ashy floor. He leans over and his lips meet your lips. He tastes like ash and smoke. The gray powder floats up in the tumble of tossed clothes and writhing bodies. The bodies are coated with a faint gray film and maybe this isn't love, maybe it's only desire, loneliness, infatuation, maybe it's just the body's need, maybe it isn't even happening, maybe you have already been cremated and you are bits of ash creating this strange dream but maybe you are really here, flesh to flesh, ash to ash, alive, breathing, in the possibility of love.

Later, you lie alone on the clean white sheets in your room. You are waiting. Either he will come for you or they will. You stare at the ceiling. It is dimpled plaster dotted with specks of gold. You think it is beautiful.

Suddenly there is knocking on the door.

You open it but it isn't the Doctors or the police and it isn't him, it's Renata.

Are you naked or dead? she says.

You slam the door. Your ash print remains on the bed, a silhouette of your body, or *the* body. She is knocking and knocking. You tell her to go away but she won't. Exasperated, you grab your ash pants from the floor, step into them, zip and button the fly, open the door.

She is almost entirely bald now, but she still wears that ridiculous paper crown. She sees you looking at it. She reaches up to fondle the point. One of the children made it for me. Behind her you see the evidence of your indiscretion. Your ash footprints reveal your exact course. The hallway is eerily empty.

Where are the children now?

They're gone, she croaks, stepping into the room, a few orange hairs wisping around her. Haven't you noticed how quiet it is?

It is. It is very quiet. All you can hear is her breath, which is surprisingly loud. This place...you say, but you don't continue. You were going to say it gives you the creeps but then you remember Farino. Where is he now? How can you hate this place when this is where you found him? You may as well relax. Enjoy this while you can. Soon you will be out there again. Just another dying body without any more chances left.

She opens your closet and begins searching through it. Have you seen my kimono? The one I was wearing when I arrived?

You tell her no. She steps out of the closet, shuts the door. They say it's just like changing clothes, you know.

You nod. You've heard that as well, though you have your doubts.

She sighs. If you see it, will you let me know? She doesn't wait for your reply. She just walks out the door.

You count to ten and then you look down the hall. There is only one set of ash footprints, your own. Are you there? you whisper. Are you there? Are you? Is anyone?

You cannot control the panic. It rises through your body on its own accord. Your throat tightens and suddenly it's as though you are breathing through a straw. Your heart beats wildly against your chest, Let me out, let me out. The body is screaming now. Anyone? Anyone? Is anyone here? But the hall remains empty except for your footprints, the silent ashy steps of your life, and this is when you realize you have not loved enough, you have not breathed enough, you have not even hated enough and just when you think, well, now it's over, the Doctors come for you, dressed in white smocks spotted with roses of blood and you are pleading with them not to send you back out there with this hopeless body and they murmur hush, hush, and don't worry. But, though they say the right things, the words are cold.

They take you down the long white halls, following your footprints, which, you can only hope (is it possible?) they have not noticed, until, eventually, you pass the room your footprints come out of, smudged into a Rorschach of ash as though several people have walked over them.

Hush, hush. Don't worry. It won't hurt any more than life. That's a little joke. OK, we're turning here. Yes, that's right. That door. Could you open it, please? No, no, don't back out now. The instruments are sharp but you will be asleep. When you wake up the worst will be over. Here, just lie down. How's that? OK, now hold still. Don't let the straps alarm you. The body, you know, has its own will to survive. Is that too tight? It is? We don't want it too loose. Once, this was a long time ago, before we perfected the procedure, a body got up right in the middle of it. The body has a tremendous will to survive even when it goes against all reason. What's that? Let's just say it was a big mess and leave it at that. The cigarette? Yes, we know about that. Don't mind the noise, all right? We're just shaving your head. What? Why aren't we angry? Can you just turn this way a little bit? Not really much left here to shave is there? We're not angry; you did your assignment. What's that? Oh, Farino. Of course we know about him. He's right there, didn't you notice? Oh, hey, hey, stop it. Don't be like that. He's fine. He just got here first. He's knocked out already. That's what we're going to do for you now. This might – look, you knew what you were getting into. You already agreed. What do you want? Life or death? You want Farino? OK, then relax. You've got him.

You are on a train. Your whole body aches. You groan as you turn your head away from the hard glass. The body is in agony. Your head throbs. You reach up and feel the bald scalp. Oh! The body! The dream of the body! The hope of the body for some miracle world where you will not suffer. You press your open palms against your face. You are not weeping. You are not breathing. You are not even here. Someone taps your shoulder.

You look up into the hound face of the train conductor. Ticket?

I already gave it to you.

He shakes his head.

You search through your pockets and find a wallet. The wallet is filled with bills but there is no ticket. I seem to have lost it, but look, here, I can pay you.

The conductor lifts the large walkie-talkie to his long mouth and says some words you don't listen to. Then he just stands there, looking at you. You realize he thinks he exists and you do too. The train screams to a long slow stop. He escorts you off.

You can't just leave me here. I'm not well.

Here's your ride now, he says.

The police cruiser comes to a halt. The policeman gets out. He tilts the brim of his hat at the conductor. When he gets close to you, he looks up with interest, Well, well, he says.

There's been some sort of mistake. Please, I'm not well.

The conductor steps back onto the train. The windows are filled with the faces of passengers. A child with enormous ears points at you and waves. For a second you think you see Farino. But that isn't possible. Is it?

The policeman says, Put your hands behind your back.

These aren't my hands.

He slaps the cuffs on you. Too tight. You tell him they are too tight.

The whistle screams over your words. The train slowly moves away.

Aren't you going to read me my rights?

The policeman has bratwurst breath. Just 'cause you shaved your head, don't think I don't know who you are. He steers you to the cruiser. Places one hand on your head as you crouch to sit in the backseat.

I know my rights.

He radios the station. Hey, I'm bringing something special.

You drive past cows and cornfields, farmhouses and old barns. The handcuffs burn into your wrists. The head hurts, the arms hurt, the whole body hurts. You groan.

Whatsa matter? The policeman looks at you in the rearview mirror.

I'm not well.

You sure do look beat up.

I've been in a hospital.

Is that right?

You look out the window at an old white farmhouse on a distant hill. You wonder who loves there.

The station is a little brick building surrounded by scrubby brown grass and pastures. The policeman behind the desk and the policewoman pouring coffee both come over to look at you.

Fucken A, they say.

Can I make my phone call?

The policewoman takes off the handcuffs. She presses your thumb into a pad of ink. She tells you where to stand for your picture. Smile, she says, we got you now Farino.

What?

What is this body doing with you? What has happened? They list the crimes he's committed. You insist it was never you. You never did those things. You are incapable of it. You tell them about the hospital, the Doctors, you tell them how Farino tricked you.

They tell you terrible things. They talk about fingerprints and blood.

But it wasn't me.

Farino, cut this shit and confess. Maybe we can give you a deal, life, instead of death. How about that?

But I didn't. I'm not like that.

You fucking monster! Why don't you show a little decency? Tell us what you did with the bodies.

I was in a hospital. He switched bodies with me. He tricked me.

Oh fuck it. He's going for the fuckin insanity shit, ain't he? Fuck it all anyway. How long he been here? Oh, fuck, give him the fuckin phone call. Let him call his fuckin lawyer, the fuckin bastard.

You don't know who to call. They give you the public defender's number. No, I have money. In my wallet.

That ain't your money to spend, you worthless piece of shit. That belonged to Renata King, OK?

Renata?

What? Is it coming back to you now? Your little amnesia starting to clear up?

How'd I end up with Renata's wallet?

You fuckin ape. You know what you did.

But you don't. You only know that you want to live. You want to live more than you want anything else at all. You want life, you want life, you want life. All you want is life.

What if this is really happening? What if you are really here? What if out of all the bodies, all the possibilities, you are in this body and what if it has done terrible things?

You look up at the three stern faces. They hate you, you think, no, they hate this body. You are not this body. The stern faces turn away from you. What can you say anyway? How can you explain? You sit, waiting, as though this were an ordinary matter, this beautiful thing, this body, breathing. This terrible judgment. This wonderful knowledge. The body breathes. It breathes and it doesn't matter what you want, when the body wants to, it breathes. It breathes in the hospital, it breathes in the jail, it breathes in your dreams and it breathes in your nightmares, it breathes in love and it breathes in hate and there's not much you can do about any of it, you are on a train, you are in an operating room, you are in a jail, you are innocent, you are guilty, you are not even here. None of this is about you, and it never was.

Author Notes

AIMEE BENDER received an MFA in fiction writing from the University of California at Irvine. Born in 1969, her first story collection *The Girl in the Flammable Skirt* appeared in 1998. Her other books are *Willful Creatures* (2005) and the novel *An Invisible Sign of My Own* (2001). She teaches fiction writing at the University of Southern California.

MICHAEL CHABON, born in 1963, grew up in Columbia, Maryland. He received a BA from the University of Pittsburgh and an MFA in creative writing from UC Irvine. His novel *The Amazing Adventures of Kavalier & Clay* won the 2001 Pulitzer Prize for Fiction; *Summerland* (2002) won the 2003 Mythopoeic Fantasy Award. He has also written a number of small comics projects, primarily for Dark Horse Comics, and co-wrote the story for *Spider-Man 2*. He lives in Berkeley, California.

TED CHIANG, born in 1967 in Port Jefferson, New York, is a graduate of Brown University and a winner of the Nebula, Hugo, and World Fantasy awards. His collection *Stories of Your Life* appeared in 2002. He works as a freelance technical writer in Seattle, Washington.

Born in 1921, CAROL EMSHWILLER grew up mostly in Ann Arbor, Michigan, but also in France. "For a while it was back and forth every other year...eight years old in France, nine and ten here, then eleven in France, twelve back here...etc." She began publishing her short stories in science fiction magazines in 1955. In the 1960s she and her husband were active in the New York avant garde art world. Her books include the novels *Carmen Dog* and *The Mount,* and the story collections

Verging on the Pertinent, Report to the Men's Club, and most recently *I Live with You.*

At SUNY Binghamton, JEFFREY FORD tried to get into one of John Gardner's writing classes after the deadline date for enrollment. Gardner refused to let him in. "As I was walking away from his office, for some reason, I have no idea why, he came out into the hallway and called me back and said, 'OK, I'll give you a chance.'" Born in 1955 in West Islip, Long Island, Ford is the author of the World Fantasy Award-winning novel *The Physiognomy* (1997) and four other novels. His collection *The Fantasy Writer's Assistant* was published in 2002.

Born in 1950 in Bloomington, Indiana, KAREN JOY FOWLER attended UC Berkeley in the late 1960s, where she studied political science, with a special interest in China and Japan. Her first stories appeared in science fiction magazines in the 1980s; her most recent novel is the bestselling *The Jane Austen Book Club.* Her earlier books include the novels *Sarah Canary* and *The Sweetheart Season,* and the collection *Black Glass.* She lives in Davis, California.

Born in Budapest, Hungary, in 1968, THEODORA GOSS spent her childhood moving from country to country, and spoke Italian and French before she spoke English. She attended the University of Virginia, and after a brief internment in Harvard Law School and working as a corporate attorney, returned to school to study for a Ph.D. in English literature. She has published short stories and poems in a number of magazines and anthologies, including *Realms of Fantasy, Alchemy, Polyphony, Strange Horizons, Lady Churchill's Rosebud Wristlet,* and *The Year's Best Fantasy and Horror.*

JONATHAN LETHEM was attending Bennington College on an art scholarship when he began writing his first attempt at a novel. Born in 1964, he is a recent recipient of a MacArthur Fellowship. His novels include *Gun, With Occasional Music, As She Climbed Across the Table, Motherless Brooklyn* (winner of the National Book Critics Circle

Award), and most recently *The Fortress of Solitude*. His story collection *The Wall of the Sky, the Wall of the Eye*, appeared in 1996, *Men and Cartoons* in 2004. He lives in Maine and Brooklyn, New York.

KELLY LINK, born in 1969, is the author of two widely praised story collections, *Stranger Things Happen* (2001) and *Magic for Beginners* (2005). She holds a BA from Columbia University and an MFA in creative writing from the University of North Carolina at Greensboro. With her husband, Gavin Grant, she runs Small Beer Press and the magazine *Lady Churchill's Rosebud Wristlet*, which has made them an irresistible force in the world of slipstream publishing.

Born in 1959, the deceptively quiet M. RICKERT lives in upstate New York, where she works as a nanny and writes. Her stories have appeared frequently in *The Magazine of Fantasy & Science Fiction*; her story collection *Map of Dreams* will be published in October 2006. She says that her life is much more mellow than that of her characters.

BENJAMIN ROSENBAUM was born in 1969 in Long Island Jewish Hospital, but his family soon moved to Arlington, Virginia. After graduating from Brown University, where he majored in computer science and religious studies, he worked as a computer programmer for many software start-ups while writing stories that have appeared in *McSweeney's*, *Harper's*, *Lady Churchill's Rosebud Wristlet*, *Strange Horizons*, *The Magazine of Fantasy & Science Fiction* and *The Infinite Matrix*. He has lived in Italy, Switzerland, and Israel, but currently resides with his wife and children in Falls Church, Virginia.

GEORGE SAUNDERS was born in 1958 and raised on the south side of Chicago. In 1981 he received a BS in Geophysical Engineering from Colorado School of Mines. From 1989 to 1996 he worked for an environmental engineering firm as a technical writer and geophysical engineer. He has also worked in Sumatra on an oil exploration geophysics crew, as a doorman in Beverly Hills, a roofer in Chicago, a convenience store clerk, a guitarist in a Texas country-and-western band,

and a knuckle-puller in a West Texas slaughterhouse. He is the author of the short story collections *CivilWarLand in Bad Decline, Pastoralia,* and *In Persuasion Nation.* He teaches Creative Writing at Syracuse University.

BRUCE STERLING, born in 1954 in Brownsville, Texas, began writing at the age of twelve in what he would later describe as "a frank bid for attention." When he was fifteen, his family moved to India, where his father worked on a fertilizer plant project. He has been publishing fiction since 1976. His novels include *Schismatrix* (1985), *Holy Fire* (1997), and *Distraction* (1998); story collections include *Crystal Express* and *A Good Old Fashioned Future.* He is the founder of the Viridian design movement (*www.viridiandesign.org*), which attempts to make reducing global carbon emissions trendy.

JEFF VANDERMEER was born in 1968 in Pennsylvania, but spent much of his childhood in the Fiji Islands, where his parents worked for the Peace Corps. His published works include *The Book of Lost Places* (1996), *Why Should I Cut Your Throat?* (2004), and *City of Saints and Madmen* (2001) and he is the editor of *The Thackery T. Lambshead Pocket Guide to Eccentric & Discredited Diseases* (2004). He lives in Florida with his wife, writer and editor Ann Kennedy.

"Fishing is one of the main things in my life," says HOWARD WALDROP. "Writing and fishing – that's about it." Born in Mississippi in 1946, Waldrop has spent most of his life in Texas. He has been publishing his elliptical fictions since the early 1970s, including the collections *Howard Who?* (1986), *All About Strange Monsters of the Recent Past* (1987), and *Going Home Again* (1997).